POWER PLAYS

Malcolm Kandall makes no secret of what he has the power to do if Laura pursues her investigation of where his campaign finances come from. The ruthless master politician has the muscle and the money to bring her newspaper to financial ruin. He knows secrets of sex and scandal that can spell disgrace and even worse for those nearest and dearest to her. And he has friends in high and low places who can get away with murder when it comes to a nosy newspaperwoman.

But his nephew, glamorous photojournalist Ted Kandall, poses an even greater threat. Laura may have hated him at first sight, but he broke down her defenses one by one. And now she knows what kind of perilous power he wields over her.

It is a power of passion ... but Laura desperately tries to remind herself what danger might lie in the arms of this man who makes her forget everything but desire. . . .

NEVER S

NEVER
SAY NEVER

Christiane Heggan

AN ONYX BOOK

ONYX
Published by the Penguin Group
Penguin Books USA Inc., 375 Hudson Street,
New York, New York 10014, U.S.A.
Penguin Books Ltd, 27 Wrights Lane,
London W8 5TZ, England
Penguin Books Australia Ltd, Ringwood,
Victoria, Australia
Penguin Books Canada Ltd, 10 Alcorn Avenue,
Toronto, Ontario, Canada M4V 3B2
Penguin Books (N.Z.) Ltd, 182–190 Wairau Road,
Auckland 10, New Zealand

Penguin Books Ltd, Registered Offices:
Harmondsworth, Middlesex, England

First published by Onyx, an imprint of Dutton Signet,
a division of Penguin Books USA Inc.

First Printing, August, 1996
10 9 8 7 6 5 4 3 2 1

 REGISTERED TRADEMARK—MARCA REGISTRADA

Printed in the United States of America

PUBLISHER'S NOTE
This is a work of fiction. Names, characters, places, and incidents either
are the product of the author's imagination or are used fictitiously, and
any resemblance to actual persons, living or dead, events, or locales is
entirely coincidental.

In memory of my father

WITH DEEP APPRECIATION

to Eileen Reynolds of the *Philadelphia Inquirer,* for giving me the grand tour and sharing her vast knowledge of the newspaper industry;

to staff photographer Ed Hille, for graciously answering all my questions;

to Ed Brown of the *Central Record,* for his personal insight and invaluable assistance;

and to Anne Klein Associates, for opening so many doors for me.

Count not upon forgiveness,
by adding sin to sin.

—Ben Sira,
Book of Wisdom

Prologue

By the time Laura Spencer realized someone was trying to kill her, it was too late. The car that had barely missed her seconds earlier was turning around, tires screeching.

In the cavernous grayness of the parking garage, Laura's high heels echoed hollowly as she ran. Mildred's car was parked just down the ramp. If she could only reach it . . .

Before she could finish her thought, the brown sedan was back.

Acting on sheer reflex, Laura leaped between two cars, crying out in pain as her knees slapped the hard concrete. A blast of exhaust fumes hit her as the car roared by, once again missing her by inches.

Fear gripped her stomach and she pressed her forehead against the door of the blue van she had landed next to. *Don't panic,* she thought, taking a few ragged breaths. *You've been in worse situations. And you've always survived.*

This silent pep talk momentarily calmed her. Shaky but clearheaded, she pulled herself up just enough to have a clear view of the ramp. Nothing.

Not even a sound. Did her attacker think he had hit her? Or was he just waiting for her to step out in the open again?

As she remained crouched, afraid to move, she heard hurried footsteps coming down the ramp.

"Are you all right?" an anxious male voice called. "Miss? Are you hurt?"

Laura heaved a sigh of relief as an elderly couple peered around the back of the van. "No. I don't think I'm hurt." She glanced down at her knees. They were badly scraped and bloody, but other than that, she was fine. She was alive.

"That man was heading right toward you," the woman said in an outraged tone as she and her companion helped Laura to her feet. "My husband and I saw the whole thing."

"I know." Laura looked around her and listened for the sound of a returning car. The garage was silent.

"Did you get a look at him?" the man asked, eyeing her intently.

She nodded. "I think I know who it is."

"Then you'd better go back inside the building and call the police. We'll come with you." He glanced at his wife who nodded. "You'll need witnesses."

"Thank you." Laura brushed the dirt off her skirt. She was shaking, and her mouth felt dry, but other than that, she was unharmed. How stupid of her to have come here alone. After ten years' experience as a crime reporter, she had fallen for the oldest trick in the book. She had responded to a call without verifying its source.

She was about to step from behind the shelter of the van when she saw him.

He stood no more than twenty feet away, his body partially hidden behind a support column.

The woman followed her gaze. "What is it, dear?"

As the man moved from behind the column, Laura's legs went weak. Frozen in fear, she could do nothing but stare at the gun that was aimed at her.

1

Sitting at a table in the dark, empty nightclub, Laura smiled as she watched her mother give her sultry rendition of Peggy Lee's "Fever."

Glad to escape the chaos at her newspaper, the *Austin Sentinel,* for an hour she had come along to the audition to offer moral support, something Shirley needed constantly, even after all her years as a performer.

She hasn't lost her magic, Laura thought as her mother's smoky voice filled the room. Or her looks. Even now, at fifty-three, Shirley Langfield couldn't walk on a stage without creating a stir. She had ash blond hair she wore in a mass of curls and tendrils, huge brown eyes Laura's stepfather had once claimed could melt Alaska, and a figure a *Playboy* model would die for.

Her wardrobe, on stage or off, was as flamboyant as the woman herself—short skirts that showed off her spectacular legs, sequined gowns in a rainbow of colors, and enough rhinestone cowboy hats to match every outfit she owned. For today's audition, she had chosen a relatively tame outfit, a fringed purple jacket over a black cat suit, and a purple Stetson worn at a rakish angle.

Except for the piano player at the far end of the stage and the man sitting next to Laura, the Golden Parrot was deserted at this noon hour, open only for auditions.

"Isn't she wonderful, Joe?" Laura asked, turning to face the club owner.

Joe Fielding, a retired Air Force colonel with a military crew cut and a Karl Malden nose, nodded without taking his eyes off the woman on the stage. "I'll admit she's better than I thought. She has a good voice and lots of sex appeal. The problem is . . ." He didn't meet Laura's eyes. "She's not exactly what I had in mind."

"You mean you want someone younger."

"I didn't say that."

He didn't have to. After accompanying her mother to a half-dozen auditions in the past eight weeks, Laura had realized that when it came to age discrimination, the entertainment field was brutal.

Because the former military man was an old friend of her stepfather's, she didn't mind forcing his hand a little. "Why don't you give her a try, Joe? See how the audience reacts to her?"

"I don't know, Laura . . ." He shook his head. "I'd be taking a big chance."

Laura leaned across the table, dropping her voice a little. "I'll make you a deal. You give her a six-week contract and you and I can work out that advertising package you claim you can't afford. A series of ads in the *Sentinel*'s Friday edition for, say, . . . half price?"

Joe, his arms crossed over his broad chest and his index finger curled around his mouth, chuckled softly. "Did anybody ever tell you that you drive one hell of a bargain?"

"What can I tell you? I trained with the best."

"Speaking of your stepfather, the old goat, how's J.B. doing these days?"

"Enjoying his retirement."

"I'm glad to hear it. Give him my best, will you?"

"Sure." Laura's gaze drifted back to the stage. "What about my mother? Do we have a deal?"

This time, Joe's laugh was gusty. "No wonder you brought that newspaper around so quickly. You're totally relentless."

She gave him a coy smile. "Is that a yes?"

He was thoughtful for a moment, his lips pursed as he continued to watch Shirley. Then, nodding a few times, he said, "Alright, young lady. Yes. You've got yourself a deal. But if it doesn't work out ... If I start losing customers ..."

"My end of the deal will still stand." She rose just as Shirley was bringing the song to a rousing finish. "You won't regret this, Joe. And by the way," she added as she and the club owner shook hands, "I would appreciate it if you kept this conversation strictly between us."

"I understand." As Shirley took a bow, he stood up and clapped loudly. "Bravo!" he exclaimed, making his way toward the stage. "Your daughter told me you were going to knock my socks off and by God, she wasn't lying. You're terrific, little lady."

Shirley beamed as Joe helped her down from the stage. "Thank you," she said in her breathless Marilyn Monroe voice. "Does that mean I'm hired?"

"How does a six-week engagement sound?"

Shirley brought her clasped hands to her mouth, like a child who had been granted her dearest wish. "It sounds wonderful. When do I start?"

"Tuesday. The first show is at eight, the second at ten-thirty. Come a little early so we can take care of the paperwork." He glanced at his watch. "Now if you'll both excuse me, I have to settle an argument between two of my waiters before they tear this place apart."

Shirley took his hand in both of hers and shook it earnestly. "Thank you so much, Mr. Fielding. I don't know how I can ever repay you."

"Just fill the joint with big spenders and we'll be about even." He winked. "And call me Joe. Everyone does."

Fifteen minutes later, Laura and her mother were walking across the cobblestone courtyard of Serano's, a popular Tex-Mex restaurant on Symphony Square. As usual, the place was packed with an elegant, youthful business crowd, and the air was fragrant with the aroma of the restaurant's famous specialties.

As they made their way toward a patio table overlooking the outdoor stage, Laura waved at an editor from the *Austin American Statesman*, unaware of the admiring glances she and her mother were drawing as they walked.

Although she never thought much about her

looks, thirty-two-year-old Laura Spencer had the kind of relaxed, natural beauty that made heads turn. She had a slender but curvaceous figure, long flaming red hair, and huge amber eyes she had inherited from her father, a magician who had seduced audiences all over the world with the power of his gaze. A sexy black mole she no longer tried to conceal sat just above the right corner of her upper lip.

But more than her beauty, it was her energy that people found mesmerizing. Whether she walked across a restaurant or conducted a high-level meeting, the vibrancy and passion that pulsed from her was almost palpable. A person couldn't be in her presence without feeling drawn in by all that intensity, a trait that made her perfect for her job as the *Austin Sentinel*'s publisher.

After both women had ordered lunch, Shirley leaned back with a satisfied sigh. "I still can't believe that wonderful man hired me. Do you know how many auditions I've been to since I came back to Texas?"

"I should. You dragged me to half of them." Laura watched her mother bite on a warm tortilla chip, bypassing the delicious but calorie-laden *chili con queso*. She looked radiant, and a far cry from the tearful woman who had called her in the middle of the night eight weeks earlier.

"Hantz is letting me go," she had sobbed from five thousand miles away. "He says I'm too old. He's bringing in a new girl, some bimbo who doesn't even know who Peggy Lee is."

It wasn't until Laura, in a moment of weakness,

had suggested Shirley come back to Austin that she had finally stopped whimpering.

Reaching across the table, Shirley patted Laura's hand. "And don't think I'm not grateful, baby," she said in answer to Laura's remark. "For everything. Today included."

Laura raised an eyebrow. "Today?"

"Oh, don't give me that innocent look." Shirley waited until the waiter had brought their seafood salads nestled in giant tortilla shells before continuing. "I know you talked Joe Fielding into giving me that job. What I don't know is how you did it." She snapped a crisp red napkin open. "However, since I was never one to look a gift horse in the mouth, I won't ask."

Because Shirley couldn't carry on a conversation without instilling a little drama in it, she allowed her eyes to fill with tears as she gazed tenderly at her daughter. "Thank you, baby."

Knowing further denial was pointless, Laura smiled. "You're welcome."

Shirley speared a plump shrimp with her fork. "You know, I wasn't sure how it was going to be between the two of us," she said as she chewed. "I mean, I wanted to be here, close to you, but I didn't think you'd want me around on a permanent basis."

Laura hadn't been sure either. After living apart all those years, the two women were more like distant friends than mother and daughter. Yet it would have never occurred to her not to lend a helping hand. Shirley may not have been the best mother in the world but Laura loved her—faults and all. "I'm the one who asked you, remember?"

"I know. But let's face it, I laid a lot on you that night when I called. No wonder you took pity on me."

"I did what any daughter would do."

Shirley took a sip of her margarita. "After the way I hurt you, another daughter would have hung up on me at the first sob."

Laura waved her fork. "That's all behind us now; and anyway, we didn't come here to talk about what happened sixteen years ago. We came here to celebrate your new gig. So cheer up."

Shirley, ever the consummate performer, underwent a total transformation. "You're right," she said, her tone bubbling with excitement. "In fact, I want to have a *real* celebration. A dinner party. At my house. You, me, and that handsome new fiancé of yours."

Laura winced inwardly. Stuart, a Texas blue blood whose family tree was said to go back to England's King George III, considered Shirley more of an embarrassment than an asset. His opinions, which he didn't even try to conceal, were a constant source of disagreement between them. "I wouldn't plan anything around Stuart if I were you, Mom. You know how busy he is these days."

Shirley heaved a sigh worthy of Sarah Bernhardt. "Do you realize that I never see him? I've invited both of you three times since your engagement party last month, and something always comes up." She made a moue that would have looked silly on most women her age. "If I didn't know better, I'd swear he was avoiding me."

"Now, Mom. You know that's not true," Laura lied. "Since being appointed Burnet County assistant prosecutor, he's been working day and night."

"I didn't realize there were that many criminals to prosecute in Burnet."

"No hard core criminals, but there are enough minor incidents throughout the county to keep him extremely busy."

"And you're okay with that?"

Laura avoided her mother's scrutinizing gaze by busying herself with her salad. "Of course."

"Well, will you please tell him this dinner is important to me and I'd like him to make an effort to be there? I'll even plan it around his schedule, how's that?"

Laura smiled. "That's very sweet of you." Anxious to change the subject, she waved her left hand in front of her mother's nose. "Do you realize you haven't said one word about my ring. What's the matter, not big enough for you?"

Shirley gasped as she took Laura's hand to admire the stunning three-carat solitaire. "Oh, my stars! I guess he wasn't kidding when he said the wait would be worth it. This baby must have cost him a fortune." She looked up expectantly. "So, you two set a date yet?"

Laura claimed her hand back. "No."

The happy smile faded. "Why not? Don't tell me he's too busy to make wedding plans."

"No. We just want to make sure the date we choose won't interfere with our schedules, that's all. Stuart may have to try the Halloway arson case in a few weeks and there's no telling how long that will last."

"He's not stalling, is he?"

"Of course not."

"And you *do* love him."

Laura laughed. "Of course I love him. Why would I have agreed to marry him if I didn't?"

"Oh, I don't know. In *my* days, people married for love. But nowadays with men and women so focused on their careers, who knows why young people do the things they do?"

"Well, I don't know about other people, but I can assure you that Stuart and I are in love. Totally."

But Laura heard a disturbing lack of conviction in her own voice as she recalled Stuart's matter-of-fact proposal. How had he put it? *You and I have a lot in common, Laura. We're both ambitious, intelligent, and we enjoy each other's company. So why not make it official?*

It wasn't the most romantic proposal in the world, but then Stuart had never been one to waste time on words of endearment. Whatever passion simmered beneath his cool exterior, he saved for the courtroom.

Shirley gave a resigned sigh. "Just don't wait too long. The man's one hell of a catch, and as long as you don't have a wedding band next to that ring . . ." Shirley wiggled a crimson-tipped finger at her. "Some pretty young thing can still snatch him away from you."

"I'll remember that." A group of diners at a

nearby table stood up to leave, and Laura glanced at her watch. "Oh no, look at the time." She wiped her mouth. "I've got to go."

"You haven't finished your salad," Shirley protested.

"I know, but I have a newspaper to run, remember?"

"Coward." She offered her cheek. "You're afraid that if you stay, I'll get you to commit to a wedding date."

Laura bent over to kiss her. "Good-bye, Mom. And congratulations again. I'll get the check on my way out."

Although it was still hours away from the eleven o'clock deadline, the newsroom was already in a state of frenzy when Laura returned to the *Sentinel.*

She had passed through its doors countless times since becoming publisher eight months ago, yet she still looked around her with pride at the thought of all she had done in that short time.

Visually speaking, the newsroom of the eighty-seven-year-old newspaper hadn't changed very much. It was still huge, with bright overhead lights, half-a-dozen partitioned offices along the east wall, and broad, crowded desks lined up along the two narrow aisles.

What had changed was the attitude of the staff as well as that of the readers. With the new, more sensational format she had implemented, reporters and editors now regarded the *Sentinel* as an exciting, aggressive publication rather than the stodgy, behind-the-times, newspaper it had become over the years.

As phones rang and reporters scrambled from their desks to cover late-breaking stories, Laura felt a surging thrill. No other place she knew could compare with the raw, unrelenting excitement of a busy newsroom.

She had almost reached her office when someone called her name. Laura turned to greet Nicki Cochran, the foreign desk editor she had hired a few weeks ago.

"We just received this picture from Associated Press," Nicki said, handing a copy of a photograph to Laura. "It was taken by Ted Kandall just as he was leaving Sarajevo." Nicki hesitated. "Do you mind if we run it instead of the one from Reuters?"

Laura took the photograph and studied it for a moment. It was a remarkable shot. Taken from a helicopter, it showed dozens of airport officials scrambling for cover as snipers opened fire. In the background, another helicopter was in flames. It was gutsy and dramatic—just the kind of photograph that had made Texas's very own Ted Kandall a household name. "It's a great photo. Why should I mind?"

The woman flushed. "I know about the long-standing feud between the *Sentinel* and his uncle and I thought . . ."

"You thought I wouldn't want to use anything with the name Kandall on it," Laura finished.

"Something like that."

"I'd be cutting my nose off to spite my face if I did that." After another glance at the photograph, she handed it back with a smile. "You have a good eye, Nicki. By all means run the shot, and make sure Ted Kandall gets full credit, not just AP."

Laura walked over to her secretary's desk, just outside her office. "Any messages while I was gone, Mildred?"

Although she had just celebrated her sixty-second birthday, Mildred Masters didn't look a day over fifty. Conservatively dressed, she was a trim, elegant woman with dark hair she always wore in a French twist, intelligent brown eyes, and a motherly way about her.

Devoted to J.B., who had been the *Sentinel*'s publisher for more than forty years, Mildred had rolled with the paper's transition easily and was now one of Laura's strongest supporters. Which was no small feat considering the resentment Laura had met when she had returned to her Texas roots eight months ago to assume her stepfather's position.

"Four calls." Mildred handed her the pink memo slips. "The first two are from the president of the Ladies' Auxiliary at Breckenridge Hospital. She wants to know if you would speak at their fall luncheon next month. The third is from Tom Grant, the six o'clock anchor at KYZZ. He needs a cohost for a Christmas benefit. The fourth call is from J.B. He had your car checked and the transmission is fine. The clutch, however, is shot, and it's about time you got yourself another car." She smiled. "That last remark was his, not mine."

Laura chuckled as she skimmed through the messages. This wasn't the first time J.B. had questioned her car's reliability. But Laura couldn't bring herself to part with her old jalopy—a 1974 yellow Ford Mustang she had bought while attending the University of Texas thirteen years ago and had never sold.

"I'll think about it. Meanwhile, would you call the president of the Ladies' Auxiliary and tell her I'll get back to her in a couple of days with a definite answer?"

"What about Tom Grant?"

"I'll call him myself."

She continued into her office. As usual, her desk was piled high with newspapers from all over the country, interoffice memos, budget projections, and requests for charitable contributions.

It was a large, sunny room with a view of the Colorado River on one side and a glass wall overlooking the newsroom on the other. J.B. had wanted her to take his office on the fifth floor; but she had turned it down. As a hands-on publisher, she liked to be where the action was—in the newsroom.

She was studying a budget sheet for the next quarter when Ken Malloy poked his head through the partially open door. "Got a minute?"

"Of course." Ken was fifty-four, a thirty-year veteran at the *Sentinel,* and one of the best advertising men in the business. Her welcoming smile faded when she saw the grim expression on his face. "What's wrong?" she asked with a sinking feeling in her stomach.

Selecting a chair across her desk, Ken sat down. "We lost another major account."

She let the budget sheet drop from her hand. "Which one?"

"Schwartz Homes."

"Damn." One of the largest developers in Central Texas, Schwartz Homes was responsible for more than one million dollars in yearly advertising revenues. It was the third major account they had lost this week. If the trend continued, the *Sentinel* would be out of business by year's end.

"Did they give you a reason?"

"Same as the others. Sales are down. They have to cut costs."

"By cutting advertising?" Laura asked incredulously. "Are they crazy, or do they think I'm stupid?"

"Neither. Schwartz Homes's two latest quarters were their highest in the last three years. I'm telling you, Laura, this is a conspiracy to put this paper out of business. And Malcolm Kandall is at the root of it. I'd stake a year's salary on it."

Laura nodded grimly. The first cancellation had occurred only four days ago, the same day her column, "Eyes on You," had focused its attention on gubernatorial candidate Malcolm Kandall, questioning the sources of some of the donations that had been made into his campaign funds.

"I don't know how much longer we can last with these kinds of setbacks," Ken continued, echoing her thoughts of a moment ago. "I was on the phone all day yesterday, trying to drum up new business, but . . ." He shook his head. "I struck out."

"Well then, maybe it's time I confronted the

enemy, don't you think?" Not one to let an impulse go unattended for very long, Laura picked up the telephone on her desk. "Mildred, please call Malcolm Kandall's campaign headquarters and tell his secretary I want to see him. Today."

2

His hands behind his back, Malcolm Kandall stood at the window of his plush campaign headquarters on the seventeenth floor of the Carlisle building. Located in the heart of Austin, it overlooked the state capitol, a grand Renaissance-style palace that had housed some of the most colorful statesmen in Texas history. On a wall behind him, a television set, tuned in to CNN, provided him with constant news and the latest political poll results.

At fifty-six, Malcolm Kandall could have easily passed for forty-five. His brown hair had just begun to sprout a touch of gray, and thanks to a vigorous exercise regimen, his body was trim and fit.

An injury he had sustained in his youth had left him with a slight limp. Although the deformity was barely visible, he was deeply conscious of it and tried to conceal it by always walking slowly when he was campaigning and stopping often to talk to his supporters.

He came from a long line of ambitious Texas politicians, and although his own career had suffered a mild setback several years ago, he had more than made up for the loss of time. A charismatic man many compared to Richard Nixon, his landslide victory in the last mayoral election was attributed to his now famous slogan "Kandall Cares," and his ability to make the people of Austin believe it.

A frisson of pleasure coursed through him as his gaze fastened on a second-floor window of the capitol building. Soon, *he* would be the one sitting in the governor's office, making state decisions, meeting with the world's leaders, and attending lavish functions. After years of hard work and ass-kissing, he had finally made it to the top. Well . . . not quite to the top. It was still a long way to the White House. But judging from his rising popularity in the polls, his victory over the incumbent governor was almost a certainty. And after that, he thought, his skin prickling with excitement—Pennsylvania Avenue.

Provided Laura Spencer didn't destroy him first.

Despite his earlier happiness, he felt a bitch of a headache beginning and pressed the bridge of his nose between his two fingers. It wasn't the first time he and the *Sentinel* had locked horns. Sixteen years ago, when Malcolm had been running for county freeholder, J.B. Lawson had linked him to an insurance fraud during his term as city councilman and disclosed his findings in a front-page article.

The scandal had cost Malcolm the election, forcing him to return to his law practice. In time, the public had forgotten the incident and Malcolm eventually reentered politics. But he had never forgiven J.B. for his vicious exposé.

And now his stepdaughter, a tabloid journalist of all things, was threatening to do the same thing to him. Unless he stopped her.

The buzzing of the intercom on his desk pulled him out of his thoughts. "Yes, Lillian."

"Miss Spencer is here, sir."

"Send her in."

The politician was sitting at his desk, looking as relaxed and elegant as he did in his television commercials when Laura was ushered in by his secretary.

"How are you, Laura? It's been a while, hasn't it?"

Ignoring his outstretched hand, Laura planted herself firmly in front of him. "Cut the bull, Malcolm. This isn't a social call. I want to know what the hell you think you're doing."

His charismatic smile stayed plastered on. "Am I supposed to know what you're talking about?"

"I'm talking about the three accounts I just lost—Orbach Motors, Bradley Department Stores, and the lastest casualty, Schwartz Homes. The owners are all good friends of yours, I believe."

"I'm sure that's a mild exaggeration." He tilted back in his chair. "You know how it is when a campaign is going well. Everyone wants to be your friend."

"Don't play games with me, Malcolm. I know you're responsible. And I know why you did it."

He steepled his fingers and held them in front of him. "I'll humor you. Why?"

"You found out I was investigating your campaign funds and you don't like it. You figure if you flex your muscles a little, show me how powerful you are, I'll back down, like a good little girl."

"Why would I want to interfere with the press? I have nothing to hide."

"Really? You mean you see nothing wrong with the fact that three Austin businessmen, who donated huge sums of money to your gubernatorial campaign, are the same people who were awarded big city contracts during your term as mayor?"

Although everything she had said so far was true, Malcolm managed to act properly shocked. "I've done nothing of the sort," he said, his voice ringing with indignation. "Everyone knows that all contracts for city jobs, regardless of their size, have to adhere to strict requirements, and for you to imply otherwise is simply insulting."

"But true."

"No it's not. And I dare you to come up with one person who will support those allegations."

She had already tried. Unfortunately, all interested parties had too much at stake to blow the whistle on their benefactor. "I will," she said with more assurance than she felt at the moment. "And your trying to run me out of business isn't going to stop me."

Malcolm heaved a pained sigh. "Oh, my dear girl. You have it all wrong." He swung gently from side to side as he continued to look at her. "In fact, quite the opposite is true, which is why I agreed to meet with you. I was hoping we could put our differences aside, at least temporarily, and reach some sort of truce."

Because their dislike for each other went back a

long way, the suggestion threw her off balance. "Truce . . . ? You and I?"

"I know there's been a lot of bad blood between our two families in the past. But things are different now; and, contrary to what you believe, I don't wish you or the *Sentinel* any harm. In fact, I would be glad to talk to Al Schwartz and the others." He smiled. "As a sign of good faith."

"Then you do admit to having pressured them."

"Here you go again, jumping to conclusions. All I meant to say was that I would put in a good word for you. The rest, of course, would be up to them."

He's good, Laura admitted to herself. Smooth as silk on the surface and lethal underneath. "I see." She raked him with a scornful look. "And would you be doing this out of the goodness of your heart or would you expect something in return?"

His good humor seemed to have returned. "Well, now that you mention it, a little favorable press once in a while would be nice."

"And it goes without saying that you would expect me to drop my investigation."

"I wouldn't want to see you waste your time on something so trivial when there are so many important issues your newspaper needs to address." His blue eyes, a legacy all the Kandall men had inherited, bored into hers. "But that would be entirely up to you."

Their gaze held and for a moment, Laura was reminded of how devastating his revenge could be, of how swiftly and mercilessly he could strike. It would have been so easy to do as he suggested, to look the other way as others had done. Especially when the jobs of five hundred people were at stake, people who counted on her, people who had families to support.

She could not take the easy way out, though. She had too much respect for her profession to use it as a negotiating tool. Malcolm Kandall hadn't changed. He was as unscrupulous and manipulative as ever. She might not be able to prove it just yet, but she would. Until then, she'd find a way to keep the *Sentinel* going—with or without his help.

"Favorable press is something one earns," she said in a calm, even voice. "And until you've done that, I'll stick to what I do best—report the truth."

This time, his gaze revealed his hatred. Ignoring it, she marched toward the door. She was about to open it when he called out her name.

One hand on the knob, Laura turned around.

"Don't be a crusader, Laura. You'll find it doesn't pay. Not in my town."

His mouth set in a tight, angry line, Malcolm watched the door close behind her.

That nosy, self-righteous little bitch, he thought, expelling a long, trembling breath. She was as much of an idealistic fool as her stepfather. And just as dangerous.

It wasn't what she suspected that worried him, but what she *could* discover if she were allowed to continue with that damned investigation of hers.

He hit the desk with his fist. He would *not* allow her to destroy him. Not when he was so close.

Of course it was still possible that once she'd had time to think about his offer of a truce, she would realize her only chance of survival was to cooperate.

If she didn't, he would have to resort to stronger measures.

Traveling west on Highway 71, Laura waited until she had safely passed an eighteen-wheeler before shifting back to cruising speed. The sights and sounds of the city had disappeared, giving way to Texas hill country, an exclusive wooded paradise west of Austin, which, until a decade or so ago, had been a well-kept secret.

J.B. Lawson, who came from a long line of German settlers, had inherited his ten-thousand-acre ranch in Burnet County from his grandfather and had used it as a weekend retreat until eight months ago, when he had retired and moved to the country permanently.

Laura didn't blame him. The air was fresher here, the temperature cooler, the pace more relaxed, decidedly Western. Feeling miles away from civilization, she took in the unspoiled scenery, the distant limestone hills dotted with green mesquite and juniper, the sunflowers and wild petunias lining the road, and the fields of pampas grass.

She had spent the best years of her life in this part of Texas. Even after J.B.'s short marriage to her mother had ended, Laura continued to regard Lost Creek as her home; and when J.B. had suggested she move into the guest house eight months ago, she had gladly accepted.

As she turned onto Cattle Trail, the mile-long access road that led to the ranch, Lost Creek came into view, first the fenced-in pastures with their famous Texas longhorns grazing the rich grass, then the main house, a three-story log cabin J.B.'s grandfather had built himself, log by log.

She parked her stepfather's Suburban in the detached carport, which doubled as J.B.'s workshop, and went into the house, delightedly aware of the smell of roast turkey and freshly baked bread. Those occasional dinners at the ranch were one of the pleasures she had missed most during her ten years in New York, and although she often worked late at the *Sentinel,* she tried to eat at the ranch at least two night a week.

She slipped out of her green suit jacket, tossed it on a chair, and stepped into a bright, log-walled room. It featured a huge stone fireplace, massive carved oak chests J.B.'s ancestors had collected over the years, and colorful Navajo rugs scattered over the century-old hardwood floor. On the walls were the mementos that had delighted her childhood—a set of antlers above the mantel, a canister lamp J.B.'s grandmother had made herself, and an old portrait of early Burnet settlers.

"Hey, hey, hey, how's my star publisher?"

At the sound of her stepfather's cheery voice, Laura turned around and smiled as he hurried toward her in that endearing bow-legged walk of his. In spite of two recent heart attacks, sixty-six-year-old J.B. Lawson was still a handsome, virile-looking man with snow white hair that curled up at the neck, a face the color and texture of old leather, and eyes as bright and blue as the Texas sky.

To strangers, he was as intimidating as he was big; but one only had to spend a few moments with him to realize that beneath that rugged exterior lay a heart of gold.

"Not feeling much like a star today," she replied in answer to his question.

J.B. slid an arm around her waist and led her toward a grouping of cushy brown sofas and chairs facing the fireplace. "In that case, why don't I make you one of my special cure-alls? I guarantee that will perk you up in no time."

"Sounds wonderful." Smiling, she watched him step behind a gleaming burlwood bar at the end of the room. Although J.B. no longer drank hard liquor, he still enjoyed playing bartender.

A martini in one hand and a bottle of Lone Star beer in the other, he came to sit across from her, watching her as he took a sip of beer. "What's bothering you, kiddo? You look lower than a gopher hole."

She fished the olive from her drink with two fingers and popped it in her mouth. She had never been able to keep anything from him for very long. "I went to see Malcolm Kandall this afternoon."

At the mention of his archenemy's name, the expression in J.B.'s eyes cooled. "Why?"

"Because we lost another account—Schwartz Homes—and I wanted to tell him what I thought of his underhanded tactics."

"What did he say?"

"He denied it, of course." She told him about her conversation with the gubernatorial candidate and how he had tried to buy her silence. "He was very clever about it. Even if I had remembered to bring a tape recorder with me, I couldn't have proved a thing."

"I'm not surprised. Malcolm was always a sly bastard." J.B. took another sip of his beer. "How bad is it, Laura?"

She sighed. "I'm not sure. I've got a few ideas that might keep us afloat for a while; but if Malcolm decides to tighten up the pressure, it could get sticky."

J.B. was thoughtful for a moment. "I could try to talk the bank into extending me another loan if you think that will help."

Laura wasn't sure it would. Two years ago, when the *Sentinel* had been in need of a new, more auto- mated printing plant, J.B. had applied for a large loan, putting the ranch and the *Sentinel* up as col- lateral. Even if he could get a loan, which she doubted, it wouldn't be enough to save the newspa- per. "There's no need to do that at the moment," she said, not wanting to create undue stress for him. "However, I scheduled a meeting of our executive committee first thing tomorrow morning. I sure could use your input, J.B."

"I'll be there." Setting his beer bottle on the coffee table, he leaned forward. "You know that I trust you implicitly, don't you, kiddo? And that whatever decision you make, I'll back you all the way."

She threw him an amused glance. "Why do I have the feeling there's a 'but' coming?"

He shook his head. "No 'but.' I just want you to know that if you decide to back off from that Kandall investigation, I'll understand. Running a newspaper is a big responsibility."

"Do you *want* me to back off, J.B.?"

"I didn't say that." His gaze was solemn as he continued to watch her. "But I know you. I know how much you've come to care about the *Sentinel,* and the people who work for it."

"As much as you do."

"Precisely. So if your heart wins in the end, and you decide to back off, don't feel you're letting me down, or that you're compromising your integrity. Sometimes, integrity is knowing when to make the tough choices."

Laura gazed into her unfinished martini. She didn't have to ask him what his decision would have been if he had been in her shoes. She knew. J.B. was a fighter. Always would be.

After a while, she looked up. "I have no intention of backing off."

J.B. leaned back in his chair as his chest filled with fatherly pride. He had known all along she was perfect for the job of publisher. She hadn't wanted to take it at first. She hadn't wanted to leave New York and the *Herald* where she had worked since her graduation from the University of Texas. And the brass at the *Herald* hadn't wanted to lose their star reporter either. After ten years with the famous paper and two Pulitzer prizes, crime reporter Laura Spencer had become a household name. Even Hollywood had come calling. She had told them no. Unlike her mother, who thrived on attention, Laura detested being thrown in the limelight.

But it wasn't until he had told her the *Sentinel* was dying a slow and painful death that she had begun to show interest in his proposition.

She had been recuperating from a gunshot wound she had sustained while covering a bank robbery in lower Manhattan. Worried about her, he had flown to New York, hoping to convince her to come back home with him.

"This past recession killed me, kiddo," he had told her as he sat on the edge of her hospital bed. "As a result, advertising revenues and circulation have slipped to an all-time low. All my good writers are jumping ship. Even my editor is threatening to quit. I think the paper can be saved; but it needs new blood. And a younger, more energetic publisher at the helm."

He didn't tell her that the other reason he was offering her the job was to get her the hell out of New York City. He wanted her back on safe, friendly ground, where she wouldn't be risking her life every time she went after a story.

"I'll even make you a partner," he added, trying to sweeten the pot, although he knew money wasn't important to her. "Twenty shares of the *Sentinel* now and thirty more at the end of one year, if you decide to stay."

When the reaction he had expected didn't come, he had played his trump card. "Oh, and you have carte blanche to change the paper any way you see fit."

Her eyes had shone brighter than fireworks on a Fourth of July. "Does that mean I can change the format?"

Turning the *Sentinel* into a more sensational publication was something Laura had urged him to do for years. But J.B. had always resisted the idea. Austin was an old-fashioned town with old-fashioned ideas and changing the newspaper format from broadsheet to tabloid could have catastrophic results. But with profits sinking at such an alarming rate, he no longer had a choice. "If you think it will save the *Sentinel*," he replied. "Go right ahead and do it."

And she had. With flair and energy and a relentlessness that had paid off beyond his wildest expectations. Within six weeks, the advertisers she had courted herself had returned in force, and her weekly column, "Eyes On You," was one of the most avidly read editorials in all of Texas. Although not a political column, it dealt with issues and people in the news, and since she wasn't one to mince words, the replies were always heated and made for much entertainment in the editorial page.

Twirling her martini, Laura was watching him. "Why the smile?"

"Because you remind me a lot of myself when I was young, full of passion and ideals." His eyes filled with sadness. "Just make sure you don't get hurt the way I did. Know exactly how to protect yourself from Kandall."

"We're not talking about the paper anymore, are we?" she asked softly.

"No." He looked out the window for a moment, lost in his thoughts. "How's your mother?" he asked at last.

"On cloud nine. She found a job. A six-week engagement at the Golden Parrot."

"Joe's club? I thought he was trying to sell the place."

"He may not have to now that Mom is his star attraction." Her eyes brightened. "Oh, J.B., you should have heard her sing "Fever" at the audition. Joe was mesmerized."

J.B. nodded slowly as memories of that song flashed through his mind. "I'm glad for her." Then, before nostalgia set its claws into him, he rose to his feet. "What do you say we go see how Lenox is coming along with that turkey he's cooking? I'm starved. And maybe after dinner, I could have that chess rematch you owe me."

"You're on." She linked her arm with his as they headed toward the kitchen. "But I warn you. You'd better come with your pockets full. I feel lucky tonight."

3

In a closet he had converted into a darkroom, Ted Kandall lifted the last print from the final wash and clipped it to a line to dry, next to the others.

Not bad at all, he thought, leaning forward to closely examine the shots. All the photographs had been taken in the mountainous landscape above Sarajevo during a battle between Bosnian Serbs and Croatians twenty-four hours earlier. The fighting had been so fierce that his helicopter to England he had boarded moments later had been hit twice, fortunately not seriously enough to abort the flight.

One of three photojournalists to be allowed into Serb territory, Ted had spent two months with a small group of militia soldiers, the youngest of whom had been fourteen. He had sent dozens of rolls of film back to London every week, and Lloyd, the Associated Press senior photo editor for whom Ted did most of his freelance work, had raved about every one of them.

"I haven't seen anything this good since Robert Capa did his Indo-China war series back in the fifties," the transplanted American had told him over the phone. "I don't know about you, but I smell another Pulitzer."

Covering the Bosnian Serbs had been one of the most dangerous yet rewarding assignments Ted could remember. Not because it had taken his career to a new level, but because, through his lens, he had been able to tell another side of the war in Yugoslavia, a side few even suspected existed.

He was pulling off his disposable gloves when the doorbell of his London flat began to ring insistently.

"Coming!" he shouted, turning off the red safety light.

His scowl at being interrupted disappeared the moment he swung the door open. Standing on the landing, a grin on her pretty face and an overnight bag slung over her shoulder, was Sandra, his twenty-two-year-old sister. "Goldilocks!" he exclaimed using the nickname he had given her long ago.

Sandra threw herself in his arms. "Hi, big brother. Glad to see me?"

"You bet. Let me take a look at you." Grinning, he took in the cap of blond curls, the big brown, laughing eyes, and the small, turned-up nose. As always her clothes, while not high fashion, certainly made a statement. For her Atlantic crossing, she had chosen baggy jeans, work boots she claimed were the latest rage on campus, and a green army jacket she had bought during her last foray through a London flea market four months ago.

She spread her arms wide. "You like my outfit?"

Ted laughed. On you, yes," he replied. Taking her bag with one hand, he encircled her waist with the other. Together they walked back into the living room. "Why didn't you tell me you were coming? I would have come to the airport."

"There was no time." Sandra collapsed on a deep red sofa and let her gaze sweep over the several black-and-white photographs of various world events that adorned the walls. She noted they were new, which didn't surprise her. Ted, as restless with his surroundings as he was with his personal life, changed them regularly. "I left Austin as you were taking off from Sarajevo."

"How do you know when I left Sarajevo?"

"I called Lloyd." She gave him a smug smile. "You're not the only one with brains, you know."

"Obviously not."

Sandra pulled him down on the sofa, forcing him to sit. "It's my turn to check you out." She frowned as she studied the handsome face, the unruly, dusty blond hair, the deep cornflower blue eyes he had inherited from their father, the day-old beard, and the strong, square jaw. "Mmm. You look tired. But I suppose I ought to be thankful you're alive, considering what I heard on the news."

"What did you hear?"

"That a British helicopter with several journalists on board had taken off from Sarajevo under heavy gunfire. That was you, wasn't it? You were on board that helicopter."

"Stop frowning, Goldilocks. Or you'll get wrinkled before your time. Does it matter what helicopter I was on? I'm here now. Safe and sound."

Sandra remained stern. "Honest to God, Theodore, if you keep this up, I'll not only have wrinkles but I'll be the only coed in my graduating class with white hair. And all because I worry so much about you."

"So stop worrying."

"Easy for you to say. You're not the one with a thrill-seeker for a brother."

"Thrill-seeker, hell. I'm just trying to make a living."

"Then why can't you make it some other way, a safer way, like fashion photography? You'd make gobs of money."

"I would also die of boredom within a week."

"Boredom?" she scoffed. "With Claudia Schiffer prancing around in her underwear all day long?"

Leaning one arm over the back of the sofa, he gave a disinterested shrug. "Oh, you know what they say. You've seen one fashion model in her underwear, you've seen them all."

Although that may have been a mild exaggeration, Sandra knew that nothing could stimulate Ted more than what he was doing now. Fifteen years her senior, he had earned his stripes as a photojournalist during the U.S. invasion of Grenada. In 1986, while freelancing for the *London Times* he had received critical acclaim for his stunning photographs of two Arab gunmen bursting into an Istanbul synagogue and killing twenty-one worshipers. Now, nine years later, he had not lost any of his passion for his work, although she could see a new expression in his eyes, a sadness she didn't remember noticing during her last visit. The war in Yugoslavia had really taken its toll on him.

Ted stretched his long legs across the coffee table. "So tell me, Goldilocks. How's college?"

"Fine. Daddy's finally reconciled himself to the idea that I won't be going to law school."

"I take it you still have your heart set on a teaching career."

"More than ever. And Daddy always knew it. It just took him some time to accept it, that's all."

"Did he give you a hard time?"

"Not as hard as he gave you when you announced you were going to become a photojournalist, but he was disappointed." She laughed. "I think deep in his heart, he always believed I would be the next Ann Richards."

"So start riding a Harley."

Sandra laughed as she leaned her head on his shoulder. "Oh, Ted, you always know how to make me laugh."

He looked down at her, wondering what had brought her to him this time. "Is that why you traveled five thousand miles? For a good laugh?"

When she didn't answer, he took her chin between two fingers and forced her to look at him. "Something wrong, sis?"

"No. I mean . . ." She jumped to her feet. "Could we go for a walk? After eight hours cooped up in a plane, I need to stretch my legs."

"Sure." He stood up. "Where do you want to go?"

"I don't know. How about that tea shop I like on Goldborne? Beauregard?"

Ted took a brown leather bomber jacket from the back of a chair and slipped it on. "Beauregard it is."

Moments later they were strolling through lively Portobello Market where, on a Saturday afternoon, one could find anything and everything from vintage typewriters and antique books to African masks.

Back in the days when Ted had first moved to Notting Hill, the area had been in a state of decay, with seedy streets, dilapidated houses, and neglected parks. But a decade of renovation had changed all of that. Now, the streets blossomed with new boutiques, art galleries, and trendy restaurants, all patroned by a clientele that was the very essence of urban chic.

Beauregard, the fashionable tea salon on Goldborne Road was one of Sandra's favorite places in all of London. He had taken her there the first summer she had come to stay with him, and her face, as she had stared at the pastry case, had been a delight to see. And to photograph.

The establishment was packed when they arrived, but thanks to a waitress Ted knew, they were ushered to a table within a few minutes.

After both had ordered a pot of Earl Grey tea and a tray of assorted pastries, Ted rested his arms on the table. "Okay, what's wrong, Goldilocks? Your boyfriend giving you a hard time? If he is . . ." He made a big production of cracking his knuckles. "Let me know, and I'll take care of him."

"I don't have a boyfriend at the moment." Sandra's gaze drifted toward an elderly gentleman and a little boy, obviously his grandson, as they slid behind a nearby booth. After a moment, she returned her attention to Ted. "It's Daddy."

He had already guessed that much. Although Sandra came to London several times a year, she wasn't in the habit of popping in unannounced. "Is he ill again?"

She nodded slowly. "He's dying."

He wasn't sure what hit him first—disbelief or pain. He had always thought of his father as indestructible. And he had just reason. Now sixty-three, the former state senator had survived the Korean War, two terrorist attacks, and a helicopter crash that had claimed the lives of three American congressmen. If there was one man in this world capable of defying death, it was Charles Kandall.

Ted swallowed to chase away the knot that had formed in his throat. "The cancer came back?"

Sandra nodded. "He hadn't been feeling well for some time—mild pains in his side, fatigue ... Finally, he got tired of my nagging and agreed to have a checkup." Her voice cracked. "This time the disease has settled in the liver. It's inoperable."

"Damn." He waited until the waitress had brought their order before speaking again. "How much time does he have?"

"Six months at best. Maybe less." Picking up the porcelain pot, she filled their cups. "He'd kill me if he knew I told you. But I had to." Tears she could no longer control ran down her cheeks and she set the teapot down. "I'm sorry," she said, wiping her face with the back of her hand. "I didn't mean to fall apart like that."

"You can cry in front of me." He stirred a spoonful of sugar into his tea. "How is Dad taking it?"

"Oh, you know Daddy. He's acting as if it's no big deal. He's even campaigning for Uncle Malcolm. Can you believe that?"

Ted wasn't surprised. Charles had always been devoted to his younger brother. Years ago, when the two had been playing a friendly game of football on the family lawn, an unlucky tackle on Charles's part had sent Malcolm crashing against a two-hundred-year-old oak. The fall had broken Malcolm's hip, leaving him with a slight limp and cutting short the youth's dream of making the high school football team. Charles, devastated by the accident, had assumed full responsibility for it, and Malcolm, true to form, had never allowed him to forget it.

Reaching across the small, round table, Ted took Sandra's hand and held it. Only six when their mother had died, she had grown up idolizing her father. "I wish there was something I could do, sis."

"There is." Their gazes locked. "Come home, Ted."

If it hadn't been for the way she looked at him, with that grief-stricken face, he would have thought she was joking.

"I know what you're thinking," she continued, talking in a low, urgent voice. "That you wouldn't be welcome, that he wouldn't want to see you."

"Bingo." He made no attempt to disguise the bitterness in his voice. "The answer is no, sis. I won't set myself up for another rejection."

"It'll be different this time. He's sick—"

"Bull. He could be at death's door and it wouldn't change a thing. I know. I tried to reconcile with him years ago, remember? I even sent him an invitation to my first stateside exhibition. Not only didn't he show up, he never even bothered to RSVP. He treated the event as if it were some insignificant happening, unworthy of even a passing thought."

Although he seldom allowed himself to think about that day, he remembered it with crystal-clear clarity. He had been so proud of his accomplishment, so certain his father would be, too, in spite of their differences. When he had called the house a week later to make sure the invitation had been received, Lucinda, the Kandalls' housekeeper had answered the phone. "I don't think you should count on him being there, Teddy," she had said, her voice heavy with sorrow. "He threw the invitation away."

He had never called home again.

"He was still angry with you over what happened at Mom's funeral," Sandra said, desperately trying to divide her loyalties.

"That's right. And he'll never stop being angry. And he'll never stop hating me."

"You're wrong. He's changed. He's ... mellowed."

But her voice lacked conviction. "Men like him don't change because they get sick, Sandra. They just grow meaner."

"You wouldn't be saying that if you saw him. Oh, he's still self-sufficient, and some days, you can't even tell he's sick. But I know that deep down he's afraid of what's happening to him, of what's waiting down the road."

"He has you and Lucinda to look after him."

"That's not enough. He needs male support. He needs your strength, your courage. He needs you, Ted."

Unexpectedly, images of his mother flashed across Ted's mind. He remembered the way she had looked the last time he had seen her alive. He had been attending the University of Louisiana and she had flown to New Orleans to spend the weekend with him as she often did. Dressed in tan slacks and a white blouse with the sleeves rolled up, she could have passed for a coed. She was so different away from home, so full of life. They had spent those two days walking around the French Quarter, sampling gumbo and listening to Dixieland jazz.

On Sunday night at the airport, she had slipped a five-thousand-dollar check into his shirt pocket, hushing his protests with a scented finger. "Stop being so damned hardheaded and take the money this time. I know you need it."

Two weeks later he had seen her again. This time, she was lying in a coffin.

"Ted, did you hear me?" Sandra's low, urgent voice brought him back.

"I heard you, but I couldn't get away now even if I wanted to," he lied, looking for an easy way out. "I told Lloyd I'd go to Haiti to cover the return of President Aristide."

"You're a freelancer. You can get out of it."

"Dad would know I came back because of his illness."

"No, he wouldn't. I've got that part covered."

Ted raised an eyebrow. "You have?"

"Uh-huh. There's a new photo gallery in Austin. You may have heard of it. The Luberick? If you could arrange an exhibition there in the next couple of weeks, it would be the perfect excuse for you to be in town."

"Oh, sis, Dad will see right through that flimsy excuse."

"No, he won't."

Her determination touched him but did little to change his feelings. It was too late for him and Charles. "He's built this wall between us . . ." he said more to himself than to her.

"Walls were made to be torn down." She watched several expressions flit across his face and although she understood what he was going through, she knew, deep in her heart, that he wanted to come home. "I know it'll be difficult to face Daddy at first, but you can do it." She smiled. "If you can charm your way out of an Iraqi jail, I know you can do this." Sandra paused before continuing.

"I know you love him, Ted," she said. "So you can stop trying to deny it."

He wanted to. He wanted to tell her he hated the old man for rejecting him all these years, for not loving him enough to forgive and move on.

Sandra brought her gaze back to Ted. "It's time to forget the past, Ted. It's time to be a family again."

Because he had never been able to refuse her anything, he felt himself waver. "I'm going to regret this," he muttered. "As surely as I'm sitting here, I'm going to regret this."

Sandra's shoulders sagged with relief. "Does that mean you'll come?"

After a while, Ted nodded. "Yes, I'll come."

"Mmm. Something smells wonderful," Laura said as Stuart rummaged through his kitchen drawer for a corkscrew. "Coq au vin?"

"Chicken marengo," he corrected her. "It's a recipe Napoléon's chef invented during the famous Marengo battle against the Austrian army, using whatever he could get from the field—a chicken, a few root vegetables, and of course, brandy."

Laura, who had no particular interest in food, French or otherwise, half listened to his chatter as he inserted the two-pronged corkscrew into a bottle of white Bordeaux and neatly popped the cork.

Stuart Fleming was every bit as handsome as her mother kept proclaiming. Tall, lean, and green-eyed, he looked more like a college athlete than a thirty-six-year-old prosecutor.

She had met him last February when J.B. was hosting a party to celebrate her homecoming. Stuart, who had just been appointed Burnet County assistant prosecutor, had been one of the guests, and she had noticed him instantly. He was intelligent, career-oriented, and could argue any topic from the legalization of drugs to the merits of the rain forest. But it was his selfless devotion to the less fortunate and his passion for justice that had won her heart in the end.

"Here we go." Smiling, he filled two balloon glasses with the golden wine and handed her one. "A 1989 Graves, perfectly chilled."

She touched her glass to his and took a sip. Her tastes leaned more toward hearty reds, but Stuart was a wine enthusiast as well as a gourmet cook, and he would have been terribly disappointed by anything less than total approval.

"Well?" he asked expectantly. "What do you think?"

"Delicious. It will go great with the chicken." Coward, she thought. Why don't you just tell him you don't give a damn about a wine's pedigree as long as you like it?

After checking the gleaming red pot on the stove and lowering the heat, Stuart took Laura's hand and led her back into the living room. His town house was a handsome duplex only two minutes from the Burnet town center that offered all the amenities for an up-and-coming young professional—a state-of-the-art kitchen, a living room, and a bedroom that doubled as study.

Sitting down on a blue-and-white-striped sofa, he pulled her beside him. "Now, what is this about dinner at your mother's? You sounded very mysterious over the phone."

She took a sip of her wine. "It's a celebration dinner. Mom is now gainfully employed. She starts work tomorrow."

His expression remained neutral. "Really. Where?"

"The Golden Parrot. She just signed a six-week contract—"

"The Golden Parrot is a dive," Stuart declared in his usual blunt way as he let go of her hand.

"It is not. It's a perfectly respectable nightclub, owned and managed by one of J.B.'s oldest friends."

"I don't care if it's managed by the pope, it's still no place for my future mother-in-law. I can't believe you allowed Shirley to sign that contract."

Laura bristled, which was often the case when they talked about her mother. "*Allowed*?" she echoed. "You talk as if she were a child instead of a grown woman."

"That's because she acts like a child. This decision of hers proves it. It's another disaster waiting to happen."

She knew exactly what other disaster he was referring to. Twenty-five years ago in Dallas, one of Shirley's former lovers had entered her dressing room while she prepared to go on stage and attacked her at knife point. Somehow, she had managed to wrestle the weapon away from him, accidentally stabbing him in the arm as they struggled. A few days later, both had dropped their respective charges against each other. "What happened in Dallas was an isolated incident," she said. "Nothing like that has ever happened since."

"You should have stopped her," he said stubbornly.

"Since when have I ever been able to tell my mother what to do?"

His expression turned scornful. "Did you even try?"

"No. I think this job will be good for her. It enables her not only to earn some money but to do something she loves."

"Have you given any consideration to what that might do to my future? Having my fiancée's mother singing torch songs in a nightclub that caters to horny GIs isn't exactly the kind of publicity that will enhance my career—"

Laura slammed her glass down on the coffee table. "Dammit, Stuart, why must you always equate everything my mother does or doesn't do to how it will affect your career? Why can't you think of her once in a while?"

The rebuttal brought a flush to Stuart's cheeks and for a moment, he had the grace to look embarrassed as he gazed into his drink. "I'm sorry," he said after a moment. "I guess I was a bit harsh." He looked up. "And anyway, I doubt if people will make the connection between her and me."

That's all that matters to him, Laura thought, saddened that in spite of her efforts, he would never fully accept her mother as she was. It was true that Shirley was a bit shallow and self-absorbed; but she could also be, on occasions, tender, forgiving, and generous to a fault.

"Forgive me?" Stuart leaned over and nuzzled her ear. "I'll even accept your mother's dinner invitation if that will bring a smile to your face."

Because Laura wasn't one to hold a grudge for very long, she didn't pull away. "And you won't make any snide remarks about her new job? Or about the way she dresses?"

He drew the sign of the cross over his heart. "Scout's honor. I'll even bring flowers and champagne."

The engaging smile melted the last of her resistance. "She'll love that. She has a soft spot for you, you know. She thinks you're the best thing that ever happened to me."

"I hope you believe her." Not giving her a chance to answer, he put his glass down, then drew her into his arms, kissing her long and deep. "Friends again?" he asked when he finally released her.

"Mmm. I don't know." She gripped the collar of his shirt and pulled him back. "Maybe if you did that again . . ."

Later that night, Laura lay in her bed, thinking about the argument that had almost ruined her and Stuart's evening.

Like many people in Burnet County, Stuart's judgment of Shirley Langfield was influenced by events that had taken place long ago when J.B., then one of Burnet's most eligible bachelors, had met the sultry Dallas chanteuse.

The townspeople had watched in disapproval as she had swept him off his feet, married him, and then a year later, had abandoned him and her sixteen-year-old daughter to pursue a singing career in Europe.

What Stuart, and most people, didn't know, was that Malcolm Kandall had engineered the breakup.

Angry at J.B. for writing an exposé about him, the politician had gone after the only person J.B. loved more than anything—his new bride.

Knowing that Shirley's career wasn't going anywhere at the time, Malcolm had arranged for her to meet a European promoter he knew. Two weeks later, Shirley had signed a one-year contract to tour military installations in Germany, swearing the move was only temporary and that she would be back at the end of the tour.

Laura had pleaded with her not to go. "How can you do that to J.B.?" she had asked. "Can't you see you're breaking his heart?"

She might as well have talked to a brick wall.

"I'm only going away for a year, baby, not forever."

"What about me? I need you, too."

"Look, why don't you try staying at Lost Creek for a while? If you don't like it, or if you miss me as much as you think you will, I'll send for you. There's an excellent American school in Frankfurt."

But Laura knew she would have been in the way. And she didn't want to leave J.B., whom she loved like a father, or Lenox, J.B.'s English butler who hovered over her like a mother hen.

As she suspected, Shirley's one-year contract turned into a second, then a third until it became obvious she had no intention of returning home. That same week J.B. had found out about Malcolm's involvement in the affair and how he had paid the German promoter to offer Shirley a contract she couldn't refuse. But by then it was too late to do anything about it. Disgusted, he had filed for divorce and life at the ranch had continued without Shirley.

It had taken Laura a long time to forgive her mother. But eventually she had; and when Shirley had called from Germany eight weeks ago, devastated at the realization that her career was over, Laura hadn't had the heart to turn her away.

Stuart had been against the idea from the very beginning. "What possessed you to invite her to come back here?" he'd asked. "After all the pain she's caused you and J.B. And where is she going to stay anyway? Surely not at your house. That's J.B.'s property for God's sake."

Fortunately, where to stay hadn't been a problem. Shirley, an astute businesswoman, had put her divorce settlement money to work for her, and by the time she came back to Austin, she had amassed a tidy sum.

But even though she lived far enough away from the Hill Country, her return to Texas had caused mixed reactions amongst the people of Burnet County. Many had gone as far as openly expressing their anger in the editorial pages of the *Hillside,* Burnet's weekly paper.

Now, with this new job, the possibility of an even greater conflict between herself and Stuart seemed stronger than ever. What if Shirley was a hit? Would her success irritate Stuart even more? Or would he learn to live with it?

With a sigh of frustration, Laura gave her pillow a few hard punches, then plopped her head onto it, hoping that by the bright light of day, her worries would evaporate. Some of them anyway.

4

Sitting behind her desk, Laura gazed at the members of her operating committee as she briefed them on the situation between her and Malcolm Kandall and how it would affect the *Sentinel*.

All were veteran newspeople who had been devoted to J.B. and who, at first, had taken her ideas for change with a great deal of skepticism.

Yet, change had been desperately needed. Despite J.B.'s attempts at more efficient management, the *Sentinel*'s newsroom had been badly run, swimming in rigid editorial bureaucracies that dated back to the early 1960s.

Laura had changed all that. She had cleaned house by cutting down on unnecessary personnel, defining duties and responsibilities, and reorganizing the structure of the newspaper, a move that hadn't exactly endeared her to the staff, but that had produced results.

Three weeks after she had assumed her position, the new *Austin Sentinel* was out in the street. Readers had received it with mixed emotions at first, but it hadn't taken Austinites long to realize that the

newspaper was not only informative, but for the
first time in years, fun to read.

And now, all eyes were turned toward her once
again. Having performed a small miracle, she was
expected to perform another—that of defeating the
mighty Malcolm Kandall.

It was a tall order. The three lost advertisers had
generated combined revenues of more than four
hundred thousand dollars a week. Without that
money, and with no new accounts to fill the void,
the *Sentinel* wouldn't survive.

Of the six people in the room, Ken Malloy, the
advertising director, and J.B. were the only two
people who were already aware of the latest problem facing the *Sentinel.* The other four, Marianne
Lyons, chief financial officer, Johnny O'Toole, the
general manager, Leo Brunnel, the marketing director, and Milton Shank, her editor, took the news
calmly, but their faces were grave, their eyes cloudy
with worry.

"What happens if we can't replace those three
advertisers?" Marianne asked. "Or if we lose others? How long will we last? Six months? Less?"

Laura and J.B. exchanged a glance. "More like
three."

"I talked to a friend of mine at the bank to try
to borrow some money," J.B. said, meeting Laura's
quick, disapproving glance. "Enough to see us
through the crisis." He shook his head. "Unfortunately the board turned me down." He sighed.
"Sorry, guys. If I hadn't sunk so much money into
that printing plant, we wouldn't be in this mess
right now."

"You did what you had to do at the time, J.B.,"
Johnny O'Toole said. "It's Kandall who galls me.
Who the hell does he think he is telling us what to
print and what not to print?"

Leo Brunnel tilted his chair back, resting it
against the wall. "You handled that sleazebag just
right, Laura. Personally, I'd be tempted to expose
him for what he is—a low-life blackmailer. The
problem is, it would be your word against his."

"We could always corner him in some dark alley
and show him how we deal with vermin like him in
the marines." The remark came from editor Milton
Shank, a former drill sergeant who often went by
the nickname of "Bulldog."

Laughter rippled through the room.

Ken Malloy, whose advertising department had
been badly shaken up by the loss of their three
biggest accounts, refused to join in the laughter.
"What are you proposing to do, Laura?"

"No layoffs if that's what you're worried about,
but effective immediately, travel will be restricted
to trips that are absolutely necessary and all confer-
ences and marketing seminars will be canceled."

Laura watched as heads bobbed in agreement.
"I also have a couple of ideas I'd like to run by
you." She glanced around the room. "First of all, I
think raising advertising rates as I thought of doing
earlier, would be a mistake. They're already over-
priced, and raising ours would only drive potential
new accounts elsewhere."

J.B. looked up. "Didn't the *New York Herald* go
through a similar crisis a few years back?"

Laura nodded. "In 1991. The board of directors

decided to cut costs by downsizing the paper. We could do the same. As you all know, besides salaries, newsprint is our biggest expenditure. Cutting even a few pages a day could make a huge difference."

"You're not talking about eliminating any specific sections, are you?" Johnny asked.

"No. For now we could just shorten the articles."

Milton nodded. "It could work. Today's readers are busy people. They want their news in brief, easy-to-digest ways. Although . . ." He scratched his head. "I doubt that will be enough to offset our losses."

"True." Laura shuffled a few papers on her desk. "Which is why we're going to need new advertisers. And to do that, we must increase our readership."

Marianne, anticipating a request for additional funds, frowned. "How do you propose to do that without spending money?" she asked suspiciously.

Laura pulled a notepad from her briefcase and skimmed through the notes she had jotted down the night before. "I was thinking of running a few daily radio commercials—something short and catchy to plug our cover stories."

Marianne groaned. "Laura, a radio campaign will cost a fortune."

"Not if we team it up with a special introductory offer for new subscribers. The last time we did that, we signed more than a thousand new readers. The added revenues would more than pay for our radio campaign."

J.B. nodded. "The advertising director at KYZZ

is a friend of mine. Why don't I give him a call and see what he can do for us?"

Laura looked at the other five people. "Any objections?"

Leo was the first to express his approval. "None from me. We could even take it one step further and send a survey team out in the streets, see what people like and don't like about the new *Sentinel.* If it's more human-interest stories they want, or more local news or more sports, then that's what we should concentrate on."

"What about a contest for kids?" Milton suggested. "We could do something with the Power Rangers, like offering a free poster with the purchase of a Sunday paper. We could triple our Sunday circulation with that alone."

Laura felt herself relax. The doubts that had shaken her self-confidence earlier were replaced with a feeling of elation. She knew why this newspaper had survived so many crises, and the reason was right here, in this room—enthusiastic, talented people whose creativity and guts made her proud to be part of their team.

And that, she thought with a pleased smile, was something Malcolm Kandall hadn't counted on.

Wearing a trenchcoat, dark glasses, and a low-brimmed hat, Malcolm Kandall waited until the cab had stopped at the back entrance of Capri, a lower Manhattan nightclub on West 10th Street, before pulling a few bills from his pocket and paying the driver.

God, how he hated this part of town. By day, it

was grim and decaying. By night, it was filled with dangerous punks, whores, and junkies. Why Enzio would chose this neighborhood for a headquarters was beyond him; but he wasn't here to question the man's tastes. He was here because Enzio had summoned him to New York, and although Malcolm's schedule allowed very little time for un-scheduled trips, he had come anyway.

No one turned down a summons from Enzio Scarpati.

Malcolm had met the mob boss eighteen months ago when both men had attended a party hosted by Malcolm's good friend, Jerry Orbach of Orbach Motors. Jerry, a former New York car salesman, had sold Enzio his first fleet of luxury cars and had kept in close contact with him over the years.

Although not as notorious as men like John Gotti, Anthony Salerno, or Carmine Persico, New York-based Enzio Scarpati was nonetheless a pow-erful man whose political connections were said to extend as far as the West Coast.

Before the evening was over, Enzio, a diminu-tive, impeccably dressed man with a penetrating stare and a large mole on the side of his nose, had managed to pull Malcolm aside. "So," he had told him point-blank. "I hear you want to be governor."

He spent the next half hour explaining to Mal-colm how he could help him in a way that would guarantee his election, even going so far as naming a handful of politicians he had already taken under his wing.

Malcolm, who until that moment had been cer-tain he would need a second term as mayor before

he could successfully win his party's nomination,
had remained cautious. "What happens if someone
finds out you're financing my campaign?"

"What? You think I'm stupid? No one's going
to know that. The donations will be made through
several of my legitimate businesses in Texas and
other states. Even if someone got suspicious, they
wouldn't be able to prove a thing."

Malcolm was barely able to conceal his excitement, and even though he knew a favor like that
didn't come without a price, he was willing to pay
it. No matter how high. "What do you want in
return?"

Enzio smiled confidently, as if the deal had already been sealed. "A small favor. When you get
elected, *I* name the state attorney general."

It had taken Malcolm less than twenty-four hours
to get back to Enzio with an affirmative answer.
Not because he had to think the offer through,
since his mind was already made up, but because
he didn't want Enzio to think he was an easy mark.

The following day, amid much fanfare and tons
of press, Malcolm had made his gubernatorial announcement. Almost simultaneously, Enzio had
begun funneling huge sums of money into Malcolm's campaign funds. As Malcolm's exposure
grew, so did his popularity, and it hadn't taken long
for the Republican party to realize that only one
man could beat the incumbent governor in November—Malcolm Kandall.

Now, as the taxi that had dropped him off disappeared into the night, Malcolm walked toward a
door marked "Private" and knocked. A minute

later, a stony-face Hawaiian, built like a sumo wrestler, opened the door.

Malcolm removed his dark glasses. "Enzio is expecting me."

Without a change of expression, the man, a deaf mute by the name of Hino, let him in and led him up a flight of stairs. Sitting in front of an unmarked door, two other men, smaller than Hino, but just as lethal looking, glanced up from their card games. Each had a .357 Magnum strapped under his arm.

As they quietly surveyed him, Malcolm did his best not to look nervous. He wished he could meet Enzio on more neutral territory, like a hotel lobby or a crowded bar. But Enzio, who had survived three attempts on his life in the last fifteen years, kept his traveling to a minimum. When he did travel, whether it was out of state or to the other end of Manhattan, the three thugs stuck to him like glue.

Enzio was sitting behind his desk when Malcolm came in. As usual he was impeccably dressed in a tan, pin-striped suit Malcolm knew had come from Savile Row, a white silk shirt, and a white camellia in his boutonnière. His pinky was adorned with an enormous diamond ring.

"Good to see you, Enzio." Removing his hat, Malcolm approached the desk, hand extended.

Enzio offered only his fingertips, then motioned toward a chair. "Sit down."

He didn't say please and he didn't smile. Malcolm felt his armpits begin to dampen.

Enzio, who he knew took great pleasure in making people nervous, opened a black leather box with his initials embossed on the lid and pushed it across the desk. "Relax, Malcolm. Here, have a cigar. A friend of mine in Havana just sent me a new shipment. They're excellent."

Although Malcolm hated cigars, he took one anyway and ran it slowly under his nose. "Mmm. You have expensive tastes, Enzio."

The Italian-born American held the flame of a solid gold lighter to the tip of his own cigar and puffed gently. "My mother, may she rest in peace, claimed I was born with expensive tastes." He took another puff and snapped the lighter shut before handing it to Malcolm. "Unfortunately, we didn't have two *centesimos* to rub together. Which is why I had to become rich."

A trickle of perspiration ran down Malcolm's spine. He didn't like this small chitchat. Whatever Enzio had called him here for, he wished he would just get on with it.

"So," Enzio said at last, leaning back in his chair. "How's the campaign going?"

"Couldn't be better." Malcolm resisted the impulse to loosen his tie. "Nine points ahead in the latest poll."

"Mmm." Enzio tilted his head back and blew a perfect smoke ring. "What's this I hear about the *Austin Sentinel* investigating your campaign funds?"

So that was it. He had heard about Laura's snooping. To underplay the seriousness of the situation, Malcolm chuckled. "You needn't worry about that, Enzio. Laura Spencer and I have had a long-standing feud and once in a while she likes to stir up the waters, in search of mud."

"It wouldn't help your campaign any if she succeeded."

"She won't. As of this morning, Laura Spencer has a new priority in her life—saving her newspaper."

Anxious to show off his initiative, he told Enzio how he had dealt with the young publisher. "So, you see," he said when he was finished, "Laura Spencer should no longer be a problem. In fact, I wouldn't be a bit surprised if the *Sentinel* disappears from circulation by year's end."

Enzio's reaction wasn't the one he had expected. "That was a stupid move, Malcolm. The elections are still a month away. She could do a lot of damage between now and then." His gaze turned hard. "Some broads are funny that way. When they go down in flames, they like to take someone down with them—usually the person who brought on their demise."

The air in the room seemed to grow thicker, more difficult to breathe. Malcolm ran a finger under his shirt collar. "You don't know her like I do," he said, forcing himself to keep his voice even. "She's just like her old man. All she cares about is the newspaper."

"I thought you said she couldn't possibly save it."

"She can't. But she'll die trying." Because the cigar was beginning to make him sick, Malcolm set it in the ashtray. "I swear, Enzio, I'll be the last person on her mind."

Leaning over the desk, Enzio pointed his cigar at him. "Just don't underestimate the woman, Malcolm. We're not talking about some two-bit reporter here. Spencer is responsible for sending a powerful friend of mine to prison when no one else could."

Enzio's penetrating, ruthless stare made Malcolm wish he had a drink to soothe his nerves. "I'm keeping an eye on her."

Enzio nodded slowly. "You do that. I would hate to think that all the time and effort I've invested in you, not to mention the money, was in vain."

Malcolm began to relax. "It hasn't been in vain, Enzio. You can be sure of that."

"Then I'm glad we had this little chat." Enzio glanced at his gold Rolex. "You came on Jerry Orbach's jet?"

"Yes."

"Then you'd better get back before your wife misses you." He waited until Malcolm had stood up before adding, "By the way, how's that little problem of hers?"

Christ, Malcolm thought as a chill settled in his gut. Was there anything the man didn't know? "That's under control, too, Enzio." Then, as if to reassure himself, he repeated. "Everything is under control."

When Kandall was gone, Enzio buzzed Tony Cordero, his loyal gofer who occupied the office next to his. Within seconds, Tony strutted in and came to sit on the edge of Enzio's desk.

"You want me, boss?"

He was a small, wiry Puerto Rican with Latin good looks, slick black hair he wore in a ponytail, and cold, shiny eyes that made him look as if he always had a fever. Also a smart dresser, he wore slate-gray trousers, a black silk shirt, open at the neck, and black dress boots.

"I want you to go to Austin for a few weeks, Tony."

"We've got problems there, boss?"

"That's what I want you to find out." Enzio laid the cigar in the ashtray and leaned back in his chair, his hands folded over his flat stomach. "You remember a reporter by the name of Laura Spencer?"

Tony's thin mouth pulled at one corner. "How could I forget her? It was her investigation of Vince Denardi that sent him to the slammer."

"She's the publisher of the *Austin Sentinel* now."

"No kidding." His expression didn't change. Few things in this world affected Tony Cordero. "Is she a problem, boss?"

"She could be, although Kandall swears she's not." Enzio inspected a perfectly manicured fingernail. "She's investigating his campaign funds, and I don't like the way Kandall's handling the situation."

"What did he do?"

"He got some big-shot friends of his to cancel their contract with the *Sentinel* in the hope that the subsequent lack of advertisers will put the paper out of business."

"But you don't think she'll back off."

Enzio studied the diamond on his pinky. "Broads like her never do."

"Maybe Kandall is more trouble than he's worth," Tony suggested. "You thought of that, boss?"

"I have. And believe me, if we were talking about any state but Texas, I would drop him without a second thought. But there's much too much money to be made, Tony. And that makes Kandall worth the trouble."

He wasn't exaggerating. The marijuana alone, smuggled across the Rio Grande on rafts by Mexican "river rats," was the most lucrative trade in the area, representing millions of dollars in revenue a year. All he needed to get his share of the wealth, was the support of influential state officials—people like Malcolm Kandall, and the man Enzio had selected to become the next state attorney general.

"What do you want me to do, boss?" Tony asked.

"When you get to Austin, check in with Luigi. He'll arrange for you to have a car, a gun, and whatever else you might need while you're there. Once you're settled in, find out how much this Spencer woman knows and who gave her the information. And most importantly, see if she's got anything that might connect Malcolm to me."

Tony's face remained impassive. "And if she does?"

"Get rid of the evidence." Enzio paused. "Then get rid of her."

5

Enzio watched Tony as he swaggered back to his office. Of all the people he had working for him—bodyguards, henchmen, and a battery of lawyers, Tony Cordero was the only man he could fully trust.

Enzio had found him outside the Capri ten years ago, bleeding from a gunshot wound. Rather than call the police, he'd had Hino bring him in and had called his personal physician.

Tony, only eighteen at the time, was a small-time hood with a wise mouth and a police record a mile long. He was also smart, quick-as-a-whip, and willing to do anything for a roof over his head and an opportunity to join the big time. Enzio, trusting his good instincts about people, had provided him with both.

Tony had come up through the ranks quickly, and it hadn't taken Enzio long to realize that the kid had both guts and initiative. His only weakness was the ladies. He seemed to have a new one every week, and although he swore each was the new-found love of his life, they kept coming and going with dizzying regularity.

Enzio would have preferred a less libido-motivated assistant, but as long as the women didn't interfere with Tony's job performance, he didn't give a rat's ass how many broads he screwed.

Enzio picked up his cigar again and relit it. Sending Tony to Austin was a smart move. He would do the job right.

Friday morning, sitting under an umbrella-covered table on the outdoor patio of the Four Seasons Hotel, Laura glanced at her watch. Bill Smolen was twenty minutes late for their breakfast date. Not a good sign, she thought, especially since the CEO of Choice Food, the largest grocery store chain in Texas, was known for his punctuality.

Although Bill Smolen had not severed ties with the *Sentinel* the way the other advertisers had done, he was dragging his feet about the renewal of his advertising contract. Laura hoped the deal she was prepared to offer him would turn things around.

She was trying to decide whether or not to call his office when she saw him standing in the doorway. As he saw her, he waved and made his way toward her table.

"Sorry I'm late, Laura," he said, lowering his heavyset frame into the chair across from her. "My daughter dropped off the grandchildren this morning and things were a bit hectic for a while."

"No problem." She smiled brightly as she handed him the extra menu. "I'm told the Southwestern omelet is excellent."

"I never eat before a golf game." He turned to

the waitress who had come to take their orders. "Just coffee, please."

Disappointed at the realization that her time with him would be limited, Laura closed her menu. "Same for me."

As soon as the waitress had disappeared, Laura leaned forward. "I know you're a busy man, Bill, so I won't waste your time with a lot of preliminary nonsense. I heard you'll be opening a new store in South Austin soon and I'm here to make you an offer I hope you won't be able to refuse."

As she was about to make her pitch, Bill shook his head. "I'm sure it's a very generous offer, Laura. Unfortunately—and this is difficult for me to say because J.B. and I go back a long way—I'm not planning to renew my contract with the *Sentinel.*"

Her heart sank. "Why not?"

He removed his glasses and wiped them slowly with a corner of his napkin. "Because in spite of the new store, business at other locations has been sluggish. As a result, I've had to cut my advertising budget."

"You've been advertising every day in the *American Statesman.*"

"That's because my contract with them runs until next spring. If business picks up by then, I'll be more than happy to talk to you at that time. But for the next few months, caution must prevail. He put his glasses back on. "I hope you understand."

The waitress brought their order but Laura pushed her cup aside. "No, Bill, I don't understand. I don't understand why you've been playing hide-

and-seek with me for the last week, or why you feel you have to lie about your budget cuts. I can guess though. You're too embarrassed to tell me the truth."

He blinked repeatedly, as if he had suddenly developed a nervous tic. "What truth? What are you talking about?"

Resting her elbows on the table, Laura leaned forward. "I'm talking about the man who already cost me three large accounts. The same man who is trying to put me out of business because he doesn't like what I'm doing."

Bill raised his hand. "Look, Laura. I don't really want to continue this conversation. What's going on between you and Malcolm Kandall has nothing to do with me—"

"How do you know I was talking about Malcolm? I never said his name."

A flush rose to his cheek. "I assumed . . . I mean, everybody knows . . ."

"Why don't you tell me the truth, Bill? He got to you, too, didn't he?" Not really expecting an answer, she added, "I don't know what Malcolm has on you, or what he promised you if you agreed to play by his rules, but I know you. You're a honest, honorable, hardworking man. Is this what you really want? To pledge alliance to a man with no scruples? A man who manipulates people as though they were puppets?"

Bill's gaze drifted toward the hotel's lush gardens where an elderly couple, arm in arm, walked along a flower-lined path. "This has nothing to do with Malcolm Kandall," he said flatly.

But she knew by the way he kept avoiding her
eyes that she had guessed right. He was in as deep
as Schwartz and the others. The only difference
was that, with a little effort, she might be able to
reach him. "What if I told you that with your help,
I could stop Malcolm Kandall from being elected
governor?" she asked in a low, earnest voice.
"Would you agree to talk to me then?"

Bill was silent for a moment, allowing her hopes
to soar. But as he brought his gaze back to her, he
shook his head. "I'm sorry if I gave you the wrong
impression, Laura. But there's nothing to tell. It's
as simple as that."

Holding back a sigh of frustration, she straight-
ened up. It had been unrealistic of her to believe
she could have persuaded him to tell the truth.
Once Malcolm had someone under his thumb, he
held him there forever. "Fine," she said, scrawling
her name on the check. "I won't pressure you anymore. Just don't come complaining to me a few
months from now when you realize the man you
and the others elected is nothing but a dirty crook.
I won't be in the mood to listen."

Then, rising, she gave him a curt nod and left
before he had a chance to stand up.

"Laura, what in the world has gotten into you?"
Stuart asked, a bewildered expression on his handsome face, as Laura dragged him to the sofa.

She wasn't sure. Her day had gone from bad to
worse. Feeling depressed, she had intended to go
straight home from work and soak in a warm bath.

But at the last minute, she had turned the car around and headed for Stuart's town house instead.

With deft fingers, Laura removed his tie and tossed it over her shoulder. "I've had a hard day." She opened his shirt and splayed her hands over his smooth, tanned chest. "A man I was counting on to give me some much needed business didn't come through, and one of my brightest editors resigned."

"That's too bad."

"Yes." She looked up. "Perhaps you can think of a way to take my mind off of it?"

Stuart licked his lips. "How?"

"By making love to me." Pushing aside her inhibitions, she gave him a gentle shove. As he toppled on the sofa, she fell on top of him. "Right here. Right now."

"Laura ... This is a bit unexpected ..." He watched her fingers as they unbuckled his belt. "At least let's go upstairs where we'll be more comfort—"

"Nope." She unzipped his fly and pushed his trousers over his hips. "I want to make love down here, with all the lights on. I want to do things we've never done before."

His Adam's apple bobbed up and down. "Like what?"

"Like ... this." With a smile that was full of promises, she unbuttoned her red coatdress and tossed it on the floor.

"Laura!"

She smiled at the sight of his growing erection. Prude or not, he was getting turned on.

With nothing left on but black panties, a black lace bra, and thigh-high stockings, she straddled him. "Take me for a ride, cowboy. A long one."

Stuart unhooked her bra. Then, pulling her to him, he took her nipple into his mouth, moaning softly as he sucked. Unfortunately, by the time he moved to the other breast, he was fully aroused. And when Stuart was aroused, his needs had to be satisfied quickly, often at the expense of her own.

Well, not tonight, she thought slowly stretching her legs along his. Tonight she wanted to be made love to slowly, lovingly. She wanted to be held, comforted, and told that everything would be all right. "Do you want me, Stuart?"

"Sure."

"How badly?"

"Let me get inside you," Stuart panted. "And I'll show you."

"Not yet." She nibbled on his earlobe as her hands slid slowly down the length of his body.

The nibble did it. With a groan that was half pleasure, half regret, he closed his eyes and sank into her. She tried to pull back, but he wouldn't let her. "You bad girl," he said, pumping in and out in that fast, powerful stroke that meant he had reached the point of no return. "You did that on purpose, didn't you? To make me come."

For a moment, her frustration was so intense that she almost withdrew. But he was already too far gone, clinging to her breasts and murmuring wild passionate words so that she didn't have the heart to break his spell.

With a skill she had perfected over the last six

months, she began to move with him, although she was certain that if she didn't, he wouldn't notice the difference.

He came in a matter of seconds and when he was done, he did what he always did. He kissed her cheek and said, "Wow."

With a small sigh of disappointment, she rested her cheek on his chest. Maybe it was her fault. All that black lace and sexy talk. The poor guy hadn't stood a chance.

Because she enjoyed being held as much as she enjoyed the sex, she snuggled close to him and started to tell him about her day, from its hopeful start to the end when Jan Newcomb had told her she was leaving.

"If only I could find a way to expose Malcolm Kandall," she said as her fingers drew small circles around his nipple. "The story would be hailed as the best piece of investigative reporting since the Watergate break-in, assuring us millions of sales. The *Sentinel* would be saved."

Sighing, she waited for Stuart's words of encouragement. When he remained silent, she raised her head and glanced at him.

He was sound asleep.

6

It had taken Ted's agent only a few days to arrange an exhibition of Ted's work at the Luberick Gallery. The owner, a former curator at the Museum of Modern Art in New York, had been thrilled at the thought of featuring "one of today's most important photographers."

It was the first time in sixteen years that he was setting foot on Texas soil. Now, as he drove toward the old homestead in a black BMW he had rented at the airport, he was filled with nostalgia as he took in the familiar landscape.

Although the town had undergone many changes over the years, West Avenue, regarded by many as Austin's most prestigious address, remained the same.

The old stately homes were still there, still shaded by majestic oaks and fronted by impeccably manicured lawns; and while vintage Bentleys had been replaced by shiny new Mercedes, the feeling of old money still prevailed.

At the end of the street, Ted pulled the car along the curb and stopped. The Kandall house, a two-and-a-half-story Victorian Gothic, had been built in the late 1800s by a man who had served as a Confederate captain. In 1903, Ted's great-grandfather, then a district judge, had bought the house, which had remained in the family ever since.

Sitting behind the wheel, Ted took a cigarette from the pack of Marlboros in his shirt pocket and lit it, drawing deeply.

He had mixed emotions about the house and the memories it evoked. There had been good times here; but they were eclipsed by the memory of too many arguments, too many accusations, and too many damned threats.

He remembered how he had sworn never to set foot here again, and yet here he was, back where his life had begun, and where a part of him had died.

After hesitating a moment, he flipped open the ashtray, extinguished his cigarette, and got out of the car.

Before he could even ring the doorbell, he heard the sound of hurried footsteps inside the house and then Lucinda, who had been the Kandall's housekeeper for more than thirty years, threw the door open. "*Dios mio!*" she cried, opening her arms and hugging Ted to her ample bosom. "It is you. It is really you."

"In all my ornery flesh, Lucy."

Releasing him, she held his hands, inspecting him from head to toe. "Oh, Teddy, I've missed you so much."

"And I've missed you, Lucy. More than you know."

A tear rolled down her dark round cheek, and

she wiped it away. "I have been so worried about you, going from one place to another, dodging bullets all the time." She shook her head. "It isn't healthy."

"I thought you and I had an understanding. I take good care of myself and you don't worry."

"Ahh, but I know you too well, Teddy. I know how restless you are, and how you love to flirt with danger."

His arm still wrapped around Lucinda's shoulders, he gave her an affectionate squeeze. "And *you* are still as gorgeous as ever," he said, changing the subject. "That husband of yours is a lucky man."

She giggled and, in a gesture as old as time, patted her thick black hair, now generously laced with gray. "Oh, stop it." But he could tell the compliment had pleased her. Then, her expression growing more serious, she added, "I was so glad when Sandra told me you had agreed to come." She heaved a heavy sigh. "Your poor father."

"How is he, Lucy?"

"Some days he's good and others . . ." She shook her head. "Just the sight of him breaks my heart."

"Is he home?"

She nodded. "In the library. He's working on a campaign speech for your uncle."

Ted's tone turned bitter. "What's the matter? Can't Uncle Malcolm afford a speechwriter now?"

"This is a speech your father will be giving himself at the Chamber of Commerce on Friday. He has been very active in your uncle's campaign, you know."

"Sandra told me."

As Ted paused, still not sure he was ready to face his father, Lucinda put an end to his indecision by giving him a gentle but firm push forward. "Go, *hijo*," she whispered. "It's time."

The door to the library was ajar and he pushed it open slowly, letting his eyes roam over the wood-paneled room with its brown leather chairs, its massive rosewood desk, and its floor-to-ceiling bookcases crammed with old law books.

Nothing had changed. Which didn't surprise him. A staunch conservative, Charles Kandall had always been averse to change, a policy he had enforced in the Senate as well as in his home.

His father stood at the window, gazing at the vast backyard which, in happier days, had been the scene of countless family picnics and games of touch football.

"Hello, Dad." It had been so long since he had said that word that it almost died in his throat.

Ted saw his father's shoulders stiffen and it seemed like an eternity before he finally turned around. When he did, Ted was shocked to see how the illness had ravaged him. He was almost completely bald and his face was pale and etched with lines. Not a big man, he had always appeared taller and stronger than he was by holding himself erect, a stance that had greatly contributed to his appeal as a state senator. But there was no sign of that strength now. He looked sunken and aged.

Only the eyes, and the expression in them, hadn't changed. A deep cornflower blue, they stared at Ted as if he were a stranger.

We might as well have been apart for a million years instead of sixteen, Ted thought. Still, he forced a smile. "Lucinda told me I'd find you here."

"What do you want?" Although his voice was weaker than Ted remembered, it was calm, cold, totally devoid of emotion.

Under the hard, dispassionate gaze, Ted felt ten years old again. Why the hell had he let Sandra talk him into going through with this charade? It was obvious he wasn't welcome here. He never would be. "The Luberick Gallery will be showing some of my work next week, and since I was in town, I thought I'd stop by and say hello."

"Why?"

Ted cleared his throat. "Because I wanted to see how you were."

"Since when do you give a damn?" Charles asked, making the question sound more like an accusation.

"I never stopped giving a damn." He hadn't planned to say that. He hadn't wanted to lay his feelings bare so Charles could sneer at them. Yet, now that he had, the task ahead seemed less insurmountable. "We need to talk, Dad."

His father's chin went up, making him look more like the old Charles. "We said everything we had to say to each other sixteen years ago."

"No we didn't." Ted walked into the room slowly, stopping a few feet away from where his father stood. Up close there were even more changes—dark circles under the eyes, deep lines bracketing his mouth. "At least I hope we haven't."

He took Charles's stony silence as a sign of encouragement. "There have been so many things I've wanted to tell you over the years; but you would never let me. That's why I came. I thought that if I spoke to you face to face instead of doing it in a letter, you'd listen."

Without the slightest change in expression, Charles turned back toward the window, his hands still behind his back. If it hadn't been for Sandra, Ted would have walked out. Instead, he took a deep breath and slowly counted to five before speaking again. "I know I said some harsh things to you the day of Mom's funeral. I'd like to apologize for that, although to tell you the truth, I've drawn a blank as to the exact words—"

Charles made a slow half turn. For the first time, his face seemed to come alive. "In that case allow me to refresh your memory. Your exact words were: 'I'll never set foot in this fucking house again as long as I live. You're nothing but a fucking murderer and I hope you rot in hell.'" Charles raised a thin white eyebrow. "Does that ring a bell?"

Pain speared through Ted as the long forgotten words echoed in his head. How could Charles ever forgive something he remembered with such devastating clarity? "I was hurting that day," he offered in his defense. "I wanted to hurt back." He paused. "I was also very young."

"So now that you're presumably older and wiser, you've come crawling back for forgiveness? Is that it?"

The words made him bristle. "I'd hardly call it crawling—"

"Or perhaps you heard that I was sick and you came to see how close you were to getting your inheritance." His mouth pulled in a tight, almost cruel smile. "Is that a better guess?"

Ted felt a flush rise to his cheek. "It's a lousy guess," he snapped, not bothering to deny knowing about Charles's illness. "Since when do I give a damn about your money? I make a decent living now, Dad. You'd know that if you had bothered to keep up with my career."

Charles waved an impatient hand. "If you came here to boast about your achievements, you've wasted your time—and mine. I don't give a damn about your career, how much money you make, or how successful you are. I stopped caring about you long ago."

The control Ted had been hanging onto, slipped away as the old resentment resurfaced. *"Caring?"* He let out a sarcastic laugh. "You've never cared about anyone in your entire life. You were always too busy campaigning or meeting with presidents. There was never time for me, or for Mom, or even for Sandra. But of course no one knew that. In the eyes of the entire country, we were the perfect family for the perfect senator. Well, I've got a news flash for you, *Dad.* You weren't perfect. Far from it."

Charles's eyes filled with fury and he pulled himself erect as if he were about to strike him. "You worthless little punk. Get out of my house. Get out before I kill you."

"Gladly!" His hands balled up into tight fists, Ted turned on his heels and was out of the room in two long strides. In the hallway, he nearly collided with Lucinda.

"What happened?" she cried as her gaze shot from Ted to his father.

"Why don't you ask him?" Then, without a backward glance, he pushed past her and stormed out of the house.

Back inside the car, he gripped the steering wheel, holding it so tightly his knuckles turned white. That son of a bitch had done it again. He had known exactly what button to push to make him lose control. It was a gift all the Kandall men seemed to have. Himself included.

He waited for his breathing to return to normal before turning on the ignition. Then, ignoring the woman across the street who was watching him from her front porch, he drove away, heading west toward J.B.'s ranch.

This time not even a SWAT team would bring him back.

As he did every morning at this time, Malcolm Kandall sat on the deck of his luxurious lakefront home in posh west Austin, enjoying a light breakfast of toast, fresh orange juice, and black coffee.

It was a gorgeous morning, and although Barbara's hangover had threatened to ruin his day, a brief look at the latest polls, which still placed him comfortably ahead of the incumbent governor, had brought everything back into perspective.

A sailboat glided by, its blue sail billowing gently in the morning breeze, and as its two occupants waved, Malcolm waved back. He could not afford to be unfriendly. Especially with the elections less than four weeks away.

As he finished his coffee, his housekeeper, always attentive, came to refill his cup. "Will Mrs. Kandall be joining you, sir?"

"I expect her down shortly, Dolores." He picked up a slice of buttered toast from a silver basket. "She's not feeling well, however, so you may want to check in on her from time to time."

"I don't need checking after, darling," a cheery voice said behind them. "I'm perfectly fine."

As Barbara strolled onto the deck, Malcolm quickly rose to his feet. "So I see." He pulled her chair and held it until she had sat down, relieved to see there was no sign of her hangover. Her short brown hair was now stylishly combed and her green eyes, although still a little bloodshot, looked much clearer than they had an hour ago.

Malcolm kissed her cheek. "You look wonderful, darling. New dress?"

At the compliment, Barbara flushed with pleasure. "Yes. Mother saw it in a Paris boutique last month and bought it for me. Do you like it?"

Although Malcolm loathed his mother-in-law, he had never questioned her good taste. "Red looks wonderful on you. You should wear it more often." He waited until Dolores had set a plate of fresh fruit in front of Barbara before adding, "I'm so glad you're feeling better, darling. Does that mean you've changed your mind about canceling your appointments?"

"Everything is back on schedule." Picking up a thin slice of cantaloupe with her fingers, she nibbled on it. "You can tell Clive to pick me up at nine-thirty. We'll go straight to UT."

Malcolm was pleased. Young voters had become increasingly important over the last few years, and last-minute cancellations, even on the part of a candidate's wife, didn't improve one's image. "Excellent," he said, mentally going through his own busy schedule. "And don't forget tonight's dinner at the Aldens. I have to fly to El Paso to meet with some of my campaign workers there, but I should be back by six."

"I haven't forgotten, although . . ." She paused, clearly ill at ease. "Would you mind terribly going there alone, dear? I don't think—"

Malcolm's good humor faded. "Of course I would mind. What would it look like if I showed up there without you?"

"I'm sure Joan would understand."

"That's not the point. The Aldens have invited some of Texas's most influential men and their wives to this dinner. One of them is Senator Babcock and I don't have to tell you how important he is to my campaign."

She gave him an imploring look. "Malcolm, be reasonable. We've been out every night this week. I'm exhausted."

"I realize that. But we knew from the start that this campaign wouldn't be easy." He heard the edge in his voice and immediately caught himself, reverting to his role of the understanding, caring husband. Reaching across the table, he took Barbara's hand. "I know you've been keeping a grueling schedule, darling, and believe me, I'm deeply grateful. All I'm asking is that you hang in there a little while longer."

In a rare gesture of impatience, Barbara yanked her hand free. "Joan and Skip Alden are beginning to get on my nerves. They're always hovering over me, watching me, asking me if I'm all right, if I need anything. You'd think I was an invalid."

"But, darling, that's because they care about you. And they worry. Just as I do."

Dolores reappeared, carrying a portable phone. "It's for you, Mrs. Kandall. It's Mrs. Alden."

Barbara rolled her eyes and took the phone from the housekeeper's hand. "Hello, Joan."

While Barbara talked to her friend, Malcolm stirred his coffee, once again astounded at her quick recovery. Another woman wouldn't have been able to get out of bed. Not Barbara. No matter how badly she felt, her commitment to his career always came first.

From the moment he had met her eighteen years ago, he had known she possessed all the qualities an ambitious politician could want in a wife— charm, intelligence, and an impeccable lineage. The money had been important, too. So important that when he had found out Barbara wouldn't be getting the bulk of her mother's fortune until Deirdre's death, he had almost called the wedding off.

Fortunately for him, he had quickly come back to his senses, telling himself that Deirdre Fenton, fifty-nine at the time, wouldn't live forever. He had been wrong. Only weeks away from her eighty-first birthday, Deirdre Fenton looked as if she might indeed do just that.

The fact that he didn't love Barbara hadn't marred their relationship one bit. Whether it was in front of a crowd of voters or in the privacy of his own bedroom, Malcolm was a master of the game and could play any role on cue.

One of his greatest performances had been his sorrow at the announcement that, after two miscarriages, Barbara would not be able to bear children. While he knew that a large family was an important part of a politician's image, the news that he would never have to deal with grimy paws and snotty noses had made him a very happy man.

The only cloud in their otherwise "perfect" marriage was Barbara's drinking which, naturally, Deirdre blamed him for.

"If you spent more time with her," she had told him one Sunday after one of Barbara's famous binges, "she wouldn't have to look for comfort in a bottle."

The Aldens, who were their closest friends, had been equally frank and had urged Barbara to seek professional help. But Malcolm had been dead set against it. Unveiling his wife's drinking problem would end his career. Later, perhaps, once the elections were over, he would see that she entered a rehab center. Not one of those celebrity dry-out "spas" where the *National Enquirer* and other rags hung around in search of juicy headlines, but a discreet, reliable clinic abroad.

Until then, he would do nothing that might jeopardize his career. Unlike his brother, who had resigned his Senate seat after Elizabeth's death, he didn't intend to let anything, or anyone, stand in his way.

The sound of the telephone dropping into its cradle snapped his attention back. Barbara's hands were clenched against her mouth. All the color had drained from her face.

Alarmed, he lowered his cup. "What's the matter?"

"Ted is back," she said in a voice so low he could barely hear it.

"Ted?" He leaned back in his chair. "It can't be. Charles would have said something."

"He's here. Joan saw him come out of your brother's house." She began to tremble. "Oh, Malcolm, what if he came back to find out the truth about his mother?"

This time, Malcolm took both her hands and held them tight. She could not crack now. "Don't be silly," he said in his most reassuring tone. "I'm sure it's nothing like that. He must have found out Charles was sick and come back for a visit, that's all."

She didn't seem to have heard him. "Oh, dear God, what am I going to do if he comes here? How am I going to face him?"

7

"Here, son. Take this." Standing at the bar, J.B. handed Ted a tumbler of Wild Turkey on the rocks. "Looks like you need it."

Ted didn't think a drink would do him much good, but he took a generous swallow anyway, waiting for the liquor to settle in his stomach before walking over to the sofa and sitting down.

He had always felt at home here. For many years as life on West Avenue grew more and more tense, Lost Creek had been a haven to him, the only place where he could truly relax. And dream.

"So what's your father done now?"

Knowing he could trust J.B., Ted told him about Charles's illness and Sandra's recent visit to London.

As Ted talked, J.B. sipped his beer. He had never cared much for the Kandalls. Even in the best of circumstances, they were a pain in the ass. But he sure loved that boy. He loved his drive, his sensitivity, and his passion for adventure, which, combined with his extraordinary talent, had made him one of the best photojournalists in the business.

Ted's childhood had been fraught with disappointments. Gentle by nature, he had craved a parental affection neither Elizabeth nor Charles had been able to give him.

J.B. had met the youth years ago during an amateur photo contest the *Sentinel* had sponsored. Ted's whimsical picture of a squirrel family had caught his attention, and although the photograph hadn't won first prize, it had showed an unusual eye for detail.

Afterward, J.B. had taken the boy under his wing, giving him books on photography and inviting him to spend a few hours each week in the *Sentinel*'s photo department. Ted had honed his craft there, and although he had often said that's where he wanted to work after he finished college, J.B. had known all along that the boy was destined for bigger and better things. And he had been right.

Except for monthly phone calls between assignments and an occasional visit to England, J.B. hadn't seen much of the boy over the years. But the bond was still there, stronger than ever.

"How does Charles look?" J.B. asked.

"Bad. That's another reason I wish things had turned out differently between us. I might have been able to convince him to slow down, to take a little better care of himself."

"Sometimes that's easier said than done." J.B. took a sip of his beer. "A man who's been in the public eye all his life never fully readjusts to the routine of an ordinary citizen."

"He did when he resigned from the Senate after my mother's death."

"He was younger then. And he still had his law practice to keep him busy."

"Well ... I'll never know whether I could have helped him or not, will I? I failed miserably."

J.B. continued to watch him. It pained him to see that after all these years the kid still regarded his father's failings as his own. "What are your plans now?"

Ted shrugged. "The exhibition at the Luberick is next week. I'll hang around until then. After that, I'll go back to London. And then maybe Haiti to await President Aristide's return."

"Or ..." J.B. gave him a sidelong glance. "You could stay here for a while, slow your own pace a bit. Seems to me that after those two months in Bosnia, you could use a little R and R. And what better place to take it than right here, under that big blue sky?"

"I was never the idle type, J.B. You know that."

"Who said anything about being idle? I have a barn that needs painting, fences that need repairing, and stalls that need cleaning." He grinned. "Of course, if you want your old job at the *Sentinel* back, I'm sure I could arrange something. It's not the kind of action you're used to, but you might find the change interesting. Come to think of it, you and my new publisher would make one hell of a team."

"I didn't know you had a new publisher. Who is he?"

"It's a she. Laura. My stepdaughter."

"Your stepdaughter? I thought she worked for one of those tabloids."

J.B. chuckled. "Don't let her hear you call the *New York Herald* a tabloid. Or the *Sentinel* for that matter." Briefly, he told him how, by changing the format, Laura had breathed new life into the rusty newspaper, saving it from extinction.

Ted had already left for England when Shirley and Laura had moved to Lost Creek, and therefore had never met either one of them; but J.B. had talked about his spirited stepdaughter often and with great pride. He had almost brought her to London once, then at the last minute, she had gone to Germany instead to visit her mother. "I'm glad you found someone reliable to carry on, J.B. I wish you both the very best."

J.B. propped his feet on the table and leaned back in his chair. "So what do you say, son? You're staying a spell?"

From behind them came a discreet cough. "Perhaps I could persuade Mr. Ted to stay by offering to make one of my shepherd's pies. Or an English trifle."

At the sound of the clipped, well-bred, English-accented voice, Ted jumped from the sofa. "Lenox!" Laughing, he took the butler's extended hand and pulled him forward in an affectionate embrace. "God, it's good to see you. How are you?"

"Very well, sir. Thank you."

Lenox was a tall, slender man with an impeccable carriage and diction that would have made Richard Burton proud. His thick black hair was thinner now and had even begun to recede a little, but the thin, elegant mustache was still there and the gleam in his eyes was as bright as ever.

He had come to Lost Creek thirty years ago, after his employer of five years, a local rancher, had died, leaving the young butler with no job and an expired visa. Feeling sorry for him, J.B. had hired him even though he had no idea what a butler was supposed to do. According to J.B.'s hilarious recount of those first few weeks, the new partnership had taken some time to develop. But once it had, neither had been able to do without the other.

"English trifle, huh?" Ted asked, as he released him. "You make them as good as ever?"

"There's only one way to find out, sir."

"Mmm." Ted felt himself relax. The whiskey, J.B.'s warm smile, and now Lenox's not so subtle coaxing, were beginning to have a soothing effect on him. Maybe J.B. was right after all. There was no hurry to get back to London. And if he didn't make Aristide's homecoming, so what? Some things in life were more important than work. Besides, it would be good to spend time with J.B., working around the ranch, playing cards at night while catching up on small-town gossip.

It sure beat sitting in his London flat, mopping around thinking about his dysfunctional family.

Picking up his glass again, he twirled the ice a few times before downing the rest of his drink. "All right," he said, looking from one man to the other. "You two talked me into it. I'll stay. For a little while."

Ted was in a foul mood when he returned to Lost Creek a little after five that same afternoon. He had gone to the Luberick Gallery to oversee the placement of his photographs when a reporter had snuck through a back door and started to ask him questions.

Out of respect for the gallery owner, he had answered them, even going as far as explaining some of his photographs to him. It wasn't until the reporter had brought up the incident at his mother's funeral that Ted had put an end to the interview by escorting the uncouth journalist out.

Damn scandalmongers, he thought as he raced through the countryside. Hadn't they had their fill of juicy headlines sixteen years ago? Didn't they have anything better to talk about than old family feuds?

Ignoring the posted speed limit, he turned onto Cattle Trail. A hundred feet or so ahead of him, a yellow Mustang bounced up and down the meandering, rocky road, taking great pains to avoid the puddles left by an apparent earlier storm.

Without slowing down, Ted leaned on his horn and pressed on the accelerator as he barreled past the slow-moving car.

The driver, a pretty redhead, threw him a furious look and blasted her own horn in response. Ted ignored her. Women. They were so much more emotional here than in the UK.

J.B. was in the carport, sharpening an old saw when Ted pulled in a few minutes later.

The ex-publisher pushed his safety glasses into his mop of white hair and put the saw down. "What's the matter with you?" he chuckled. "You look as if you could start a fight in an empty house."

Ted leaned against the BMW and lit a Marlboro. "I ran into a vulture." He took a deep, soothing drag, held the smoke in his lungs for a moment, then released it toward the sky. "Funny though, nowadays, they call themselves *reporters*."

"Oh." J.B. smiled. "You didn't punch him, did you?"

"Not this time. But I came close." Remembering he was trying to quit, he dropped the cigarette on the ground and crushed it with the tip of a black Reebock. "I swear if I see another reporter within a hundred feet of me while I'm here, you excluded that is, I'll—"

He was interrupted by a screech of tires. Turning his head, he saw the yellow Mustang lurch to a stop as the redhead slammed on the brakes.

"You lunatic," the woman shouted as she got out of the car and marched toward him. "You nearly ran me off the road."

Despite his bad mood, Ted took in a few details he hadn't noticed when he had passed her—mainly that she was small but exquisitely proportioned. Even under that stylish black suit, one could see she had a dynamite body. And the face wasn't bad either—eyes the color of thick honey, a full mouth, painted a bright red, and the sexiest little mole he'd ever seen, perched just above her upper lip.

But it was her hair, a glorious, flaming red that set her apart from other women he knew, even redheads. His blood, which had been boiling a moment ago, dropped down to a simmer as he imagined his fingers running through that wild, fiery mane.

"Did you hear what I said?" she asked, both fists on her hips. "Or are you in some kind of stupor?" Her gaze turned suspicious. "Unless you're drunk."

Still leaning against the fender of the BMW, Ted crossed his arms and gave her another head-to-toe look, a slow one this time, so he could visually savor every inch of her. "Yes to the first question and no to the other two," he said, amused that under his scrutiny, her face had turned beet red. "I was merely trying to reach my destination."

"At ninety miles an hour? On a road where the speed is posted at thirty-five?"

"Well, well," J.B. said, wiping his hands on a rag as he stepped between them. "I see you two have met." A gleam of amusement flashed in his eyes as he glanced from one to the other. "At least informally."

"You know this bozo?" Laura asked.

"I sure do. Ted, this is the new publisher I told you about, my stepdaughter, Laura Spencer. Laura, this is Ted Kandall. He's going to be staying at Lost Creek for a week or two."

Ted Kandall. No wonder she hadn't recognized him. He looked nothing like the newspaper photographs she had seen of him in recent years. Most of them showed him either in a nightclub or on the slopes of some fancy winter resort, always accompanied by a stunning, leggy blonde. Sometimes two.

His was a strong, handsome face, made even more unique by its combination of boy-next-door charm and blatant sex appeal. A little over six feet tall, he had a muscular build, dark blond hair tousled by the wind, and eyes that were a stunning cornflower blue. The light stubble gave him a roguish look that somehow added to his sexuality.

"So this is the famous Laura." Flashing a disarming grin, he extended his hand. "No hard feelings I hope."

Remembering he was J.B.'s friend, as well as his houseguest, Laura took the offered hand and shook it. "Of course not," she said, her tone only half serious. "I always enjoy having my car splashed with mud after it's been Simonized."

He glanced at the Mustang's driver's door. It was covered with mud. "Now, I really feel like a bozo." Reaching inside the BMW, he pulled out a pen and a business card from the glove compartment and scribbled something on it before handing it to her. "Maybe this will help me redeem myself."

"What is it?"

"An IOU for a Kandall wash and wax job. I promise you won't be disappointed. Just ask J.B."

"He's right, kiddo. No one took care of my old Ninety-eight better than Ted."

"There you go. Am I forgiven?"

Amusement lent his voice a playful, almost sensual quality that put Laura instantly on her guard. Charm was an inbred characteristic with the Kandalls; and if rumors were to be believed, this Kandall's romantic exploits numbered in the dozens.

She pulled her hand free and avoided answering his question by asking one of her own. "Are you here on business, Mr. Kandall? Or pleasure?"

"Actually neither. I'm just here."

Mmm. Enigmatic. Maybe that's why he was so

popular with the ladies. Some women were suckers for the sexy, mysterious type.

So that he would not mistake her for one of his adoring fans, she pushed a strand of hair from her face, making it a point to use her left hand.

Ted was nearly blinded by the rock on her finger. So the lady was taken. In a big way. Without being sure why, he felt a small pang of regret. "Who's the lucky guy?" he asked, nodding toward the ring.

J.B., who had witnessed the unfolding exchange with a great deal of interest, rested his elbow on Ted's shoulder. "Laura is engaged to Stuart Fleming. You remember him, don't you, Ted? I believe the two of you attended Westberry High together."

"Fleming," Ted said, remembering a handsome but pretentious kid with few friends. "I think I do. Was he the one claiming to be related to English royalty?"

Laura's lips twitched. Somehow, the image of Stuart flaunting his pedigree was as easy to imagine as it was amusing.

"He's an assistant D.A. now," J.B. continued. "Right here in Burnet."

"No kidding." Ted threw another glance at the ring. It was as ostentatious as the snobbish boy he remembered. And for some reason, on that small, delicate hand, the damned thing looked obscene. "Have you set a date yet?" he asked for lack of anything more original to say.

"No, but we will." Laura tucked the business card in her jacket pocket. "Soon."

Ted nodded. For an engaged woman carrying thirty grand worth of rocks, she sure didn't sound very excited. "Well, tell him I said hello, will you? And if he ever wants a replay of that tennis match he said I won unfairly, I'm willing to take him on. Without a referee this time." Then, with a pat on J.B.'s shoulder and a promise to see him later at dinner, he gave Laura a two-finger salute and went into the house.

Laura's gaze followed the photojournalist until he had disappeared. "So what do you think of my protegé?" J.B. asked, coming to stand beside her.

"He oozes charm. Just like his uncle."

"Oh, you're wrong there, kiddo. He may be charming but he's nothing like his uncle. The real resemblance is between him and his father, although Charles is too damned stubborn to see it."

"What is he doing here anyway?"

He told her about the exhibition at the Luberick Gallery next week and Ted's attempts to reconcile with his father. He didn't think it necessary to mention Charles's illness.

"Does he know I'm investigating Malcolm?"

"I doubt it. Although he's bound to find out sooner or later. Why?"

"How will he feel toward you when he does?"

"If you're worried it might affect our friendship, don't. There's never been any love lost between Ted and his uncle. And anyway, he's not the type to hold a grudge against people trying to do their job, even if that job is investigating a member of the Kandall family."

J.B. walked toward a small refrigerator he kept next to his workbench, retrieved two Perriers from it and untwisted the caps. "Do I dare ask how that

investigation is coming along? Or is your flare-up
of a moment ago indication enough?" He handed
her one of the bottles.

Laura took a long, thirsty swallow. "I'm making
no headway whatsoever. Wherever I go, people
clam up." She told him about her unsuccessful
meeting with Bill Smolen.

"Fear is a powerful emotion, kiddo. And greed
an even greater one. No one knows that better than
Malcolm." Then, because he sensed she had
stopped by for a little moral support, he added,
"It's going to be all right. Just give those ideas you
and the operating committee came up with time
to work."

"You're right." Feeling better already, she
sniffed the air. "Is that Lenox's shepherd's pie
I'm smelling?"

"It certainly is. He's preparing a special dinner
in honor of Ted's return. You'll join us, won't you?
I know the two of you didn't hit it off as well as I
had expected, but after a nice dinner and some fine
wine, I have a feeling things will improve."

She smiled. "You wouldn't be trying to set me
up by any chance, would you? Because if you are,
I should remind you that I'm already spoken for—
to a man *you* introduced me to."

J.B. sighed. "A mistake I've been trying to cor-
rect ever since."

It was true. From the moment she and Stuart
had started dating, about six months ago, J.B. had
made no secret of how he felt toward the attorney.
"The boy has no fire," he had told her once. "He's

ambitious, handsome, and rich. And that's about it. You'll be bored with him within a year."

However, when she had announced, a couple of months ago that she had accepted Stuart's proposal, J.B. had put his objections aside, given her a warm hug, and promised her the "biggest damned wedding Texas had ever seen." But she knew that deep down, his feelings hadn't changed. Occasionally, it showed.

"So what do you say, kiddo?" he asked, wrapping a thick arm around her shoulder. "You're staying?"

"Can't." Laura downed the rest of her Perrier before taking it back to the carport. "Mom is having a little celebration dinner of her own tonight and Stuart is due to pick me up in a few minutes."

"Stuart is going to your mother's? How much of your soul did you have to sell?"

"None of it," she replied, feeling honor bound to defend her fiancé. "He's coming of his own accord. Because it's important to Mom and to me."

"Good for him. But mark next Friday night on your calendar, will you? I'm having a big barbecue for Ted. Stuart is invited but if he can't make it, you come anyway, you hear?"

She laughed. "All right."

He walked her to her car. "Have a good time tonight, kiddo. Oh, and say hello to your mother."

8

Dressed in gray sweatpants and a cropped black T-shirt, Ted braced his stomach against the paddock fence and aimed his Nikon at a herd of grazing longhorns.

It had been years since he had photographed anything as peaceful as the scene in front of him now. It felt odd to have time to take position, to study, to focus. Odd, but not unpleasant.

He had awakened at the crack of dawn, not because of jet lag, which no longer affected him, but because he couldn't get his father out of his mind. Was there anything he could have done to prevent the fiasco of yesterday? He had tossed the question around and around in his mind for hours.

The answer, of course, was a resounding yes. If he hadn't taken the bait his father had so cleverly provided, maybe things would have been different. That damned temper of his had brought him nothing but trouble over the years, and few people could trigger it better than Charles.

As the sun had begun to rise, he had taken a quick shower, thrown some clothes on, grabbed his camera, without which he felt naked, and gone for a brisk, soothing walk.

He loved the countryside at this time of the morning. He loved the fresh smell that rose from the damp earth, the pearling of dew on the grass, the way everything turned a pale shade of gold as the sun began its slow ascent over the horizon.

"Here, boy," he called out, pointing his lens toward a longhorn who was staring in the distance. "Look this way, will you? That's it. Slow and easy. Right into the camera. Yeah, good boy."

The talk, more for himself than for his subject, came naturally, a habit left over from his early days as a department store portrait photographer.

Walking along the fence, he took another half-dozen shots, gave the indifferent longhorn his two-finger salute, and resumed his walk down the narrow, rocky road.

He was taking deep gulps of that wonderful morning air when he saw her.

She stood on her porch, sipping coffee and gazing at the same longhorns he had been photographing a moment earlier. The cool sophistication that had exuded from her yesterday was gone. She wore a pair of skimpy denim shorts and a pink T-shirt that molded her high round breasts. Her glorious hair was gathered up into a topknot from which a few tendrils had escaped.

There was an intriguing look about her—different from yesterday. She seemed more pensive, almost troubled as she kept staring into the distance.

Ted held his breath. In the early-morning haze,

the image had an almost unreal quality as if it might disappear in an instant.

Almost unconsciously, he raised his camera, gave a slight twist of his telephoto lens to adjust the focus, and pressed the shutter. Then, as always when he was faced with a fascinating subject, he forgot where he was, and even who he was, as he became totally absorbed with his task.

Moving quickly, he shot her again, as she pushed a wisp of hair from her face, and again as her gaze followed the flight of a buzzard high in the sky. He kept shooting until he had exhausted the last of his film. Then, he just stood there, one foot braced against a big old oak and kept watching her, unable to take his eyes off her.

After a while, she glanced into her cup and walked inside. Following an impulse, he started toward the guest house.

Built in a grove of live oaks five hundred yards from the main house, the guest house was a small replica of the log cabin with beamed interiors, chintz-covered chairs, and lots of windows to let in the brilliant Texas sunshine.

Wearing her Sunday morning favorite attire—shorts and a T-shirt—Laura stood at the counter of her small but efficient kitchen as she refilled her coffee cup. She started to leave, then, with a shrug, she reached into the cookie jar and pulled out one of Lenox's delicious shortbread cookies. It wasn't the healthiest breakfast in the world for a hard-working woman, but anything more complicated than that would interrupt her train of thought.

Back on the wraparound porch where she had been working since early this morning, she walked slowly toward the glass-topped table as she sipped her coffee. After a minute, she sat down and studied the yellow pad with the names of people she had hoped would help in her investigation of Malcolm Kandall.

Unfortunately, she hadn't been able to get anyone to cooperate. Even friends of J.B.'s, people she had thought she could count on, had remained as tight-lipped as Bill Smolen, claiming they hadn't been aware of any irregularities.

Fund-raising documents obtained by the *Sentinel* in recent months had revealed that in the last year, Malcolm Kandall had received 62,000 contributions totaling more than fifteen million dollars. While most of the donations came from single individuals and ranged from ten dollars to ten thousand dollars, eighty-two companies had contributed a total of more than ten million dollars, twice the amount the incumbent governor had raised so far.

Of those eighty-two businesses and large corporations, half were located in Texas and the rest in New York, New Jersey, California, and Washington, D.C. The identity of the largest contributors hadn't come as a surprise. Names like Orbach of Orbach Motors, Bradley Department Stores, and Schwartz Homes appeared near the top of the list. But there were others Laura had never heard of—a construction company in Queens, a cable television executive in California, and a restaurant chain headquartered in Laredo.

It was those contributors she needed to concentrate on. Who were those people? Did they support other politicians? Or just this one?

"Hi, there."

Startled, Laura looked up. Ted stood a few feet away, his arms folded, one foot on the lower step. Trying to be inconspicuous, she tucked her pad under her briefcase. "Good morning." She glanced at the camera hanging around his neck. "Found anything interesting to photograph?"

He smiled. Up close, with no makeup, she was even lovelier. For a moment, he was tempted to find out if that ripe, sexy mouth with the little black mole over it was as soft as it looked. Then, remembering she was engaged, he tempered his impulses. "More than I expected in this quiet patch of Texas."

To keep his thoughts from straying any further, he glanced toward the Mustang. The mud had been washed off but the hood was open. "Something wrong with your car?"

"The battery is dead, I think. Lenox will give me a jump later."

"Mind if I take a look? It could be something else."

"Are you handy with cars?"

"I used to be."

She shrugged. "Then go right ahead. But don't ask me to supply any tools. With the exception of the car jack in the trunk, I don't have any."

Unhooking his camera from around his neck, he ran up the few steps and laid it on the table. He flashed that dazzling smile again. "Guard that with your life."

She watched him walk over to the Mustang. He had a quick, springy step that reminded her of a basketball player she had dated in high school. But that's where the resemblance to any of the men she had known ended. Maybe it was the way his smile carried all the way to his eyes, softening them that made him different, or the way he talked in a totally unaffected way. It would have been easy for someone with that degree of fame, someone whose work was displayed in the world's most famous galleries, to be at least a tiny bit full of himself. Not Ted Kandall. J.B. had been right after all. The man was as different from his uncle as night and day.

Because she didn't feel comfortable working on Malcolm's investigation with him here, she pulled her laptop computer toward her, punched a key to recall her column, and started to write copy. This week she had devoted "Eyes On You" to the recent Houston floods and the courageous group of volunteers who had helped pull dozens of stranded people to safety.

Five minutes later, she heard the purr of an engine. Looking up, she saw Ted snap the hood shut. She leaned back in her chair. "I must say, I'm impressed."

"Don't be. It was only a loose wire." He tossed the cloth he'd used to wipe his hands in the trunk and closed it. "That engine is in remarkably good condition for a car that old."

"Try telling that to J.B. He thinks I'm too sentimental about the car, that I should junk it and buy myself a real one—something big and powerful. And reliable."

Without being invited, Ted pulled out the chair next to her and sat down. "Was it a gift from someone?"

"No. I paid for it with my own hard-earned money, while I attended UT. When I got the offer from the *New York Herald* after graduation, I left the car here, with the intention of selling it— eventually."

"But 'eventually' never came."

She laughed. "No. Lenox, bless his heart, kept it in tip-top shape for me. He drove it once a week, made sure the oil was changed regularly, and even gave it a wax job once or twice a year."

He watched her as she talked. Now that she had dropped some of her earlier reserve, there was something mesmerizing about the way she expressed herself, with small hand movements and quick, warm smiles. She smelled fabulous, too. Not perfumy like so many women he knew, but a clean, powdery scent that reminded him of an English garden. Someday, he would have to photograph her again. Not in repose but in action. Shaking off his mood, he glanced at the computer in front of her. "What are you working on?"

"My next column."

"Ah, yes. The much-talked-about "Eyes On You." Excellent piece of journalism. The approach is fresh and the subjects intriguing. I particularly liked that piece on drugs and border patrols along the Rio Grande. Very gutsy."

The compliment made her blush. "I wasn't aware you kept up with your hometown newspaper."

"I don't. J.B. had several back issues at the house

and I thought reading your columns would be a good way to get to know you better."

"Why would you want to do that?"

He shrugged. "Professional curiosity."

She met his gaze squarely. "And was that curiosity satisfied?"

"Not entirely. I found out you're a good journalist, painfully honest and hardworking, which explains why J.B. thinks so highly of you. But I'm sure there's a lot more to Laura Spencer than meets the eye."

She laughed. "Good journalist, hardworking. This is high praise coming from a Kandall."

She had a great laugh, he thought. Throaty and sexy as hell. "I'm not a typical Kandall. Some say I'm worse."

She watched him pull out a cigarette from a pack tucked into his waistband. He didn't light it. Instead, he ran his fingers up and down the length of it, slowly. It was a sensual, slightly disturbing gesture, although totally unintentional.

"What do you think?" he asked.

She pulled her gaze away from his strong, tanned hands. "About what?"

"My being the worst of the Kandall bunch."

"Oh." She struggled to get her thoughts back on track. "I try not to judge people on first impressions."

"In that case, I hope I'll have a chance to make a second impression."

His eyes challenged her, half serious, half amused. Sensations she shouldn't have felt tugged and pulled at her. She was trying to think of a harmless, noncommittal reply when she heard the powerful roar of an engine coming up the road. "Stuart!"

One eyebrow up, Ted turned his head. A shiny red Porsche had come to a stop beside the Mustang. Stuart Fleming stepped out of it, his tall frame managing the exit from the low sports car gracefully. His eyes narrowed slightly when he saw Ted.

Ted watched him approach. Except for a few changes—shorter hair and a stronger physique—he didn't look much different than he had twenty years ago. He still had that same measured way of assessing those he perceived as lesser human beings with one cold, all-encompassing look.

Other than that, he was very handsome and it was easy to see why Laura, or any woman, would have fallen for him. And the smell of money didn't hurt either. Christ, it was everywhere, from the fancy red toy to the white Armani jacket with the sleeves pushed up à la Don Johnson and the solid gold watch around his wrist. It was hardly the kind of everyday stuff one could afford on a deputy D.A.'s salary. Obviously the Fleming trust fund was alive and well. And Stuart wasn't shy about using it.

Ted stood up. "How's it going, Stuart?"

At the bottom of the steps, the attorney stopped. "Do I know you?"

Laura sauntered down to meet him, smiling affably, much like a mediator trying to prevent a battle. "Stuart, this is Ted Kandall. You heard he was in town, didn't you?"

"No." He circled Laura's waist and held her close as they climbed the steps. There was no tenderness in the gesture, Ted noted. Just a message that said, "hands off." In what seemed like an afterthought, Stuart leaned forward and offered his hand. "How have you been, Ted?"

Ted shook it and for a moment the two men measured each other like two old adversaries. "I can't complain."

"The Luberick Gallery in Austin is showing an exhibition of Ted's work next Saturday," Laura said brightly. "The whole town is talking about it."

"Is that so."

The lack of enthusiasm made Ted smile. That, too, hadn't changed. Stuart's motto had always been "if it's not happening to me, it's not worth talking about." "I hope you and Laura will come."

Stuart wrinkled his nose as if he had smelled something foul. "I doubt we'll be able to make it."

"Free champagne," Ted said in a teasing tone. "The good stuff."

"We'll pass." He smiled down at Laura. "We're both very busy."

"So I've heard." Ted perched one hip on the railing. "Deputy D.A. huh?" He bobbed his head a few times. "Impressive. Although I was surprised to hear you had taken the job. I was always under the impression your tastes leaned more toward a private practice—preferably with a prestigious, well-established firm."

The remark brought a flicker of annoyance to the otherwise dispassionate green eyes. "That was then. I'm a different man now. I suppose I could have gone to work for a big firm, but I chose to do something more rewarding instead."

Ted held back a smile. Translated, that meant there had been no offer and he'd had to settle for whatever he could get.

"What about you?" Stuart's chin tilted upward. "Have any of your childhood aspirations come true yet or are you still waiting for that big break?"

Mmm. Not a bad comeback. Maybe some day the two of them could sit down and have a serious insult-trading session like in the old days. The winner could walk away with Laura. But before Ted could think of an equally smart reply, Stuart had turned to Laura, dismissing him totally. "Darling, you look positively delicious, but surely that's not what you're going to wear?"

Laura's eyes grew mildly alarmed. "Are we going somewhere?"

Stuart's handsome features registered instant dismay. "You forgot my parents' anniversary party?"

Laura groaned inwardly. How could she have forgotten something as big as the Flemings' fortieth wedding anniversary? Stuart must have mentioned it a dozen times during the last week.

She saw the wry amusement on Ted's face and blushed. "I'm sorry, Stuart. I did forget."

Stuart kissed the tip of her nose. "No harm done, darling. How long will it take you to get ready?"

"Ten minutes at the most."

"Go ahead then." He flashed a smile in Ted's direction. "Ted and I will entertain each other, talk about the good old days."

And be bored to death? No, thanks. "Maybe some other time," Ted said. "Right now I have some photographs to develop." His gaze drifted back to Laura. "Thanks for the conversation. Oh, by the way, you don't mind if I stop by the *Sentinel* some morning, do you? I'd like to say hello to the old gang."

"No. Of course not." For a moment, she almost added, "Thanks for fixing my car," then remembered that Stuart was there and changed her mind. "Come any time."

9

Although Ted wasn't fond of his uncle, he had always felt a deep affection for his aunt Barbara. She was a gentle, caring woman, a little high-strung perhaps, but who wouldn't be, married to a man like Malcolm Kandall?

A uniformed maid he didn't know opened the door when he rang the bell on Monday morning, and eyed him suspiciously. "May I help you?"

"I'd like to see Barbara Kandall, please. I'm Ted Kandall—her nephew."

The woman's expression didn't change. "I'll let her know you're here." After a moment's hesitation, she opened the door wider and let him into the huge foyer. "Please wait here."

She wasn't gone more than thirty seconds when Ted heard the crash. Reacting instinctively, he ran toward the drawing room where the sound had come from and threw the door open.

Barbara stood in the middle of the room. Her face was white, her eyes filled with an expression that stopped him cold—a mixture of despair and terror. The remains of a shattered glass lay at her feet.

"I'll go get a broom," the maid murmured as she hurried out of the room.

In a few long strides, Ted was by his aunt's side, taking her hands in his. "Barbara, are you all right?"

When she nodded, he kissed her on the cheek. Then, hoping to relieve some of the tension, he said, "If I had known my visit would have had such an effect on you, I would have made a less dramatic entrance."

The housekeeper had returned, carrying a whisk broom and a dustpan. Still holding Barbara's hands, Ted pulled her away from the debris. "Can I get you anything? Water? A drink?"

"I'm fine." To his relief, the blood was slowly returning to her cheeks. "It's good to see you, Ted," she said with a weak smile. "I was wondering when I'd be hearing from you."

"You knew I was in town?"

"Joan Alden saw you come out of your father's house the other day. She lives across the street, you know." Her hands went to her throat, massaging it gently. "What brought you back to Austin, Ted?"

"Sandra told me Dad was sick," he said, seeing no need to keep his knowledge of Charles's illness a secret any longer. "So I decided to make another attempt at establishing peace in the family."

"Did you succeed?"

"The visit was a complete flop. After five minutes, we were at each other's throats again." He let out a mirthless laugh. "Old habits die hard, I guess."

Barbara's fingers, still trembling, played with the

teardrop diamond around her neck. "Are you planning to stay in Texas long?"

He looked at her. Her reaction, or lack of it, puzzled him. Barbara was a compassionate woman. From the moment she had joined the Kandall family almost two decades ago, she had been a constant source of encouragement to him, urging him to be patient with Charles, certain that eventually he would come around regarding Ted's choice of career.

There was none of that compassion now, no warmth. She looked almost . . . distant. "A week," he said in answer to her question. "Maybe two."

He told her about the exhibition and J.B.'s invitation to stay at Lost Creek. "After that, I'll probably go back to London." He studied her for another few seconds. "Are you sure I can't get you anything?"

She smiled as she patted her hair and for an instant, the old Barbara was back. "Why? Do I look that bad?"

"You look terrific, just a little more nervous than I remember, that's all. Is it me?" he asked as an afterthought. "Would you rather I weren't here?"

"Oh, no." Her face softened. "I'm glad you came. It's been so long. Malcolm will be sorry he missed you."

"Where is he, by the way?"

"He's campaigning at Bergstrom Air Force Base. I was supposed to go with him, but I was too tired. You have no idea how exhausting a campaign can be. In fact, I was about to take a short nap when you came in."

It was the gentlest of hints, but a hint just the same, and he took it, rising to his feet. "Then I'll let you rest. Perhaps we could have lunch one day before I leave? And you'll come to the exhibition, won't you? Sandra will be there."

"I'd love that. And so will Malcolm."

But her voice lacked conviction and she couldn't quite meet his gaze. He would give her a day or two to get over whatever was bothering her and then he would call again.

He was about to say good-bye when Malcolm came in. He was slightly out of breath, as if he had been running. When he saw Ted standing in the middle of the drawing room, he stopped. "Ted."

"Hello, Uncle Malcolm." Ted was the first to offer his hand and although Malcolm shook it, there was no warmth in it, no welcome in the guarded smile. "I hope you don't mind my stopping by. I wanted to say hello to Barbara."

"Of course not." He threw his wife a quick glance. Then, setting his briefcase on a console by the door, he said, "I talked to your father this morning."

Ted thrust his hands in his pockets. "Did he tell you how well we hit it off?"

Malcolm ignored the sarcastic remark. Looking a little more relaxed now, he sat down in a green brocade chair and crossed his legs. "Look, Ted, the last thing I want to do is get between you and your father. But I would like to give you a small piece of advice if you don't mind. Go back to England. Your father is a sick man, and while your coming here to try to patch things up was an honorable gesture on your part, it didn't work."

"Did my father tell you that?"

"He didn't have to. The sound of his voice on the phone was enough to make me realize how much your visit has upset him." He studied the tip of his shoe for a moment, before looking up again. "What I'm trying to say, as diplomatically as I can, is that it would be best for all of us if you went back to England as soon as possible. If you don't, your father's health could be in serious jeopardy. I'm sure you don't want that."

Barbara, who hadn't said a word since Malcolm had walked in, came to stand beside her husband. More or less recovered from whatever had spooked her, she laid a hand on his shoulder. "Malcolm is right, Ted. We have to think of Charles."

Ted looked from one to the other. Since when did Malcolm give a damn about his brother's well-being? Everybody, including Charles, knew he had always been fiercely jealous of him, that the only reason he had worked for him all these years was to advance his own political career.

This scene is all wrong, Ted thought. It's been wrong from the moment I set foot into this house.

As the atmosphere grew more stifling, he only wanted one thing—to get out of there. "Thanks for the advice, Uncle Malcolm." In an attempt at civility, he gave him a pat on the shoulder. "I have no idea what my plans are at the moment. When I do, I'll let you know."

Because Malcolm was a master at concealing his true feelings, Ted couldn't tell whether the remark annoyed him or not. But he couldn't miss Barbara's reaction as she gripped her husband's shoulder and bit down on her bottom lip.

Pretending he hadn't noticed anything, he kissed her on the cheek. "Don't bother to show me out," he said softly. "I know the way."

Back in his car, he glanced in the rearview mirror. Malcolm stood at the window, watching him.

What the hell is going on with this family? he thought irritably as he drove off. Are Sandra and I the only sane ones here? Or are we going bonkers as well?

Malcolm, who had cut short his visit to Bergstrom Air Force Base after Dolores's call, let the curtain fall back and turned around. "What the hell did he want?"

Her hand shaking, Barbara walked over to a cart displaying several brands of bottled water and poured herself a glass of Evian. "You mean Dolores didn't tell you when she called?" she asked in an uncharacteristically icy tone. "She must be slipping."

Realizing his mistake, Malcolm quickly came to her. "I'm sorry I snapped at you, darling. I guess my nerves aren't much better than yours. But, please, don't be mad at Dolores for doing her job. You and I agreed you needed someone to watch over you while I was away campaigning, remember?"

Her eyes closed briefly. "I know. It's just that . . ." She let out a hopeless sigh. "I wish things were different."

"What do you mean?"

"I'm tired of being supervised, Malcolm, of being treated like an irresponsible child. I want to be strong again, the way I used to be before . . ." She let the sentence trail and gazed into her drink.

Malcolm stroked her hair. "Shhh. You're doing just fine."

"No, I'm not. I'm a mess. When Dolores told me Ted was here, I was so upset, I dropped my iced tea." She turned imploring eyes toward him. "I want to check into a rehabilitation clinic, Malcolm. I need it so badly. That way, I wouldn't have to run into Ted again—"

"And what would we tell the voters? Or the thousands of volunteers who devoted every minute of their time to this campaign?"

"I don't know . . ."

As tears welled up in her eyes, he took her hand and brought it to his lips. "What happened, Barbara? What did Ted say to make you feel this way?"

"He had a terrible row with Charles and he's so torn up about it. I know he came to me for comfort and I couldn't give it to him—because I was afraid." She met his watchful gaze. "He knew something was wrong, Malcolm. He kept looking at me in that quiet, serious way of his. He's so intuitive, you know, so much like his mother in that respect."

"Shhh." He stroked her hair. "Don't think about Elizabeth. Don't even say her name. You'll only make yourself sick."

She continued to gaze silently into her drink.

When she spoke again, her voice was hollow with despair. "What about you, Malcolm? Don't you ever think about her?

"No," he said truthfully. "The past is the past. We can't afford to look back. Just think of all the lives that would be shattered if we did—not just ours, but Charles's as well. And Sandra. You don't want to hurt Sandra, do you?"

Barbara shook her head.

"Then you must never bring up the past again." He squeezed her hand. "Do it for me, Barbara. Do it for us."

Her eyes closed, she nodded.

Laura was in the middle of dictating a letter to Mildred when she heard the commotion outside her office. Glancing toward the newsroom, she saw that more than a dozen reporters had left their desks and were crowding around a grinning Ted Kandall for what appeared to be a hero's welcome.

Even from this distance, his presence was potent. With his face freshly shaven, there was something thrilling about him, about the way he captured attention and held it, effortlessly.

"Will you look at him?" Mildred said as she watched Ted shake hands. "It's as if time had stood still, as if he'd never left."

"The staff certainly seems to be crazy about him."

Mildred's chest swelled up, like that of a proud mother. "He's always had that effect on people. Even when he was a boy."

"You've known him a long time, haven't you?"

"I met him when he entered that photo contest. He was only fourteen at the time, but he was already so focused, so sure of what he wanted to do. I never had a moment's doubt he would go far. In spite of his father."

Her eyes still on Ted, Laura bit gently on the end of her pencil as he continued to dazzle the small crowd with anecdotes punctuated by laughter.

Piecing what she knew about him from J.B. and from what she had read, she tried to imagine him as a boy, this young rebel who had turned his nose up at the family fortune and announced one day he wasn't going to law school.

His father had been furious and had threatened to disown him, but that hadn't changed Ted's mind. A few weeks later, with little more than the clothes on his back, he had enrolled at the University of Louisiana, supporting himself by working as a photographer's assistant in a department store.

It wasn't until his mother's tragic suicide on Aspen Mountain in Colorado sixteen years ago, that the feud between him and his father had escalated. Every newspaper in Texas and across the nation had told its own version of the incident, repeating in lurid details how, in front of four hundred mourners, Ted had accused his father of being a murderer.

Shortly after that, he had moved to England and, except for J.B., no one had ever seen him again. Until now.

"He never married, did he?" she asked, swiveling slowly in her chair.

Mildred shook her head. "No."

"Surely it can't be for lack of women. From what I heard, he's quite a ladies' man."

"Oh, I don't know about that." Mildred watched Ted through the glass window. "It's true that there's been a few women in his life over the years, all beautiful. But I don't think he's ever felt strongly about any of them. He would have told J.B."

"You think he's too fussy?"

"That may be part of it. Or it could be that he doesn't want to be tied down. He's got the wanderlust, you know. He can never stay in any one place for very long."

Through her open door, Laura heard Ted mimicking someone with a strong German accent. The newsroom exploded with laughter.

As Ted turned around unexpectedly, their gaze met. Laura felt herself blushing as if she had been caught doing something wrong. Well, aren't you? she thought. Questioning Mildred about every detail of his life?

She pulled her gaze away and busied herself by shuffling through the papers on her desk. "That will be all for now, Mildred. I'll call you later if I need to dictate another letter."

"But Laura ..." Looking puzzled, Mildred glanced from her pad to Laura. "You didn't finish this one."

Laura felt herself blush again. "You're right. I'll ... do it later. Why don't you go say hello to Ted. I know you're dying to."

As Mildred walked into the newsroom, Laura's gaze followed her. She saw Ted turn around. In an instant, he had lifted the secretary off the floor and was twirling her around, much to Mildred's delight.

Because she was beginning to find the man much too fascinating, Laura pulled her gaze away and returned to her work.

"So what did you think of the movie?" Stuart asked as the Porsche's powerful beams sliced through the night. "Erotic enough for you?"

Although his tone was light, almost detached, Laura knew the sensuous foreign thriller had stimulated him—if not mentally, at least physically. She had sensed it in the way his whole body had seemed to gravitate forward during the seductive shower scene, and again later when he had dropped his popcorn.

"More so than I expected," she said with a chuckle. "Although that's not the reason I chose this movie."

"Liar." In the dark, Stuart's eyes shone brightly. "You took me to see that film in the hope I'd get all hot and bothered."

"I didn't think you needed outside stimulation for that," she teased. Then, slanting him an amused glance, she asked, "Did it work?"

Stuart laughed. "You wench. You know it did."

They had reached the guest house and after Stuart brought the car to a stop and shut off the engine, he turned to face her. "And for your information, I do *not* need outside stimulation. You turn me on all by yourself." His finger touched her mouth, trailed gently toward the opening in her blouse. "Why don't we go inside so I can show you?"

Laura held back a sigh of disappointment. She loved him dearly, but he was so predictable. And so damned tame—even in a state of arousal. Why couldn't he forget his inhibitions for one night and just ravish her right here? In the Porsche?

Was that what she wanted? she wondered as her heart skipped a beat. To be ravished in the Porsche?

The thought made her smile. Stuart treasured that car. The idea alone of using it for something as primal as sex, and possibly soiling it, was unthinkable.

"What do you say, hon?" Warm lips touched hers.

For a moment, just a moment, she was tempted to be the aggressor, to rip his Izod shirt and attack his body and his senses with all the passion she could muster.

But he was already pulling away from her and groping for the door handle. "Hurry."

Well, well, she thought as she stepped out of the car. He *was* hot and bothered. Maybe taking him to that movie hadn't been a total waste of time after all.

Her heart beating in anticipation, she opened the screen door. As she did, a large manila envelope that had been tucked between the two doors slid down.

"What's that?" Stuart asked.

Laura bent down to pick up the envelope. "I don't know." She turned it around as they both walked in. There was no name, no return address, and of course, no postmark. "Why don't we take a look and see?"

Unfastening the metal clasp, she peered inside and saw that the envelope contained eight by ten photographs. "It must be from my photo editor. Although I can't imagine why he would hand deliver ..." She gasped as she pulled out the first print. "What in the world ..."

Behind her, Stuart made a hissing sound.

Emptying the envelope, Laura spread the rest of the black-and-white photos on the coffee table. There were an even dozen of them, all of herself and taken apparently at the same time, although in various poses. She had never seen herself like that, had no idea she could look so ... sensual? Was that the word she was looking for?

Her heart thundered against her chest as she picked up one of the shots. The photographer had captured her in profile as she stood on her porch and gazed into the distance. The morning light had wrapped her in an iridescent glow, giving the shot a strange, almost dreamlike quality. Her hair looked soft and wispy, the color of silver dust. Her lips were moist and half parted, and through the T-shirt's thin fabric, the outline of a hard nipple could be seen.

"What the hell is going on here?" Stuart snapped. "Who took those pictures?"

"I can think of only one person. Ted Kandall."

"What do you mean, 'you think'? Don't you know? You posed for him, didn't you?"

Laura's cheeks colored. "No, Stuart. I didn't

pose for him. I didn't even know he was there. Not until he said hello anyway. He must have taken those before that . . . while I was working."

"It sure doesn't look to me as if you were working."

"I was thinking, which as you know is part of the working process."

Stuart made a scornful sound. "Thinking about what, I wonder."

She whirled around, cheeks on fire, eyes flashing. "Look, Stuart, I don't like what you're implying. I'm not the one you should attack here. I'm as surprised by this as you are."

"Well, that settles it." Stuart marched toward a small console by the window. "I've never liked the guy. And now I know why. For all his so-called talent, the man is nothing but a camera-toting sicko who gets his jollies from photographing unsuspecting women."

"What are you doing?"

"Calling the police. I'm having Ted Kandall arrested."

She hurried across the room. "What for?"

"Voyeurism. Trespassing. Breaking and entering. You name it, I'll—"

With the tip of her index finger, Laura disconnected the call.

It was Stuart's turn to redden. "What do you think you're doing?"

"He didn't break and enter, Stuart. And he didn't trespass. This is J.B.'s property, remember? And he is J.B.'s houseguest."

"Are you aware that forty-five percent of rapists

live within a three-mile radius of their victims? And that—"

"Oh, for God's sake, Ted Kandall is not a rapist."

"How do you know? Look at those pictures. Tell me they're not the work of a pervert."

"I'm not going to stand here and analyze Ted Kandall. Or his motives. I'll deal with that part later. But *you* are not calling the police."

"Why not? Why are you defending him, Laura?" His eyes narrowed suspiciously. "What is he to you?"

"He's nothing. I'm doing it for J.B. Ted is his guest. And his friend. How would it look if I had him arrested?"

"What about me? How will it look if that jerk starts to pass those photos around town? Or worse, if he decides to include them in his exhibition on Saturday? How do you think people will react when they see my fiancée plastered on the walls of the Luberick Gallery, looking like some . . ." He gestured toward the photos. "Some overheated hussy."

"And you," Laura shouted back, "are behaving like a jealous, irrational, stupid jerk."

"Oh, really? Then maybe I should leave."

"Fine. You know the way out."

"Fine." His arms held rigidly at his sides, he crossed the room. At the door, he turned to throw her one last murderous look. When she didn't call him back, he left, slamming the door behind him.

Laura gave a vicious kick to one of the photographs that had fallen to the floor.

So much for a night of wild, unbridled passion.

1 0

By the time Laura arrived at the main house the following morning, the place was already buzzing with activity in preparation for J.B.'s barbecue.

Dozens of workmen rushed from one end of the property to another, hammering the bandstand, erecting tents, setting up tables, and stringing colorful lanterns in the huge oaks.

She found Ted down by the wells, checking the stock-tank levels. He stood near the top of the tank ladder, wearing nothing but a pair of snug jeans, boots, and a black Stetson she vaguely remembered seeing on J.B. years ago.

"Ted!"

Glancing down, he raised his hand in a salute. "Be right down."

She watched him climb down the narrow ladder with the ease of an old ranch hand. Once on firm ground, he tossed the clipboard on a nearby bench next to a pair of work gloves he had apparently decided not to wear and grinned. "Howdy."

His chest, broader than she had realized, was covered with a thin sheen of perspiration. Not bothering to answer his greeting she pulled her gaze away and held out the manila envelope. "Would you care to explain this?"

Ted felt the electricity around them crackle. He wondered if she felt it, too. "What is there to explain? I'm a photographer. You're a beautiful woman. I gave in to an impulse, that's all."

"It never occurred to you that I might not like to be photographed without my knowledge? Or that I might be offended?"

He let his gaze skim over the lovely, angry face, the delicate throat, the crisp white pantsuit. "Frankly, no. I thought you might enjoy seeing yourself as an artist sees you—sexy, vulnerable."

"Well, I don't. And you would do well to curb those impulses of yours in the future. This one almost landed you in jail."

His brow lifted. "You were that upset?"

"Stuart is the one who wanted to call the police."

Without being sure why, he felt mildly disappointed. His work wasn't something he wanted to share with Stuart Fleming. "I didn't realize you showed them to him."

"He was with me when I found them. And he didn't approve of your artwork any more than I did."

With the flick of a finger, he pushed the Stetson back on his head. "Does that mean a job at the *Sentinel* is out of the question?"

Her body stiffened instantly. "What are you talking about?"

"J.B. thought you might want me to shoot a few pictures for the paper while I'm here."

He could see that the remark had thrown her.

For a moment, she looked confused, lost for words. Then, almost as quickly, she was in charge again. "I'm afraid that's impossible. My staff wouldn't appreciate having some hotshot photographer step into their space. Even for a few days."

Another publisher might have jumped at the chance. The fact that she didn't made him like her even more. He shrugged. "No problem. Like I said, it was just a thought. If you change your mind, just give me a holler."

The lazy, almost caressing sound of his voice was beginning to make her forget why she had come here. She waved the envelope she still held. "Where are the negatives for these?"

"In my room."

"I want them."

The smiled deepened as he walked slowly toward her. "All right. If you don't mind giving me a ride to the house, I'll get them for you."

His proximity made it difficult for her to concentrate. For one startled moment, she felt herself swaying toward him, as if pulled by a magnet. Summoning all of her willpower, she squared her shoulders and took a step back. "That won't be necessary. Just leave them with Lenox and I'll pick them up later."

Then tugging the edges of her suit jacket in an attempt to look dignified, she murmured a quick good-bye and walked back toward her car.

In a nondescript, slightly run-down motel half a mile from the Austin airport, Tony Cordero stood

in front of a cracked bathroom mirror as he began
to tie the knot of his Bill Blass tie.

Tony loved clothes. Not the foul-smelling rejects
he used to salvage from his neighbors' trash years
ago, but the good stuff. And this, he thought, glancing appreciatively at the navy pinstripe his East Village tailor had made for him, was very good stuff.

He hadn't been too thrilled to hear he would be
spending the next four weeks in the Texas capital,
and Henrietta, the curvaceous fitness instructor he
had been dating for the last month, hadn't been too
happy either. Henrietta was a lady who demanded
continuous attention. If it hadn't been for his con-
siderable powers of persuasion, and the expensive
little trinket from Tiffany's, he'd be history right
now.

Tony sighed as he secured the Windsor knot. He
missed her already. Just the thought of that firm,
strong, flexible body next to his was enough to
drive him crazy.

Maybe this job wouldn't take as long as Enzio
thought. Maybe once he got his hands on the information he needed, and had taken care of Laura
Spencer, the boss would tell him to come home,
give him a big fat bonus for a job well done, and
send him back into Henrietta's arms.

In a better mood already, he took a step back to
admire his handiwork. He looked terrific. For this
particular assignment, he had chosen to reprise his
role as Enrico Garcia, head of Garcia Creations. It
was a role that suited him well, and all that had
been needed was a few minor adjustments to fit
the part to the circumstances.

With both palms, he smoothed his slick ponytail back and grinned at his reflection. This job would be a cinch.

Fifteen minutes later, as Tony stood in the lobby of the *Austin Sentinel,* he let out a sigh of relief. The pretty brunette sitting behind the reception desk was a Latina. How lucky could a guy get?

Flashing what Henrietta called his John Travolta smile, he rested his briefcase on the girl's desk and immediately slipped into his role. "How do you do, Miss Rodriguez," he said after glancing at her nameplate. "My name is Enrico Garcia." He let the r's roll off his tongue. "You may have heard of Garcia Creations? The Los Angeles fashion house?"

Before she could say no, he let his gaze run appreciatively over the simple two-piece white jersey. "Lovely suit."

"Thank you." She smiled back. "What can I do for you, Mr. Garcia?"

"I'm here to arrange a promotional campaign for a chain of boutiques I plan to open throughout Texas next month. I wonder if I could talk to the person in charge of your advertising department?"

"That would be Mr. Malloy. Ken Malloy." She rested her fingers on the switchboard. "Would you like me to call him for you? He might be able to see you right away."

"Thank you." He watched as she dialed a number and told Ken Malloy about the visitor in the downstairs lobby.

She was smiling when she hung up. "Mr. Malloy

said for you to go right up. Third floor—second office down the hall."

"Thank you, Miss Rodriguez."

"You're welcome."

Aware that her gaze was following him, he walked briskly, hitting the elevator button with a little flourish. So far so good.

Ken Malloy welcomed him warmly, listened to Tony's phony story about his chain of exclusive boutiques, and told him he would be glad to oversee the project personally.

Although Tony found the conversation excruciatingly boring, he nodded eagerly as Malloy outlined several options for the campaign. To stay in character, Tony showed him a few of the sketches he kept in his briefcase.

Half an hour later, Tony stood up, shook the man's hand, and promised to get back to him after he'd discussed the *Sentinel*'s ideas with his two partners.

The business card Tony left with Malloy, with an L.A. address and phone number, was as phony as the rest of the story. But by the time Malloy would realize that, Tony would have the information he needed and would be long gone.

Back in the lobby, he went straight to Angela Rodriguez's desk again.

"How did it go?" she asked, obviously delighted to see him again.

"Very well. It looks as if Garcia Creations and the *Sentinel* are going to be doing business together after all."

"I'm glad to hear it."

"And to show you my appreciation ..." He opened his briefcase and pulled out an exquisite silk scarf with a black-and-white geometric design and the Garcia label attached at one end. "Allow me to present you with a small gift."

Her pretty face turned a deep shade of red. "Oh, I couldn't I mean ... I didn't do anything." But he could see from the way her gaze kept returning to the silky square that she was tempted.

He didn't blame her. The sucker, a French design whose label he had removed and replaced with his own, had cost him a hundred smackers. Had the lady worn blue, red, green, or a mixture of colors, he would have chosen one of the five other designer scarfs he had carefully selected for this type of con. "You are underestimating yourself, Miss Rodriguez. It is Miss, is it not?"

"Yes ..."

Gently, he draped the scarf over her shoulders. "Perfect. It was made for that suit." He let his eyes bore into hers. "And for you."

"Oh." Still blushing, she touched the silky fabric as she gazed down at it. After a few seconds, she looked up. "If you're sure it's all right."

"I'm sure. In fact, I think we should put it to the test."

"To the test?" She shook her head. "I don't understand."

"Have lunch with me. We'll go somewhere crowded and see how others react." It wasn't exactly what Enzio would have called being unobtrusive but the quicker he secured the information he needed, the quicker he'd be back home with Henrietta.

He saw a look of regret pass through Angela Rodriguez's eyes. "I can't," she said with a sigh. "The girl who fills in for me is sick. I'll have to stay in today."

"That's too bad." He was thoughtful for a moment. So he would have to wait a few more hours. It wouldn't kill him. But it might be safer to take her some place *not* so crowded after all. "Then how about dinner? I have to catch a seven-thirty flight back to Los Angeles, but if you don't mind eating early . . ."

Her face brightened. "Not at all. I quit at five. I could meet you somewhere."

The cautious type. That was fine with him. Picking her up at the *Sentinel* now that he had met Malloy would have been too risky anyway. Remembering a quiet-looking restaurant a couple of blocks from the Blue Moon Motel, he asked, "Do you know where the Top Hat is?"

"Sure. I could be there by five-thirty."

"Then I'll see you this evening." Gallantly, he bent over and took her hand, brushing his lips against the soft brown skin. "Until later, Angela." He smiled under half-lowered lids. "May I call you Angela?"

"Yes." He saw her holding back a delighted giggle. "You may."

By the time Tony said good-bye to Angela Rodriguez at seven o'clock that evening, he knew where Laura Spencer lived, what make of car she drove, and what sort of schedule she kept. He had also learned that she was engaged to a Burnet County assistant prosecutor, and that her family consisted of a stepfather, now retired from the *Sentinel,* and her mother, a nightclub singer presently under contract at a place called the Golden Parrot.

Settling behind the wheel of the black Toyota Luigi had provided, Tony let out a sigh of satisfaction. This job was going to be almost too easy.

11

Laura was getting ready for bed when Stuart called on Thursday evening. "Hi." His tone was apologetic, almost caressing. "I'm sorry about the way I blew up last night. I shouldn't have taken my anger out on you."

"You're damned right."

"We wasted what could have been a great evening."

She twisted a curl around her index finger. "*You* wasted what could have been a great evening."

There was a soft chuckle. "You're never going to let me live this down, are you?"

She felt herself soften. "Not until you redeem yourself."

"Oh, Laura, believe me I'd like nothing better. But the Halloway case is going to trial and Ed assigned me to it."

"Meaning?"

"Meaning we're not going to be seeing much of each other for the next few weeks."

"Not even on weekends?"

"I'm afraid not. This is a very complicated case and Halloway hired a very sharp, very tricky attorney."

She let out a resigned sigh. Stuart had told her about this trial, and how crucial it was to his career, months ago. To complain now would be pointless.

"I'll call you as soon as I can get away," Stuart told her. "We might be able to squeeze in a quick dinner one night."

She started to laugh. For a moment, she thought he was going to say 'We might be able to squeeze in a quickie.' "What about J.B.'s barbecue tomorrow night?"

"I'll stop by for an hour or so."

Considering how busy he was, that was more than she had expected. "I'll see you there then. Good night, Stuart."

By the time darkness fell on Friday night, the much anticipated Lost Creek barbecue was in full swing. The buffet table brimmed with American and Mexican specialities, including Lenox's famous no-bean chili, one of the few authentic dishes he had learned to make during his thirty years at the ranch. From the glowing barbecue pit, the aroma of sizzling steaks permeated the night while on the bandstand a lively combo entertained the more than one hundred guests.

Standing on the porch, next to J.B., Laura sipped a frozen margarita. To comply with the theme of the evening, she had worn black leather pants Stuart called her rock star pants and an embroidered black vest over a simple white blouse. Silver-studded black boots and a cowboy hat hanging behind her back complemented the outfit.

"It's a terrific party, J.B.," she said, watching a

neighboring rancher pull his wife to the dance floor for a two-step. "You've outdone yourself with this one."

J.B. caught the semiwistful expression on her face. "Then, why aren't you having any fun, girl?"

"I will." She let her gaze sweep slowly around the crowded lawn. "As soon as Stuart gets here."

"That could take hours." Ignoring her protests, J.B. took her hand and dragged her through the crowd until he found the person he was looking for.

"Ted," he said, pulling the photographer away from a small group of people, "I have a very bored young lady here. Think you can do anything about it?"

Like an actor answering a cue, Ted immediately slipped an arm around Laura's waist. "I'll certainly try." Smiling down at her, he asked. "What's your pleasure? A walk in the moonlight? A dance?"

Being alone with him in the moonlight was the last thing she wanted. "Dancing seems like a better choice, although I must warn you, I never did master the two-step."

"I'd offer to teach you, but I'm not much of an expert myself. Which leaves us only one alternative." Keeping a firm grip on her waist, he led her toward the bandstand where he whispered a few words into the guitarist's ear.

As the band suddenly struck up the first few chords of Julio Iglesias's "*Amor*," Ted opened his arms. "Is that more like it?"

She wasn't sure of that either, but rather than turn him down after all the trouble he had gone to, she murmured what she hoped was a noncommital "that's fine," and slid effortlessly into his waiting arms.

The contact with his hard chest, as he drew her close, sent a jolt through her entire body. I'm just lonely for Stuart, that's all, she reasoned as she glanced helplessly around her in search of her fiancé. It's *his* arms I want around me. *His* breath I want to feel next to my cheek.

Almost as if he had read her mind, Ted pulled away just enough so he could look into her eyes. "Where's Stuart?"

"Working late. He should be here soon."

"I hope so." He drew her close again, cupping her right hand and bringing it to his chest. "I'd hate him to miss seeing you in this outfit."

She smiled. "You're not thinking about taking more pictures, are you?"

"I think about it every time I see you. But I'll control myself. Unless you tell me it's okay."

Laura began to relax. He wasn't coming on to her. He was just a nice guy, trying to make small conversation. J.B. was right. She was too uptight these days. She needed to have more fun.

"Mind if I cut in?"

At the sound of Stuart's voice, she almost heaved a sigh of relief. "Stuart," she said as soon as Ted released her. "I'm so glad you could make it."

"I told you I would." As he talked, his eyes remained on Ted. "Thanks for filling in for me, old man," he said, a trace of sarcasm in his voice. "Now if you don't mind, my fiancée and I will finish this dance together."

Reluctantly, Ted let go of Laura's hand. "By all means. Have fun."

He watched them move across the dance floor, two lovers gazing fondly into each other's eyes. Something deep in his gut stirred. What the hell was the matter with him? Why was he getting so damned worked up over this woman? She was engaged, for Christ's sake. And from what he could see, she was happy.

As a waiter, carrying drinks on a tray stopped by, Ted helped himself to a bottle of Corona and took a long swallow. Then, spotting J.B. on the other side of the dance floor, he made his way toward him.

The Luberick Gallery on Congress Street was packed when Laura and J.B. arrived there on Saturday afternoon. Austin's glitterati, along with some of the best-known art critics in the state, were in attendance as they crowded to admire more than two hundred black-and-white photographs taken during the course of Ted Kandall's meteoric career.

Laura hadn't wanted to come, and had tried to beg off by claiming she had work to do. But J.B. had refused to let her off the hook. "You can take a couple of hours off," he had told her. "If you don't you'll burn yourself out and then where will the *Sentinel* be?"

Now, as she studied the photograph of a Somalian woman watching a convoy of American troops pass by her shack, Laura understood why critics all over the world hailed Ted Kandall as the new Robert Capa.

This was much more than a photograph. It told an entire story. Through his camera lens, Ted had captured an incredible range of emotions—awe, fear, curiosity, and hope.

It was that hope, which reappeared over and over in all his photographs, that made the devastating images of war seem less tragic. There were others, candid shots taken in Nicaragua, in South Africa on the day Nelson Mandela was released from prison, and in Libya during an uprising. All had that same quality, that same blend of suffering and hope.

"This one almost got him killed," J.B. said, pointing at a photo taken in Sarajevo's infamous Sniper Alley.

Laura looked at the half-dozen bodies scattered in the street, the women fleeing under the blast of machine guns. "Was he shot?"

"In the thigh. But instead of running for cover, he grabbed hold of a wounded United Nations soldier and together they limped to safety. And this one ..." They stopped to look at a grouping of smaller photographs simply entitled "Tumbling Gate." "Ted took those during the historic opening of the Brandenburg Gate in November of 1989. By the time he resurfaced from the chaos, he had been bruised, scratched, and even stomped on, but the photographs he brought back were the most incredible I have seen of that event."

Before she could comment, J.B. waved at someone across the room. "That's Ring Farley," he told Laura. "I haven't seen that rascal in years. Why don't you go on? I'll catch up with you later."

"All right." Laura moved on and stopped in front of another photograph. This time it was that of a small boy, crouched in a street filled with debris from a recent explosion. There was fear in his eyes as he looked up at the camera, and an air of possessiveness as he clutched the torn teddy bear he had rescued from beneath a pile of debris.

"This is one of my favorites."

She didn't have to turn around to know Ted was standing directly behind her, close enough for her to smell his aftershave. "It's an extraordinary picture," she said in a husky voice. "I feel as if I know this boy."

"You would like him." He stepped up beside her, moved by the glistening of tears in her eyes as she turned to look at him. "His name is Elrak. He's Croatian, seven years old, and knows where to trade a pack of American cigarettes for a loaf of bread." He patted his breast pocket where she could see the outline of a pack of Marlboros. "That's why I haven't been able to give up smoking."

That last sentence startled her, for that was a side of Ted Kandall she hadn't expected—a tender side that had nothing to do with the wild, adventurous playboy the press so often described. "You're right," she said. "I do like him." She looked at the picture again, finding it difficult to move away. "What will happen to him?"

Ted shrugged. "It's hard to say. He's survived so far, although his home was destroyed. Before I left Sarajevo, I found a new place for him and his family. Hopefully, he'll be safe there."

"Tell me about the other photographs."

"Sure." Cupping her elbow, he guided her across the room, stopping in front of the various displays. He described each scene for her, making them come alive with touching, sometimes amusing anecdotes.

It's his way of blocking out the ugliness, she mused as she stole quick glances in his direction from time to time. His way to make it more bearable.

"Hi, big brother!"

At the sound of the cheery, youthful voice, Laura turned around and saw a lovely young woman come forward and wrap an arm around Ted's waist. She wore a very short, very clingy black dress, high-heeled clogs with gray socks, and a mischievous smile that looked remarkably like Ted's.

"Goldilocks!" Ted hugged her warmly. "Did you come alone?"

"Are you kidding? All my friends are here, free-loading on finger sandwiches and champagne." She nudged Ted in the ribs as she glanced at Laura. "Aren't you going to introduce me?"

"Oh." Ted laughed. "Sorry. This is Laura Spencer, J.B.'s stepdaughter as well as the *Sentinel*'s new publisher. Laura, meet my kid sister, Sandra."

"Hey," Sandra said, elbowing him in the ribs again. "Watch who you call a kid." Then, offering her hand to Laura, she added, "It's a pleasure to meet you, Laura. My brother has told me a lot about you."

Laura shot Ted a surprised glance. "He has?"

"Uh-huh. Don't worry. It was all very flattering,

which is quite surprising, considering how he feels about reporters."

"I see." Laura was beginning to like this girl. "And how *does* he feel about reporters?"

Sandra snatched a canapé the size of a quarter from a passing waiter and popped it in her mouth. "Hates them," she said, licking some of the shrimp mousse from her finger. "With a passion. he hit one in the mouth years ago. Gave him a bloody lip and broke two teeth. The man was going to sue us, but after my father talked to him, he agreed to settle out of court."

"You must excuse my sister," Ted said, ruffling the cap of blond curls. "She is a born gossip. We used to call her Louella."

"That's not gossip, it's the God's honest truth . . ."

Suddenly, all three were jostled as a camera crew pushed its way toward them. In a few seconds, Ted and Sandra were surrounded. "Could we have a shot of you and your sister, Mr. Kandall?"

"How about a few words for our six o'clock news, Mr. Kandall? How does it feel to be back in Texas after all those years?"

As Ted started to answer, Laura discreetly backed away. But as she resumed her stroll through the gallery, she heard a sharp curse. It was followed by a crash and then a flurry of activity as people rushed to where Ted and Sandra had been standing.

There was a moment of stunned silence.

The gallery owner, a woman by the name of Claire Logan, glanced helplessly around her. "What happened? Where did he go?"

A flustered reporter rearranged his glasses while a cameraman inspected his equipment. "The man is nuts," he spat, running his fingers through his hair. "All I did was ask if the feud between him and his father was over, and the next thing I knew, he had knocked my cameraman to the ground."

"You weren't supposed to talk about anything but the exhibition," Mrs. Logan said sternly. "That was cleared with your station days ago."

"Well no one told me."

Laura knew from the way the reporter averted his eyes that he was lying. Recognizing a photographer from the *Sentinel* in the back, she approached him. "Where did Ted Kandall go?" she asked.

The young man gestured toward the door. "He and his sister went that way, Miss Spencer. That's all I can tell you."

Impulsively, Laura went after them.

She caught up with Ted at the end of the street as he was about to cross Congress Bridge. There was no sign of Sandra. "Mind if I join you?" she asked as she fell into step with him.

He didn't answer. Hands deep in his pockets, he went down the steps that led from the bridge to the Town Lake's Hike and Bike trail, a popular five-mile loop along the Colorado River that offered a spectacular view of the city.

"Where is Sandra?"

"I put her in a cab." He kicked a twig out of the way. "That damned reporter had her in tears. I could have wrung his neck."

"Lucky for you you didn't. Although you may have to spring for a new camera."

"It's his own damn fault. If he had stuck to the questions we agreed to, none of that would have happened."

"What did he ask you?"

He didn't seem to have heard her. "Why the hell can't they leave us alone? Why do they have to resort to such underhanded tactics to get their free shot?"

"You have to understand that the Kandalls have always held a great deal of fascination for the media. They're considered the Kennedys of Texas. Powerful, wealthy, bigger than life."

"And that makes them newsworthy?"

"Not necessarily, but the public thinks so, and as long as it does, the media will react accordingly."

"The media sucks."

She smiled. "At one time, I may have been tempted to agree with you. Lord knows, J.B. and I had our share of the limelight when my mother left. I suppose I look at it differently now."

"You would have never stooped to that reporter's level."

The compliment touched her more than any other he had made so far. "What did he say to you?" she asked again.

Ted paused to watch a lone sculler glide by, barely making a ripple in the water. "He wanted to know if my father had forgiven me for my behavior the day of my mother's funeral."

"I take it that's a sore subject with you."

"Only when I don't want to talk about it. And

NEVER SAY NEVER   151

he knew I didn't want to talk about it. His station manager and I had agreed there would be no questions about my family during the interview, that we would talk only about my work and the exhibition."

She came to stand next to him as he continued to gaze at the river. "If you want to talk about it now, I'll be glad to listen. People say I'm pretty good at that."

He didn't doubt it. There was something genuine about her, a goodness and decency he had sensed right away. Maybe that was part of the attraction he felt for her. In his world, the women he met, although beautiful and intelligent, were somewhat brittle and superficial. That's why he had never been able to stay with any one of them for very long.

"My father and I never got along," he began, then shook his head. "No, that's not true. There was a time when we were inseparable. But after a while, his work started to get in the way. There were long absences from home, trips to Washington with my mother, late-night meetings. By the time I was thirteen, I hardly saw him anymore. Or my mother for that matter. To make things easier, they sent me to boarding school, but I managed to get expelled within the first three months."

Laura smiled, wondering what he had done to prompt such a serious punishment.

"I didn't know what I wanted to do with my life then," he continued as they slowly resumed their walk along the shaded path. "But I knew one thing—I didn't want to become a politician. And I didn't want to go to law school. That's when my father and I started to drift apart. Years later, when I told him I wanted to become a photographer and travel around the world, he threw a fit. My mother tried to intervene, but he wouldn't listen. So I enrolled at the University of Louisiana and never saw him again until the day of my mother's funeral."

She remembered reading the account of that tragic death. Charles Kandall had flown about a hundred campaign volunteers to his chalet in Aspen for the weekend. That Sunday, in the middle of the festivities, his wife went upstairs, walked onto a balcony, and jumped to her death. "It must have been awful for you."

He let out a sarcastic laugh. "I almost didn't hear about it. I was spending the weekend with friends in Florida and after a few attempts to locate me, my father gave up. If it hadn't been for Lucinda, I would have missed my own mother's funeral."

"And you were angry."

"I was furious. I arrived in the middle of the services. I practically had to punch my way through the security guards to get to where the rest of the family sat. And when I did, my father wouldn't even look at me. Later I found out the police had suspected foul play at first, but when they didn't find anything to support that theory, they declared the death a suicide."

"J.B. told me you never bought that theory. Is that true?"

"I didn't at first. I couldn't imagine my mother doing that to herself. She seemed so full of life, a real party girl, but she was a great mother, too."

He smiled, a sad smile that was quite touching. "People adored her."

They moved aside to let a mother pushing a baby carriage pass by. "I wasn't invited to go back to the house after the graveside services," he continued in a flat tone. "But I went anyway. Looking back, I realize I could have patched things up with my father if I had tried. For the first time in years, we had a mutual bond—our grief. Instead, I told him it was his fault Mother was dead, that if he had been a better, more attentive husband, she wouldn't have killed herself."

"But you don't feel that way anymore?"

He shook his head. "He wasn't responsible. She enjoyed the lifestyle he provided, and all the perks that went with it. Why she chose to end it all, that way, will always remain a mystery to me."

Even though Laura had heard the story before, she she had never heard it told with such poignancy. There was no expression on his face, no emotion in his voice, but the pain she sensed drove right through her. "And your father never forgave you for that day."

"No. Not even last week when I went to see him."

She laid a hand on his arm. "I'm sorry, Ted."

Without breaking his stride, he patted her hand. "I know you are. Thank you." He glanced at her and for the first time since she had caught up with him, she saw the hint of a smile tug at his mouth. "People are right. You *are* good at this."

Next to them, a little girl pointed an excited finger toward the bridge. Dusk had fallen and from the girders where they lived, a colony of Mexican free-tailed bats came flying out in a continuous, undulating dark ribbon. It was a spectacle Austinites never tired of. Every night at dusk, people came by the dozens, standing on the bridge or sitting on the riverbanks, waiting for that exact moment when the bats came out for their nightly foraging.

"It's still the greatest show in Austin, isn't it?" Laura murmured beside him.

"Yeah." Ted's gaze followed the lengthening stream as it stretched over the river. "My father brought me here once. I couldn't have been more than five or six. It was so crowded he had to hoist me on his shoulders."

Later that night, it took Laura hours to fall asleep. She kept seeing the expression in Ted's eyes as he talked about his photographs and what they meant to him, what he hoped they would mean for those who saw them. And she thought of the way he had talked about his father, not with anger, but with a longing that had made her wish she could help him.

It bothered her that she had never felt that sort of compassion for Stuart. But why should she? Stuart had always gotten along well with his parents. Of course, he worked hard at it. Even if he had dreamed of becoming something other than an attorney, he would have given up that dream in a heartbeat to please his parents. That's how he was.

12

"What in the world is that?" Laura asked as her mother poured a suspicious-looking green mixture into a loaf pan.

Looking very domestic in a frilly pink apron over lavender jeans and a white T-shirt, Shirley carried the pan to the stove. *"Gâteau d'épinards à la Parisienne."*

"What's a *gâteau d'épinards?"*

"Spinach loaf, but it loses its pizzaz in the translation. Stuart gave me the recipe."

"Stuart? My Stuart?"

"He and I have made tremendous progress since that little dinner last week." She slid the loaf in the oven and set the timer for twenty-five minutes. "Especially after I told him I was taking a gourmet cooking class."

"When did you start taking a cooking class?"

"I didn't. But inventing a common bond seemed like a good way to make him like me, so I made the whole thing up." She gave Laura's cheek an affectionate tweak. "And stop looking at me as if I had stolen the crown jewels. It's just a harmless little fib."

"Stuart hates fibs."

"Well, what he doesn't know won't hurt him, I always say."

Shirley opened a drawer, pulled out two silver place mats, and took them to the kitchen table by a window that overlooked the UT campus. "In fact, he was very sweet to me over the phone. He even promised to come and hear me sing sometime."

So, Laura thought. That little rift she and Stuart had had the night they found Ted's pictures had done some good after all. "He really said that?"

"I'm telling you, baby, he's a new man. In fact, he's been so nice to me, I'm actually thinking of making him a proposition."

Laura lowered her glass. "What kind of proposition?"

"It has to do with Joe selling the Golden Parrot."

"I wasn't aware he was still trying to sell. I thought business was great."

Picking up a carafe from the gleaming white counter, Shirley poured Laura a glass of iced tea. "It is. But he's tired. He wants to spend more time with his grandkids."

"What does that have to do with Stuart?"

"Joe has a prospective buyer—a young, snotty entrepreneur who plans to turn the club into some sort of rock and roll hangout—which means, if I want to save my job, I'll have to buy the Golden Parrot."

Laura almost choked on her tea. "Buy the Golden Parrot? With what?"

Unfazed at Laura's reaction, Shirley continued to set the table. "Joe told me if I can get one hundred thousand dollars for the down payment, he'll finance the rest himself. Now before you go nuts on me," she added as Laura's eyes grew wide with disbelief, "hear me out." She untied her apron and laid it out neatly on the countertop. "First of all, I know that starting a business at my age is risky. But the Golden Parrot already has an established clientele. I've seen the books. I know how much Joe nets out every week."

"Do you have any idea of the time and energy it takes to run a supper club? Supervise employees? Deal with suppliers? Cranky customers?"

"I'm not afraid of hard work, Laura. All I want is a chance to prove what I can do. But first I need a hundred thousand dollars for the down payment."

"And that's when you thought of Stuart?"

"The thought crossed my mind. Although to tell you the truth, Stuart was my second choice."

"Who's the first?"

"J.B."

Laura stared at her incredulously. "You can't be serious."

"He's helped a lot of people get started with their own business over the years—some of them he hardly knew. Why wouldn't he do it for me?"

"I don't believe what I'm hearing," Laura said, shaking her head. "How can you expect a man you've hurt so badly, a man you walked out on after only one year of marriage, a man you haven't spoken to in sixteen years, to suddenly forget the past and hand you over a hundred thousand dollars?"

"First of all, he doesn't have to hand me over anything. I'll be glad to sign a promissory note. Just as I would for Joe."

"J.B. will never do it."

"How do you know? He loved me once. And deep down, I know he still cares. You told me so yourself."

The timer rang. Slipping two oven mitts on her hands, Shirley walked over to the stove. "Look, if he turns me down, I'll go someplace else. Maybe to Stuart. But for now, J.B. is my best bet."

Laura started to voice another objection, then stopped. J.B. was a big boy. He knew how to say no. Even to Shirley. And if he didn't, if indeed he still cared enough about her to want to help her, that was his decision to make, not hers.

"Here we are." Shirley turned around, the steaming green loaf proudly held in her mittened hands. "Let the feast begin."

From the public phone outside his motel room, Tony dialed Enzio's number in New York. The boss wasn't going to be happy. But what could he do about it? It wasn't his fault he hadn't found anything.

"About time you called," Enzio said when he finally answered. "What did you find out?"

"Not a thing, boss. I searched Laura Spencer's house from top to bottom and found zilch. No names, no incriminating documents, and nothing to connect Kandall to you."

"What about her office?"

Tony laughed. "Boss, that place is busier than

Times Square. Day *and* night." He paused. "Maybe there ain't nothing to find."

"Mmm." Enzio was silent for a moment. "That could be. Luigi tells me there hasn't been anything more in the *Sentinel* about Kandall's campaign funds."

"Not a word. I wouldn't be a bit surprised if Laura Spencer realized she bit off more than she could chew and dropped the whole thing."

"You could be right." There was another pause. "How is Kandall holding up?"

"Like a charm. I saw him on a news program this morning and let me tell you, the guy's got style. They also say he's a shoo-in on November 8."

"Let's hope so."

"What do you want me to do, boss?" He prayed Enzio would tell him to come home. There was nothing for him to do here.

"Stay where you are. And keep searching Laura's house—every day. If she keeps records in her office, she's bound to bring them home one of these nights. And it wouldn't be a bad idea to tail her from now on. Just so I know who she sees."

Tony sighed. "All right, boss."

"I can't believe I have to come all the way to Burnet County to see my own brother." Closing the door of her blue Firebird, Sandra walked toward Ted as he came out of the house to meet her. "You might as well still be in England for all I've seen of you these past few days."

"Sorry, Goldilocks. J.B. keeps me busy." Wrapping an arm around her waist, he led her toward the house. "How are you doing, sis?"

"Pretty well." She glanced at him. "What about you? Did you get in trouble with the television station?"

"No. I agreed to appear on one of their morning shows and in exchange they promised not to sue."

"What if they do the same thing again when you're on camera?"

"They won't. I have the station manager's word on that."

Under the broad archway that connected the foyer to the family room, Sandra stopped and let her gaze sweep over the large room. "God, I forgot how much I liked this place, how warm and comfortable it felt, not like that mausoleum we were raised in."

"Watch it. You're beginning to sound like me. Dad won't like that."

Choosing a chair that was drenched in sunshine, Sandra kicked off her clogs and tucked her legs under her. "Where's J.B.?"

"Playing a round of golf with Sheriff Wilson." Ted sat across from her and draped an arm over the back of the chair. "Something on your mind, sis?"

"Daddy is on my mind. And you."

Ted raised a hand to silence her. "Oh no, you don't. That subject is closed. For good."

"You haven't even heard what I came to tell you," she protested.

"I don't have to. The look in your eyes says it

all. You're here to make another pitch for poor old Dad, and the answer is no."

"That's not why I came. Well ... not exactly."

"What does that mean?" Ted asked, then immediately regretted the question.

"It means that after you hear what I have to say, you'll have another opinion of Daddy."

"Oh, Sandra. If I didn't love you so much, you would already be out of here. But since I do love you and since I know you won't go away until you've had your say ..." He made a grand gesture. "Go ahead. But I warn you, you're wasting your time."

"This isn't going to be easy." She took a deep breath, held it for a moment, then exhaled. "There's something you don't know. Something I should have told you long ago."

Ted's mouth pulled into an ironic smile. "More deep, dark family secrets from the Kandalls' closet?"

"This secret is about Mom."

Ted's smile faded. "What about Mom?"

"You remember how you chastised Daddy on the day of Mom's funeral, how you told him that if he had paid more attention to her, she wouldn't have killed herself?"

How could he forget? "I remember saying something to that effect, yes."

"Well ... Mom wasn't as lonely as everyone thought she was."

"What the hell does that mean?"

"She was having an affair."

A bomb exploding on Ted's lap couldn't have stunned him more. "Run this by me again."

Sandra moistened her lips. "You were away at school, so you couldn't have known, but a couple of weeks before Mom's death, Daddy found out she was having an affair—"

"That's bullshit. She loved Dad!"

"Apparently that didn't stop her from committing adultery."

He threw her a vicious look. "Has Dad been brainwashing you again? Filling your head with lies about her?"

"No. He has no idea I know."

"How *do* you know?"

"I heard them fight in their room one night, and every night after that—terrible fights that frightened me so much I used to hide under the covers. But I could still hear them. I could hear Daddy demanding to know who the man was."

"Jesus, Sandra."

"It's true. He was like a madman, screaming and threatening to beat it out of her if she didn't tell him."

"Did she?"

"No. She kept denying it."

"There you are. It was just his jealousy talking. You know how he got when he saw other men looking at her."

Sandra shook her head. "It was more than that, Ted. One night, after a particularly nasty fight, Mom finally admitted she was having an affair and that she wanted out of the marriage. Daddy was in shock. I know because there was a long silence.

Then after a while, I heard their bedroom door slam. The following morning at breakfast, he was very quiet and his eyes were red, as if he had been crying. I wanted to say something to him then, but I didn't know what to say. So I kept quiet. I thought by pretending nothing had happened, all the ugliness would go away. And it did. Mom went to Aspen with him and I thought everything was fine." She brushed away a tear. "That following Sunday, she was dead."

Ted sank back against the chair. "Are you sure this is how it happened, Sandra? It isn't some nightmare your six-year-old subconscious mistook for reality?"

She shook her head. "It wasn't a nightmare. It really happened."

"Why didn't you tell me this sooner?"

"I was afraid to. I'm not even sure I understood the full meaning of what had happened between them. So, I pushed it all out of my mind. I never thought about it again. It wasn't that hard. I was so broken up when Mom died, anything else seemed insignificant. It wasn't until years later when I read a biography of Daddy; and what a perfect marriage he and Mom had, that I was able to face the truth."

"You said Dad doesn't know . . ."

She shook her head. "I could never bring myself to tell him. I figured he had buried the past along with Mom and it was better to let things be."

"And Mom never revealed the identity of the man?"

"No. That's one secret she took to the grave with her."

"You don't remember anyone coming to the house on a regular basis? Any telephone conversations?"

"Nothing."

"Dammit, you must have." Ted jumped from the chair and jammed his hands in his pants pockets as he paced the huge room. "You were always with her."

Ted's sudden outburst brought a flush to Sandra's cheeks. "I was six years old! The last thing I would have done was spy on my own mother."

"Sorry." He raked his hair back, feeling like a heel for taking his anger out on Sandra. "It's just that . . . It changes everything, you see. If she was involved with someone else, then her death may not have been a suicide after all . . ." Sandra's eyes widened in horror. "What are you saying?"

"I'm saying that she could have been murdered."

"Ted, the police made a thorough investigation. They found no reason to suspect foul play. That's why they concluded she had committed suicide."

"And you know something? I never bought it. Mom wasn't the type to throw herself from balconies. Or to kill herself any other way. She loved life too much." His voice softened. "And she loved you. She would never do that to you."

"But who would want to kill her?"

"Maybe her lover. Maybe she had a change of heart about leaving Dad, and the man got angry and killed her." Forcing himself to stand still, he added, "You realize we have to tell the police, don't you?"

Her eyes filled with alarm. "Tell them what?"

"That there was another man involved. They would want to know that."

"But what difference could it possibly make now? It's been so long."

"Aren't you the least bit interested in what really happened that day? If someone did kill Mom, don't you want him punished?"

"Of course I do. But what about Daddy? What will such a scandal do to him?"

"I would think he'd want to know the truth as much as we did."

Sandra didn't answer.

"He should have told me," Ted said half to himself. "He shouldn't have let me walk away the day of the funeral without telling me the truth."

"You never gave him a chance. You were so angry. Even if he had wanted to tell you, you wouldn't have listened."

It was true. He had been like a madman, with only one thought in mind—to lash out.

"I had made up my mind to tell you when I came to London that last time," Sandra continued. "But when you agreed to come home, there was no need for it. Especially since I knew how much it would hurt you. The reason I told you now is because . . ." She gave him a hesitant look. "Because it's my last card, my last hope that you'll give Daddy another chance."

"Why does it always have to be me? Why can't *he* give me a second chance?"

"Ted—"

"He could have come to the exhibition, Sandra.

He could have ended this stupid feud once and for all."

Sandra lowered her head. There was nothing she could say to that, nothing that would soften the bitterness in Ted's heart.

"Where are her things?" Ted asked abruptly.

The question took Sandra aback. "Whose things?"

"Mom's clothes, her books, her mementos. Everything."

"Daddy gave her clothes away. I have the jewelry. You're welcome to take anything you want," she added, misreading his question.

He shook his head. "I'm more interested in things like photo albums, old letters that may have been saved."

"Lucinda packed everything in boxes and put them in the attic. I haven't been up there in ages, but all the boxes are marked."

"I'd like to take a look at them."

"Go ahead."

"When Dad is not there."

"Oh." She was thoughtful for a moment. "He's playing bridge with General McGough tomorrow afternoon. I could let Lucinda know you'll be coming."

He nodded. "Thanks, sis."

Her soft brown eyes locked with his. "You're not doing that out of sentimentality, are you? Looking through Mom's things I mean."

"Not exactly."

"What are you hoping to find?"

Ted shrugged. "If I'm lucky, a clue as to the man's identity."

"You really think this mystery man had something to do with Mom's death?"

"I don't know. What I do know is that I can't stand by and do nothing. I'm going to get to the bottom of this mess. For Dad," he added quietly. "I owe him that much."

Other than a thick coat of dust and a few cobwebs, the attic was the same as Ted remembered. Amid the clutter was an assortment of old relics that brought back a flood of memories—an old ten-speed with one wheel askew, a model airplane he had crashed and repaired time after time, a worn baseball glove, Sandra's dollhouse with the paint chipped off.

Half-a-dozen boxes with the name Mrs. Kandall scrawled on the front were stacked against a far wall. Ted made his way there, sat on the floor, and started to go through each container.

It was all there—books Elizabeth had loved, some of them autographed by the authors, framed photographs of her grandparents, a dozen embroidered handkerchiefs, her collection of pill boxes, even a penholder Ted had made for her in kindergarten. But there was no journal, no photographs, no address book. Nothing that could have given him a clue as to the identity of his mother's mysterious lover.

Disappointed, he put the last box back in place and stood up. As he looked around the attic, his gaze fell on a golf bag lying on its side.

He felt a quick stab of pain. The set had been a gift from Elizabeth to Charles for their tenth wedding anniversary. According to Lucinda, he had been playing with those golf clubs the morning of Elizabeth's death.

Following the tragedy, Charles had put the clubs away and had never set foot on a golf course again.

Gripping the handle, Ted brought the dusty bag to an upright position and propped it against the wall. A nine iron stood in the forefront, its number engraved on the steel head. His mouth curved into a smile as he remembered the day his father had tried to teach him the game.

"It's all in the wrist action, son." Charles had demonstrated his technique, but Ted, only nine at the time, had never mastered the game. Eventually, he had stopped trying and taken up tennis instead, much to his father's displeasure.

Unable to resist, he pulled the club out of the bag, and as he did, his heart stopped.

Wrapped around the dry, cracked leather hand grip was a gold chain he recognized instantly. It had belonged to his mother.

Stunned, he uncoiled the chain, being careful not to pull on it, and let it slip into his open palm. It was a family heirloom, a thin rope of Florentine gold Elizabeth had inherited from her grandmother. She had worn it the day she died, yet it hadn't been around her neck when the police had recovered her body.

The missing necklace hadn't changed the police opinion that Elizabeth had committed suicide. They had simply concluded it had come off during the fall.

Ted looked at the chain again, closer this time. Only then did he realized it was broken, torn from the clasp, as if someone had yanked it off. "What the hell . . ."

He glanced from the necklace to the golf bag. If the chain had been found, what was it doing in this old golf bag? Why hadn't it been repaired and given to Sandra with the rest of Elizabeth's jewelry?

The truth hit him like a fist.

Charles. Charles had put the chain in here.

Charles had killed Elizabeth.

1 3

Sandra, who had left school before the end of her last class so she could get home early, ran into Ted as he was coming down the staircase. "Did you find anything?"

She could tell from the grim expression on his face that he had.

Ted sat on a step and waited until Sandra had done the same before handing her the chain.

"Mom's necklace," Sandra whispered. She took it as if it were made of delicate glass and stared at it for a long time. When she looked up again, some of the color had drained from her face and her eyes were filled with tears. "Where did you find it?"

"In the attic."

"But how can that be? After Mom died, Daddy hired a team of mountain climbers to try to find it. They came back empty-handed, so how could it have been put away with the rest of her things if it was never recovered?"

"I didn't find it with her things."

"Then where?"

"Dad's old golf bag. It was twisted around the handle of a nine iron."

Her eyes grew wider. "How did it get there?"

He gave her a long, scrutinizing look, wondering if she was up to hearing the truth. She not only adored her father, she had always been fiercely protective of him. But Ted also knew that she hated to be handled with kid gloves. "Mom's killer put it there."

Mom's killer. Ever since hearing those two words yesterday, Sandra had been haunted by them. In class today, she hadn't been able to concentrate knowing Ted was at the house, searching for something that would reawaken this horrible nightmare. "You talk as if you know who he is."

"I do."

Sandra swallowed. There was an odd look on Ted's face, a hard, forbidding expression that frightened her. "Tell me." When he remained silent, she gripped his arm, sinking her nails into it. "Tell me," she repeated.

"It's Dad."

A look of horror shot through Sandra's eyes as her face turned white. "No." She just kept shaking her head.

"Can't you see how it all fits?" He was wound up now, like a mechanical toy that couldn't be turned off. "Dad's rage when he found out Mom had betrayed him, his pain when she told him she was leaving him and now ..." He glanced at the chain Sandra still held in her palm. "Now this."

Sandra shook her head. "Someone, anyone, could have put it there. Even the murderer, if there *was* a murderer."

"Then why didn't that someone tip off the police? If he or she had wanted to implicate Dad, a simple anonymous phone call would have done the job."

"But if you're right," Sandra said, her voice rising in despair. "If Daddy did it and then put the chain in his golf bag, why didn't he retrieve it later? Why did he leave it there where it could be found?"

"I don't know, sis. Maybe he forgot where he put it. The shock, or the guilt, could have done that."

She gazed at the chain, stroking it gently with her fingertips. "I can't believe he would kill her."

"Not intentionally maybe. But he could have pushed her accidentally, in a moment of anger."

"But that's the whole point. He wasn't angry anymore. Mom went to Colorado with him. Doesn't that prove they had made up? That she wasn't leaving him after all?"

"Maybe. Or she could have agreed to go for the sake of their guests. Dad could have misinterpreted the gesture. That afternoon, she could have taken him upstairs and told him nothing had changed. He became angry. Things got out of hand. Maybe he pushed her, or maybe she just lost her balance and he tried to stop the fall. But all he could get hold of was the chain."

The picture he described was so vivid, she could almost see it. Still, she refused to believe her father could do something so horrible, even in a moment of wild rage. "If it was an accident," she persisted. "Why didn't he tell the police? They would have believed him."

"Not if they knew she was leaving him for another man. Jealousy is the most damning motive of all, sis. Ask any cop."

She met his gaze squarely, defiantly. "Then he would have faced the police and taken his punishment. Daddy is not a coward."

"I know that." Ted's tone softened as he looked at Sandra's anguished face. "The fear of going to prison is not what kept him from turning himself in."

"Then what?"

"You, Goldilocks. He wanted to spare you additional pain. I'm sure that's why he resigned from the Senate. So he could take care of you properly."

Sandra was crying softly now, her head buried in her hands. Gathering her in his arms, Ted held her.

After a while, she took the handkerchief he handed her and dried her eyes. "We have to keep this to ourselves," she whispered when her sobs began to subside. "We won't say anything. To Daddy or to the police." She took his hand and squeezed it hard. "Swear, Ted. Swear you won't call the police."

Ted was silent for a moment. Up in the attic, he had fought with his conscience for nearly an hour, torn between his need to avenge his mother's death and his loyalty to his father.

It wasn't until this very moment, until he saw his sister's imploring eyes that he knew he didn't have a choice. She had been hurt enough. He would not add to her pain by sending her dying father to prison.

"No," he said gently, stroking the soft golden hair. "I won't call the police."

* * *

Leaning against the fence, Ted watched as the sun sank lower and lower into the Western sky. He had no idea how long he had been standing here, watching the distant hills.

"So that's where you've been hiding."

Although he recognized J.B.'s voice, he didn't turn around. "Were you looking for me, J.B.?"

"Sort of. I saw you wandering off a couple of hours ago and became concerned when you didn't come back." Coming to stand by the fence, next to Ted, he leaned forward, resting his forearms over the top railing. "Something troubling you, son?"

Ted didn't answer. Not because he didn't trust J.B.—he knew his secret would be safe with him— but because he had no idea how or where to start.

J.B. continued to watch him, a concerned expression on his face. "Sometimes, it helps to talk."

Ted already knew that. After his conversation with Laura on Saturday night, a tremendous burden had been lifted from his shoulder. The talk hadn't changed how he felt toward his father, but it had eased off some of the guilt Ted had carried along all these years.

"Would it have anything to do with your father?" J.B. persisted gently. "Or with Sandra's earlier visit?"

"Right on both counts."

"How serious is it this time?"

Ted continued to gaze into the distance. The sun had completely disappeared and the landscape was slowly turning a muted, dusky shade of blue as it often did at this time of night. "Charles killed my mother."

For a moment, J.B.'s only reaction was his stunned silence. When he spoke again, his voice was low and husky. "How do you know that?"

His eyes riveted on a single point on the horizon, Ted told him everything, including the promise he had made to Sandra not to tell the police.

"Sweet Jesus." J.B. shook his head in disbelief. He continued to look at Ted, who hadn't made eye contact with him yet. "Look, son, you know I'm not much on advice. I've tried to be there for you when I thought you needed it and I've tried to steer you in the right direction whenever possible, but I've never told you what to do."

"You've been a good friend, J.B."

"I hope you'll continue to think that because I'm about to break my own golden rule."

Ted didn't answer.

"You have to come clean with this thing, Ted," J.B. went on. "You and Sandra can't go through the rest of your lives not knowing what happened."

"I know what happened. He killed my mother."

"You don't know the circumstances. You have this image of your father as a cold-blooded murderer but it could be an entirely different scenario. You owe it to yourself, and to your father, to find out *exactly* what happened that day."

Ted shook his head. "That's impossible. If you saw my father, you would understand why. He's a sick man, J.B. A shock like that could finish him off. Whatever he did, I've come to terms with it. It's done. Nothing I can do now will change that."

"It's a terrible burden to carry, son."

"It would be worse knowing I was responsible for his death."

The two men were silent for a moment, each lost in his own thoughts. After a while, J.B. laid his big, callused hand on Ted's shoulder. "Come on, son. Let's go home."

The sound of a chair scraping against wood boards awakened Laura with a jolt. She sat up, nerves taut, and glanced at the illuminated clock on the bedside table. One-thirty. Who could be walking around her porch at this time of night? She excluded J.B. Although he suffered from insomnia and often went for a late-night walk, he wouldn't be coming this way. Besides, tomorrow was the MediaTech conference. He always went to bed early when he had a function to attend the following day.

Pushing the covers aside, she got out of bed and tiptoed to the window. It was a clear night, filled with shadows. In the distance the main house was just a dark silhouette.

She raised the window sash halfway and poked her head through the opening and felt the back of her neck prickle. One of the porch chairs was askew, as if someone had walked into it. Was that the sound she had heard? Or had she imagined it?

From the corner of her eye, she caught a movement and whipped her head around to glance in that direction. Something, or someone, moved through the cluster of live oak next to the guest house.

She shivered at the thought that a prowler might

have been trying to get in while she slept, and quickly withdrew, snapping the window shut. Knowing no robber worth his salt would dare come into a house brilliantly lit, she walked back to the bed and turned on the light. Then she ran downstairs and did the same there.

Not sure what to do next, she stared at the phone for a moment, tempted to call the police. But by the time they arrived, whoever had been lurking around would be gone. What could she tell them except that she had seen a shadow run through the trees?

A check of the front door convinced her the lock hadn't been tampered with, although the simple dead bolt would hardly be a deterrent for a sophisticated burglar.

Maybe she *had* imagined that noise after all. Maybe those ten years in New York, where breakins were a daily occurrence, had made her paranoid.

Had she felt comfortable enough about it, she would have called Stuart. He lived only a few minutes away. But she already knew what he would say. *"It's just the wind rustling through the trees, Laura. Go back to bed."*

He was so sensible. And she was so . . . so what? Foolish? Was that the word she was looking for?

She gave a short, nervous laugh. What was she doing analyzing herself at one-thirty in the morning?

Go back to bed, Laura.

Leaving all the lights on, just in case, she walked back upstairs.

14

The MediaTech conference held each year at the Palmer Auditorium and Convention Center, was one of the largest in the state, featuring more than a thousand exhibitors and the latest in high-tech communication technology.

Although J.B. had been a sponsor for years, he hadn't planned to attend this year's event until learning that the luncheon speaker would be none other than Barbara Kandall.

He and Barbara were old friends. They had met nineteen years ago when she had brought her third grade class to tour the *Austin Sentinel*. He had been struck not only by her charm, but by the way she interacted with the children, challenging their minds and encouraging them to ask questions.

Her wedding to Malcolm Kandall a year later had been a disappointment, not because he had hoped to marry her himself as some had believed, but because he couldn't understand how a gentle, caring woman like Barbara Fenton would want to spend the rest of her life with a man as self-centered and superficial as Malcolm Kandall. Yet, oddly enough, the marriage had lasted. Whether or not she was as happy as she appeared to be was another matter.

He loved to watch her address a crowd. Although she didn't have the social savvy of other political wives he knew, her passion when discussing important issues was both endearing and uplifting.

Now, sitting between the president of Carmel Computers and a publishing executive, J.B. watched Barbara as she sat at a nearby table.

For a woman who, only a few minutes ago, had delivered a rousing speech, she was surprisingly restless. Her eyes kept darting across the room, following the waiters as they stopped from time to time to refill wineglasses.

J.B. was one of the few people in Austin who knew about Barbara's drinking problem. A few years ago, when he had realized the addiction was getting out of hand, he had urged her to seek help.

"I can't do that," she had told him with a firm shake of her head. "If my drinking problem were made public, it would be the end of Malcolm's career."

Although he had pointed out to her that her health was much more important than her husband's career, she had remained undaunted. Malcolm came first.

They had never talked about her drinking again after that. But now, watching her become more jittery with each passing second, he realized how far the problem had escalated.

He was about to go to her when the president of Carmel Computers called his attention to a brochure he was reading. It wasn't until minutes later, when he heard Barbara's rich, throaty laugh, that he became alarmed at the change in her. Her cheeks were flushed and she talked rapidly, taking frequent sips of what he suspected was white wine, without bothering to put the glass down.

The lady was in bad shape and unless he got her out of here fast, some overzealous reporter was bound to see it, too.

Excusing himself, J.B. stood up and quickly made his way to the next table. "Hello, Barbara." He kissed her lightly on the cheek.

"J.B.! My old friend." Her voice was much louder than usual. "I thought you might be here."

Not giving her a chance to say another word, he took her hand and pulled here up to her feet. "I wonder if I could have a word with you? In private." He saw her hesitate and added, "It's urgent."

As inconspicuously as possible, he took the glass from her hand and set it back on the table. A small black clutch purse lay next to her plate. He took it and handed it to her. "Let's go."

She followed him docilely, waiting until they had reached the lobby before asking, "What's going on, J.B.? Where are you taking me?"

"Home."

The green eyes registered surprise. "Home? But I can't." She hiccuped and giggled as she covered her mouth in apology. "I have to give a speech."

"You already spoke, Barbara. And you did a great job." Leaning closer, he whispered into her ear. "The problem is, you've had a little too much to drink."

"You know something?" She gave him a sweet smile and hiccuped again. "I think you're right."

At that moment, an old friend of J.B.'s, Elliot Fitzpatrick, stepped out of a phone booth across the lobby and walked toward them. "Is something wrong with Barbara?" he asked.

"She's just coming down with some stomach bug," J.B. reassured him. "Nothing to worry about."

"Can I help?"

"That's all right, Elliot. I can handle it." Wrapping an arm around Barbara's waist, J.B. steered her toward a back door he knew led to the garage.

"You're always so good to me, J.B." Barbara leaned against him as they walked. "Why is that?"

"Because you and I are friends. You would do the same for me."

In the garage, it took him only a minute to locate the Suburban. Keeping a firm grip on Barbara, he helped her into the passenger seat, buckling the seat belt around her before closing the door. "Did Clive drive you?" he asked as he slid behind the wheel.

She shook her head. "No. I took the SL."

"I'll have someone take it back to your house later, okay?"

" 'Kay." She pressed her fingers to her temples. "Things are spinning a bit."

"Keep your eyes open and don't lean back."

"I'm drunk," she announced in a serious tone.

J.B. smiled as he stopped to pay the cashier. "I know."

"Do you think that man in the lobby noticed?"

"You don't have to worry about Elliot. He's the soul of discretion." He waited until he had turned onto Barton Springs Road before speaking again. "What happened, Barbara? The last time you and I talked, you told me you had this problem of yours under control."

She started to cry softly.

Cursing his lack of sensitivity, J.B. reached for her hand, which lay limply on her lap. "I'm sorry, kiddo. I didn't mean to sound so critical. I care about you. All I really want to do is help you."

"Oh, J.B." In spite of his advice not to lean back, she did just that. "You can't help me. No one can help me. It's much too late."

"It's never too late to turn over a new leaf. I know an excellent rehabilitation clinic in Dallas. Eight short weeks from now, you could be a new woman."

She kept shaking her head. "Can't do that. Not with the elections so close . . ." She was beginning to slur her words and as the car climbed the hills of West Austin, her head lolled sideways.

"You never used to drink in public, Barbara. What happened today? Everything was going so well for you."

"Dragons," she murmured.

He shot her a quick glance. "Say that again?"

She gave him a glassy look. "Do you slay dragons, J.B.?"

He smiled. "I would for you." Then more seriously, he added, "Talk to me, girl. What's bothering you?"

"Can't. It's too ... ugly. And it hurts."

His mouth closed in a tight, angry line. How could he have been so blind? How could he have been her friend for all those years and not seen what she was going through? "Does it have to do with Malcolm?" What a stupid question. How could it not have something to do with Malcolm?

"You'll hate me if I tell you." She sounded like a repentent child.

"I could never hate you, Barbara. You know that."

There was a long silence. When she spoke again, her voice was barely above a whisper. "It happened ... so long ago."

"What did?"

"Malcolm," she slurred. "And Elizabeth. They were in love."

Malcolm and Elizabeth. Sweet Jesus.

"I followed them to the library," she continued. "They didn't know I was there ..."

"Where was that?"

"Aspen."

His blood chilled.

"I saw them, J.B. And I heard them. I heard ... I heard everything." She hiccuped again but this time there was no giggle, no coy smile. "She was so pretty in that white dress. Much prettier than me ..."

"That's not true."

"Malcolm wouldn't agree."

"Malcolm is a fool." J.B.'s voice was gruff, angry.

That bastard. That dirty, rotten, good-for-nothing bastard.

"I hated her," she said with a passion that startled him. "Wanted her to die." She was breathing hard now, and her hands kept clenching and unclenching. "Wanted to ... push her off that balcony."

J.B. jammed his foot on the brakes and came to a screeching halt. He turned to her. "My God, girl. What are you saying?"

She rested her head against the window and closed her eyes. "Can't talk about it. Too awful."

J.B.'s first reaction was denial. It couldn't be. Not sweet, gentle Barbara. He had misunderstood. He sat there, looking at her. She looked so innocent, and so tormented. "Barbara?" His thick fingers went to her cheek. "Talk to me, girl. You know you can trust me."

She let out a trembling sigh but did not answer him.

"Barbara?" He shook her gently, then more forcefully. "Barbara?"

It was useless. She was out cold.

J.B. fell back against his seat and tried to think, to make some sense out of what he had heard. But the images his mind conjured were too impossible to fathom.

His face grim, he put the Suburban in drive again and began the slow, spectacular descent down Scenic Drive until he reached the Kandalls' house.

A severe-looking woman in a maid's uniform opened the door. "I'm J.B. Lawson," he said, as she gave him a blank look. "Mrs. Kandall was taken ill during the MediaTech luncheon." He handed her Barbara's purse. "She's asleep now, so if you'll show me the way to her room, I'll carry her up."

Not waiting for an answer, he walked back to the car, cradled Barbara's slender body in his arms, and followed the tight-lipped maid up the stairs.

In the green and gold bedroom, he lowered Barbara onto the bed and waited until he had caught his breath before turning back to the housekeeper. "Her car is still downtown. I'll have someone bring it back—"

"That won't be necessary," the woman said with a pinched expression. "Mr. Kandall will want to do that himself."

J.B. shrugged. "Suit yourself." After one last glance at Barbara, who had begun to snore gently, he stepped out of the room, closing the door behind him. "When do you expect Mr. Kandall home?"

"Not before dinner."

"When he comes in, please tell him I want to talk to him."

Although the woman's expression didn't change, she inclined her head to signify she would relay the message.

Back in the car, J.B. glanced toward the upstairs windows. "Oh, Barbara," he murmured as he turned on the ignition. "What in God's name have you done?"

Malcolm, who had been called away from a meeting with the mayor to answer Dolores's urgent call, was pacing like an angry bull when Barbara began to stir two hours later.

In two long strides, he was by her side. "Barb? Wake up." He patted her on the cheeks.

She moaned and pressed a hand to her stomach. "I'm not feeling well."

"Serves you right," he spat, not bothering with his usual bedside manners. "Of all the dumb things you've ever done in your life, getting drunk at the MediaTech luncheon, in front of five hundred people, had to be the dumbest."

"Didn't mean to—"

"And whatever possessed you to let J.B. drive you home? The man hates my guts, for Christ's sake. He's probably writing an article right now. Can't you just see the headlines? 'Wife of gubernatorial candidate gets roaring drunk.'"

Barbara opened her eyes, squinting a little as she tried to focus. "J.B. wouldn't do that."

"How the hell do you know?" When she didn't answer, he sat down on the bed. "You didn't tell him anything, did you?"

"Can't remember . . ."

"You must remember if you talked to him."

"Talked . . . yes."

"About what?" He tried to control his anger. In her present condition, shouting would only make her withdraw more. "Did you tell him anything about Elizabeth and me? Try to concentrate, Barbara. It's important."

"Why?"

"Because J.B. wants to see me, that's why. He hasn't spoken a word to me in sixteen years, but all of a sudden he wants to see me. Does that tell you anything, Barbara?"

Slowly, using her elbows, she propped herself up.

"That a girl." Malcolm forced a smile. "Now, try to remember what you and J.B. talked about. Did Elizabeth's name come up?"

Her complexion had turned a sick shade of gray. "I don't know ... Maybe."

"What did you say to him, Barbara?"

"Can't remember."

"Barbara!" he cried in exasperation.

"Don't feel well." One hand on her stomach, she pressed her head against the mound of green pillows. "Talk later."

"Damn." Raking his fingers through his hair, Malcolm stood up and glared at her for a full minute. He had seen her in this condition enough times to know that trying to get her to remember anything after a binge like that was useless. It could be days until her conversation with J.B. became clear again. Which meant he would have to face the old fox without knowing how much she had told him.

He would volunteer nothing, he decided as he watched Barbara sleep. He would let him do all the talking. That way he would be safe.

Feeling somewhat more confident, he walked over to the phone and dialed Lost Creek. J.B. answered the phone himself.

"I understand you want to talk to me," Malcolm said, not bothering with civilities. "So talk."

J.B.'s voice was cool. "Not over the phone. We can meet at my house or yours. Your pick."

"There are too many people at my house. I'll come to the ranch, provided we don't have an audience."

"We won't. Lenox goes to bed early and Ted is in Dallas, visiting friends. I don't expect him until late."

Malcolm glanced at his watch. "I have to attend a reception at the Four Seasons. If I leave at ten, I can be at Lost Creek by eleven."

"I'll be waiting for you." J.B. hung up.

It was eleven-fifteen when Malcolm arrived at Lost Creek. Parking his black Corvette next to J.B.'s Suburban, he walked to the front door. It was a moonless night and a cool breeze blew in from the south, bringing with it the smell of rain.

He took a few deep breaths then knocked, waiting until the door had opened before pasting on his smile. "Hello, J.B. Playing butler now?" Whatever animosity he felt toward the older man, Malcolm had decided not to let it show. Not tonight.

"As I said, Lenox goes to bed early."

Malcolm followed him into a softly lit study that reflected J.B.'s simple country tastes—plaid furniture, a big oak desk, and a gigantic bookcase filled with old books. There was even a cozy fire in the brick fireplace to ward off the night's chill.

J.B. walked around his desk, sat down in a brown swivel chair, and leaned back. "How's Barbara?"

He's playing with me, Malcolm thought. And enjoying every second of it. "Fine. She's sleeping." He cleared his throat. "Thanks for bringing her home, J.B."

Malcolm's grateful remark went unnoticed. "She needs help, Kandall. Professional help."

"I know." Malcolm sighed, summoning every ounce of acting ability he may have had. "I can't begin to tell you how many times I've said those same exact words to her. She won't listen."

"I find that hard to believe. Barbara is a sensible woman. And she knows she has a serious problem. With a little encouragement on your part, she could have been in a rehab clinic years ago."

"It's not as easy as you think. Barbara can be very stubborn at times. When she makes up her mind about something, she rarely backs down."

J.B.'s gaze was hard. "What happened the day Elizabeth died, Malcolm?"

Malcolm's face blanched. "What?"

"I said, what happened the day Elizabeth died?"

"How the hell should I know?"

"Because you were there. And so was Barbara."

"We were at the chalet that day, true, but as for knowing what happened, I don't know any more than the rest of the guests."

"You're lying." J.B. leaned forward, his eyes gleaming viciously. "You and Elizabeth were on that balcony—together."

Malcolm forced a mocking laugh. "Where did you get that crazy notion?"

"Barbara told me."

"Barbara was plastered, for God's sake! Are you saying you believe the ramblings of a drunk?"

"When those ramblings reveal a secret that might be at the root of her problem, you're damned right I do."

"What the hell are you talking about? What *secret*?"

"Barbara never used to drink. It started later, right after Elizabeth died as a matter of fact. My guess is that her sister-in-law's death and the events that led to it were so traumatic, she had to drink in order to forget them."

He paused, measuring his old adversary, wondering what it would take to break down his awsome resistance. The truth, he decided. In the end, the truth was always the best weapon.

"Barbara killed her, didn't she?" he asked. "She pushed Elizabeth off that balcony."

1 5

Malcolm felt as if he had been punched in the gut. Unable to utter a word, he just stared at J.B.

"That's what happened, isn't it?" J.B. asked. "And that's why Barbara drinks. The guilt is killing her."

"You're insane," Malcolm finally managed. "You know as well as I do that Barbara couldn't hurt a fly. Much less another human being."

"That's the saddest part of all." J.B.'s tone was almost mournful. "And what's even sadder is that she did it for a skunk like you."

"Now just a minute—"

"Oh, don't just-a-minute me. And don't you dare, not for one moment, try to shirk your responsibility in this sick tragedy. Sleeping with your brother's wife! How low can you get, Malcolm?"

"I didn't sleep with my brother's wife!"

"Like hell you didn't. Barbara may have been drunk this afternoon, but I know pain when I see it. And she was in pain. She hasn't stopped hurting since the day she found out you and Elizabeth were having an affair."

"Barbara didn't say that."

"She said enough. You and Elizabeth were in the upstairs library, on the balcony. Barbara walked in on you and she snapped. A woman, who indeed, couldn't hurt a fly, turned into a killer. All because of you."

Malcolm gripped the edges of his chair. "You're crazy—"

"You covered up for her, not to spare her, but to save yourself from a scandal you knew would end your career."

"That's all speculation on your part," Malcolm sneered. "The product of an overactive imagination. You don't have an ounce of proof."

"I have enough to get the Aspen police to re-open the case."

Malcolm almost stopped breathing. "You wouldn't do that to Barbara. She's your friend."

"It's true then?"

Oh, God, what now? Denial? It would be as useless as it was risky. J.B. had a low level of patience. There was no telling when he would stop talking and start calling the cops himself. Praying the old man's affection for Barbara was enough to ward off a disaster, he let his shoulders sag. "Oh, God."

"Am I right?"

Malcolm nodded. "It was an accident. You must believe that. It happened so quickly, I couldn't do anything to stop it until it was too late. One moment, the two women were clawing at each other, the next . . ." He closed his eyes. "The next, Elizabeth was falling."

"Why the hell didn't you try to stop them?"

"I told you, I couldn't. It happened too fast. It was an accident. A stupid, senseless accident."

"Then why didn't you tell that to the police?"

"I couldn't." He spoke rapidly as he walked back and forth in front of J.B.'s desk. "I couldn't risk having my wife thrown in jail."

"Bullshit. You weren't thinking of her. You were thinking of yourself. Of your career."

"No! I swear to God my career was the last thing on my mind at the time. All I cared about was Barbara."

A sardonic smiled pulled J.B.'s mouth as he saw the sweat pearl on the politician's forehead. "You lying son of a bitch," he said, his voice dripping with contempt. "You're not worth spit, you know that? All these years, you saw what the guilt was doing to her. You knew why she drank. But you didn't do anything to help her."

"She didn't want to be helped." Malcolm's face was white as a sheet. The famous arrogance was gone, and the voice that had charmed millions of Texans during the past year had turned frail.

"*You're* the one who didn't want her treated. I know because I talked to Deirdre a couple of years ago. She told me how you had convinced Barbara that the two of you could handle the problem all by yourselves.

"Look. . . ." Malcolm swallowed. "Where are we going with this? You want me to put her in a clinic? Is that it?"

"That's only part of it."

"What else do you want?"

J.B. leaned back and let his gaze bore into Malcolm's. "I want you to call the Aspen police and tell them what happened that day."

Malcolm stood very still. "You can't be serious. Barbara will be thrown in jail. She'll be put through a horrendous trial. Do you have any idea what that will do to her?"

"And what about what the guilt is doing to her now? It's killing her, Malcolm. Look at her, man. She's running on empty."

Cold sweat dripped down Malcolm's armpits. "You're right. I'll see to it that she enters the best clinic money can buy. Just don't ask me to turn her in."

When J.B. didn't answer, he played his last card. "Look, I'll make a deal with you. I'll pay you whatever you want if you promise to keep this thing quiet. I know the *Sentinel* is in bad shape right now—"

"Thanks to you."

"I know." He might as well admit to it now, to show he was sincere. "What I did was stupid and inexcusable. But I can fix it, J.B. One call to Orbach and the others and everything will be as before—even better. And I'll give you money to get back on your feet. Just say how much."

"You have no money, Malcolm. You squandered your trust fund a long time ago. And Barbara won't get anything until Deirdre's death. So how can you stand there and talk to me about a deal?"

"My brother will give me whatever I need. I know he will. He doesn't want another family scandal."

J.B. smiled. There had been a time when he

would have killed to have this man reduced to such a quivering mass. But not now. Now there were others to consider—Barbara certainly, but also Ted. He wouldn't let that boy go the rest of his life thinking his father was a murderer.

"Let it go, J.B." Malcolm circled the desk and came to stand directly in front of his old enemy. "Do it for Barbara."

Silently, J.B. pushed a small square of paper toward Malcolm. Then, he picked up the phone and handed it to him. "That's the number of the Aspen sheriff. Go ahead, Malcolm. For once in your life, do what's right."

Malcolm gave a frantic shake of his head. "I can't . . ."

"If you don't, I will."

Malcolm was drenched in sweat. That son of a bitch was mean enough to do it. And the sheriff would listen to him. Even if he didn't believe the story, there was enough there to justify reopening the investigation. What then? How long would Barbara last under police questioning?

He ran a trembling hand through his hair. He would be finished. All his dreams would be reduced to a pile of ashes—all because of a stupid, vengeful old man. He couldn't let that happen. He couldn't.

His gaze darted around him, stopped on the desk. What looked like a hunting knife J.B. might have been using as a letter opener, lay next to an opened envelope.

"Well, Malcolm?"

There was no time to think. Only to act. As he pretended to reach for the receiver J.B. was holding, Malcolm's hand abruptly shifted course. In one quick motion, he scooped up the knife.

He saw the look of shock in the older man's eyes, but before J.B. could move, Malcolm raised his arm. Then, with all the speed and strength he could muster, he plunged the knife into J.B.'s chest.

The phone dropped from J.B.'s hand and his mouth opened in a desperate effort to call for help. But all that came out was a gasping sound.

Malcolm took a step back. His breath came out in shallow gasps as he stared at the blood that was slowly, steadily seeping out of the wound.

He's not dead, he thought, watching J.B.'s hand clutch the knife's handle, instinctively trying to pull it out. Oh, God, how long is it going to take?

Another thought brought the taste of bile to his mouth. *What if he didn't die?*

Then, as if someone had answered his prayers, J.B.'s eyes rolled upward, then closed. He slumped back in his chair, his head tilted at an odd angle. Malcolm kept staring at him, incapable of moving.

Get out of here. The silent command brought everything back into focus. Slowly, his brain began to function again. he listened for the sound of footsteps. Lenox's quarters were in the back of the house, but he could have heard them argue.

There was nothing but the silence. And the crackling of the fire in the hearth.

His movements stiff, he took a handkerchief from his pocket, and shook it open as he walked back toward the slumped body. The smell of blood, as it continued to flow, made him gag.

Gritting his teeth, he pried J.B.'s fingers from the

handle and wiped it clean. He did the same with the desktop, although he didn't recall having touched it, and the chair he had occupied earlier.

Still holding the handkerchief, he backed out of the room. At the door, he threw one last glance around. Had he forgotten anything? When he was sure he hadn't, he took a deep steadying breath and hurried out.

He was halfway to his car when he remembered the bull's head knocker on the front door. With a half groan, he went back to wipe it off. Then, moving as fast as his bad leg would permit, he ran toward the Corvette.

The persistent ring of the telephone pulled Laura from a deep sleep. " 'Lo?"

"Oh, Miss Laura, you must come right away. Something . . . Something terrible has happened."

Remembering only two other times when Lenox had sounded this distraught, Laura bolted to a sitting position. "What is it? Did J.B. have another heart attack?"

The butler's voice, usually so strong and sure, was trembling. "No. He . . . he's been murdered, Miss Laura."

The words slammed into her, and for a moment, she couldn't react. Even breathing was difficult. When she could finally talk, all she could manage was a weak "No."

"The police are here . . ."

She remained still for a full minute, unable to absorb the information. Or accept it. Not J.B. Not

this giant of a man who had laughed at death by
surviving two heart attacks.

"Miss Laura?"

She had already hung up.

The house was brilliantly lit and filled with police
and paramedics when Laura arrived. Sheriff Amos
Wilson, who had known J.B. since the third grade,
was there with two of his deputies. He rushed
toward her, blocking the entrance to the study. He
was a big man, although not as big as J.B., with a
craggy, tanned face, unruly gray hair, and a pro-
nounced paunch that attested to his fondness for
Tex-Mex food and homemade ice cream. On his
uniform shirt, his sheriff's badge shone brightly.

"I'm sorry, Laura," he said, his voice husky with
grief as his arms closed around her. "So very
sorry."

She began to tremble. "Then, it's true." For an
irrational moment, as she sped toward the main
house, she had hoped that it was all a horrible mistake, that she would find J.B. standing there, hear
his booming voice. *"What in God's name are you
doing up at this time of night, kiddo?"*

"I'm afraid it is." Amos's voice reached her
through a fog.

"How? What happened?"

"I don't have all the details yet. I've only been
here a few minutes."

"I want to see him."

He held her back. "Not now. The coroner and
the D.A. are in there."

The coroner. The D.A. Words she had heard

hundreds of times before, suddenly made no sense to her. They didn't belong here. Not in this house. "Who did this to him, Amos? Who?"

The sheriff's eyes filled with an expression she didn't quite understand—a mixture of sadness and compassion. "Let's go in the other room," he said, leading her gently down the hall. "I'll explain—"

"Laura!"

The heart-wrenching cry stopped her cold. She spun around, and gasped at the scene before her.

Flanked and held in a solid grip by two deputies, was her mother. Her hair was in total disarray. Tears and mascara had smeared around her eyes, making her look like a raccoon. Her gown, a long sheath of gold lamé, was covered with blood. There was more blood on her hands, her face, even her hair.

Something cold and hard lodged itself in Laura's stomach. "Mom!" she breathed. "What—"

"They're arresting me for murder, Laura! They say I killed J.B.!"

1 6

Stunned, Laura looked from her mother to Amos. A nervous chuckle she couldn't hold back escaped from her lips. "What is she talking about, Amos? What kind of sick joke is this?"

"It's no joke, Laura." The sheriff's face was solemn. "All the evidence points at your mother."

"What evidence—"

"I didn't do it!" Shirley cried. She tried to jerk her arms free from the two deputies' grip, but they held her firmly. "I just came to talk to J.B. He was already dead when I got here—"

Laura quickly raised a warning hand. "Don't say another word."

But Shirley was too overwrought to listen. "Is everybody deaf? I didn't do it!"

Laura turned to Amos. "Please, Amos. Tell your deputies to let go of her."

"I can't do that, Laura. I have to take her in."

"Not until I've talked to her."

"Laura—"

Inside the study, she saw the flash of a camera as a police photographer walked around the room, photographing evidence. "Amos, please. Just ten minutes. That's all I ask."

Amos sighed, glanced at Shirley who was still wrestling with the two deputies, and then back at Laura. "All right. Ten minutes, not one second more." He nodded at his men. "Let her go."

The moment Shirley was free she ran into Laura's arms. "Oh, baby!" she sobbed. "Help me."

"I will. Come on." Her arm wrapped around Shirley's quivering shoulders, Laura guided her toward the family room. She tried not to think of the last time she had been in here. J.B. had been full of life then, and playing bartender.

"Sit down, Mom."

Shirley did as she was told.

"What happened?" Laura asked, sitting beside her. "What are you doing here?"

Shirley buried her head in her hands. "Oh, Laura. If only I had listened to you."

"What are you talking about?"

"I came here to ask J.B. to lend me the down payment for the Golden Parrot."

"Oh, Mom."

"I know, I know." She dried her tears with the palms of her hands, making an even bigger mess of her face. "It was a crazy idea—one chance in a million he'd say yes. But I was desperate, Laura, you know that." She caught another tear with the tip of her middle finger. "And desperate people do stupid things."

"Why did you come here at this time of night? Didn't you have to work?"

"It was a slow night. Joe said I didn't have to

do the second show; and I knew J.B. never went to bed until late. I figured the worst that could happen was that he would throw me out.''

"Is that what he did?"

"No!" She looked up, her eyes bright with indignation. "I never got a chance to even talk to him. He . . ." She ran both hands through her disheveled hair as if to rearrange it but only succeeded in making it look wilder. "He was dead."

"All right." Laura took a handkerchief from her pocket and handed it to Shirley. "Tell me everything, starting with what time you got here and how you got into the house."

Shirley took a deep breath and released it slowly. "I got here at twelve-twenty. I know because the radio station I was listening to paused for a commercial and gave the time." She dabbed her eyes before continuing. "I was walking toward J.B.'s front door when I saw the light streaming from the study window. So I circled around the house. The French doors were closed but I could see him, sitting at his desk. His back was to me and his head was slumped a little to the side, as if he were sleeping." A sob caught in her throat and she pressed the balled hanky to her mouth. "I can't talk about it," she said with a shake of the head. "It's too horrible."

"You have to talk about it," Laura said sharply. "And you have to do it quickly, before your mind has a chance to block out vital information. That's the only way I can help you, Mom."

Shirley didn't reply. With her eyes closed and her hands tightly clasped together as if in prayer, her look was so tragic, that at any other time Laura would have smiled. Shirley was, had always been, the ultimate actress. But she wasn't acting now. "Mom? Did you hear me?"

"Yes." She pulled her hands from her mouth. "The French doors were unlocked, so I went in and called out his name. When he didn't answer, I came closer. He was motionless and a knife was sticking out of his chest."

At the realization that J.B had been stabbed to death, Laura briefly closed her eyes. "Go on."

"I didn't take time to think. I just ran to him and tried to revive him. When he didn't respond, I tried to pull the knife out. I was screaming and pulling at the same time, but the damn thing wouldn't budge."

Laura held back a groan. Shirley's fingerprints were on the murder weapon.

"I realized he was dead," Shirley continued in a broken voice. "So I took him in my arms. I was crying and rocking him, and telling him I was sorry, sorry for all the bad things I had done to him in the past. I told him that if I could take them all back, I would." She paused. "That's when Lenox came in."

"Lenox found you there?"

Shirley nodded.

Laura could imagine the scene. J.B., with a knife in his chest. Shirley all bloody, crying, saying she was sorry. "What did he say?"

"That fool's only words to me were: 'Dear Lord, what have you done?' Then, he rushed to J.B., realized he was dead, and called the police. I tried to tell him I had nothing to do with that stabbing. But the man was like a stone." She squared her shoulders. "He never liked me, you know. He never thought I was good enough for J.B."

"How much of this did you tell Amos?"

"All of it." Her expression turned nasty. "He tricked me, Laura. I thought he came here as a friend and so, when he questioned me, I told him the truth, just as I told you. His entire demeanor changed then. He became Sheriff Amos Wilson, the lawman. He even had the nerve to bring up that Dallas incident with Luke Mendez twenty-five years ago. Can you believe that? The way he talked, you'd think I had a habit of stabbing people."

"Didn't Amos tell you you didn't have to say anything without an attorney present?"

"I don't know ... I think so."

"Why didn't you listen to him?"

Shirley's gaze turned resentful. "What's the matter with you? You talk as if I were guilty. Haven't you heard a word I said? I didn't kill J.B. Which means I have nothing to hide. Besides, where am I going to get an attorney at one o'clock in the morning? In this godforsaken town where everybody treats me like I'm Typhoid Mary."

Laura squeezed her hand. "I know an attorney."

Before she had a chance to say anything more, Amos was walking toward them. "Are you finished, Laura?"

Laura stood up just as the paramedics rolled a stretcher out. All she could see was J.B.'s bulk, wrapped in a plastic bag, but it was enough to make tonight's events even more real. She pulled her gaze away. "Yes, I'm finished for now."

Shirley held her arm in a deadly grip. "You're not going to let me go to jail alone, are you?"

"I just have to make a phone call, Mom. You go on with Amos and I'll meet you there in a few minutes."

"What are they going to do to me?"

"Routine things—fingerprints, photographs." Gently, she pried Shirley's fingers from her arm. "You'll be there only for a little while, Mom. I promise everything will be cleared up very shortly. Just remember not to say another word or sign anything until I come back with your attorney."

Shirley nodded.

When Amos and the deputies were gone, Laura expelled a slow breath and turned to look at Lenox, who had quietly reappeared. His face was a white, rigid mask. His eyes were bright with tears and grief. Shirley's earlier comment that he had never liked her was, as many things Shirley said, an exaggeration. A cautious man, Lenox had been a little suspicious of the singer at first, until he had realized J.B. had never been happier. The dislike had come later, when Shirley had announced she was leaving.

For the first time since she had known the Englishman, she felt a mild resentment toward him. No doubt his statement to the police hadn't done anything to strengthen Shirley's position. But this was no time to start a debate. Later, after things had quieted down, she would talk to him.

"Where is Ted?" she asked.

"He went to Dallas to see a friend. I was able to reach him not too long ago. He's on his way."

"Good." She crossed over to the bar, picked up the phone, and dialed Stuart's number. After the fourth ring, his machine clicked on. "Stuart, are you there?" She paused to give him a chance to pick up. When the silence dragged on, she took a deep breath. "Stuart, J.B. has been killed and my mother was arrested for his murder. I need you desperately, so please call me as soon as you get in. I'm at the ranch." Then, afraid she'd break down, she hung up.

When she turned around, Lenox had disappeared. Down the hall, she could hear the forensic team walking around, dusting for prints and gathering various evidence.

She glanced at the mantel clock. One forty-five A.M. Where could Stuart be at this time of night? He never stayed at the office past six. He preferred to work at home, sometimes until the early morning hours. But if he *was* home, why hadn't he answered the phone?

After ten minutes had passed, she dialed his number again. This time, when the machine came on, she let out an exasperated sigh and hung up.

Then, knowing she'd go insane if she stayed inactive a minute longer, she grabbed her car keys and left.

Stuart's town house was dark when she pulled her car into an empty parking space, but his Porsche was there, gleaming under the glow of the streetlight.

She rang once, then, when there was no answer, she pressed the bell repeatedly until finally a light went on in the upstairs bedroom. A few seconds later, the door was thrown open. Stuart wore a navy velour robe over pale blue pajamas. His initials, scrawled in old English style, were embroidered on the breast pocket.

"Laura." He ran a hand through his hair. "What in the world are you . . .?"

She didn't let him finish but pushed past him and then whirled around. "Why didn't you answer your phone?"

He closed the door and turned to face her. "I guess I didn't hear it. My allergies started acting up again so I took an Allerest before I went to bed. It must have knocked me out." He thrust his hands in the robe's patch pockets. "Why? What's wrong?"

Something about his tone of voice and the way he kept his distance put her instantly on her guard. She glanced behind him, toward the end table where he kept his answering machine.

The red light indicating a message had been recorded was not blinking.

Her mouth opened as she met his gaze. "You got my call," she said, so astonished at his bold lie that she could barely find the words to express her shock. "You played back my message .. and then what?" She shook her head, unwilling to accept the facts. "You went back to bed? Is that it?"

His face was red with embarrassment. "I was going to call you first thing in the morning."

"*First thing in the morning*? My mother is in jail,

Stuart, accused of a crime she didn't commit. You're the only person I can turn to. The only person who can help us, and you don't even call back?"

"Laura—"

"I'm your fiancée, for God's sake! Not some pro bono case. How could you listen to my message, knowing what had just happened, what I was going through, and then go back to bed?"

"You're overwrought. Let me make you some tea—"

"I don't want tea! I want your help. I want you to come to the county jail with me and bail my mother out."

From under his even tan, his face paled. "What?"

She closed her eyes, then reopened them. "What am I speaking Swahili? I want you to represent my mother, Stuart."

He laughed, a short, perplexed laugh as if she had said something very stupid. "Laura, I prosecute criminals, remember? I don't defend them."

"My mother is not a criminal. She didn't do it."

"Nevertheless, I can't—"

"You can take a leave of absence from the D.A.'s office to defend a case. It's done all the time and you know it. I'll retain you," she added, not giving a damn if she was insulting his pride. "I have some money saved."

"It isn't a question of money."

He took a few slow steps around the room, then came to stand directly in front of her. His hands were still in his pockets and it struck her then that he hadn't said one word to express his sorrow, not one word of comfort, not one tender gesture to ease her pain, to reassure her that everything would be all right, that he would take care of everything.

Laura's face became wary. "Then what is it?"

"I can't defend her ..."

"Why not?"

"Ed called ... He took me off the Halloway case."

"Yes?"

She saw his Adam's apple bob up and down as he swallowed. "I've been assigned to prosecute your mother."

1 7

If he hadn't looked so damned guilty, she wouldn't have believed him. Aware her mouth was open, she closed it, waiting for him to continue, to say he had turned down the request. But he just stood there, his hands in his pockets, a defensive expression on his face.

"When did you find out about this?"

"Earlier."

"How much earlier? Before my phone call? Is that why you didn't answer?"

He turned away so that all she could see was his rigid back. "I didn't want to tell you over the phone."

"You could have come to the ranch. You knew I was there." His silence only confirmed what she already knew. He had made up his mind to prosecute without even talking it over with her. "Tell me you turned down the request," she said, refusing to believe he could be so callous.

He spun around. "Laura, please, put yourself in my place. I'm thirty-six years old. My greatest achievement so far is this job of deputy D.A. for Burnet County. You think I like it? You think I don't realize that most of my law school classmates are already junior partners in big, prestigious firms? That their names are constantly being mentioned in newspapers?"

"You said you loved your job."

"My job sucks. I took it because that's all there was."

"All right. You hate your job. What does that have to do with my mother?"

"It has everything to do with your mother. This case could bring me the recognition I need. I would be noticed, watched for the entire length of the trial. And afterward, I'd be able to pick whatever firm I chose to work with. They'll be coming to me on bended knees."

"The same thing could happen if you defended her."

He shook his head. "No. They would say I took the case out of compassion for you. I'd be accused of not using my head, of not seeing the hopelessness of the case. No one would ever take me seriously after that."

"It's not a hopeless case." She started to reach for him, but the expression in his eyes stopped her cold. "I know it looks bad for my mother," she continued bravely. "But she didn't do it. The evidence is all circumstantial. Come and talk to her, Stuart, and you'll see."

He stook his head. "Only a fool would take this case and hope to win it. I'm sorry, Laura."

She stood in the middle of his living room, her arms hanging at her sides. She thought of all the other times she had been here, eating, working, sometimes laughing with him. What a difference a few hours made. She felt as though a huge tidal wave had washed over her, sapping her of all her strength. "You really mean it. You're not going to help me."

"I'm sorry," he said again.

"And I thought I knew you. I thought you loved me. I thought you would have done anything for me, as I would have for you. But I was only fooling myself, wasn't I? All that matters to you, all that has ever mattered to you, is your career."

"Don't resent me for being practical, Laura. If you were in my shoes, you'd do exactly the same thing."

"I would have *never* turned my back on you!" Even though he had erected a physical barrier between them, she walked right up to him, forcing him to look at her. "How could this case be assigned to you anyway? Isn't prosecuting your fiancée's mother a conflict of interest?"

This time, there was no doubt in her mind. He *was* averting his eyes. "Stuart?"

He cleared his throat. "We need to talk, Laura."

Her legs weakened. Only her pride kept her from sitting down. "Talk."

"You're right. There would be a conflict of interest. That's why I'm sure you'll understand why I have to . . ." He bit his lips and looked at her helplessly. "Why I have to do this."

His words were like a slap in the face. "You want to break our engagement."

He seemed relieved that she had said it, not him. "It's for the best, Laura. It wouldn't have worked.

In time you would have come to hate me for prosecuting your mother. I want to spare us that."

"Oh, Stuart." Beneath the anger, she could feel the first stabs of pain.

"It's for the best," he said again.

"Of course." Walking much slower now, she walked past him and headed toward the door. "Consider yourself disengaged."

"Laura?"

She turned around, one eyebrow up.

"Uh . . . The ring?"

Laura almost laughed. He looked so damned pathetic. What was he afraid of? That she would want to keep his flawless diamond? Or was he afraid of what his parents would say?

God. What kind of spell had she been under not to notice how shallow he really was? How spineless?

Slowly, she removed the ring and dropped it on the table by the front door. Before he could thank her, she left.

Although it was nearly three A.M. when Laura came out of the county jail, more than a dozen reporters from various newspapers and television stations had gathered around Riddel Park to wait for her.

They surrounded her in an instant, pushing microphones in her face, training their camera lenses on her. She remembered all the times she had acted in the same fashion, shouldering her way to the front of the horde, trying to get a statement, a sentence, anything she could use for a quote. Now, *she*

was the center of attention, and she had no idea
how to handle it.

"Miss Spencer, did your mother admit to killing
J.B. Lawson?"

"Did she tell you why she did it?"

"Is is true that she stabbed a lover twenty-five
years ago?"

Blinded by the bright lights, Laura tried to walk
past the crowd of reporters, but they kept coming
closer, hurling questions at her. "I have nothing to
say. Please let me through."

Suddenly, a strong arm wrapped around her
shoulders. "You heard the lady," Ted said in an
authoritative voice. "Let us through."

"Aw, come on, Mr. Kandall. We're just doing
our job. You know how it is. So does Miss
Spencer."

"Miss Spencer is very tired. I'm sure after she's
had a chance to rest, she'll be glad to answer your
questions. Right now, I'd like to take her home."

Astounded, Laura watched the crowd part in
front of them.

"Come on." Ted hurried her along, keeping her
close to him as they walked toward the BMW.
"Let's get out of here before they change their
minds."

She didn't ask what he was doing there, or how
he had found her. Inside the car, she pressed her
head back against the leather headrest and closed
her eyes, barely aware that they were moving. She
tried to shut everything out, but strange images
kept pushing through, images that made no sense—
her mother covered with blood, the stretcher being

wheeled out, the heavy cell door clanging shut as Laura watched helplessly, the crowd outside jostling her, demanding to know if Shirley had killed J.B.

J.B. Grief stabbed through her, swift and raw, stronger than before. How could he be dead? There was so much they hadn't done yet, so many things that had been left unsaid.

"I want to see him." She barely recognized the sound of her voice as she spoke. "I want to see J.B."

Ted gave her a sharp look. "You don't have to do that."

"I won't believe he's dead until I see him." She stared straight ahead, her eyes dry. "Take me to him."

The visit to the county morgue was short but painful. J.B.'s body was still on the stretcher, covered with a white sheet. When the attendant on duty pulled it back, Laura stared at the white frozen face for a full minute, then without a word to Ted or the attendant, she walked out and climbed back into the BMW.

It took Ted only a few minutes to make the drive back to Lost Creek. Because he didn't want her to be alone, he drove directly to the main house. The police cars were gone. He parked next to J.B.'s Suburban, as he had done so many times in the last several days and turned to look at Laura. She was pale and her eyes were dry and vacant as she stared into the night. He wasn't even sure she realized they were no longer moving.

He had to think of her now. He had to put his grief aside and help her get through the difficult days ahead. He took her hands in his. They were cold and unyielding. "Tell me how I can help you."

The pain he saw in her eyes made his own even more acute.

"Tell me it didn't happen," she said tonelessly. "Tell me it's all a horrible nightmare and I'm going to wake up."

"I wish I could."

"I loved him so much," she murmured. "He wasn't like any man I have ever known. He changed my life from the moment I met him. He didn't care that I was quiet and unresponsive at first, almost to the point of being rude. He understood. And he loved me just the way I was."

"That's because he believed in people. He saw something in them no one else saw. That was one of his most endearing qualities."

Ted's voice was low, controlled. Laura looked at him. The handsome features were taut, filled with a misery she understood only too well. She had been so wrapped up in her own grief, she hadn't thought of his. "Oh, Ted, I'm sorry. You loved him, too."

He pulled a cigarette from his pocket, looked at it for a moment, then lit it, using the lighter on the dash. He inhaled deeply, letting the strong, hot smoke fill his lungs. "J.B. bought me my first Nikon. It was shortly after I lost a photo contest the *Sentinel* had sponsored. Of course, he didn't call it 'losing,' but 'winning second place.' He handed the camera to me and in a gruff voice said,

'I never want to hear you say the word 'loser' again, do you hear? You're a winner, kid. Don't you ever forget it.' "

He took another deep drag on his cigarette. "His faith in me was an incredible boost to my shattered ego. In subsequent years, whenever things didn't go quite the way I had hoped, I would remember his words."

It was her turn to soothe and comfort. "I'm glad you had a chance to spend some time with him. It's been many years since I've seen him this happy."

When he didn't answer, she added, "I'm going to find out who did this to him, Ted. I don't care what I have to do . . ."

The look in his eyes, a mixture of sadness and surprise, stopped her. She let go of his hand as if it had bit her. "You think my mother did it, don't you? You and the whole county."

"Laura, I only know what Amos told me—"

"I don't give a damn what Amos told you!" Her voice vibrated with anger. "She didn't do it. It just . . ." As if she had suddenly realized the awesome odds her mother faced, her shoulders sagged. "It just looks that way."

Ted's voice softened. "Why don't you tell me what happened?"

His gentle tone, along with the compassionate expression in his eyes, were like a soothing potion. For the first time since this nightmare had begun, she felt herself relax. She repeated what Shirley had told her, the way she had looked. After a short hesitation, she even mentioned the one hundred thousand dollars Shirley had come to borrow from J.B.

"I know how incriminating it all sounds," she said when she was finished. "But I believe her. Shirley is incapable of killing anyone, and for Amos to suggest she would do so in a moment of anger is ludicrous. She doesn't even have a temper."

Ted nodded slowly. In spite of all the physical evidence Amos had mentioned, the story was just too pat. Why would Shirley kill J.B., then stay at the scene of the crime and be caught? It didn't make sense.

"If your mother didn't do it," he said. "Then who did?"

"I don't know. I'm sure J.B. had his share of enemies. But I can't think of anyone who would want to kill him. Unless .."

He was instantly alert. "Unless what?"

"The other night . . ." She frowned. "It was very late. I was awakened by a noise outside my house. When I looked out the window, I saw someone running through the trees."

"Did you report it to the police?"

"No. At the time, I wasn't sure if the shadow was that of an animal or a prowler. He, or it, was gone before I could make up my mind."

Worry clouded Ted's blue eyes. "Were you and J.B. working on a special story? Something dangerous perhaps?"

"Just my investigation of your uncle, but I never thought of that as particularly life-threatening."

"You'll have to tell Amos and your mother's attorney about the possible prowler. That's probably something they'll want to check into."

"I will." She wasn't ready to tell him Shirley didn't have an attorney, that the one man she thought she could count on had turned his back on her. Right now all she wanted was to be alone with her grief.

"I asked Lenox to prepare a room for you and bring some of your clothes from the guest house," Ted said, as if he had read her thoughts. "I hope that's all right."

She unbuckled her seat belt. "That's fine. Thanks, Ted."

They both got out of the car in silence. Once inside the house, Ted hesitated. He wanted to take her in his arms and hold her until that anguished look in her eyes disappeared. But something about the stiff way she held her body told him the gesture wouldn't be welcome.

"I'll see you tomorrow," he said.

Laura nodded, then walked up the staircase.

18

The phone rang on Sheriff Wilson's desk. He glanced at the clock on the wall. Only the D.A. would call this early in the morning. He was right.

"How's the Lawson murder investigation coming along?" Ed Cavanaugh asked. "Got anything back from the lab yet?"

Amos could almost see the nasty little gleam in the man's eyes. "Yes."

"Well? Are Shirley Langfield's fingerprints on the murder weapon?"

Amos sighed. "Yes, Ed. They're also on a small table, on J.B.'s chair, and on one of the French doors."

"Excellent, excellent. Her attorney show up yet?"

"She doesn't have an attorney."

"Well then, see that she gets one, will you? I want a signed statement from that woman by noon."

"Look, Ed." He paused, bracing himself for the fight. "I need to talk to you about something."

"Make it quick. I'm busy."

"I don't think Shirley Langfield did it."

"What?"

"It doesn't make sense. She would have run away. She would have worn gloves, or at the very least, she would have wiped off her fingerprints and gotten rid of that dress."

"That's it? That's what you base your opinion on? What she should have done and didn't do?"

"A jury will want to know why some areas were wiped clean—like the knocker on the front door— and others were not."

"That door knocker probably hasn't been used in years. Half the time, those suckers are there for decoration. You know that."

"J.B.'s desk was clean, too."

"So the guy was a neat freak. Or maybe Shirley started wiping her prints off and then lost her nerve. It happens."

Amos scratched his head. "I'm having a problem with that theory, Ed."

"Look, Amos." The D.A.'s voice turned cold. "I don't give a shit about your problems. I have an election coming up and I intend to win it. Now, you know that's not going to happen if I pussyfoot around. You have more evidence than you can shake a stick at, so build me a case that will win me a conviction or by God, Amos, I'll have your badge." He hung up.

Heaving a sigh of frustration, Amos stared helplessly at the phone.

Malcolm had been unable to fall asleep after returning home from his clandestine visit to Lost Creek. Staring at the shadows on the ceiling, he lay in the dark, reliving the events of the past few hours moment by moment, worrying over clues he may have left behind.

He hadn't. Looking back, he was certain he had been meticulous and thorough. Still, sleep continued to elude him and when the telephone rang at five-fifteen, he was almost relieved. The wait was over.

He glanced at Barbara as he picked up the receiver on the bedside table. She was sleeping soundly. "Hello?"

It was Clint, his campaign manager. Usually quite calm, Clint now spoke in an agitated voice. "You'll never believe what I just heard."

Tensing slightly, Malcolm prepared himself. From now on, his performance had to be flawless. "I don't play guessing games at five o'clock in the morning," he said in the gruff voice of one who has just been awakened from a sound sleep.

Clint didn't let Malcolm's apparent bad mood faze him. "J.B. Lawson is dead," he announced bluntly. "He was found murdered at his home last night."

Although Malcolm had anticipated the news, the words still left him shaky. "Murdered?" Not sure he sounded stunned enough, he added, "Dear God. Who did it? Why?"

"The reason is still sketchy. All I know is that the police have arrested J.B.'s ex-wife, Shirley Langfield."

Shirley. *They had arrested Shirley Langfield.* He almost laughed out loud. That was priceless. He couldn't have found a better fall guy, a fall *gal*, if he had tried. The people of Burnet County had never forgiven her for walking out on J.B. years ago. Finding an objective jury would be one hell of a task.

"Holy shit." Falling into the act, he ran his hand through his hair. "I can't believe this. J.B. Lawson . . . murdered. Unbelievable."

Never one to let a golden opportunity pass by, Clint said, "We're going to milk this news for all it's worth, Malcolm."

"What are you talking about?"

"Your platform, Malcolm," Clint said with a touch of impatience in his voice. "Your *law and order* platform? The press is going to want your reaction. A prominent Texas man has been the victim of yet another violent crime. Politicians are going to be flooded with letters from irate citizens, demanding changes in our crime laws. This is your chance to pitch your views at a time when they'll do the most good. Remember the incumbent governor wants the death penalty in Texas abolished. *You* want it enforced."

"Good thinking, Clint. You're finally beginning to earn that outrageous salary I'm paying you."

Under control now, Malcolm's mind began to work feverishly again. "Have funeral arrangements been made yet? If so, find out if we should send flowers or make a donation to one of J.B.'s favorite charities. In case of the latter, our contribution should be a generous one—at least a couple of thousand dollars. And make sure that amount leaks out to the press."

He could hear Clint chuckle. "I'll let you know what I find out and call you back."

After hanging up, Malcolm glanced at Barbara who was still sleeping. The news of her old friend's death was going to be a terrible shock to her. He would have to tell her gently. And he would have to keep a close eye on her. At least until after the elections.

He began to relax. He had done it. Not only had he eliminated his biggest threat, but someone else was about to take the rap for his crime.

Smiling, he leaned back against the pillows.

How was that for luck?

It was seven o'clock that morning when Tony called Enzio in New York.

"What the hell is going on out there?" Enzio said as a form of greeting. "I just heard on the news that J.B. Lawson was murdered."

"You heard right, boss. I just went out for coffee and the whole fucking town is talking about it."

"They say his ex-old lady did it."

"Yeah, but the broad's denying it."

"Has Kandall made a statement yet?"

"I'll say." Tony chuckled. "The man was brilliant. If I didn't know any better, I would have sworn his best friend had just kicked the bucket."

"Any chance *he* did it?"

Tony was silent for a moment as he pondered the question over. "That's possible," he said after a while. "If the old man was working with Laura on the investigation and he found out something damaging, Kandall could have panicked. But I don't think so. He doesn't have the guts to do something like that. Besides, if Laura had something on him, you know it'd be out by now."

"I guess you're right. What about you?" Enzio took a noisy slurp of his morning coffee. "Did you find anything?"

"Yeah. A list of names she finally brought home. All are names of people we know—Orbach, Andover, Canton, Massuela, and a few others. The good news is that all those names have been crossed out with a notation next to them saying: "dead end," which means she couldn't get any of those people to talk."

"I would hope not. I pay them a lot of money to keep their mouths shut."

"I'm telling you, boss, the woman's harmless. And anyway, from what I've been hearing this morning, she won't rest until she finds her stepfather's murderer, which means she won't have the time, or the inclination, to continue the Kandall investigation. There ain't much for me to do down here now, is there?" he asked hopefully.

"There's plenty for you to do. For one thing, I want you to start tailing Laura. I still don't trust her. If there's any chance Kandall is involved in that murder and she finds out about it, we're in deep shit, so keep an eye on her and keep reporting to me every day."

Tony sighed disappointedly. "Yes, boss."

Laura hadn't been able to fall asleep. By morning, tired of tossing and turning, she got out of bed, showered, and dressed in the jeans and sweatshirt

Lenox had brought from the guest house. If she was going to stay here for a few days, she would need more clothes.

Her living room was just as she had left it a little less than eighteen hours ago—silent, tidy, and full of memories.

Still unable to cry, she glanced at the chair where J.B. always sat, remembering the last time he had been here. It was shortly after her engagement to Stuart. Over a pizza and a half gallon of Pepsi, she had told him about her plans to revamp the *Sentinel*'s Sunday supplement with the addition of a comics page.

Her heart heavy with grief, she began walking around the room, touching the furniture, straightening a pillow, centering the candleholder on the small end table. In front of the large wall-to-wall bookcase, crammed with books and old mementos, her gaze fell on a ceramic vase in various shades of gold and amber. It was a birthday gift from Stuart.

"The colors reminded me of your eyes," he had told her.

There were other gifts from him—a brass swan, a small replica of the Statue of Liberty he had picked up in New York, a porcelain rose he bought for her at an antiques show, a book of poems by Robert Frost.

She picked up a framed photograph of the two of them. It had been taken this past Labor Day aboard the Flemings' forty-foot sloop. That evening, Stuart had asked her to marry him.

"Bastard." She flung the photograph across the room, watching it shatter as it crashed against the wall. With hardly a pause, she picked up the amber vase and subjected it to the same fate. Within moments, the rose and the other presents had been discarded in the same manner.

Not bothering to glance at the debris, she ran upstairs, threw the closet door open, and started yanking Stuart's clothes from the hangers. When everything lay in a pile on the floor, she scooped it up, marched to the window, and threw it all out.

Breathing hard, she sat on the bed, wishing she could cry.

Ted was about twenty yards from the guest house when he saw the pile of clothes scattered across Laura's lawn. Having heard on the morning news that Stuart Fleming would be prosecuting Shirley Langfield, he had no difficulty guessing who the clothes belonged to.

He found Laura sitting on the bed. Her face was white and she was staring at her hands, which were tightly clenched in her lap. For a moment, all he could do was look at her. He had never been very good with others' pain.

But something about the way she looked, not stoic as she had last night, but lost and defeated, stirred something deep inside of him in a way he had not expected. He moved toward her, a little awkwardly at first, and sat next to her on the bed. "Can I help?"

"No."

He didn't let her sharp tone faze him. "I just heard Stuart is going to prosecute your mother."

This time, her hands balled up in tight little fists. "Bastard."

"Me or him?" When she didn't answer, he reached for a strand of hair that lay across her cheek and pushed it back, hooking it behind her ear.

"He dumped me," she said after a while. "Did you hear about that, too?"

He stared at her in total disbelief. "No. I wasn't aware of that."

"He did it so he wouldn't have a conflict of interest." Her voice trembling with emotion she could no longer conceal, Laura told him about her visit to Stuart's town house, her plea for help, the way he had turned her down and finally, the last blow when he had announced the wedding was off.

"Why didn't you say something to me last night?"

"Last night was for J.B.," she whispered.

Before she could anticipate the gesture, he had gathered her close, easing her head onto his shoulder. Although pity was the last thing she wanted right now, she gave in to the gentle pressure.

All at once, her defenses, her pride, everything she had been trying to hold onto for the last several hours, came unglued. With a sob that seemed to rise from her very soul, she buried her head against his chest and wept helplessly.

1 9

The news of J.B.'s death spread through the Hill Country like brushfire. For the next two days, while funeral arrangements were being made, hundreds of friends, neighbors, and colleagues—people whose lives he had touched—came or called to offer their condolences.

For Laura, who had had to deal with the double tragedy of J.B.'s death and her mother's arrest, the outpouring of sympathy was a constant reminder of the ordeal that still lay ahead.

Through J.B.'s long-time lawyer, she had retained one of Texas's most successful criminal attorneys, a man by the name of Quentin March. Although he had been optimistic, his efforts to get Shirley out on bail had failed. Stuart, who avoided all eye contact with Laura during the bail hearing, had convinced the judge that Shirley was a flight risk and bail had been denied.

The preliminary hearing was set for Friday, October 28.

Ted's quiet, unflappable strength had been a godsend. Thanks to him, Lenox and Mildred, who, although inconsolable, had insisted on helping out, the arrangements for J.B.'s burial had been made expeditiously and tastefully.

Now, as Laura stood at the small Burnet cemetery where Reverend McCord was conducting graveside services, she gazed at the solemn faces around her, wondering if one of them belonged to J.B.'s murderer.

More than four hundred mourners had come to pay their respects. Amongst them were some of Texas's most influential citizens—the governor of Texas, the CEO of Consolidated Oil, a couple of senators, even a television evangelist Laura remembered meeting years ago.

Behind Senator Babcock, she caught a glimpse of Malcolm Kandall and his wife, Barbara. Barbara was crying softly and Malcolm, his head bowed and his hands folded in front of him, looked properly mournful.

Because of her vow to find J.B.'s killer, her investigation of the gubernatorial candidate would have to wait. Did he realize that? she wondered as their gaze met. Was he relieved or indifferent? As usual his expression revealed nothing. As a news crew that was filming the services from a discreet distance inched closer, Malcolm took his wife's hand and held it.

No doubt that picture would make the six o'clock news with part of the comments Malcolm had made during an earlier news broadcast: "J.B. Lawson was a great man. He and I didn't always see eye to eye, but I respected him and admired his talent as a newsman. He will be greatly missed."

Suddenly, inexplicably, Laura felt a chill. It was a

feeling she had experienced often during her crime reporting days in New York City, one she associated with imminent danger.

Instinctively, she glanced over her shoulder. The hearse that had brought J.B.'s casket to the cemetery was still there. Behind it was a long stream of cars waiting to take the mourners back to Lost Creek.

It was then that she saw the car. It was a nondescript black sedan that stood slightly ahead of the hearse. Its windows were rolled up except for the one on the passenger's side, which was halfway open.

She caught a glimpse of a man behind the wheel, and of jet black slicked-back hair. Before she could see anything more, however, the window rolled shut and the car slowly drove away.

Someone had been watching her.

"Oh, baby, it's so good to see you," Shirley said as the matron ushered Laura into a visitor's room. She wore the standard prison blues issued by the Burnet County jail. Her blond hair was pulled back and without makeup, she looked more vulnerable than ever before.

"How was J.B.'s funeral?" she asked.

"Crowded." Laura managed a wan smile. "Everybody ate and drank and gossiped. J.B. would have loved it."

"Was Stuart there?"

For the first time in three days, Laura didn't feel the stab of pain at the mere mention of her ex-fiancé's name. "Yes, but we didn't speak. He didn't even come forward to offer his condolences."

"That rat." Shirley's eyes sizzled with fury. "And to think I treated him like a son, that I was about to entrust him with my most prized possession."

"I don't want to talk about him anymore."

"Okay, baby." Shirley started to reach for Laura's hand across the table, then as the matron cleared her throat in warning, she withdrew it.

"How are you doing, Mom?"

Shirley's expression turned sour. "Miserable. This place is the pits. And so damned noisy, forget about getting any sleep. I've been waiting for Amos to show his face so I can tell him what I think of his accommodations, but that snake has been laying low ever since he brought me here."

Addressing the matron at the door, she raised her voice. "What's the matter? Is he afraid I'll scratch his eyes out? Or maybe I'm hiding a knife. A big one. And I'm waiting for just the right moment to plunge it into that mean, old heart of his."

"Mom, will you please shut up?" Laura whispered as the matron shot them a nasty look. "This is exactly the kind of attitude that will get you into trouble."

"I'm already in trouble, Laura. And I'd like to see you sitting in a four by four twenty-four hours a day, having to pee for all the world to see. Do you know they won't even give me a privacy screen? The ice maiden here shot down my request by saying 'this ain't the Ritz.' "

Laura held back a smile. At least her mother's

spirits were back. "Are you going to answer a few questions or are you going to spend our ten minutes bitching about the accommodations?"

Shirley's attention perked up. "Why? You found out something?"

"I just want to know if you saw a car coming from the opposite direction when you drove to Lost Creek the other night. The coroner has established the time of death between twelve-fifteen and one A.M. You said you arrived at the ranch at twelve-twenty. If the killer drove west toward Kerville, you wouldn't have seen him. But if he drove *east*, toward Austin, you had to have passed him."

Shirley frowned in concentration. "Now that you mention it, I did see a car. I had just passed the Clermont Peach farm. I was maybe . . . ten minutes or so from the Lost Creek turnoff."

"Did you notice what kind of car it was? The make? Color?"

Shirley shook her head. "It was too dark. And he was driving too fast." Her eyes grew wide. "My God, Laura. You think it was the murderer?"

"It could have been. What about the headlights? Were they set high like on a pickup truck or a van? Or low as in a sports car or sedan?"

"Low." Her gaze shot up. "I remember something else."

"What?"

"It made a lot of noise as it went by. Like one of those fancy racing cars."

"That's good, Mom. Now what about the color? Could it have been black?"

"Maybe." Shirley frowned in concentration, then

shook her head. "I don't know for sure. Why did you pick black?"

Laura told her about the car she had seen at the cemetery earlier.

"Oh, my God! Are you saying you're being stalked?"

"No—"

"Laura, you called the police, didn't you?"

"Shhh. Keep your voice down. I'm not in any danger."

"How do you know?"

"Because if that man wanted to harm me, he would have already done so."

Shirley wasn't convinced. Leaning forward, she stared hard into Laura's eyes. "Don't do anything crazy, okay? I couldn't bear it if something happened to you."

"Nothing is going to happen to me. I'm too tough, remember? Besides, Ted insisted I move into the main house, and with him and Lenox watching over me, I'm safer than Fort Knox."

Shirley continued to watch her. "You like this Ted Kandall a lot, don't you?"

"I guess I do. He's been a great source of comfort these past few days."

"You're not falling for him, are you? Because that wouldn't be very smart considering—"

"I'm not falling for him, Mom. I've had it with men; and if there is one thing you can be sure of it's that I'll never fall in love again."

"Never is a long time, baby."

"Ted and I are just friends," Laura said, with a

touch of impatience in her voice. "Don't make any more of the relationship than there is."

"I won't say another word about it."

"Good." Laura tugged at the edge of her jacket before adding, "Now, I need to talk to you about J.B.'s will. I suppose it won't come as a surprise to you that he left me practically everything he owned—two-thirds of the *Sentinel* and the ranch."

"Oh, Laura, that's wonderful." Then, making a quick recovery, she asked, "Why only two-thirds of the *Sentinel*? Who gets the rest?"

"Two of the newspaper's senior employees own ten shares each, and as you know, I received twenty shares when I became publisher. J.B. left the remaining shares to Ted and me. Forty shares to me and twenty to Ted."

"Ted, huh?" Shirley arched a thin, blond brow. "How do you feel about that?"

Laura shrugged. "I have no problem with it. Ted and I had a long talk. He said he wasn't much of a businessman and would be glad to leave the affairs of the paper in my hands and remain more or less a silent partner."

"That's a very smart decision on his part."

"And now that brings us to you."

Shirley made a dismissive gesture. "If it's about the hundred thousand dollars J.B. left me as part of my divorce settlement, you tell the lawyer he can keep it. I don't want it. Maybe that way the D.A. will believe me when I say I had forgotten about that clause in the will."

"Before you make any rash decision," Laura replied, "let's wait and see what happens at the trial.

What I came to discuss with you is how the money will be handled. You know you can't collect it until you're released, don't you?"

"Quentin told me."

"Good. Now . . ." Laura rested her arms on the table. "As I suspected, J.B. was cash poor. His only revenues came from the land he leased to another rancher and from the sale of a few heads of cattle every now and then. After going over the books with J.B.'s foreman, I decided the best way to increase those revenues is to lease additional land. The money will be used for the upkeep of the ranch, mortgage payments, etc. Any extra will be put aside toward your inheritance and Lenox's. It shouldn't take too long—"

"Lenox!"

Laura smiled. "Yes, Mom. J.B. left him a hundred thousand dollars also."

Shirley made a small sarcastic sound. "Well, I guess you're going to be looking for a new butler soon."

"That's up to Lenox."

Shirley nodded slowly, then, leaning back in her chair, she folded her arms. "So, if I can't collect my hundred thousand, how will I pay for my attorney's fees? All I have in the bank is twenty thousand dollars."

"That's enough for now. For the rest, Quentin has agreed to wait until you collect your inheritance."

"Provided I'm found innocent. What happens if I'm found guilty?"

In spite of the matron, Laura patted her mother's hand. "Let's think positive, okay?"

Shirley expelled a long, trembling breath. "Do you really believe I'm going to get out of this hole, Laura? You hear things in jail, you know. And one of the things I hear is that your ex-fiancé is building one hell of a case against me."

"Quentin is a good man, too. Have faith in him."

"If you say so."

Laura rose. "I'll stop by tomorrow. Take care."

"You, too. And if you see Amos, tell him I'm getting ulcers from the junk they call food in this joint. Tell him that after all the fine dinners he ate at our house, the least he could do is throw in a steak every once in a while."

"I'll tell him, Mom. Meanwhile, behave yourself and stop giving the guards a hard time. They're only doing their job."

Later that night, after Ted and Lenox had gone to bed, Laura, too restless to sleep, walked quietly down the stairs and went to sit on the porch swing where she and J.B. had spent so many quiet evenings, discussing her plans for the *Sentinel.*

She would never hear the sound of his voice again, she thought, gazing at the stars he had taught her to recognize years ago. Or that rolling laughter that was so contagious. J.B. was gone and whatever lay ahead for the newspaper, good or bad, he would never be a part of it again.

"You shouldn't be here by yourself."

She turned her head. Ted stood just behind her. He was still dressed in the casual clothes he had changed into after J.B.'s funeral. "That's a bad habit you have, you know," she said. "Sneaking up on people."

"Sorry. Something I picked up in the trenches." He pointed at the seat next to her on the swing. "May I?"

"Sure."

"Couldn't sleep either, huh?"

He watched her as she shook her head. God, she was beautiful. Even with those dark circles under her eyes and the sad slant of her mouth, there was something mesmerizing about her. "You used to spend a lot of time here with J.B., didn't you?"

"Tons of time. This is where he taught me how to truly appreciate the countryside." She continued to stare into the night. "I don't know if I can save the paper without him, Ted. Without his moral support. I don't want to fail, but—"

The despair in her voice made him want to gather her in his arms again. He couldn't remember ever being affected so deeply by a woman before. It scared the hell out of him. Until now, women, necessary though they were, had never been a priority in his life. They came and went at regular intervals. Most of the time, they were the ones to end the relationship, claiming his lack of commitment and vagabond life were too irritating.

So why was he so damned preoccupied with *this* woman? "You won't fail," he said softly.

"How can you be so sure of that?"

"Because you're made of tough stock. Just like your mother."

A smile curved her lips as she looked at him.

"Is this another thing you learned in the trenches? Comforting women?"

"No. That's something I learned from hanging around my little sister." As she fell silent again, he reached for her hand and held it. "Look, Laura, about the *Sentinel*. I'm not a rich man, but I have a couple of hundred thousand dollars saved. Just say the word, and it's yours."

His generosity touched her deeply. "Thanks, Ted. Unfortunately, the money would only keep the *Sentinel* afloat for a few more weeks. What this newspaper desperately needs is credibility and the only way to do that ..." She bit her lip.

"Is by exposing my uncle," he finished for her.

"We don't need to talk about that. I realize the subject puts you in a difficult position, even more difficult now that you own part of the *Sentinel*."

Ted couldn't hold back a sarcastic smile. "My uncle and I aren't exactly bosom buddies. I've never cared for his politics. I'm not too crazy about the man either. And for what it's worth, I agree with you that a juicy exposé would give the *Sentinel* the kick it needs to get back on track."

"And you wouldn't resent me for printing the story?"

"Nope. I have a stake in that newspaper now, Laura. I want to see it protected." Seeing that she was beginning to relax, he added, "Do you really have something on him?"

"Nothing I can prove."

Sensing she didn't want to discuss the matter any further, he didn't push her. Pressure of any kind was the last thing she needed right now.

He stood up and extended his hand. "Come on. I'll make you some hot cocoa. J.B. told me once that hot chocolate could cure anything. Even insomnia."

Without a word, she took his hand and followed him inside.

A somber hush greeted Laura when she walked into the newsroom on Monday morning.

Because it was the first time she had been in her office since J.B.'s death last Wednesday, her desk was piled with correspondence and phone messages she probably would never have time to get to.

Within moments, Mildred, her features taut from trying to hide her pain, came into her office. "Johnny and Leo would like to see you," she said. "Shall I let them know you're here?"

Laura dropped the sheaf of messages on her desk. "Sure. I need to talk to them, too."

Through the large glass panel, she watched as the two men approached her office. They were the *Sentinel*'s most senior employees, each having joined the staff in the late fifties within months of each other. Ten years ago, as a reward for their outstanding service, J.B. had sold each of them ten shares of the business and given them a voice in all decisions regarding the *Sentinel.*

She knew J.B.'s bequest wouldn't come as a surprise to them, but she wasn't sure how they would react at the news that Ted Kandall was now a major stockholder. That's what she wanted to talk to them about. "Good morning, gentlemen," she said when they came in.

Although they replied in unison, both seemed ill at ease.

Whatever they want to talk to me about, it's serious, she thought or they wouldn't be looking so grim. Holding back a sigh, for she wasn't sure she could handle another disaster, she squared her shoulders. "You wanted to see me?"

Leo glanced at Johnny. Guessing he had been appointed spokesman, Laura focused on him. "Johnny?"

After a short, uncomfortable silence, the general manager cleared his throat. "I hate to have to bring this up at such a time, Laura. But I don't have any choice."

She was filled with a mild feeling of apprehension. "Just come right out with it."

"All right." This time, he did meet her gaze. "A big West Coast publisher approached Leo and me on Friday, and offered to buy our shares of the *Sentinel*."

Laura tensed. "Which publisher?"

"Carl Hansen of Hansen Publications."

Although she had never met the publisher, she knew his reputation as a wheeler and dealer. Based in San Francisco, the publishing giant owned more than two dozen newspapers across the country and scores of magazines—none of which he had founded himself. He preferred to wait until a newspaper was in desperate trouble. Then, he and his team of sharks would come in, buy the paper for a song, and put it back on its feet. "I hope you told him that no part of the *Sentinel* was for sale."

Johnny fidgeted in his seat and said nothing.

"Actually we didn't," Leo said, coming to his friend's rescue. "The truth is, both of us are considering selling our shares to Hansen."

Laura felt the blood drain from her face. "You can't be serious. You know as well as I do that J.B. never intended for those shares to go outside the company—especially to a sleaze like Hansen."

"We know that," Leo said. "And up until a few weeks ago, we would have never thought of betraying that trust. But things have changed, Laura. The *Sentinel* is in serious trouble and Hansen is our only hope. He would bring in dozens of advertisers—which we badly need. The *Sentinel* would be saved, Laura. You wouldn't have to lay off a single employee. And you would still be the majority stockholder. You could still make all the decisions."

"Not for long. You saw what he did with the *Phoenix Star*. His people came in nice and meek and within weeks, they had that place in an uproar, with employees picketing for reforms and threatening to quit unless Hansen was allowed to become the majority stockholder. That's how that conglomerate works, Leo. By using strong-arm tactics. I know. I've watched them doing the same thing to a number of newspapers all over the country. I'm not going to let it happen to the *Sentinel*."

Johnny shook his head. "I know you mean well, Laura, but with all due respect, your good intentions aren't going to save the paper. Not this time. And where will that put us? Where are we going to find another job at our age?"

"You won't be guaranteed a job if Hansen takes

over. They like to bring in younger people at half the salary."

"Hansen said he would keep us on, and every other employee as well. He's ready to put that in writing."

They had already made up their minds, Laura realized. And there was nothing she could do. Eight months ago, while reviewing the financial status of the *Sentinel,* she had discovered that the sale agreement between J.B. and his two employees did not preclude Leo and Johnny from selling their shares to an outsider. When she had pointed that error out to J.B., he had shrugged her concerns off.

"Those two are like family, Laura. They would never do anything to hurt me."

Johnny leaned foward, his expression earnest. "Don't think we're being disloyal, Laura. What we're doing is as much to save our jobs as to save the *Sentinel,* and the five hundred people who work for it."

Laura gazed into the newsroom where reporters and editors were hard at work, unaware of this new crisis. She remembered something J.B. had told her not too long ago. "Sometimes integrity means knowing when to make the tough choices."

Maybe the choice had been made for her. And maybe Johnny and Leo were right, but dammit, she wasn't going to give up without a fight. "How much time did Hansen give you to make up your mind?" she asked.

"Until Friday."

"Can you stall him?"

Johnny and Leo exchanged an uneasy glance. "Why? And for how long?"

"If I could have a couple of weeks, I might be able to break that story on Malcolm Kandall."

"That would make one hell of a headline," Johnny admitted. "The sales would go through the roof." He glanced at Leo who nodded. "How do we stall him?"

"Tell him there are some legalities to deal with regarding the terms of J.B.'s will. Tell him you need until . . ." She glanced at her calendar. "Until November eight."

"What if he checks our story?"

"I'll alert J.B.'s attorney as well as his banker. Both are old friends. They won't mind covering for us. Even if it means telling a little white lie." Seeing an opportunity to bring them up to date on the contents of J.B.'s will, she did so, stressing that Ted had no intention of interfering with the business of the *Sentinel* in any way.

Showing no resentment at all, the two men congratulated her warmly. "You've been a good publisher, Laura," Leo said. "And a true moral booster. I hope everything works out the way you want it to."

"Thanks, Leo." As they rose, she did, too. "And if you hear anything that might help my investigation, any lead at all, let me know, will you? This is a team effort."

"We'll do that," Johnny said.

After they were gone, she turned her computer on, quickly inserted the file she kept in the *Sentinel*'s safe, and went down the list of Malcolm's financial supporters. Halfway down, she stopped. The nagging feeling she'd had ever since Johnny had told her about Hansen Publications had been justified after all. The conglomerate was listed as one of Malcolm's contributors. To date, it had donated close to two hundred thousand dollars to the campaign.

Another thought flashed through her mind, sending a chill down her back.

What if the gubernatorial elections and J.B.'s murder were related?

20

Laura immediately left the *Sentinel* and headed back to Lost Creek to talk to Lenox, whom she had been avoiding since the night Shirley was arrested. It was time to put an end to that nonsense. Lenox couldn't help what he had seen and heard. Nor could he help if he was an honest man.

Now, standing in the kitchen doorway, one shoulder leaning against the jamb, Laura watched as he brought down a stack of dishes from a cupboard, and set them on the kitchen counter.

Grief had added years to his face and to his posture. This man, who days ago had walked as straight as an arrow, now looked as if the weight of the world sat on his shoulders.

"Hello, Lenox."

Startled, the Englishman turned around. "Miss Laura. Forgive me. I didn't see you standing there."

"I didn't want to make any sudden move until you had unloaded your cargo." She tilted her head sideways. "All right if I come in?"

The request took him aback. "Of course." He

stood a little stiffly, much like a servant who didn't know what to expect.

Laura looked around the huge country kitchen with its gleaming copper pots hanging from a rack above the blue-tiled island, the oak table and chairs, the French windows overlooking a vegetable garden Lenox planted himself every year. She had spent many enjoyable after-school hours in this kitchen, eating Lenox's famous English scones and drinking mugs of steaming cocoa.

"I'm sorry about the way I've treated you these past few days," she said. "Avoiding you, acting as if you weren't even here."

"There's no need for you to apologize, Miss Laura."

"Yes, there is. I should have realized sooner that you are a man of honor, that you had no choice but to tell the police what you saw and heard the night my stepfather was killed."

The Englishman inclined his head. "Thank you for saying that."

"You and I have always had a special relationship. I would hate to think my stupidity destroyed that bond between us."

"There is no chance of that, Miss Laura."

"Then I hope you'll stay on at Lost Creek?"

He bowed his head, once again the perfect butler. "If that's what you want, I would like that very much. It's no secret that I've come to regard this house as my home."

"And I couldn't imagine it without you." Then, setting her purse on the kitchen table, she sat down. "Now that that's settled, why don't I come straight to the point? You know that I'm investigating J.B.'s death, don't you?"

He smiled. "Sheriff Wilson told me. He said you were being more stubborn than a Hill Country mule."

"You tell him he hasn't seen me kick yet." Reaching into her purse, she pulled out a small notebook and a silver Cross pen. "Would you mind answering a few questions?"

"Not at all."

"Good." She paused. "Did J.B. ever mention the possibility of selling the *Sentinel*?"

"Not that I recall. Although I'm certain this is something he would have discussed with you rather than me."

"I suppose so." She tapped her pen against the notebook. "What about visitors? I know the police already questioned you extensively about that, but could you repeat it for my benefit?"

"Of course. Other than you, Sheriff Wilson, who stopped by occasionally, and Mr. Ted, I've seen no one here in recent weeks. Mr. Lawson spent most of his time out on the range with his men or working on the wells."

"What about the day he died? Did you happen to overhear a phone conversation by any chance? Or catch the name of the caller? Or callers?"

If the suggestion that he may have eavesdropped offended him, he didn't show it. "No. As you know, Mr. Lawson attended the MediaTech luncheon that day. He did not return until four-thirty."

"Four-thirty? Why so late?"

"I don't know. When he got back, he went into

his study as always and I went to prepare his dinner." He tapped his lip. "I do remember the phone ringing a few minutes later, however, but by the time I reached the kitchen extension, Mr. Lawson had already answered it."

"So you don't know who called."

He shook his head. "I'm afraid not. I hung up as soon as I heard Mr. Lawson say 'hello.' "

"What happened after that?"

"Nothing out of the ordinary. Mr. Ted was in Dallas that evening and you were working late, so I served Mr. Lawson's dinner in the study at seven o'clock."

"What was he doing?"

Lenox frowned in concentration. "Standing at the window. He seemed distracted. I asked him if he had enjoyed the luncheon and he said he had. Then, he said something rather peculiar."

"What's that?"

"He said, 'Things have finally come full circle, Lenox.' "

Laura wrote down the sentence. "Did he say what he meant by that?"

"No. I lingered a little while longer, in case he felt like talking, as he often did, but when it became obvious he wanted to be alone, I left. I must have put his remark out of my mind because I didn't remember it until just now."

"Did you talk to him again after that?"

"I went back to the study at eight o'clock to pick up his dinner tray. He was reading and told me he didn't need anything else and that I could retire if

I wanted to. That was . . ." He cleared his throat. "That was the last time I saw Mr. Lawson alive."

The cold hollow inside Laura's stomach grew colder. "You were more fortunate than I was. I didn't see him at all that day."

Lenox didn't seem to have heard her. "If only I had stayed up instead of going to bed . . ."

"What happened is not your fault, Lenox. I'm convinced that whoever came here that night fully intended to kill J.B. Whether it was premeditated murder or a last-minute decision I don't know, but the intention was there. You might have delayed the outcome, but you couldn't have prevented it."

She made another entry in her pad before she looked up again. "What was the first sound that woke you up, Lenox?"

Although the question clearly made him uncomfortable, since it meant implicating Shirley, he answered it without flinching. "A woman crying. Sobbing actually. I jumped out of bed, threw on a robe, and ran to the study where the cries had come from. When I opened the door, I saw Miss Langfield kneeling in front of Mr. Lawson's chair. She was holding him in her arms. She was crying and talking at the same time. She kept repeating she was sorry and begging him to forgive her."

"But you didn't hear her say anything about stabbing him?"

"No. I told the police that."

Laura nodded. "Did you hear anything else prior to those cries? Footsteps? A door closing? The sound of a car?"

"No, Miss Laura." His eyes grew apologetic. "I'm sorry."

She made another entry in her notebook. "Can you remember anything else, Lenox? A small detail you may have forgotten to mention to the police?"

"Not at the moment."

She stood up. "All right, but if you do, will you let me know?"

"Of course." He walked with her to the door. "Please be careful, Miss Laura. I know you're anxious to catch the person who killed Mr. Lawson, but perhaps you ought to leave that task to the police. Investigating a murder is not . . ."

Although he stopped himself in time, she guessed what he had been about to say. Charming though he was, Lenox was from the old school. He firmly believed that certain professions were best handled by men. "Is not women's work?" she finished for him.

His cheeks colored slightly. "I didn't mean any disrespect."

"I know, Lenox." She smiled. "And you needn't worry. I'm not a rooky. I know what I'm doing." Impulsively, she leaned over and kissed his cheek. "But if it'll make you feel better, yes, I intend to be very careful."

That evening at dinner, Laura told Ted about Hensen Publications's attempts to buy into the *Sentinel*. She did not, however, mention Carl Hensen's substantial contributions to Malcolm's campaign. She wanted to ease into that slowly and carefully.

"Can't you do anything to stop him?" He picked

up his wineglass but didn't drink from it. He just twirled it between his fingers as he talked. "Like finding a loophole that will prevent Leo and Johnny from selling?"

"I've already called an attorney I know and faxed him a copy of the agreement of sale. It's airtight. There's nothing we can do."

"I don't understand. Why would J.B. sign a contract that did not include a stockholder's agreement, knowing how he felt about the *Sentinel*?"

"There was no contract as such. J.B. made a straight sale. The agreement all three signed only outlined the price they had agreed to and the method of payment." She unfolded her napkin. "J.B. was a great newsman and he had a big heart, but he wasn't much of a businessman. He was the first to admit it."

Lenox brought a steaming tuna casserole to the table but Laura only put a spoonful on her plate. The lively dinners she had enjoyed so much in the past were now hurdles she somehow managed to get through night after night.

Ted remained thoughtful. "What puzzles me is why a man like Carl Hansen, who can buy any paper in the country, would suddenly be interested in the *Sentinel*?" He put his glass down and began to eat. "What do you know about the guy anyway?"

Laura shrugged. "Just what I read in the papers. He started his publishing empire in 1961 after inheriting the *San Francisco Sun* from his father. Five years ago, he was found guilty of mismanaging pension funds and spent three months in prison. There's even been a rumor or two that he may be connected to organized crime."

"That might make his connection to J.B.'s murder more believable, but why would he want to kill him? I've never even heard J.B. mention his name, have you?"

"Once or twice, but never as if he knew him personally."

"Then why this sudden interest in the *Sentinel*?"

Maybe now was as good a time as any to tell him the rest of what she knew. "It may be related to your uncle." Watching him closely, she told him about Hansen's two-hundred-thousand-dollar contribution to Malcolm's campaign.

At the implication that a member of his family might be connected to J.B.'s death, even indirectly, Ted's gaze cooled. "Are you saying my uncle is being controlled by the Mafia?"

"No," she said cautiously. "All I said was that Carl Hansen *may* be connected to organized crime. It's possible that he has designs on Malcolm without Malcolm even knowing about it."

"Where does the *Sentinel* fit in?"

"Buying into the *Sentinel* would be a way for Hansen to stop me from investigating Malcolm's campaign funds."

"But how? Even if Hansen gets his hands on Leo and Johnny's shares, you'd still be the majority shareholder. You'd still be free to write whatever you want."

"Not if he puts pressure on me to stop the investigation by turning my employees against me."

"He couldn't do that. They adore you. Every one of them."

"That was before, when the *Sentinel* was showing a profit and when their future was assured. It's differnt now. And it's because of me, because of my determination to go after Malcolm that the paper is in such trouble. Hansen would be quick to point that out to them. He would tell them that if they don't do something, they'll all be out of a job. That's what he did with the *Phoenix Star.* Days after he had acquired a small portion of the newspaper, two of the *Star*'s oldest board members were forced to resign and sell him their shares."

Ted was watching her intently, a worried line across his brows. "So how do you propose to stop him?"

While she sipped her wine, she told him about the two weeks she had bought for herself, and for the *Sentinel.* "If I can prove that Malcolm is profiting from illegal favors he did in the past or that he is taking money from a crime syndicate, an exclusive in the *Sentinel* would assure us millions of sales."

"Would it bring you back the advertisers you lost?"

"Most likely. No one would want to be associated with Malcolm Kandall anymore."

Ted refilled their glasses. "I'd like to help," he said casually. "I'm not sure how, but if you need me for anything, I'm here."

It was the first indication he had given her that he might be extending his stay indefinitely. The thought pleased her although she wasn't entirely sure why. Maybe she was just getting used to having him here. "Are you sure you want to be involved in this? Your family might frown on your sudden allegiance to the *Sentinel.*"

"Sandra is the only family member I wouldn't want to hurt. And I don't think she'd mind one bit if I helped you expose my uncle, provided of course he's guilty." He took another sip of his wine. "As for my father, I don't really care what he thinks anymore."

The sharpness of his tone startled her. He didn't sound at all as he had the night of the exhibition, when he had talked about growing up with his father. Something had happened between then and now. She was sure of it.

"Thanks for the offer." She tried to smile, hoping her light tone would improve his mood. "I usually work alone but in your case, I might make an exception."

She wasn't sure he had heard her.

Enzio Scarpati was at home, enjoying a cup of his morning espresso and watching joggers run through Central Park, when his phone rang at seven A.M.

He listened intently as the caller talked. When he was finished, he said, "Are you sure they aren't bullshitting you?"

"Positive. I had a banker friend of mine make some inquiries. Apparently J.B. Lawson was heavily indebted and there are certain formalities the heirs have to go through before any new transactions can be made. It shouldn't take more than a couple of weeks to straighten everything out."

"What if Laura Spencer gets wind of what you're trying to do?"

"She won't. Leo Brunnel and Johnny O'Toole gave me their word they wouldn't tell her until I say it's okay. I have no reason not to trust them, Enzio. Those two guys are anxious to sell. They're nearing sixty and scared they'll be out of a job soon." He chuckled. "The last thing they want to do is screw up this opportunity."

"All right, Carl. Let me know what happens."

After he had hung up, Enzio took his cup to the server and refilled it. His decision to ask Carl Hansen to buy into the *Sentinel* had been a stroke of genius. With him at the helm, and he had no doubt that he would soon be, not only would Laura Spencer be out of the picture, but Malcolm would now have both Austin newspapers on his side.

The two-week delay bothered him, though. It could be a trick, a bid for time while Laura continued her investigation. But Hansen was as sharp as a tack when it came to newspaper people. If he said Laura Spencer didn't know anything, he had to trust him.

Satisfied that everything was going according to plans, he downed his espresso and went in to get ready for his morning jog.

21

"There must be more than a million cars in this city," Ted said after Laura finally got around to telling him about the suspicious dark sedan she had seen at the cemetery. "Surely you must remember more about this particular one, other than its being black and having a Texas Rangers decal on the rear bumper."

The impatience in his voice almost earned him a biting reply. Just because J.B. had left him part of the *Sentinel* didn't give him the right to boss her around. One look at his face, however, at the deep crease between his brows and the restless look in those otherwise cool blue eyes, made her realize that his outburst had stemmed not from impatience toward her, but from a deep sense of frustration at their lack of progress—an emotion she understood all too well.

They sat in her office at the *Sentinel,* drinking coffee. Outside in the newsroom, with more than half the staff covering various stories, the pace was relatively slow. "The man behind the wheel had black hair," Laura said, wishing she'd remember more.

"That's all?"

"Sorry. Not everyone has your great eye for detail."

"How did you survive as a crime reporter?"

She tapped her temple. "Powers of deduction, my dear Watson. It's a gift some of us are fortunate to have. Mine has never failed me."

Irritation made way for a smile. "Okay, Sherlock. How do you propose to catch your stalker if you know nothing about him?"

"What makes you think he was stalking me? Maybe *you're* the one he's after." She sipped her coffee. "Some jealous husband perhaps?"

"I don't mess around with married women."

"Well then, he could have been a shy mourner. Or one of those weirdos who like to hang around cemeteries."

It drove him crazy that she didn't seem to take the incident seriously. "He could also be a vicious killer. Someone hired by that Hansen guy maybe."

"Isn't that reaching a bit?"

"Maybe it is. The truth is we don't know. And until we do, I'm not going to let you take any chances. From now on, you and I are a team. Wherever you go, I go."

A light danced in her eyes, the first Ted had seen since J.B.'s death. "Is that your big brother syndrome kicking in again?"

"Something like that." It was easier than to admit he was beginning to care an awful lot about her. Maybe too much. "After all, I told J.B. I'd keep an eye on you. I take my promises seriously."

"That was two weeks ago. And if I recall, it was

only a temporary assignment. Until my fiancé arrived."

"You no longer have a fiancé," he said gruffly. "So like it or not, you're stuck with me."

He had been expecting a flat refusal. She surprised him by shrugging. "All right. I guess there's no harm in you and I working together. Just as long as you remember who is Holmes and who is Watson."

Very early the following morning, while Ted and the ranch foreman were at a cattle auction, Laura showered quickly, threw on a pair of faded blue jeans and an old UT sweatshirt, and walked down soundlessly to J.B.'s study. For some reason, she could think more clearly here than anywhere else in the house, perhaps because she and J.B. had spent so much time in this room while laying out plans to reorganize the paper.

Except for the absence of the old leather chair, which had been sent to the upholsterer, and the antique hunting knife, which the police had taken as evidence, the room looked the same—cozy and masculine.

This time, Laura didn't allow the memories to intrude as they had so often during the past week. Instead, she pulled up a chair, sat down, and laid her yellow pad down on the desk, studying the sentence she had jotted down the other day in the kitchen.

"Things have finally come full circle, Lenox."

What had J.B. meant by that? she wondered as she underlined the sentence. How could it be connected to Carl Hansen when J.B. hardly knew him? And why had J.B. returned from the luncheon so late? Where had he gone between one-thirty, the time the function had ended, and four-thirty?

She tapped the end of her pencil against her lip. Maybe someone close to J.B. would know. But who? He must have been acquainted with dozens of people at that event. Which one should she call first?

Next to her pad was J.B.'s address book, which she had taken from his desk the day of the funeral. Leafing through it, she stopped at Elliot Fitzpatrick's name. Elliot was an old friend of J.B.'s and the owner of KYZZ radio. For the past five years he had been the chairman of the MediaTech conference. Laura didn't know whether or not he could help her but it was worth a try.

After a warm greeting, Elliot's wife put her through right away. "How are you, Laura?" he asked when he came on the line.

"Better. Thanks for your donation to the heart foundation, Elliot. It was very generous of you."

"You're welcome, although I would have gladly given ten times that much to have J.B. still with us."

"I know." She paused. "Elliot, I was hoping you could help me with something."

"Of course. What is it?"

"Lenox tells me that on the day of the Media-Tech luncheon, J.B. didn't return to Lost Creek until four-thirty. Did he go somewhere afterward? Either with you or with someone else he knew?"

"Not me. But I did see him with Barbara Kandall. The two of them were in the lobby. Barbara looked sick as a dog. I asked J.B. if he needed help, but he said he didn't.''

"Do you know where they went?''

"I had the impression he was taking her home.''

"Did you speak to him after that?''

Elliot sighed. "No. Those were the last words J.B. spoke to me.''

She thanked him and hung up, more puzzled than ever. Taking Barbara Kandall home because she was ill was exactly the sort of incident J.B. would have mentioned to Lenox in a casual conversation. Instead, he had made that strange remark about things coming full circle—*finally* coming full circle—and had left it at that.

Could he have been thinking about something related to Barbara Kandall? It was possible. After all they had been friends for a long time. They knew a lot of the same people, and still saw each other from time to time, in spite of Malcolm's disapproval.

After another few seconds of reflexion, she tore the yellow sheet from her pad, crumpled it, and threw it in the wastebasket. If she wanted answers to her questions, there was only one way to get them. Picking up the telephone, she dialed the Kandalls' residence.

"Thank you for seeing me on such short notice,'' Laura said as Barbara Kandall led her into an elegant rose and ivory living room filled with priceless antiques. "I know how busy you are these days.''

"Please sit down, Laura.'' Barbara indicated a

stunning set of gilded Regency chairs by a window overlooking Lake Austin. "You said this had to do with J.B.?" Although her smile was friendly, there was a guarded look in her eyes, and she seemed paler than she had been at J.B.'s funeral.

"Yes." Laura gazed at her steadily. "I'm investigating his murder."

"Investigating . . . ? But I thought . . ."

"That's all right, Barbara. You can say it. You thought the murderer was already in custody."

"Are you saying the police let your mother go?"

"No. She's still in jail. What I'm saying," Laura added, aware it was beginning to sound like an old refrain, "is that she didn't kill J.B. And the only way I'm going to prove it is by finding out who did."

"I see." Barbara moistened her lips. "What does that have to do with me?"

Laura glanced at the woman's tightly clasped hands. Was she always this nervous? Or was Laura's presence making her uncomfortable? "I'm trying to reconstruct the last hours before J.B.'s death, and I'm hoping you can help me."

"I don't see how."

Laura leaned forward, intent on catching every clue available through the woman's body language. "I understand you and J.B. left the Palmer Auditorium together after the MediaTech luncheon."

"Who told you that?"

"Someone who saw you together." Was it her imagination or had Barbara's face turned paler? "Did he take you directly home?" she probed.

"Did he make a phone call in the car? Or receive one?"

Barbara's hand moved to her throat and played with a diamond hanging from a thin gold chain. She looked elegant and cool in a jade pantsuit that emphasized her green eyes, but beneath the ladylike poise Laura sensed a great deal of tension.

"I'm afraid I wasn't very observant that day, Laura. You see, I had come down with the flu earlier and the only reason I was able to get through the morning session was because I was heavily medicated. By the time we sat down to lunch, the medication had worn off. J.B., observant as usual, realized I was sick and graciously offered to drive me home."

"Surely you remember if he stopped somewhere."

Barbara's smile was apologetic. "I don't. I fell asleep before we even left the garage and didn't wake up until hours later—in my bed. By then, J.B. was long gone." Her eyes filled with tears. "I'm sorry I can't be more helpful, Laura. I loved J.B. dearly, and if there was something I could do to bring his killer to justice, I would do it." She glanced at a grandfather clock as it bonged softly, then at her watch.

Taking her cue, Laura stood up. "I know you would. Thanks again for seeing me, Barbara."

Their steps echoed through the foyer as they walked across the magestic black-and-white marble floor. "Please let me know if you remember anything else."

"Of course."

In the Mustang, which was parked next to a black Corvette, Laura stole a quick glance at Barbara, still standing under the portico.

She's hiding something, Laura thought, watching her go back inside and close the door. But what? And more importantly, how can I get it out of her?

Her thoughts were interrupted by the ring of her car phone.

"What the hell do you think you're doing?" Ted barked at her when she answered. "I thought we had an understanding. You don't go anywhere without me."

"I know, but this couldn't wait, Ted."

"Where are you?"

"At your uncle's house. I came to see Barbara."

Her reply seemed to throw him. "Barbara? Why? What does she have to do with anything?"

She waited for a shiny cream Bentley to go by before pulling onto Scenic Drive. "I'll tell you when I get home."

"When will that be?"

"You're getting to be a royal pain, you know that?"

"Get used to it. And answer the damned question."

This time the impatience in his voice brought on a smile. Until now, she had found his protectiveness mildly irritating. She wasn't accustomed to having people question her comings and goings, and she had no patience whatsover for worriers.

These last few days with Ted had changed her completely. There was something homey and comforting about having someone fuss about her, wanting to keep her safe, calling to find out when she was coming home.

With an inward smile, she pressed on the accelerator. "I'm on my way now."

Ted was sitting on the paddock fence, waiting for her, when Laura arrived at Lost Creek an hour later. After a morning at the auction house, he looked sweaty and scruffy—but strangely appealing. J.B.'s old Stetson was pushed back on his head and a blade of grass was stuck between his teeth. He smiled as he watched her approach.

"About time you got here."

She hooked the heel of her shoe on the lower rung of the fence. I didn't know I was being timed."

Ignoring the remark, he asked, "So what's this about you and Barbara?"

After she had told him what had prompted her visit to the Kandalls' house, he jumped down from the fence, his face thoughtful. "I can't imagine she would purposely withhold vital information from you. Especially considering the way she felt about J.B."

"I don't pretend to know her as well as you do, but she was hiding something, Ted. I'm sure of it."

Ted turned toward the pasture where the longhorns were still grazing, oblivious of the changes that had taken place during the last several days. "When I was growing up, Barbara was the only relative I felt comfortable with. She's the one who encouraged me to follow my dream." A small smile tugged at the corner of his mouth. "No one knew that. It was a little secret we shared."

"She sounds like a nice lady."

"She is, but she changed. I guess it was right about the time my mother died. She became more distant. She wouldn't answer my phone calls from England after I moved there. Or my letters. It wasn't until I wrote to invite her to attend my first exhibition in London that she finally called—to say she wasn't coming."

Laura could sense Ted's sadness. There was so much for his family to be proud of. Instead they treated him like an outcast. "What do you think changed her?"

He shrugged. "Maybe Malcolm. You can't live with someone for all those years and not start looking at life, and people, the same way they do." Casually, maybe even unconsciously, he draped an arm around her shoulders as they started walking back toward the house. "Do you want me to talk to her? I can't guarantee I'll get better results than you did, but you never know."

Laura shook her head. "I don't think that's the answer, Ted. She'll think we're ganging up on her and will resent you for it. I don't want to make things worse for you."

"Then what do you suggest?"

She met his gaze. "I'm going to tell Amos and Quentin that J.B. drove Barbara home the afternoon of his death. If she won't talk to me, she'll be forced to talk to them."

He stopped walking and gently but firmly turned her around to face him. "Why the serious face? Did you think I would object?"

"The thought crossed my mind. She is your aunt, and you obviously have deep feelings about her."

"J.B. was my best friend. I would never stand in the way of an investigation, even if it meant causing a problem for Barbara. So stop worrying about me and my very strange family, okay?"

She smiled. "Okay."

He kissed the tip of her nose. "If you give me ten minutes to shower and change, I'll take you to see Amos."

Startled by the unexpected, brotherly kiss, she gazed into his eyes. "Do I have a choice?"

"Nope."

Her lips curved as she watched him run the short distance to the front door. What would it be like, she wondered, to have him around all the time? To work with him, side by side, day after day? It wasn't totally inconceivable. After all, he now owned part of the *Sentinel.* And he had made no mention of his leaving any time soon.

Irritated at the direction her thoughts were taking, she tried to shake them off. What was she doing? Why was she getting herself all worked up over something that would never happen? Ted was as likely to give up his vagabond life as she was to fly to the moon.

Unexpectedly, her mother's words of a few days ago echoed in her head. *"You're not falling for him, are you?"*

She couldn't be. Not so soon after Stuart. Not after she had sworn to never fall in love again, to never trust another man as long as she lived.

It's because of J.B.'s death, she thought. It's

brought us closer together. We're friends. Nothing more.

Then why was she standing here with this knot in her throat at the mere thought that he might be leaving soon? Would she be feeling this way if Ted were just a friend?

Pushing these thoughts aside, she walked over to the Mustang to wait for him.

"As if this case wasn't complicated enough," Amos muttered after Laura had finished describing her visit to Barbara. "Now we have the wife of the gubernatorial candidate smack in the middle of it. The D.A. is going to love this."

"The D.A. is going to love what?"

As Amos looked up, Laura turned her head. Stuart stood in the doorway, one inquiring eyebrow raised. Impeccable as always, he wore a light gray suit over an ivory silk shirt and carried a black alligator briefcase.

Although Laura no longer had any feelings for him, except contempt, she couldn't help noticing that he looked better than he had in months. The limelight becomes him, she thought, wondering why she had never noticed that about him before. He absolutely thrives in it.

Forcing herself to stay neutral, she listened as Amos briefed Stuart about the object of Ted and Laura's visit. At the mention of Barbara Kandall's name, Stuart's face turned crimson.

"What the hell are you trying to do?" he bellowed, slamming the door and walking threateningly toward Laura. "Sabotage my case?"

Before Laura could reply, Ted sprung from his chair, blocking Stuart's path. "You don't have a case, pal. Not until all the clues have been investigated."

Stuart threw him a murderous look. "I don't need any clues. I've got enough evidence right now to get a conviction."

"You have *circumstantial* evidence. Not proof. And no matter how badly you want to win this case, you can't ignore a potentially important eyewitness."

Without taking his eyes off Ted, Stuart said, "Give us a minute, will you, Sheriff? I want to talk to Ted alone."

Taking Laura's arm, Amos ushered her out of the room.

Stuart waited until the door had closed before speaking again. "Listen to me closely, Ted, because I won't repeat this. If you think I'm going to let a punk like you ruin this case for me so you can impress my ex-fiancée, you're crazier than I thought."

Ted took a threatening step forward. It took all his willpower not to grab that pompous ass by the collar and throw him out in the street. "This isn't about you and me, counselor. It's about justice."

"Bull. You've been after Laura since the first day you arrived. It didn't matter to you that she was engaged to be married. Or that she couldn't stand the sight of you. That huge ego of yours wouldn't let you take no for an answer."

"Don't give me any of that ego shit. And don't talk as if I am the reason you and Laura split up.

We all know who did the splitting and why, don't we, Fleming?"

"I'm not going to stand here and discuss my private life with you. But I'll tell you this. You *will* stop meddling in my case immediately. Or this time, so help me God, I'll throw you in jail."

Glad that he had gotten Stuart properly riled up, Ted leaned against Amos's desk and folded his arms. "Why? Are you afraid Laura and I will come up with the real killer?"

"I *have* the real killer. She's in custody."

"If you're so sure of that, why won't you question my aunt? See what she can remember about that afternoon?"

"I'm not about to embarrass myself, and my office, by interrogating a woman of Barbara Kandall's stature about an incident that has no bearing whatsoever on the murder."

"Why don't you say the truth, Stuart? We're alone now. You aren't pushing this investigation because Shirley Langfield is the one you want convicted."

When Stuart's cheeks flamed up again, Ted knew he had guessed right. "You think this case will make you a hero, don't you? You think this will finally be your ticket to fame, to the recognition you think you so richly deserve."

"You're full of shit. You always were." His sneer turned into an ugly grimace. "Well, those days are over, *pal,*" he added, mimicking Ted's sarcastic tone of a moment ago. "I'm running this show now. If you don't like it, you can pack up and go back to England."

"That's a real grown-up remark, Stuart."

"I'll say it again. Stay out of my case."

Shaking his head, Ted watched as Stuart stalked out of the office. God, he hated snobs.

Rather than wait for Ted and Stuart to end their confrontation, Laura decided to walk over to the county jail and spend a few minutes with her mother. But as she came out of the sheriff's office, she saw that more than two hundred people had lined up along Northington Street.

"What's going on?" she asked a woman next to her.

"Malcolm Kandall is filming a commercial." The woman raised herself on tiptoes. "Right here in Burnet. Isn't that exciting?"

Although Laura had better things to do than to watch a man she despised preen in front of a camera, her reporter's curiosity got the best of her. As she approached the cordonned-off area, she saw Malcolm make his way through the throng of people.

He walked slowly, favoring his bad leg. But the people hardly noticed. As usual, he was playing them like a violin, smiling affably, shaking hands, and kissing babies. Just behind him, a film crew followed his tracks.

"Good to see you," he said, nodding at random. "How are you? Thanks for coming."

To a volunteer wearing a "Kandall Cares" straw hat, he pointed a friendly finger. "You're looking great. Keep up the good work."

As someone behind Laura moved to get a better

look, she was suddenly propelled forward, into Malcolm Kandall's direct line of vision.

Their eyes met, and held. She caught a momentary look of surprise in the handsome blue eyes; then, as if someone had touched him with a magic wand, the old charismatic smile was back in place, and he moved on.

Taking advantage of a break in the crowd, Laura turned to leave and bumped into a man behind her.

"I'm sorry," she murmured. As she looked up, her heart lurched in her chest.

The man was short and wiry. His hair was black and pulled back into a slick ponytail. His features, although attractive, were thin and angular, the cheekbones high and prominent. Small, dark eyes that were unusually bright stared at her with a cold, dispassionate expression.

A shiver passed through her.

It was the man she had seen at the cemetery.

2 2

In the time it took her to recover from the shock, the man had disappeared into the crowd.

She pushed after him. Now that he had confirmed her suspicions by running away, she was more determined than ever to find out who he was and what he wanted with her. "Excuse me," she said as she struggled through the sea of people. "Please let me go. Excuse me."

But when she reached Riddel Park, the man was nowhere in sight. She looked around her, puzzled and frustrated. How could a man move so fast? And disappear so quickly?

She returned to the parking lot in back of the sheriff's office, where Ted had left her car. Her legs still shaky from the sudden encounter, she stood beside the Mustang as her gaze swept across the lot. Questions for which she had no answers spun inside her head. Who was this man? What did he want with her? And the most important question of all: Was he in any way connected to J.B.'s murder?

"Laura!"

She whipped around and saw Ted running toward her.

"What are you doing here? Amos said you went to visit your mother."

Still breathing hard, she gripped his arm. "I saw him again, Ted."

"Who?"

"The man from the cemetery. He was right here. In Burnet Square."

"Are you sure?"

She nodded. "Yes. I didn't think I had seen enough of him to give a description, but I must have because I recognized him instantly." She told him how she had bumped into him and then had lost him."

"That was a dumb thing to do, Laura. What were you going to do once you caught him? Wrestle him to the ground?"

"I don't know," she snapped. "I didn't stop to think, all right? I saw. I reacted."

"That's exactly what scares me about you, Sherlock." Then, taking her arm, he escorted her back into the sheriff's office.

"The hair is perfect," Laura said, leaning to study the sketch. "But his jaw was more angular, the cheekbones more jutting. And his eyes were shinier, like two little chunks of black coal."

With a few strokes of his charcoal pen, the police artist made the appropriate changes.

"That's it." Instinctively, Laura backed away as she had moments earlier when she had found herself face to face with her stalker. "That's him."

Sheriff Wilson, who had been quietly watching, shook his head. "I don't remember seeing him

around here. But I'll check throughout the county.
If he came to town before J.B.'s murder, and I
can find him, I'll bring him in for questioning." He
nodded to the artist. "Run me several copies, will
you, Gary?"

"And one for me," Laura said.

Amos threw her a suspicious look. "What are
you going to do with it?"

Her wide, innocent look had Ted fighting to keep
a straight face. "I want to show it to my staff," she
replied. "I want everyone to be on the alert in case
he decides to show up at the *Sentinel.*"

"If he does, you just call me, okay? Do not, I
repeat, do not try to apprehend this man on your
own. Do I make myself clear?"

"Perfectly." When the artist returned, Laura
deftly plucked a copy of the composite from the
stack in his hand. "Thanks, officer."

Although the young man seemed delighted to
oblige Laura, Amos's expression remained watchful. He knew how she operated. Once she had
made up her mind about something, nothing could
stop her. And while he was the first to admit she
was gutsy, smart, and no doubt competent, she was
still a civilian. And civilians who meddle in police
business were a pain in the ass. He didn't need that
kind of trouble. Not with the heat he was already
taking from the D.A.

"Why, that's Enrico!"

Her eyes wide with astonishment, the *Sentinel*'s
receptionist glanced from the charcoal drawing to
Laura.

"Enrico?"

"Enrico Garcia. He's a fashion designer from L.A. He was here oh ... a couple of weeks ago." Angela's fingers toyed with the scarf around her neck. "He gave me this."

Laura glanced at the scarf, a red-and-white geometric design, then back at Angela. "Is he a friend of yours?"

"Oh, no, nothing like that, Miss Spencer." Her cheeks colored slightly. "Actually he's a client of yours. At least, I think he is. He stopped here one day and said he was opening a chain of boutiques and wanted to advertise in our newspaper. So I sent him up to see Mr. Malloy."

The fashion designer. Of course. Laura had meant to check back with Ken about him but things had moved so fast after that, it had completely slipped her mind.

Angela cast a worried glance toward the sketch. "What's wrong with him? Is he a criminal or something?"

"That's what I'm trying to find out." Laura reached for the phone on Angela's desk and dialed Ken's extension. "Ken, what's the story on that L.A. fashion designer you mentioned a couple of weeks ago?" she asked when the advertising director came on the line. "Did the deal with him ever go through?"

Ken's tone was bitter. "I never heard from that jerk again. He gave me some phony business card with a nonexistant Los Angeles address and phone number on it. When I called L.A. information, I was told there was no listing for Garcia Creations *or* Enrico Garcia."

Laura's face remained expressionless. "Thank you, Ken." She handed the phone back to Angela, glancing once again at the scarf around her neck. It didn't take a genius to figure that Garcia, or whatever his name was, had come here under false pretenses and pumped an innocent receptionist for information.

"What else can you tell me about this man, Angela?"

"Well, he ..." Angela's eyes filled with embarrassment. "He took me out to dinner—to show his appreciation for sending him to see Mr. Malloy."

"Did you tell him that was your job?"

"I tried. He wouldn't take no for an answer. He was so friendly and seemed so harmless that when he suggested I meet him at this restaurant near the airport, I said okay."

"Why near the airport?"

"He said he had to fly back to L.A. that same evening."

"I see. What did you talk about?"

"Fashion. The L.A. scene." Under Laura's watchful gaze, her cheeks turned crimson again. "We also talked about you."

Laura had already figured that much. "What about J.B.? Did you talk about him?"

"A little, but not much."

"Go on."

Angela coiled the telephone cord around her finger. "It all seemed so innocent. He told me about his work, and I told him about mine. And when he threw in a question about the *Sentinel* every now and then, or about you, I didn't think anything of it." She was close to tears. "I guess I should have. I'm sorry, Miss Spencer. Real sorry."

Some of Laura's anger dissipated. Angela was just a kid. Nineteen at the most. Certainly no match for a smooth operator like this Enrico Garcia. "Did you tell him where I lived?" she asked in a softer tone.

Looking miserable, Angela nodded.

It must have been him outside her house that night, Laura reflected. The thought he may have been inside as well, going through her things while she slept, made her shiver again.

Seeing a tear roll down Angela's cheek, Laura took pity on her and patted her hand. "All right. Don't cry."

Angela looked up. "You're not going to fire me?"

"No, I'm not going to fire you. You've done a good job here, Angela. But the next time someone wants information on this company, or on any of the people who work here, you send them to me, okay?"

Angela bobbed her head in agreement. "Yes, Miss Spencer. Thank you, Miss Spencer."

Laura walked back to the grouping of chairs at the other side of the lobby, where Ted was waiting for her.

As she approached, he put the unlit cigarette he had been rolling between his fingers in his pocket and stood up. "What's the matter with your receptionist? Why is she so upset?"

Laura told him about Enrico Garcia's visit to the *Sentinel* and how he had used Angela to get information. "It's obvious he didn't leave for L.A. as he wanted her to believe," she said when she was finished, "but went back to where he was staying— probably at a hotel near the airport."

"We could check the phone book. Austin is a small airport. How many hotels can there be in that vicinity?"

Laura's eyes gleamed. "Ted, I like the way you think."

He watched her as she picked up a phone book on an end table and flipped through the yellow pages. When she reached the hotel listing, she ran a finger down a short, straight line. "Three motels, all just off I–35. That shouldn't be too difficult."

In a gesture that was as familiar as it was seductive, she flipped one side of her hair behind her shoulder and dialed a number, winking at him just before going into her routine.

"Good afternoon," she said affably. "My colleague was supposed to contact me as soon as he checked in and I haven't heard from him. Can you tell me if he arrived yet? His name is Enrico Garcia." She waited a few seconds while the desk clerk checked her computer. "Not registered?" she said, feigning surprise. "That's odd. Yes, I will check with another hotel. Thank you."

"Well done," Ted said after she had hung up. "You remind me of a papparazzi I know. He got himself into Buckingham Palace one morning and went as far as the queen's dressing room before he was caught."

"How did he get past all that security?"

"The same way you just did—with a bluff and a smile."

"We all do what we have to do, I guess." She repeated her routine with the other motels, then, after receiving a negative answer from both, she let out a sigh of frustration and hung up. "Damn."

"He could have registered under a different name," Ted suggested.

"That's true." She tapped a finger against her lip. "In which case I'm stuck, unless of course, I show the police sketch to hotel employees."

"You do remember that that's exactly what Amos warned you not to do."

"On the other hand," she said, pretending she hadn't heard him. "Flashing that drawing around could be risky. If Enrico finds out we're looking for him, he could pull another disappearing act." She glanced at her watch. "I didn't see a black car following us into Austin, did you?"

"No . . ."

"Which means he could be at his hotel. If he is, so will his car."

"What good will that do you? You don't know the make, remember?"

"But how many black sedans with a Texas Rangers decal on the rear bumper can there be in those three parking lots?"

Ted grinned. "If we're lucky, only one."

"Then what are we waiting for?" She tossed the phone book on the table and stood up. Let's go catch ourselves a stalker."

                    *   *   *

While Ted and Laura were driving toward the airport, Tony Cordero paced his motel room. From time to time, he took a sip of his beer from the bottle he had taken from the six-pack on the bureau.

Letting that broad see him had been a big mistake. But when she had walked toward Malcolm Kandall in Burnet, his stomach had done a somersault. What if she decided to do something crazy? Like shoot him? It wouldn't be the first time something like that happened.

So he had followed her a little closer than usual, ready to pounce on her if he had to. The next thing he knew, she was staring right into his eyes. Lucky for him he had quick reflexes. And fast legs.

Still, she had seen his face well enough for a description, which meant he should lay low for a while. No more tailing her until he was sure he was in the clear. He might even have to start wearing that disguise he brought with him.

The problem was Enzio. The boss didn't like it when his people screwed up. And this was a major screwup.

Well, Enzio didn't have to know. All Tony had to do was keep his mouth shut, pretend he was still tailing the woman, and report to the boss as he had been doing.

Satisfied he had every angle covered, he took one last swig of his beer and set the bottle on the dresser. The fine dinner he had planned on having this evening would have to wait. Until the heat was off, he would have to content himself with a quick bite at the joint next door.

2 3

After driving around the parking lot of two motels with no result, Ted and Laura found what they were looking for at the Blue Moon Motel just off Airport Boulevard.

"That's it!" Laura said excitedly, pointing at a black Toyota. "There's the decal."

The Blue Moon was a one-story, run-down motel that boasted a swimming pool, cable television in every room, and an early-bird special at the adjoining restaurant for $5.95.

As Ted parked the Mustang several spaces from the Toyota, Laura was already dialing Amos's office on her car phone.

"Sheriff Wilson, please," she asked when a deputy answered.

"Sheriff Wilson isn't here."

"Do you have a number where I can reach him? This is an emergency."

"What kind of emergency?"

She gave him her name, told him where she was, and how her receptionist had identified her stalker as one Enrico Garcia. "I also found out that he arrived in Austin four days *before* J.B.'s murder."

"So?"

"So," she replied testily. "Sheriff Wilson said he would have the man picked up and brought in for questioning as soon as he was located. I've located him. Right here at the Blue Moon Motel. All you have to do—"

"I don't know anything about picking up a stalker," the deputy replied in a lazy Texas twang. "Sheriff should be back soon, though. I'll tell him you called."

"Thanks." She slammed the phone down. "For nothing."

"What's wrong?" Ted asked.

"Amos's deputy, that's what's wrong. He's the D.A.'s cousin. And not about to lift one finger to help me clear my mother."

Before Ted could reply, Laura gripped his arm. "There he is!"

Ted followed her gaze. A thin, well-dressed man in his late twenties stood outside Room 123, tugging lightly at his cuff as he looked cautiously around him.

"Get down." Ted ducked, dragging her with him.

"What are you doing?" she asked, struggling to get free. "Why aren't we grabbing him?"

"Because," Ted said, holding her down. "He'll be much more useful to us if he doesn't know we're on to him." As he talked, he grabbed the Nikon from the back seat. Fortunately, shooting while trying to keep out of sight was something he'd had a lot of practice with over the years. His finger on the shutter, he took a half-dozen shots before straightening up.

"You can come up now," he told Laura as Garcia walked away from them.

She threw him a murderous look. "Why didn't you break my arm while you were at it?"

"Sorry. There was no time to be gentle."

Laura massaged her wrist. "Where is he going?"

"To have his early-bird special, I imagine." He watched the man disappear inside the restaurant.

"Good." She glanced in the rearview mirror and rearranged her hair. "That will give me time to search his room, find out where he comes from, and what he's up to."

"Are you crazy? That's breaking and entering."

She unbuckled her seat belt. "Just entering. I don't intend to break anything."

"How will you get in?"

With the flick of a finger, she extracted a credit card from her purse. "With an old and reliable standby."

Ted fell back against his seat. "Oh, don't make me laugh. You don't really expect to open a door with a credit card, do you?"

"Have you ever tried it?"

"No, but—"

"Then don't knock it. The truth is, it does work. And unless the management installed dead bolts on all the doors, which I'm sure it didn't, looking at this place, the lock should be a cinch."

Ted wasn't convinced. "I don't like it. What if Garcia comes back unexpectedly? Or if someone sees you messing around with the door?"

"Give the horn three light taps. It will be my cue to take cover."

He glanced uneasily around the deserted parking lot. "Have you ever done this before?"

"Once or twice. There's nothing to it."

"A moment ago, you were concerned about flashing a police sketch. Now you're about to break into a motel room. What happened in between Laura? What did I miss?"

"Amos's uncooperative deputy, that's what happened."

"You realize we could end up in jail."

"Do you have a better idea on how to get the lowdown on Enrico Garcia?"

He didn't. Their call for help had been ignored and the Austin police were not likely to respond to a complaint as vague as "a possible stalker."

"I guess not." He glanced back toward the restaurant. "But be quick, will you?"

Trying not to show her nervousness, she wiggled her ten fingers in front of his nose. "As quick as these babies will let me."

As she started to open the door, Ted took her shoulders, leaned over, and kissed her. This time, it was no brotherly kiss. His touch was as gentle and tender as a whisper, and, for a moment, she almost kissed him back. Then, as if she had touched fire, she pulled back. "What was that for?"

His eyes had that half-amused, half-serious look she had come to know so well. "Luck."

"Oh." Then, ignoring the pounding in her heart, she stepped out of the car and walked in long, purposeful strides toward Room 123.

On the way, she passed a young man in dark pants and a white shirt. A name tag on his breast pocket identified him as the night clerk. Worried he might later remember her, she lowered her head, but he barely glanced at her as he walked by. She waited until he had disappeared into the lobby before stopping in front of Enrico's room.

Although she was an old pro at entering premises, her hand shook when she inserted the small plastic card between the lock and the door frame. If the desk clerk came back and saw her tampering with the door, he would undoubtedly want to know what the problem was.

After a few manipulations, the latch bolt slid back.

Heaving a small sigh of relief, she let herself in and closed the door behind her. It was an ordinary room with a double bed, a dresser, and a television set on a rotating stand.

She started with the dresser first. Being careful not to disturb the neat arrangement of socks and underwear, she conducted a quick, thorough search. She found nothing of interest.

In the closet, she counted three suits, two sports jackets, and two pairs of slacks, all of excellent quality. Other than a pack of spearmint gum and a half-dozen handkerchiefs, all the pockets were empty. The labels, however, from a Manhattan tailor by the name of Ernesto Farentino, gave Laura her first clue that Enrico Garcia might not be everything he claimed to be.

She was going through the last pair of slacks when she heard the sound of approaching footsteps. Turning her head, she saw the shadow of a man stop in front of the draped window.

She held her breath. Had Enrico come back without Ted seeing him?

As her gaze shot around the room in search of a place to hide, the man bent his head and cupped his hands, as if lighting a cigarette, then moved on.

Laura let out a long sigh. Then, without wasting another second, she pulled out the single suitcase from the closet, put one knee on the floor, and unzipped it. Scattered on the bottom were an assortment of silk scarves with the Garcia Creations label on it, a thick gray wig, scuffed work boots and blue overalls—not at all what a spiffy dresser like Enrico Garcia would wear.

Obviously, the man had felt it necessary to bring a disguise with him.

Buried beneath the wig, was an airline ticket issued by a Manhattan travel agency. Enrico's name was printed at the top.

The bathroom revealed nothing of interest— toothpaste, a toothbrush, a hair dryer, shaving items, and a manicure kit. No aftershave. That was an interesting detail, Laura thought. Expensive clothes, a manicure kit, but no aftershave. Or cologne. It didn't fit.

Satisfied there was nothing else to find, she opened the door, glanced in both directions, then hurried back toward the Mustang.

"Well?" Ted said, when she had slid into the passenger seat.

"At first glance, our man seems to be exactly what he claims—a Los Angeles fashion designer by the name of Enrico Garcia. However, his airline ticket was purchased in New York and the labels

in his suits all say Ernesto Farentino—Tailor for
Men—New York."

"So he's not from L.A."

"If he is, he goes an awfully long way for his
clothes *and* his travel arrangements." She picked
up the phone.

"Who are you calling?"

"Homicide detective Joe DiVecchio. He and I
worked on several cases together." As she spoke,
she dialed the New York number, leaving the receiver in place so Ted could hear the conversation
on the speaker.

"Well, I'll be damned," the policeman said, when
the desk sergeant transferred the call. "If it isn't
Slick Laurie."

"How are you, Joe?"

"Lousy. Donna finally made good on her threat
and put me on a low-fat diet. I'm eating enough
green to exfoliate a farm. But she's happy. And
so is my doctor. How about you, kid? Won any
rodeos yet?"

"When I do, you'll be the first to know."

DiVecchio's voice turned serious. "I was sorry to
hear about your stepfather. Did you get my card?"

"Yes. Thanks." After a short pause, Laura told
him about Enrico Garcia and what she knew about
him. "I need an ID, Joe. And I need it fast."

"I'll see what I can do. Fax me a copy of the
composite so I can run it through our computer. If
the guy has no record, I should be able to track
him down through that tailor."

"Thanks, Joe."

She disconnected the call. "We can fax him the

sketch from the *Sentinel*," she told Ted as he put the car in gear. "Hopefully we'll know something about Garcia soon. Meanwhile I'll try Amos again."

"Why don't you let me do that?" Ted suggested. "If he's not there, I might be able to put a little pressure on that lazy deputy of his."

Amos was there. And he was not in a good mood. "Have you two completely lost your mind?" he barked. "Or are you determined to have me fired?"

"We tried to call you, Amos."

"Aw, you're just as bad as she is. I ought to teach you both a lesson and throw you in the can for B and E and for interfering with police business."

"Come on, Amos. We located the guy. Don't you want him?"

There was a short pause. "So who the hell is he?"

Ted told him how the *Sentinel*'s receptionist had recognized Enrico from the sketch, and placed him in Austin four days before J.B.'s murder. He also told him about the disguise in the man's suitcase. "I took a couple of good photographs of him, too. I'll stop by the *Sentinel* to develop them before I bring them over."

Amos was much calmer. "Is he in his room now?" he asked.

"No. He's having dinner at the restaurant next to the motel, a place called the Bull's Eye. He's been there since about six-thirty."

"I'm waiting for an arrest warrant," Amos said. "As soon as I get it, I'll be on my way."

Fifteen minutes after Laura had faxed Joe Di-Vecchio the sketch from the *Sentinel*, the police sergeant called back.

"Your Enrico Garcia is as phony as a three-dollar bill," he told Laura. His real name is Tony Cordero—a very mean hombre, who, for the last eight years, has been Enzio Scarpati's right-hand man."

"Scarpati as in the New York crime boss?" Laura asked.

"The one and the same. Cordero is a low-key kind of guy. You don't hear much about him, but he's slick. He used to hang around Tompkins Square with a tough street gang years ago, then he came to work for Scarpati and within a few years, became his number-one man."

"What does he do for him exactly?"

"Officially he manages Scarpati's nightclub downtown Manhattan. Unofficially, he handles a number of tasks from mayhem to murder, although, like everything else connected with Scarpati, we've never been able to prove it. The man is dangerous, Laura," he said again. "He also uses several aliases and can transform himself into anything—a GI, an affluent businessman—even a clergyman."

"What is he doing in Austin?"

"Beats me. I wasn't aware Scarpati ran an operation in the Southwest."

"Do you know of any connection between

Scarpati and a West Coast publisher by the name of Carl Hansen?"

"Nope. But that doesn't mean one doesn't exist. Isn't Hansen suspected of having underworld connections?"

"That's what I hear." Laura's fingers drummed impatiently against the desk surface. She didn't like puzzles. Especially ones with so many pieces missing.

"Thanks a lot, Joe. I'll call you if I need additional info. Give my love to Donna."

"Don't mess with this guy, Laura," DiVecchio warned. "I swear he'll make you regret it."

2 4

It was ten after seven by the time Tony returned from the restaurant. The dinner hadn't done much to lift his spirits. The steak had been overdone and the potatoes soggy. Only the wine, a rich cabernet, had made the meal passable.

As he closed the door behind him, his nostrils twitched. Then he sneezed. Not once, or twice, but four times. Standing just inside the door, he scanned the room. There was only one thing capable of triggering such a reaction on his part. Perfume. Which was why he only dated women who didn't wear any.

Someone wearing perfume had been in this room between the time he had left it, forty minutes ago, and now. He could still smell it: a subtle, vaguely familiar scent a less observant man would have missed.

Seeing nothing disturbed, he walked briskly to the closet, pulled out his suitcase, and unzipped it. The items he had left there, the scarves, the wig and clothes and his airline ticket were still there.

A thief would have taken the scarves and the ticket. And his clothes. If theft was excluded, then who had come into his room? And why?

Crossing to the bedside table, he dialed the front desk.

"This is Mr. Garcia in Room 123," he said, making no effort to disguise the irritation in his voice. "Did someone come in here between six-thirty and seven-ten this evening? A maid? A maintenance man?"

The desk clerk was immediately on the defensive. "No, sir. Most of our staff has already left for the day. Is there a problem? Is anything missing?"

"I don't know yet. But I do know that someone was here."

"I can assure you—"

"Did you see anyone *near* my room?"

"No, sir." There was a pause. "Except for that woman, now that I think of it."

Tony tensed. "What woman?"

"I had just returned from my dinner shift when I saw her, a little after six-thirty. I assumed she was a guest—"

"What did she look like?"

"Pretty. Long red hair." He cleared his throat. "If valuables are missing—"

"I'll let you know." Then, without bothering to thank the man for his help, Tony slammed the phone down.

Laura Spencer. That was her perfume he had smelled, the same perfume he had noticed in her house each time he had searched it, although it hadn't affected him as violently then.

The bitch had found him. She had sat in her car until the coast was clear and then sneaked into his room. She must have searched it, which meant she

294 Christiane Heggan

had found the wig. And the airline ticket, with the name of the New York City travel agency.

You're slipping, Tony. You're making mistakes you never used to make.

But if she had found the wig and the ticket, why hadn't she stuck around and confronted him? Or called the cops? What the hell was she waiting for?

Muttering under his breath, he sprang from the bed. He wasn't accomplishing anything by driving himself crazy with questions he couldn't answer. He had to get out of here.

Yanking clothes from the closet, he started throwing them into the suitcase, forcing his mind to think in some kind of orderly fashion. His first priority was to find another place to stay—something as far from here as possible.

The second priority was just as important.

Laura Spencer had to die.

Ted and Laura had been back at Lost Creek for a couple of hours when Sheriff Wilson's call came through. He sounded tired.

"Your guy must have gotten tipped off somehow," he said when Ted answered. "He was gone by the time my men got to the Blue Moon."

Ted's face turned grim. "I don't suppose he left a forwarding address."

"Nothing. Not even a fingerprint. He wiped the place clean, paid his bill in cash, and disappeared."

"Well, at least we had time to run an ID on him." Ted told him what they had learned from Joe DiVecchio.

At the other end, Amos let out a long, frustrated

sigh. Ted felt sorry for him. He doubted that in all his years as a county sheriff, the lawman had ever investigated a case with so many twists and turns.

"We'll find him," Amos said at last. "Copies of that sketch are everywhere, in Burnet *and* Travis county. If anybody spots him, we'll hear about it. Until then, you and Laura stay put, you hear? Your Nick and Nora Charles days are over."

Laura couldn't sleep. Even though she felt safe in this big house with two strong men watching over her, the thought that Tony Cordero, a killer and a master of disguise, was running around loose made her feel uneasy.

She tossed the Agatha Christie mystery she had been reading aside and leaned back against the mound of frilly white pillows. No wonder she felt so restless. Murder and mayhem in a small, peaceful English village wasn't exactly the kind of reading that was conducive to a good night's sleep. What she needed was something long and tedious. J.B.'s extensive library should have something appropriate.

She was getting out of bed when she heard a sound outside her door.

As her heart did a somersault, her eyes scanned the room for a weapon. The carousel music box on the dresser seemed to be the only possibility. She tiptoed to the dresser. The music box was too flimsy to do much harm, but she picked it up anyway. Any weapon was better than none.

The gentle rap at her door nearly made her jump out of her skin.

"Laura?"

She closed her eyes and heaved a sigh of relief before throwing the door open. "Damn you, Ted. You scared me half to death."

He could see that. Her beautiful face was as white as the low-cut nightgown she wore. "Sorry. I saw the light under the door and wanted to make sure you were all right." He pulled his gaze from the tantalizing cleavage and glanced at the carousel she still held. "What were you going to do with that?"

Her hand trembling, she put the music box back on the dresser. "Clobber you, I guess. I thought you were an intruder. What are you doing up anyway? I thought you went to bed hours ago."

"I couldn't sleep, so I decided to make another security check."

She was lovely. With her red hair tumbling over her shoulders, her face free of makeup and that creamy, silky gown skimming over her body, she looked as if she had risen from some long-forgotten Greek temple, a seductress sent back to earth to drive men crazy. He couldn't speak for other men, but she was doing one hell of a job on him.

"And ... does everything check?" she asked in a mildly teasing tone.

"Yes."

The sight of the unmade bed, with the sheets rumpled and the imprint of her body on the mattress, almost made him groan. Under different circumstances, he would have loved nothing more than to erase her fears by tumbling her on that inviting bed and making love to her all night.

He didn't think she would have pushed him away. Not because he thought himself so irresistible, but because he knew he hadn't imagined the attraction between them. Nor had he imagined the way her lips had parted, if only for an instant, when he had kissed her earlier.

But her recent breakup with Stuart had left her scarred and vulnerable and a romance now, however brief, would only complicate matters—for both of them.

"You don't have to worry about a thing," he continued, striving to keep his tone casual. "The house is tight as a drum, Lenox is sleeping with his Winchester next to his bed, and I'm only two doors down the hall. You're safe." He smiled. "At least from stalkers."

"I feel better already."

The intensity of her gaze as she whispered the words made his throat go dry. The restlessness he saw in those honey-colored eyes had nothing to do with night fears or even killers on the prowl. And she no longer looked fragile as she had a minute ago, not with those sultry eyes, those moist, half-parted lips.

He swallowed. If this was some sort of a test, he was failing miserably. "You think you can sleep now?"

"I can try."

As she continued to gaze at him, he felt his willpower slip away. It wasn't like him to lose control, to feel as if his fate was being decided without him having a say about it. Yet, he felt rooted to the spot, incapable of walking away from her. When he did move, it was to take another step forward. "Maybe you need an incentive."

She gave him that half smile again. "Maybe you're right."

He could smell her perfume. It was that same haunting scent he had noticed that Sunday morning on her porch, the one that reminded him of an English garden. It made him want to touch her, gently, as he would a flower. And taste her. Slowly, his gaze still fastened on her, he raised his hand to her cheek, gently stroking the petal-soft flesh.

The touch sent Laura's heart fluttering. It was impossible to deny the attraction anymore. It had always been there, in a hidden, guilty sort of way. Tonight, that attraction was even more powerful. Tonight, she yearned to feel strong arms around her, to discover the wonders of making love to someone whose passion equaled her own, someone who could make her tremble, as she was trembling now.

His hand slid to the back of her neck and cupped it. He pulled her to him, while his eyes, hot and bold, locked with hers. "Come here."

With a small, catchy sigh, she went to him, head tilted back, heart thundering in her chest. This time the kiss was different, no longer playful. Sinking his hands into her hair, he took her mouth with a reckless, hungry thrust of his tongue.

In silent accord, her lips parted beneath his. She found herself reaching for him, clinging, feeding the hunger with openmouthed kisses that left her gasping and wanting more.

Desire swept over her, making her feel as though

she was melting, liquefying. As she arched against him, his hands moved downward, in a slow, sensual motion that had her fighting for breath. When he cupped her breasts, a moan escaped her. "This is supposed to make me sleepy?"

He nipped at her earlobe. "It's not working?"

She let out a sigh. "Oh, I ... wouldn't say that. Something is definitely ... working."

With deliberate slowness, he slid a finger under the gown's thin strap and slipped it off her shoulder. He did the same with the other strap, holding it with the tip of his finger so it wouldn't fall all the way.

Eyes closed, Laura savored every sensation. His mouth felt like a feather, wispy soft and excrutiatingly exciting as it roamed from her mouth to her throat and to the swell of her breasts. She felt a rush of cool air as the gown slid down from her body, in a slow, silky, lingering caress that almost had her crying out in need.

"This is how I saw you in my thoughts," Ted murmured as he bent to take an erect nipple into his mouth. "This is how I've wanted you, hot and trembling."

He felt her shudder, and understood the need. Gathering her in his arms, he carried her to the bed and laid her down, his mouth pressed to the hollow of her throat.

He had never thought it would be so difficult to keep his own desire under control. He had done it before, dozens of times. It was different with Laura. Each sigh, each ragged breath she let out played havoc with his senses. Her needs became his needs,

her urgency, a delicious aphrodisiac that sent his
blood racing to his groin.

He gazed deep into her eyes. "Are you sure this
is what you want?"

"Yes." She spoke against his mouth. "Oh, yes."

Heat coiled in his belly as her breath brushed
against his face, sweet, hot, intoxicating as hell.
"Show me then. Show me what you want."

Her hands shook as she fumbled with the buttons
of his shirt. In her eagerness to touch him, to have
his flesh against her flesh, she was as clumsy as a
young girl.

The sight of him naked brought a lump to her
throat. He was magnificent—deeply tanned, with
strong, muscular thighs and a flat, hard belly. Her
hands, timid at first, moved to touch him, fingertips
skimming the broad chest, the taut stomach muscles, moving slowly downward.

"You're hard as a rock." She had never said anything as bold as that before, had never felt such
need to hold and caress a man the way she did now.

She knew what pleasure could do, how it could
dull the mind and ignite the body, turning it into a
mass of sensations. But she didn't know it could be
like this, that wherever she touched him a pulse
would beat, a nerve would respond, heat would
burst.

She rolled on top of him, her long hair falling to
one side like a thick curtain. The position allowed
him to feast on her breasts, and feast he did, closing
his mouth over the tight buds, moving from one
breast to the other, tongue darting, hands molding.

Laura felt her desire crest, like an enormous approaching wave that was rolling slowly, gathering in strength. Inside her, the pressure built to a pitch. Her body was slick with sweat now, just on the edge of losing control. "Now. Please, Ted, now."

In one smooth motion, he rolled her over and covered her body with his. As he drove into her, his hungry mouth found hers again. Then, grasping her thighs, he pulled them high around him and sank deeper.

They moved slowly at first, then with mounting speed. Desperate to take all he could give, Laura clung to him, fingers digging into his back. The heat was unbearable now. She could barely breathe, didn't want to breathe for fear of breaking the spell.

The climax tore into her, so potent, so complete, that for a moment she thought she would faint. When she cried out his name, he reached for her hands, held her arms flat on the bed and buried his face in her hair as his passion was released into her.

It seemed to take forever for her breath to return to normal. When it did, she let out a throaty chuckle and settled her head into the curve of his shoulder. "Now," she said, her lips moving against his damp skin. "I can sleep."

Laura was awakened by a delicious sensation—warm lips nuzzling her earlobe. "Mmm." She stirred. "What are you doing?"

"Trying to satiate my appetite."

She giggled. "I thought you did that last night."

"I guess I just can't get enough of you."

Propping himself on one elbow, he observed her.

With her hair all tousled and that sleepy look in her eyes, she looked like a little girl, soft, sweet, trusting. The latter scared the hell out of him. What exactly was she expecting from him? What if he couldn't give it to her?

"Regrets?" she asked, as though she had read his mind.

He shook his head. "None." That much was true. "You?"

She pursed her lips. "Maybe one."

"Oh?" He raised an eyebrow.

A slow smile curved her lips. "The night wasn't long enough."

He slid his hand around her waist and brought her closer. "We don't have to get up yet."

"Yes, we do. My mother's preliminary hearing is today, remember? And I need time to find her something of mine to wear. Nothing she owns is appropriate. Not for a day in court anyway."

He had forgotten all about the hearing. "Try not to worry," he said, catching the sudden look of anxiety in her eyes. "She's in good hands."

Although he believed that, he wasn't at all sure that the outcome of that preliminary hearing would turn out the way they hoped it would.

2 5

In a motel room in the northern part of the city, Tony stood in front of the bathroom mirror, securing a thick white mustache above his upper lip.

Worried that Laura Spencer might have given the cops a description of the gray wig in his suitcase, he had stopped at a wig shop and bought something entirely different. Then he had made a second stop—this time to an army surplus store where he had bought baggy khaki pants, a faded red shirt, and a hard hat.

Standing back, he admired his handiwork. As always, the transformation was uncanny. With that bushy white wig, the matching mustache, and the work boots that added two inches to his height, his own mother wouldn't recognize him.

The boots were a bit of a problem, but that's because he hadn't worn them in a while. He would get used to them.

With all the construction that was going on in this part of town, he would blend in just fine.

Now all he had to do was go over his plan with meticulous care and then carry it out quickly.

If all went as he expected, he'd be back in New

York by tomorrow afternoon, and in Henrietta's bed by tomorrow night. Leaving Austin, even with his picture being shown on all the networks, shouldn't be a problem. Luigi, who had more connections than AT&T was taking care of that little detail right now.

Getting him not to say anything to Enzio about the Laura Spencer blunder, however, had been another matter. It wasn't until Tony had explained he wanted a chance to talk to the boss face to face that the transplanted Italian had finally agreed. He had even brought him another car, a brown Buick that would allow Tony to tail Laura Spencer and Ted Kandall without being spotted.

Walking over to the bed, he opened the Austin map that had come with the Buick, spread it out on the bed, and studied it carefully.

After he had memorized the route he would be taking later today, he folded the map and tossed it in his suitcase. Because today was Shirley Langfield's preliminary hearing, he knew where Laura Spencer would be spending most of the day. What he didn't know was how long the hearing would last and where she would be going afterward.

Sitting outside that Burnet County courtroom for hours waiting for the hearing to end would be a real drag, not to mention dangerous. But he had no choice. If he wanted to wrap up this thing today, that's exactly what he had to do.

The Burnet County courthouse was packed when Ted and Laura arrived at ten o'clock that morning. Shirley, dressed in a simple blue suit and a high-collared blouse, was already sitting at the defendant's table with Quentin March.

Stuart, in his glory, now that he had made every newspaper headline in the state, was conferring with his assistant, a young man with curly blond hair and a nervous eye tic. Although he saw her, he didn't acknowledge her.

From the moment he called his first witness, Laura knew her ex-fiancé had prepared his case meticulously. Under Stuart's expert guidance, each witness testified as to what they had seen, heard, and what evidence they had collected. By the time he had finished interrogating the last of Shirley's coworkers at the Golden Parrot, the singer's need for the hundred thousand dollars she had come to borrow from J.B. had been firmly established.

Although Laura's testimony about what she had seen the night of the murder was only a reiteration of what Amos and other witnesses had already testified to, he conducted her examination with a panache that had every eye in that courtroom glued to him.

Quentin, more subdued but just as effective, did an excellent job of outlining the circumstantial evidence, showing Shirley as an innocent woman who had had the misfortune of being at the wrong place at the wrong time.

But in the end, he had been no match for Stuart's staggering evidence.

It had taken the stern-looking judge less than ten minutes to return his decision. Shirley would be bound over for trial. The date had been set for Monday, January 23, 1995.

*   *   *

It'll be different at the trial," Ted said as he, Laura, and Quentin walked toward the parking lot. "Quentin will have more time to prepare his case."

"Ted is right." Quentin, a heavyset man with a deep chest and a patrician nose, walked at a brisk pace, his head held high. "Three months will give me ample time to do all the things I couldn't do in one week."

"What did you find out about Carl Hansen?" Ted asked. "Any chance he's connected to the case?"

"I have a private investigator working on that angle right now. And another one checking Enzio Scarpati. They haven't come up with anything yet, but I'm confident they will." He glanced at Laura. "What about that car your mother saw on the way back from Lost Creek the night of the murder? Have you been able to match it with anyone you know?"

Laura shook her head. "Her description was too vague. I suppose it could be Cordero's Toyota, but she said it was loud, like a race car, so I don't know what to think."

They had reached the attorney's car, a sleek, black Mercedes. "I feel as though I should remember something important and can't," Laura said, almost thinking out loud. "It's right on the edge of my mind."

Ted gave her a quick, sharp look. "Is it about the car?"

"I don't know, but it's right there. I can almost

touch it. Something I should know. Something I *do* know."

"You're pushing too hard," Quentin said, throwing his briefcase in the back seat. "The mind is a funny thing. Like people, you've got to give it a little space once in a while."

Arms around each other, Ted and Laura watched the attorney drive away.

"What now?" Ted asked. "What have you got planned for the rest of the day?"

Laura glanced at her watch. "I have an editorial meeting at four, then another with the financial committee. Needless to say, I dread that one."

"How *is* the financial situation?"

"Grim. Our efforts to draw in big advertisers haven't paid off the way we had hoped."

"You think Malcolm is still applying pressure?"

"I'm sure he is. But I'll be damned if I can prove it." She sighed. "And meanwhile, the clock is ticking."

"You mean with Hansen."

Laura nodded. "I only have ten days left. If I can't make something happen by then, I will probably lose the *Sentinel*."

In the deputy D.A.'s office, where Malcolm had come to congratulate Stuart after Shirley Langfield's preliminary trial, the two men shook hands.

"You did a great job, Mr. Fleming, Malcolm said, grasping the younger man's hands with both of his.

Stuart beamed. "Were you in the courtroom, sir?"

"No. But I practically had a minute-by-minute

account of everything that went on." He watched
the young attorney's chest swell with self-impor-
tance. "I can only hope the actual trial will go just
as well and that justice will be served."

"It will be served, Mr. Kandall. I promise you
that."

Malcolm nodded approvingly. Then, crossing his
arms and leaning against Stuart's desk, he asked,
"Have you ever thought about a career in politics,
Mr. Fleming?"

Stuart's face turned red with excitement. "No,
sir. I can't say that I have."

Malcolm smiled. "You might want to think about
it. We sure could use someone with your talents in
the governor's office." He lowered his voice to an
intimate, conspiratorial whisper. "You win this case
and I can guarantee you any position you want."
He chuckled. "Except mine of course."

As Malcolm left the assistant D.A.'s office a few
minutes later, he knew this visit had been a good
move. There was nothing like the promise of a
golden future to turn an ambitious man into a
shark.

Being careful to obey all traffic laws, Tony followed Ted Kandall's BMW back into Austin at
three o'clock that same afternoon. Once they had
reached the *Sentinel,* Tony parked across the street
and watched as the photographer pulled up in front
of the main entrance.

A few moments later, Laura kissed him on the
cheek, got out of the car, and hurried toward the
Sentinel building.

Tony heaved a sigh of relief.

As Ted drove away, Tony put the Buick back in gear.

He was ready.

After dropping Laura off at the *Sentinel*, Ted drove to a coffee shop near the UT campus where his sister had asked him to meet her.

She was already there, sitting in a booth. "How did the preliminary hearing go?" she asked, noting his troubled expression.

"Pretty much as I expected. Shirley was bound over."

Sandra caught the eye of a waitress and ordered two cappuccinos. "I'm sorry, Ted. How's Laura taking it?"

"She's upset, but she had no false illusions." He removed his sunglasses and laid them on the table. "What's up?"

"Aunt Barbara took me out to lunch yesterday. She looked awful."

"The campaign must be getting to her." Quentin March's recent visit and his intense questioning, although unsuccessful, hadn't done much for her frazzled nerves either.

"I guess you're right." Sandra folded her arms and rested them on the table. "Anyway, she came to talk about you."

The remark surprised him. At the Luberick Gallery where Barbara had stayed only a few minutes, and then later at J.B.'s funeral, she had barely spoken to her. "Regarding what?"

"She wanted to know if your plans about staying

in Austin for only two weeks had changed." She picked up the menu, half pretending to study it. "She also wanted to know if the rumors she'd heard about you were true."

"What rumors?"

A gleam danced in her eyes. "That you and Laura Spencer are an item."

"What concern is that of hers?" he asked gruffly.

Sandra's mouth fell open. "Then it is true." It was more a statement than a question.

"You know how rumors are. You can't believe half of them."

"Don't play games with me, Theodore. I'm too smart for that." Holding the menu against her cheek so no one could eavesdrop on their conversation, she leaned forward. "Are you in love with her? You are, aren't you?"

"I didn't say that." Things were complicated enough without bringing Sandra into the picture. She was an incurable romantic. One slip on his part and she would start hounding him about a wedding date.

"Well, why don't you say it then?" Sandra asked with a touch of impatience in her voice. "What is it about the word you find so repulsive?"

"Maybe I just find it premature."

"No, you don't. I saw the way you looked at Laura that night at the Luberick Gallery. And the way you held her hand during J.B.'s funeral."

"It was a difficult time for both of us."

"It was more than that." She leaned back to allow the waitress to set a foamy cappuccino in front of her. When the girl was gone, Sandra propped both elbows on the table and rested her chin on her hands. "Does Laura feel the same way?"

Her relentlessness made Ted smile. One way or another she was going to get the truth out of him. "You'll have to ask her that yourself."

"You don't *know*?"

"I'm not a mind reader, sis."

Sandra rolled her eyes to the ceiling. "You're not supposed to *read* her mind, Ted. You're supposed to tell her you love her and she'll do the same."

He wished it could be that simple. The truth was he had no idea where he and Laura stood romantically. Yes, he cared about her. A great deal. He just wasn't sure that was enough.

"I hope this isn't another one of your meaningless flings," Sandra continued, determined to keep her thoughts in focus. "I like Laura a lot, and I would love to have her for a sister-in-law." She sighed. "Too bad Aunt Barbara doesn't feel the same way about her."

"What exactly did Barbara say?"

"She said that a romance between you and Laura at this time could only make the situation between you and Daddy worse."

He laughed. "Sandra, the situation between Dad and me *couldn't* be any worse."

"I told her that, but she didn't seem to be listening. She was acting very strange. If I didn't know better, I'd swear she had been drinking."

Ted gazed thoughtfully into his cup and didn't answer. Barbara's behavior the day of his visit had struck him as strange also, although at the time, he had attributed it to a bad case of nerves. Looking back, he wondered if Sandra's suspicions might be true. Barbara wouldn't be the first politician's wife to succumb to the pressures of a rigorous campaign. "What else did she say?"

"She asked me to talk to you, to explain that you were making things difficult for everyone. With the elections so near and the *Sentinel* so openly against Uncle Malcolm, your relationship with its publisher would prove embarrassing for him."

It had finally happened, he thought sadly. After seventeen years, warm, kind, thoughtful Barbara had become as self-absorbed as the rest of the Kandall clan.

"Maybe you could talk to her," Sandra suggested. "Tell her she shouldn't worry."

"I don't see the point—" He was interrupted by the ring of a telephone.

Sandra's eyes widened as he opened the small, black pouch he had been carrying and took out a cellular phone. "When did you get that?"

"This morning." He pushed a button. "Hello?"

"Ted, this is Amos. I wanted you to know that we still haven't located Tony Cordero. He must be holed up somewhere."

"Do you think he went back to New York?"

"Not a chance. All departure points are on alert. We even made a second sketch showing the way he would look with that wig Laura described. Oh, and I talked to his boss."

"Scarpati?"

"Yep. Surprisingly, the man couldn't have been

more cooperative. He told me that Cordero had asked for a couple of weeks off to visit his sister in Florida. He even offered to look for her phone number and call me back when he found it."

"What did he say when you told him Cordero was here in Austin?"

"He sounded shocked. And even more shocked to hear he had been tailing Laura."

"It could be an act."

"I realize that. Which is why, until Cordero is caught, I don't want you to let Laura out of your sight."

"Don't worry about that. Laura is either with me or at the *Sentinel*. She's safe."

"Good. Her mother would skin me alive and feed me to the vultures if anything happened to that girl."

Sandra's eyes were bulging with curiosity when Ted hung up. "What was that all about? Who was on the phone? Is Laura in some kind of danger?"

"I can't talk right now." He downed the rest of his cappuccino, dropped a ten-dollar bill on the table, and stood up. "Have a good day, Goldilocks."

Amos's phone call had made him uneasy. He knew Laura was safe at the *Sentinel*, especially now that every employee had had a chance to see the police sketch. But it wouldn't hurt to check on her anyway.

Laura was at her desk, studying a report of Malcolm Kandall's latest list of campaign contributions when Mildred hurried into her office.

"Ted just called," she said excitedly. "He just found evidence that can clear your mother."

"What?"

Mildred handed Laura a pink memo slip. "He said you should meet him in the parking garage of the Singleton Building right away. He'll be waiting on the third level—in front of the elevator."

"The Singleton Building? That's way up by the Balcones Research Center. What in the world is he doing there?"

"He didn't say. Or if he did, I couldn't understand him. There was a lot of noise in the background and I could only make out half of what he was saying."

"Why didn't you put him through to me?"

"He said there was no time. And then he hung up."

Laura hesitated but only for an instant. She glanced at the slip of paper where Mildred had jotted down the address of the Singleton Building. "I don't have my car with me. Do you mind if I borrow yours?"

"Of course not." Mildred walked over to her desk, retrieved a set of keys from a drawer, and came back with them. "You know my Grand Prix, don't you? It's navy blue. Parked in front."

Five minutes later, Laura was heading north on Mo-Pac Boulevard. "Dear God," she murmured, trying not to let her hopes soar. "Whatever Ted found, let it be something we can use. Let it be something that will clear my mother."

"Ted!" Mildred's bewildered gaze darted from Ted to Laura's empty office, then back to him. "What are you doing here?"

"I came to see Laura." He looked around. "Where is she?"

"She's not here. She left right after your call."

A chill went through him. "What call? What are you talking about?" He was aware that people had stopped working and were looking at him. "What the hell is going on here? *Where is Laura?*"

Mildred stood up, gripping her desk to steady herself. "She went to the Singleton Building to meet you." She had turned white as a sheet. "Oh, my God, Ted. Someone called ... He said he was you ..."

Tony Cordero. "How did she go there?"

"She took my car. A navy Grand Prix." She looked miserable. "There's no phone in it."

Realizing he wouldn't get any more out of Mildred if he kept shouting, he gripped her shoulders. "Calm down. Did she talk to the man herself? Do you know what he said?"

"I took the call ... He said she should meet him in the garage of the Singleton Building—that's north of here, on West Anderson Lane, near the Balcones Research Center. He would be waiting for her on the third level, in front of the elevator. He said he had information about her mother. ..."

Ted was no longer listening. "Call the Austin police," he shouted as he raced across the newsroom. "And tell them to hurry."

The Singleton was a newly constructed eight-story apartment building not too far from the Northcross Mall. How in the world had Ted found a link between this building and J.B.'s murder?

Laura wondered as she turned onto Anderson Lane. And why hadn't he told her about it earlier?

At the garage entrance, she stopped, took a ticket from the automatic dispenser, and waited until the barrier had risen before proceeding.

Because the building wasn't fully occupied yet, the garage was only half full. At the third level, Laura pulled the Grand Prix into an empty slot, then dropping Mildred's keys into her Gucci bag, she got out of the car.

On a wall, a red arrow, with the word ELEVATORS written above it, pointed to the left. Hooking the strap of her purse around her shoulder, Laura hurried toward it.

It was then that she heard the roar of an engine.

2 6

October 28, 1994

A s the woman screamed a shot rang out.
The force of the blow sent Laura reeling
backward against the van. Pain seared through her
and she slid down, stopping only when her rear hit
the cold, hard concrete. Clutching her upper chest,
she felt the hot stickiness of blood and groaned
silently as she thought, oh, no, not again.

Through a fog, she was aware of the sound of running footsteps, of a car door slamming shut, voices . . .

"Miss? Miss? Can you hear me?" Someone lifted
her head, cradled it gently. "Oh, God, Emma, go
get help, quick. She's losing a lot of blood . . ."

Laura didn't hear the rest. As the pain receded,
so did consciousness. With a sigh, she closed her
eyes and let herself be enveloped by the darkness.

Those damned shoes, Tony thought as he raced
down the ramp. They were slowing him down.

Behind him, he could hear the old man shouting
at the woman to go get help. Christ, he hoped
Laura was dead. With those two people there, ob-
structing his vision, he hadn't been able to aim as
well as he would have liked.

There was nothing he could do about it now. He could already hear people running from the elevators.

At last he reached the Buick, which he had left unlocked. Yanking the door open, he jumped behind the wheel. Barely missing crashing into a parked car, he pressed hard on the gas pedal as he careened around a corner, tires squealing.

Suddenly, a police siren sounded and a patrol car, lights blazing, rounded the corner, momentarily blinding him.

"Shit." Tony tried to jam on the brakes but his foot, not used to the heavy shoe, got caught under the pedal, causing him to lose precious seconds.

Frantically, as he felt the car skid out of control, he spun the wheel in a desperate attempt to avoid the concrete wall that was rushing at him.

He never made it.

As a scream of terror rose from his throat, the Buick slammed into the wall. In that fraction of a second before metal met concrete, Tony knew, as sure as the sun would rise tomorrow, that this was one mess he wouldn't be able to get out of.

Ted was halfway across the downstairs lobby when Angela, the *Sentinel*'s receptionist, called his name. "Mrs. Masters is on the phone, Mr. Kandall," she said, handing him the receiver. "She says it's urgent."

Ted nearly tore the phone from her hand. "What is it, Mildred?"

"A Sergeant Sutherland of the Austin police department just called." There was a break in her voice. "Oh, Ted, Laura's been shot."

He had never known the true meaning of blood running cold. He knew it now. "She's not . . ."

"I don't know." Mildred was crying. "They took her to Breckenridge Hospital. Sergeant Sutherland didn't know anything more."

Letting the phone drop on the receptionist's desk, Ted sprinted toward his car.

Ted had never been so scared in his entire life. As he raced across town toward Breckenridge Hospital, he kept fighting back the taste of terror that rose in his throat.

This was all his fault, he thought as he shot through a red light. He should have never left her alone. Hadn't Amos said not to let her out of his sight? Why hadn't he taken the advice literally?

At last, the huge medical structure came into view. He pulled in front of the emergency entrance in a screech of tires and jumped out.

"Hey!" an ambulance attendant called out to him. "You can't park there."

Ted tossed him the keys. "Move it."

At the desk, Sergeant Sutherland, a tall, slender man in plain clothes, was waiting for him. After telling him Laura was in surgery, he briefed him about what had happened at the Singleton garage.

"Her attacker is dead," he said in a strong Texas accent. "I'm waiting for an ID—"

"His name is Tony Cordero," Ted said as he watched the double doors that led to the emergency room. "He works for Enzio Scarpati, the New York mob boss."

"You knew the gunman?"

"Not personally. But he's been stalking Laura Spencer for days. Look," he said as a nurse came through the double doors, "why don't you call Sheriff Wilson in Burnet County? I'm sure he'll be glad to fill you in."

Before the policeman could reply, Ted had caught up with the nurse. "I'm Ted Kandall," he said, not the least bit embarrassed that for once in his life, he was pulling rank by using the illustrious family name. "Can you tell me how Laura Spencer is doing? She was brought in half an hour ago. She was shot."

"I'll go check on her condition," the nurse offered.

But when she came back, she could only tell him that Laura was in surgery and the doctor would be out to talk to him as soon as he was finished.

A few minutes later, Mildred, whom he had rudely left behind, arrived. They spent the next hour together, she drinking coffee from a nearby vending machine, he pacing the waiting room floor.

At six o'clock, a doctor in bloodstained greens came out through the swinging doors. He was a small, rotund man with compassionate blue eyes. "Miss Spencer is going to be just fine," he said in a fatherly tone. "She was lucky. The bullet missed her heart and lodged itself in the upper left side of her chest just under her clavicle. We removed it and I'm glad to report that there doesn't seem to be any nerve damage. I expect a full recovery within a month."

Relief flooded him. "When can I see her?"

"As soon as they bring her back from the recovery room. And only for a few minutes. She's going to be groggy from the anesthetic. Rest and sleep are the best things for her right now."

Laura's eyes were closed when Ted and Mildred went in to see her twenty minutes later. Her chest was bandaged and her face was deathly pale. But she was alive.

Behind him, Mildred was crying softly, one hand on his shoulder. Without taking his eyes off Laura, Ted gave it an affectionate squeeze. "She's going to be okay, Mildred."

He didn't want to think what he would have done if she hadn't pulled through. In spite of the lightness he had affected in front of Sandra earlier, Laura Spencer had become as indispensable to him as the air he breathed.

At the sound of muffled, faraway voices, Laura's eyelids fluttered open. She saw a white ceiling, white, antiseptic walls, sunlight filtering through lowered blinds. Although moving seemed to require a monumental effort, she turned her head to the left, where something sharp seemed to be jabbing in her hand. An IV bottle hung from a metal rod.

"What ... ?"

"Hi, Sherlock."

Through a dancing blur, she saw Ted's face bend toward her. He was smiling, but his eyes were filled with concern. "Ted." Her mouth felt as if someone had stuffed it with cotton. "What happened . . . ?" As she started to move, pain shot through her upper chest and made her wince.

"Easy, sweetheart." Ted held her as she fell back against her pillow. "No sudden moves, okay?"

"Okay." She saw Mildred and tried to smile. "Hi."

"Hi, yourself," Mildred said, blotting her teary eyes with a handkerchief. "How do you feel?"

"Shaky. Where am I?"

"Breckenridge Hospital." Ted pulled up chairs for himself and Mildred. "You've been shot. But you're going to be all right."

"Shot." It was all coming back to her now—the telephone call, the race across town, the brown sedan that had come barreling toward her, clearly intending to run her down, and then the gun, pointed at her, exploding. "It wasn't you . . ."

"No. It was Cordero." He took her hand, brought it to his lips, and held it there. "He won't hurt you anymore, darling. He's dead."

"You didn't . . . ?"

He shook his head. "No. Although I would have killed the son of the bitch with my bare hands if I had caught him."

"Then how . . . ?"

"His car skidded out of control as he tore down the ramp and hit a concrete wall. He was killed on impact."

She closed her eyes. "What did he want with me?"

"We don't know yet." He kissed her fingertips

again. "We'll talk about it later, okay, baby?" he added, as she began to drift off again. "Right now, you need to rest. You've lost a lot of blood."

She closed her eyes and smiled dreamily. *Sweetheart, darling, baby.* Those were words of endearment, words he had never said before, not even in the throes of passion. The sound of his voice, too, sounded different. There was a new tenderness to it, a sweetness that almost brought tears to her eyes.

She moistened her dry lips with the tip of her tongue. "I want to go home."

He laughed—a low, relieved chuckle that took off some of the chill inside her. "In due time, Sherlock. Right now you've got to rest. Doctor's orders."

Her lids were getting heavy again. "Mom . . . Don't want her to hear what happened from the guards . . ."

"Amos went to tell her himself. She's okay. You'll be able to call her tomorrow. But only if you rest."

The haze was getting thicker. "You'll stay?"

He kissed her temple. "Try to get rid of me."

Laura was sitting up in bed when Ted arrived early the following morning. He had wanted to spend the night right here in her room, but the floor nurse had convinced him to go home and get some rest.

"You're not going to be of any help to her if you're a wreck in the morning," she had told him in a gruff but gentle voice. "So why don't you go home, Mr. Kandall? If there is any change in her condition, and I don't expect there will be, I'll call you."

Now, under Laura's amused gaze, he walked across the room and handed her the huge bouquet of red roses he had bought at the downstairs flower shop. That was another first for him, and he felt awkward as hell as he extended a rigid arm. "These are for you."

"Oh, Ted, they're beautiful."

"Not as beautiful as you."

It was true. Although she still looked pale, her eyes were much brighter than they had been yesterday, and her glorious red hair had been brushed back to its original sheen.

As he pulled up a chair, he glanced at the brilliant burst of pink lilies on Laura's bedside table. "Very nice. Should I be worried about a possible rival?"

She laughed. "Not unless you feel threatened by older men." She smelled the roses once more before laying them aside. "Betty and Jim Fowley were here earlier. The elderly couple that came to my rescue?"

Ted nodded. "Two remarkable people. The doctor is almost certain that without their quick intervention, you would have bled to death."

"I'd like to do something special for them when all this is over. Like inviting them to a real Texas barbecue—in their honor. We might as well carry on J.B.'s tradition of good food and Western hospitality."

We, she thought as a quick blush rushed to her cheeks. She had said "we" as if she expected them to be together from now on. The thought, although appealing, was unrealistic. Oh, not as far as she was concerned. She didn't have to search too deeply within herself to know she was in love with Ted—completely and unconditionally. Not even the idea of a long-distance relationship between Austin and London gave her a moment's pause. But she was equally certain it wasn't the same with him. He had made it quite clear, without coming right out and telling her, that his career was too precious to give up. For any woman.

Suddenly uncomfortable, she shifted, and immediately regretted it. "Ouch."

"What is it?" Ted jumped up, knocking the chair

over. "Do you hurt? Can I get you anything? The nurse? Something for the pain?"

It spite of her discomfort, Laura smiled. "I'm fine. I just moved too fast, that's all."

"When is the last time you took a pain pill?"

"I'm not taking pain pills anymore. They interfere with my thinking process."

"Who's running this hospital? You or the doctors?"

She tilted a stubborn chin. "I'm not trying to run anything. I just happen to know what's best for me, that's all." Her back firmly cushioned against the pillows, she folded her hands over the crisp, white sheets. "Now, tell me what you learned since yesterday."

He brought the chair he had knocked down upright and sat down again. "Not an awful lot. You'll probably be getting a visit from the Austin PD soon. A Sergeant Sutherland has been investigating the incident and he's going to want to question you."

"What did he find out about Tony Cordero?"

"Nothing we didn't already know. Although I expect that's about to change."

"What do you mean?"

"Sutherland asked Enzio Scarpati to come down to Austin to identify Cordero's body."

"Shouldn't a next of kin do that?"

"Cordero's only next of kin is his sister. A month ago, she left her Florida home and went back to Puerto Rico. The police have been trying to get hold of her but she left no forwarding address."

"And Scarpati agreed to come here?"

"Not only that, but he's even agreed to answer a few routine questions. He's at the police station right now." He smiled. "Along with three bodyguards and two attorneys."

"Good. I'm curious to find out what a New York mob boss's right-hand man could possibly want with me."

"Don't be too optismistic. I don't know much about mafiosos, but a man like Scarpati didn't get where he is today by being truthful to the police. Cooperative maybe—truthful ..." He shook his head. "No way."

"You think he had a contract on me, don't you? And on J.B."

Ted held her right hand in his, stroking it gently with the ball of his thumb. "I don't know what to think anymore. This is getting more bizarre by the minute."

Before Laura could comment, the telephone on her bedside table rang. Ted answered it and handed it to Laura. "It's your mother."

"Oh, my baby!" Shirley cried. "My poor, beautiful darling. How are you? Are you in pain? You have to tell your doctor if you are. Or the nurse. Those people are not mind readers, you know."

"I'm fine, Mom."

"I don't believe it. How can you be fine with a bullet lodged in your chest?"

"The bullet was taken out. Another couple of days and I'll be as good as new."

"This is all Amos's fault," Shirley said, her animosity for the sheriff returning. "If he had protected you the way he was supposed to, none of this would have happened."

"If anybody is at fault, it's me for not listening to Amos. He had warned me not to meddle in police business. I didn't listen."

"Well, at least we no longer have to worry about the gunman. He's dead."

Laura didn't tell her she would have much preferred if he had been caught alive. There was no need to worry her unnecessarily.

"When are you going home, baby?"

"In a few days. I'll stop by to see you first."

"I'd like that. In the meantime make sure you get plenty of sleep." She heaved a sigh worthy of an Academy Award. "Oh, how I wish I could be with you. I feel so helpless in this damn cell."

"You'll be out of there soon, Mom. I promise."

"I don't like the sound of that. You're not still thinking about investigating J.B.'s murder yourself, are you? After what just happened? You would have to be crazy. You almost died, for God's sake—"

Laura closed her eyes and pressed her head back against the pillows. "Mom, will you please calm down?"

"Not until you promise to leave police work to the police. That's what we're paying them for."

"I promise. Good-bye, Mom. I'm hanging up now," she added as Shirley kept babbling away." Rolling her eyes upward, she handed Ted the receiver.

"Tough cookie, your mother." He hung up the phone.

"And bossy. Poor Amos. He must have gotten an earful."

With the gentlest of touches, Ted brushed a strand of red hair back from her forehead. "Do you feel up to telling me what happened?"

"I think so." A shadow he recognized as embarrassment passed through her eyes. "I was so stupid. I should have realized that you would never leave such a message with Mildred without talking to me first, no matter how rushed you were. And you knew I didn't have a car, so how could you expect me to dash halfway across town?"

"Cordero knew what to say to make you react, Laura. I would have done the same thing in your shoes."

"No, you wouldn't." Squeezing her fingers around his hand, she took a deep breath. "He must have been hiding ... waiting for me on the third level."

"You never saw him?"

"Not until he shot me. And even then, I didn't realize it was him. He had white hair." In a voice that had started to shake, she told him about her frantic attempts to get back to Mildred's car, the lunge behind the van, and how she had frozen when she had spotted her attacker behind the column, with the gun pointed at her.

"I always thought I had such terrific reflexes. But I couldn't move. I knew my life depended on what I would do next, and I could not move."

"You've never had a gun pointed at you before either."

That was true. The gunshot wound she had suffered outside that bank in New York had been the result of a stray bullet fired from inside the bank. She hadn't even seen the gunman.

"If only he had come at me like a man, instead of hiding like a coward, I could have taken him."

A grin tugged at Ted's mouth. "Really?"

"Laugh if you want to, but a few years ago, after a rash of late-night muggings in lower Manhattan, the *Herald*'s publisher insisted we all take a self-defense course. Everyone at the paper did, even the men." Her gaze was mildly defiant as she turned to look at him. "I could toss you down like a sack of flour if I wanted to. It has nothing to do with size or even strength. It's all a matter of leverage."

"I'll bear that in mind if you ever decide to get rough with me."

A nurse he hadn't seen before came in, carrying a stainless steel tray. "Time to change your dressing, Miss Spencer."

It was Ted's cue to leave. After kissing Laura, he walked out and went to a pay phone in the lobby to call Amos. Because J.B.'s death and the attempt on Laura's life seemed, at first glance, related, Sergeant Sutherland had agreed to let Amos be present during Scarpati's questioning, and Ted was anxious to know what the mobster had had to say.

With any luck, the mystery would be unraveled soon, but he wasn't holding his breath. Not with a man like Scarpati involved.

It was four o'clock that same afternoon when Sergeant Sutherland, of the Austin police department, came to see Laura. He was a slender man with a strong Texas accent and a sleepy look about him. After the first few questions, however, Laura decided that looks were indeed deceiving.

After she had given him her statement, it was her turn to ask questions. She did so in the same brisk, businesslike manner he had used with her. "What did you find out from Enzio Scarpati, Sergeant?"

"He maintains that he knew nothing about Tony Cordero's plans to come to Austin. As you may already know, Cordero's sister went back to Puerto Rico and we haven't been able to locate her. Mr. Scarpati claims he wasn't aware she had left Florida."

"Did Sheriff Wilson ask Scarpati if he had ever met my stepfather?"

Sutherland closed his black notebook and tucked it in his suit pocket. "Yes. Mr. Scarpati said he hadn't. He swears he's never set foot in Austin prior to today."

"He could be lying."

"He could be. Just as he could be lying about Cordero's travel plans. Unfortunately, we have no way of proving it. It's his word against that of a dead man."

"How did he react when he identified the body?"

"He seemed upset. He said Cordero was a good employee."

"Where is Scarpati now?"

Sutherland sighed. "He wasn't charged with anything. Therefore, I had no choice but to let him return to New York."

"Great."

"I'm sorry, Miss Spencer." He rose. "I know you were hoping he could clear your mother somehow, but until we can prove he's lying, or that he had something to do with the attempt on your life, my hands are tied."

They would never be able to pin anything on him, she thought bitterly. The NYPD had been trying to for years. The man was just too clever.

After he left, Laura thought about her conversation with Sergeant Sutherland as she watched the silent images of what appeared to be a press conference flash on her TV screen.

It wasn't until she realized Stuart was being interviewed that she picked up the remote control on her nightstand and turned on the volume.

". . . Regrettable as the attack on Miss Spencer was," Stuart was saying in a rather pompous tone. "It had nothing to do with J.B. Lawson's murder."

An eager reporter in a second row pushed his way to the front. "Are you aware that your fiancée vowed to find the real killer, Mr. Fleming?"

Stuart's mouth pinched in a thin, cynical smile. "Ex-fiancée. And yes, I'm aware of that statement. I wasn't upset by it if that's what you want to know. Everyone is entitled to their opinion. As far as this office is concerned, this case is open and shut."

Then, with a superior tilt of his head, he thanked the reporters assembled outside his office, and hurried toward the red Porsche.

"You jerk," Laura muttered, shutting the TV off.

"We'll see just how open and shut your case is after I'm finished with it."

Moving cautiously, she reached for the telephone and dialed the *Sentinel.* "Mildred," she said when her secretary answered. "Would you please arrange for someone to bring my personal phone book to the hospital? If I'm going to be stuck in here for a week, I might as well do some work."

28

"Miss Spencer? Can you hear me?"

The voice was male, husky, with a slight, familiar Bronx accent. Because she had only been dozing, Laura opened her eyes without further coaxing. And almost cried out in fear.

Standing at the foot of her bed was Enzio Scarpati.

Although he was a small man, he looked as formidable in person as he did on television. If anything, there seemed to be even more of him to look at—more shine in the black hair, more intensity in the dark eyes, more gold on his fingers. Even the ugly mole on the side of his nose seemed bigger.

"What are you doing here?" Her eyes darted to the door as she tried to sit up. "How did you get past the nurses' station?"

Foolish question. A man like Enzio Scarpati could get through walls if he wanted to.

He slid his hands in his jacket pockets. "No one was there."

She tried not to look afraid, remembering that part of his power was the effect he had on people.

His smile was reassuring, almost fatherly. "I assure you there's nothing for you to be afraid of," he said in that same soft, caressing tone. "I came here to put your mind at ease, not to make you more suspicious."

The silent bell attached to her bed was only a few inches away, and although she could have easily reached it, she ignored it. It wasn't an act of bravado on her part, but rather one of desperation. The case against her mother was growing more hopeless with each passing day. If there was one chance, even a remote one, that Enzio could help set Shirley free, she had to take it.

"What do you want?"

"To apologize for what Tony did to you. It was inexcusable as well as inexplicable, and I deeply regret it."

"But of course you claim no responsibility for it."

"None whatsoever. I don't know you, Miss Spencer. Or your stepfather. And I have never felt threatened by either one of you."

"And if you had, would you have ordered us killed?"

The smile that tugged at the corner of his mouth never reached his eyes. For the first time she realized how truly dangerous he was. "I'm not in the business of killing people, despite what you may have heard."

"Then how do you explain that someone who has been working for you for all these years, someone you knew and trusted, someone I understand was your right-hand man, came to Austin to kill me and you didn't know anything about it?"

Enzio had asked himself that same question. It wasn't until he had talked to Luigi that he had learned the reason for Tony's irrational behavior: Laura Spencer had blown his cover and he had been afraid of the repercussions. The fool. All he would have had to do was tell the truth and this mess could have been avoided. Enzio would have simply brought him back to New York and sent someone else in his place. No big deal. Instead, Tony had chosen to handle the matter himself. And screwed everything up in the process.

"Evidently," he replied, "I didn't know him as well as I thought. It happens."

"To others perhaps, but not to you. I know how meticulous you are when you choose your people. If you weren't, you wouldn't have survived—"

The door swung open and a handsome young man walked in, a broad smile on his face and a bouquet of flowers in his hand. The moment he saw Enzio, the smile faded, and his expression turned stony.

He gave Laura a quick darting gaze, as if to assure himself she was all right. Then, he closed the door. "What the hell are you doing here?" he asked Enzio.

Enzio calmly sized him up. "Who wants to know?"

"The name is Kandall. Ted Kandall."

Enzio's eyes narrowed. So that was Malcolm's world-roving nephew. The black sheep of the family. He wasn't quite what Enzio had expected. Malcolm's description had alluded to a spoiled, whiny, slightly obnoxious rich boy. Ted Kandall seemed to be none of those things. And even more interesting, he didn't appear afraid, or even mildly intimidated.

"I said," Ted repeated. "What are you doing here?"

"Having a civilized conversation with Miss Spencer."

Ted tossed the flowers on a chair. He would have loved to make mincemeat out of that little runt, to beat that greasy face of his to a pulp. The thought alone that he was here, talking to Laura, sent his blood boiling.

Under Enzio's calm, dispassionate gaze, Ted came to stand within inches of the man. "Well you can take your civilities and get the hell out of here. But before you do, let me give you one small piece of advice. Keep your filthy hands and those of your goons away from Laura. Because if anything happens to her, if she gets as much as a splinter in her little toe, I'm coming after you myself, *capish*?"

Enzio held Ted's angry gaze without flinching. The kid had more spunk than he had given him credit for. "You're either very brave or very foolish, Mr. Kandall. But since love may be the reason for your behavior, I'll forgive you, even though I'm not the forgiving type. And yes, I will leave. I was finished anyway."

Turning toward Laura, he gave a short, old-fashioned bow. "Again, you have my most sincere apologies, Miss Spencer."

Then, after one last, cold look at Ted, the mobster moved past him and walked out.

The house looked like a meadow in bloom when Laura returned home from the hospital on Saturday. Flowers were everywhere along with cards, telegrams, and phone messages from well-wishers. There was even an enormous stuffed panda, compliments of the old gang at the *New York Herald.*

"My goodness!" Laura exclaimed as she took in the colorful display. "I wasn't aware I knew so many people."

"There are more flowers in your room, Miss Laura," Lenox said. "And in the library." He smiled, a rare occurrence since J.B. had died. "I even had to put some in the kitchen. I hope you don't mind."

"Not at all." She picked up a card attached to a spectacular arrangement of pink glads, held it up, and read it out loud. " 'Welcome home, Sherlock. If you ever give me a scare like that again, I'll kill you. Ted.' "

She laughed and pressed a hand to his cheek. "What a lovely thing to say, Ted. Thank you."

"You're welcome."

As Laura headed toward the family room, he stopped her. "Oh, no, you don't. The doctor said *bed* rest." He turned her gently toward the staircase. "And that's exactly where you're going."

"But that's silly. Rest is rest, regardless of where you do it."

"Wrong." He gave her rear a friendly pat. "Come on, up you go. Lenox prepared a very special homecoming lunch for you." He winked at the Englishman. "And you know how cranky he gets when he's kept waiting."

Half an hour later, wearing a blue-and-white nightshirt with the Dallas Cowboys logo on the front, Laura was sitting in bed, enjoying the last of Lenox's delicious chocolate mousse while Ted played nursemaid.

When she was finished, he removed her tray and took it to the dresser. "Well, I see that getting shot didn't spoil your appetite. You pigged out as if there were no tomorrow."

"I can't help it. I always turn to food in time of crisis. It calms my nerves."

He came to sit on the edge of her bed and ran the back of his index finger along her throat. "Have you ever considered some other form of nerve-soothing therapy?"

Turning her head, she caught his finger between her teeth and bit it gently. "Such as?"

"Such as . . ." He leaned forward. "This." His mouth took hers in a slow, lingering kiss while his fingers played with the buttons on her nightshirt, undoing them slowly, one by one.

Her breath caught. "Is that another of your—"

"Or this." Bypassing the bandage, which was now much smaller, his mouth trailed down to her breast. With his tongue, he made slow, wet circles around her nipple, then drew a tight, erect bud into his mouth. "You were saying?"

She had no idea. She had lost her train of thought. As his mouth continued its sensual, searing, downward journey, she let herself sink into the mounds of pillows behind her.

"Having trouble concentrating, darling?"

"A little . . ." She was aware of an intense heat in her middle section, of hands gently prying her legs apart. Mildly alarmed, for she had never known that kind of intimacy before, she tried to stop him.

He wouldn't let her. "The doctor said no sudden movement, so please be still, darling. And enjoy."

She tried to protest and found herself gasping for breath as his tongue sent a ripple of pleasure through her entire body. He was teasing her now, nipping gently at the tender skin of her inner thigh while his fingers did wicked, delicious things to her.

When he found her hot, moist flesh, she cried out in astonishment as spark after spark of excitement shot through her. But nothing had prepared her for the sudden jolt of heat as his tongue sank deeper. All inhibition left her as she gripped his shoulders, unable to hold back. Her hips strained against him, moving shamelessly, brazenly, urging him to go on.

"Oh, God." Laura felt the climax rise. Pleasure and sensations exploded, convulsing her body, forcing her to take big gulps of air, until her lungs felt as if they, too, would explode. "Come inside me."

In an instant, Ted had shed his clothes and was bracing his arms on each side of her. He entered her slowly, taking great pains not to hurt her. As the world slowly dissolved around them and their bodies reached a crescendo that was theirs alone, she knew with absolute certainty that she would never be able to belong to anyone but this man.

Ted stood at the window, gazing into the night. From time to time, he took a drag of his cigarette. And he thought.

He had always been so sure of what he wanted

from life. He had laid out each element meticulously, by order of importance—career, family—such as it was—friends, and women.

In sixteen years, the order had never changed. His friends worried about him. They thought that his life, although perfectly structured, needed something more—like a home to come to every night, a loving wife, kids, a dog that dug up the neighbor's flower beds.

But he had no experience of such a home, or how to create one. His youth had been surrounded with parents and relatives who cared more about public opinion than family values. Even his mother, whom he had adored, had always been too busy for him.

The neglect had hurt him at first; but eventually he had learned to accept his parents' inattention to his needs, their long absences from home, the demands of a new campaign, and the chaos that always preceeded an important soiree.

The experience had forced him to become self-sufficient at a very early age. It had also left him with a very low opinion of family life. Certain that he would be no better at raising children than his own father had been, he had turned his back on marriage and commitment, filling the occasional loneliness with meaningless attachments that kept him entertained, if not fulfilled.

Although he was careful to select women whose needs matched his own, occasionally one slipped by him, either accidentally or because she believed she could change him.

Those relationships, which he terminated very

quickly, left him feeling like a heel. And if it were true that he was wasting the best years of life, as his friends claimed, he didn't care. What he had was exactly what he wanted.

Or was it?

Crushing the cigarette in the small ashtray cupped in his hand, he turned to look at Laura. She had changed everything—his philosophy on women, his priorities, and his carefully laid plans. In the space of four short weeks, she had turned his life upside down and there wasn't one damn thing he could do about it.

The thought that someone had hurt her and had tried to kill her, made him want to kill, too. Not quickly and mercifully, but with a pain-inflicting slowness that would have had that bastard begging for mercy.

A groan he couldn't identify as pain or pleasure escaped from Laura's lips. Setting the ashtray on the window ledge, he rushed to her side, touching her gently, warning her not to turn too abruptly.

She opened her eyes, smiled at him in a way that claimed another chunk of the old, defensive armor. "What are you doing up?" she murmured.

"I couldn't sleep."

"Mmm." She stretched slowly, languorously, like a cat. "I was dreaming. At least, I *thought* I was dreaming."

"I hope it was a good dream."

"The best." She coiled her arms around his neck. "You were whispering wonderful things to me."

He laughed. "Was I really?"

Her long, curly lashes fluttered seductively. "You

were saying that I was beautiful, and oh, so desirable."

"You didn't dream that. I said it." He kissed the tip of her nose. "You *are* beautiful. And desirable."

"You said something else after that."

"That you drove me crazy?"

"Mmm. *After* that."

She wasn't going to let him off the hook. And why should she? Hadn't someone told him once that women were suckers for the word "love"? That they could never hear it often enough?

And it wasn't as if he had said it in passing, or in a moment of wild passion. Oh, no, he had said it very clearly. And repeatedly, throughout the night. And with more passion than he had ever believed himself capable of.

He might as well learn to say it often. She would insist on it. He was sure of that. "I believe I said that I loved you."

Her eyes were wide open now. "Did you mean it?"

"What do you think?"

"You sounded like you did. But then again, in the throes of passion, a man will say anything." She raised an eyebrow. "Won't he?"

"Not this man."

A slow smile spread across her face as she pulled him to her. "Say it again."

He almost groaned, but he said it, waiting until his mouth was only a breath away from hers. "I love you. I love you madly, I love you completely. I love you forever."

2 9

"Where do you think you're going?" Bolting to a sitting position, Ted stared as Laura wove a thin leather belt through the loops of her gray slacks.

"You're awake." She gave him a quick smile. "And so cute with your hair all messed up."

He raked his fingers through his hair. "Don't change the subject. Where were you sneaking off to?"

"I wasn't sneaking off. I'm just going to the *Sentinel*." Glancing in the mirror, she pulled the collar of her red silk blouse and arranged it over the lapels of her navy blazer. "Why the stern look? Surely you didn't expect me to sit here day after day, doing nothing but watching soap operas and getting fat on Lenox's cooking, did you?"

"What's wrong with taking it easy for a few days?"

"Taking it easy isn't a luxury I can afford. In case you've forgotten, there are only two days left until my deadline with Leo and Johnny. If I haven't proved that Malcolm is maliciously trying to put me out of business by then along with his motivation, it's all over."

"Your life is more important than the *Sentinel.*"

"My life is not in danger anymore."

"What makes you so sure?"

"The fact that I'm still alive. Believe me if Enzio Scarpati wanted to kill me, he would have already done so." As Ted started to protest again, she stopped him with a kiss. "Instead of giving me a hard time, why don't you come to the office with me? I could use a bright, handsome assistant to help me with my tedious research."

The scowl on his handsome face slowly disappeared. When she kissed him again, he smiled. "I knew you'd take advantage of me sooner or later."

More than a dozen people rushed forward to greet Laura when she and Ted walked into the newsroom an hour and a half later. After assuring everyone she was fine and getting better every day, Laura arranged for a second computer to be brought into her office.

In a few moments, she had shown Ted how to access the Nexus database the newspaper used.

"What are we looking for, exactly?" he asked as an article dating back to January 1994 shot up on the screen.

"Proof that Enzio Scarpati lied when he told Sergeant Sutherland he had never been in Austin prior to last week."

He turned around in his chair and looked up. "I thought you were trying to nail my uncle."

"I am." As he continued to look at her, obviously waiting for an explanation, she added, "I gave this a lot of thought while I was in the hospital, and I'm convinced that J.B.'s murder, the attempt on my life, and what's been happening to the *Sentinel* are all related."

"A few days ago, you weren't sure at all. What made you change your mind?"

"Intuition. And the Carl Hansen connection."

Ted shook his head. "You're on the wrong track, Laura. My uncle is no saint, but he wouldn't touch a man like Scarpati with a ten-foot pole."

"How do you know?"

"Because he's built his entire campaign on law and order and the rights people have to live without fear. To imply that he could be associated with the mob is insane."

"I agree that at first sight it's an unlikely match. An alleged crime boss and a blue-blood politician. But you can't ignore the fact that Malcolm is not just any politician. He's an overly ambitious and, in my opinion, unscrupulous one. And look at all the money he's raised in such a short time," she continued since he remained silent. "Millions more than the incumbent governor. How did he do it?"

"The money flows where the power is, Laura. You know that. Right now Malcolm represents that power. And don't forget that a lot of his supporters were my father's friends. Naturally they would want to show their loyalty to Charles by being generous with Malcolm."

She almost sighed with relief when he took her hand. "I haven't convinced you, have I?"

Her fingers closed over his. "Does that bother you?"

He smiled. "No." Glancing back at the computer

screen, he asked, "You think the answer is in here."

"Hopefully. A man like Scarpati doesn't establish relations within a state capital without going unnoticed. I don't remember reading anything about him since I took over as publisher, but we'll double check anyway." She walked back to her desk. "If we don't find what we're looking for in the ninety-four files, we'll go back to ninety-three."

Sitting in his study, behind the large ebony desk that had belonged to his father, Malcolm glanced up, waving the sheet of stationery his brother had just handed him. "What the hell is this?"

Charles, looking paler than usual, smiled. "A concession speech."

The smile on Charles's lips sent another rush of adrenaline pumping through Malcolm's veins. "I know it's a concession speech. But what the hell am I supposed to do with it?"

"It's always a good idea to know what to say should the unexpected happen. This one happens to be excellent. It was written by my—"

Malcolm crumpled the sheet into a ball and tossed it into the wastebasket by the side of his desk. "There isn't going to be a concession speech. You know damn well that I'm as good as elected. But of course, it would kill you to admit it, wouldn't it?"

Charles briefly closed his eyes. "For God's sake, Malcolm. Don't start with that old refrain again—"

"You know what your problem is? You have no faith in me. You never had."

"That's not true."

"Oh no?" Malcolm squared his shoulders, looking twice as large as his brother. "From the moment I entered politics, you never gave me credit for doing anything right. And even before that, while I was busting my ass for you, running your campaigns and getting you reelected, somebody else always got the accolades. I was just the kid brother you felt you had to keep on out of pity."

"You're wrong. I've told you before, I don't feel pity toward you. Guilt perhaps. And regret, certainly. But not pity. And I do recognize your talents. I always did. As a campaign manager *and* as a politician."

"Then why do you always disagree with my ideas?"

"Not all of them," Charles said in a tired voice. "Just a few. But that's because we have different views. You know I tend to be a bit more liberal than you are."

"Fine thing for a Republican to admit."

"I never kept my feelings a secret."

"And they never kept you from getting elected. Time after time." His tone turned sarcastic. "How did you do it, Charles? Did you take my advice and grease a few pockets after all? Or was it just the old charm that did it?"

Charles's mouth pulled into a faint smile. "You were always more gifted in the charm department than I could ever hope to be."

"Yet you never thought I'd get anywhere, did you? Much less this far. Come on, admit it. You never thought I had enough brains, enough vision, enough determination to become governor of Texas. It must kill you to see how wrong you were, to realize that I'm not only as good as you were, but better."

The smile on Charles's face vanished. "That's all that ever mattered to you, isn't it? To be better than me."

"What's wrong with a little competition between siblings?"

"Nothing, provided that competition doesn't turn into an obsession. Or worse . . . jealousy."

"Jealousy?" Malcolm's tone was deliberately condescending. "Me? Of you? Don't make me laugh."

"Go ahead and laugh. It would be a lot better than arguing." Bracing his hands on the armrests, he pushed himself up. "Good luck tomorrow, Malcolm."

"Thank you."

When Charles was gone, Malcolm, not one to dwell for long over family disagreements, shrugged, reached for the remote control, and turned on the television in search of an update on the attempt on Laura Spencer's life a little over a week ago. He found it on CNN.

"Little progress has been made so far in unraveling the mystery that surrounded the near-fatal attack on *Austin Sentinel*'s publisher, Laura Spencer. In a brief statement given to this network yesterday, Sergeant Paul Sutherland of the Austin police, said that the search for clues would continue. In Iraq today, Sadam Hussein . . ."

No longer listening, Malcolm leaned back in his

chair, his index finger curled around his mouth. The news of Laura Spencer's attack and Tony Cordero's subsequent death had left him stunned and baffled. It wasn't totally inconceivable that Enzio had ordered the hit. But why? Laura was no threat to him. Unless, of course, Enzio knew something Malcolm didn't.

The temptation to call the Capri was almost unbearable. But he fought it. From the very beginning of their association, Enzio had made it clear that Malcolm was not to contact him unless he was contacted first. To disobey those orders now could cost him dearly.

"Malcolm?"

At the sound of his wife's voice, he swiveled around in his chair, clicking off the remote. Barbara stood just inside the door, a puzzled expression on her face.

"What's wrong with Charles? He walked out of here without even saying good-bye."

Malcolm made a dismissive gesture with his hand. "We had a mild disagreement over my schedule. He'll get over it. Don't worry about him."

"But I do worry. He's a sick man, Malcolm. And he has devoted a lot of time and energy to this campaign. The least you could do is show a little compassion."

"Compassion isn't going to get me elected."

"How can you say that? If it weren't for him, for his continued support and the support of his wealthy friends, you may never have gotten this far."

"Thank you, Barbara," he said sarcastically.

"There is nothing like warm encouragement from one's own spouse to give you a lift twenty-four hours before an election."

Barbara's voice softened. "I didn't mean that the way it sounded. You know I believe in you. Just as I believe you'll win tomorrow. I just wish you would be a little more patient with Charles, knowing what he's going through, that's all."

If her presence at the polls tomorrow hadn't been so crucial, he would have told her to go to hell as well. But he couldn't afford a wrong move right now. Since the afternoon of the MediaTech conference, she had kept her word and hadn't touched a drop of alcohol. He wanted to keep it that way. At least through tomorrow.

Rising, he smiled. "You're right, darling. As usual. I'll give Charles time to get home, then I'll call him and apologize." For the first time, he noticed the shirt she held in her hand. "Is that mine?"

"Yes." She unfolded it. "Dolores was in the process of ironing it when she noticed the bloodstain on the cuff." She held the sleeve for him to see. "She washed it in warm water along with the others and the stain must have set."

Malcolm felt as if a jackhammer had hit him in the gut.

It was the shirt he had worn the night of J.B.'s murder.

3 0

Unable to utter a word, Malcolm continued to stare at the shirt. The cuff must have become soiled when he had pried J.B.'s fingers from the knife handle. He had been in such a hurry to get to bed and forget the horrendous events of that night, the thought of checking his clothes as he undressed had never occurred to him.

Barbara was watching him, her expression one of mild concern. "Did you cut yourself that day?"

Malcolm nodded, glad for the excuse she had unwillingly provided. "Yes, I did ... I was shaving."

"With your shirt on?"

"No, of course not." He fought to keep his voice from going shrill. "The cut reopened as I was getting dressed."

His suit! he thought with a jolt. There had to be blood on the sleeve as well. Suddenly, his legs felt as if they had just run a marathon, but he managed to walk around his desk with a semblance of calm. "Get rid of it," he said, with a nonchalant wave of his hand. "It's useless to me if the stain won't come out."

"Let me see the cut," Barbara said, moving closer to him. "I hope you put something on it."

"There's nothing to see. It's practically gone." He had to go check that suit, get rid of it before Dolores, who checked his clothes at regular intervals, had a chance to send it to the cleaners.

"Malcolm, is something wrong—"

"I can't talk now, Barbara," he said as he walked past her. "I have to get ready for my appointment with Senator Babcock." Then, no longer able to conceal his urgency, he hurried out of the study.

In the master bedroom, he went directly to the walk-in closet he shared with Barbara and quickly flipped through his clothes until he found the suit he had worn the night of the Jaycees dinner—a tan herringbone.

His heart almost stopped. The underside of the right cuff was smeared with blood that had dried a dark, purplish color.

Yanking the suit from the hanger, he rolled it into a ball, looking around the room for a temporary hiding place. Tonight, when Barbara was asleep, he would worry about getting rid of it permanently. Maybe he could bury it in the backyard. Or he could sink it in the bottom of the lake. Yes, that was better, much safer. No one would ever find it there.

As he started to reach for a suitcase on the closet's upper shelf, the door opened and Barbara walked in, still holding the shirt.

"What's going on with you, Malcolm? You ran out of the study as if the house was on fire."

"I told you. I have a meeting with Babcock."

"That's not until one-thirty." Her gaze fell on the bundle he held against his chest. "What are you doing with that suit? Did you get blood on the jacket, too?"

Denying it when she could so easily verify the facts herself would have been pointless. "Yes. I . . . I was going to take it to the cleaners."

"Well, for heaven's sake, *you* don't have to take it to the cleaners. Dolores will do that." She held out her hand. "Here, give it to me."

"No." Instinctively, he took a step back. Too late, he realized that step was a mistake.

Barbara, who could, when she wanted to, be more stubborn than a pack of mules, looked at him curiously. "Why are you acting so strange, Malcolm? And why don't you want me to take care of that jacket for you?"

He could have choked her. "What the hell is this? The fucking inquisition? Can't I take care of my own clothes if I want to?"

Slowly, like a woman on a mission, Barbara came to stand in front of him. Her entire demeanor had changed. Her body had stiffened, and her eyes, usually so gentle, now bore into his with a cold determination. "What are you hiding, Malcolm?"

"Nothing—"

"Stop taking me for a fool." Before he could stop her, she had yanked the suit from his arms, discarding the pants. As he stood still, she unrolled the jacket and focused her attention on the right sleeve.

For a few seconds that seemed to stretch into an eternity, she did nothing but stare at the thick red blotch. When she looked up at last, her face had turned a sick shade of gray. "That's a big stain, Malcolm." Her voice was flat, just above a whisper.

He moistened his lips. "Why are you making such a big deal of this? I told you—"

"Because that's the suit you wore the night of the Jaycees dinner, the night J.B. was killed."

"How can you remember what I wore that night in the shape you were in?"

"I don't know, but I remember everything. Vividly. You were upset with me for letting J.B. drive me home. You said he wanted to see you, that you had to know what I had told him so you could deal with him accordingly."

"So?" He tried to make his own voice sound convincing but he knew he was failing. She had already guessed the truth.

"The following morning you told me you never had a chance to talk to him, that it was so late by the time you were finished at the Four Seasons, you had decided to contact him later." She glanced at the bloody sleeve again. "You lied to me, didn't you? And you're lying now, trying to get me to believe that you would wear a soiled jacket all day and then go to an important function wearing that same jacket. You're much too meticulous to do something like that, Malcolm."

"I didn't see it . . ." The words strangled in his throat.

"Somebody in your office had to. Look at it!" she cried, shoving the sleeve in his face. "How can you, or anyone else, miss it?"

She lowered her arm and let the jacket slip from

her hand. "You got that stain later that night, didn't you? When you went to see J.B. After ..." She blinked once. "After you killed him."

There was no point in denying it any longer. The effort was draining him. He should conserve his energy for the next battle—that of convincing her he'd had no choice, that J.B. would have destroyed them both. "Let me explain ..."

The cry that came out of her throat sounded like that of a wounded animal. Her clenched fists flew to her mouth and her eyes filled with horror. She was shaking her head, slowly, repeatedly, as if she couldn't accept what she had already guessed.

He went to her, hoping to calm her down as he had done so many times in the past. But she wouldn't let him. "You killed him!" she cried hysterically, as she took a step back. "You killed J.B.! And you're letting someone else take the bla—"

He slapped her hard. As her hand went to her cheek, she stared at him in disbelief.

"Oh, my God, Barbara, I'm sorry," he said as he rushed to her. "I didn't mean to do that ... I don't know what came over me. You were hysterical ..." He tried to pull her hand away from her cheek. "Let me see—"

She jerked away so hard, he stumbled back. "Don't touch me!" Then, as sobs erupted, she turned from him and ran.

It took him only a few seconds to pull himself together. He had to stop her. In her condition, she was capable of doing anything, including going to the police.

As he ran down the staircase, he kept calling her name, begging her to stop and listen to him.

She didn't. She ran blindly across the foyer, threw the front door open, and disappeared out of sight.

He reached the portico just as she was getting into her SL. "Barbara, for God's sake, stop!"

The Mercedes's door closed with a thud. In two leaps he was beside it, pulling on the handle. It was no use. She had already locked it.

"Barbara, don't do anything stupid. Let's talk." He banged on the window with his fist, his voice threatening one moment, pleading the next. "Please, darling. I swear, you'll understand once I—"

Staring straight ahead, Barbara gunned the engine and took off in a hail of gravel, knocking him to the ground.

Stunned, he watched the car disappear down the driveway.

3 1

It was ten o'clock on Monday evening when Laura, exhausted, pushed away from her computer. After two days spent poring over old articles, gossip columns, and city news, they had found nothing.

"No luck either, huh?" Ted stretched as he stiffled a yawn.

She pressed the bridge of her nose between two fingers. "There is no mention of Scarpati having been in Austin anywhere in those files. Yet I'm willing to bet the farm that he's no stranger to these parts. The Southwest would be a lucrative area for him. More than half the drugs in the United States come across the Texas border. Why wouldn't he want to get a piece of the action?"

"I agree. But how do *you* fit in? Or J.B.?"

"Damned if I know." As Laura started to rise, she saw Nicki Cochran, the foreign desk editor, waving at her frantically.

"What happened?" she asked as she and Ted walked over to Nicki's desk.

The editor, who was on the phone, laid her hand over the mouthpiece. "I'm talking to our London correspondent. A bomb just exploded at 10 Downing Street during an all-night meeting between the prime minister and a spokesperson for the IRA."

"Any casualties?" Ted asked.

"That's what I'm trying to find out." She let out a sigh of exasperation as she slammed the receiver down. "Damn. We got disconnected again. That's the third time." Turning back to her computer screen, she pushed a few keys to get the latest information from the wire, but nothing came up.

Ted had already picked up another extension. "All right if I call Lloyd?" he asked Laura.

"Sure. Put him on the speaker so we can all hear him."

As Ted had expected, Lloyd had heard about the incident and was already up, trying to dispatch one of his photographers to the scene.

"It's one hell of a mess." The voice of the Associated Press editor shook as it came over the speaker. "Three unconfirmed dead and no news about the prime minister *or* the IRA official."

"Anybody called to claim responsibility?"

"Half-a-dozen groups so far. My guess is that the bomb was planted by someone trying to sabotage the peace talks. Within minutes of the blast, every London newspaper received anonymous phone calls warning that similar incidents would be taking place within the next week throughout England and Ireland. You've got to go to Belfast to cover that angle, Ted. Charter a plane if you have to. I don't care how much it costs—"

Ted glanced at Laura, who was watching him

intently. "I can't right now, Lloyd. Maybe in a few days—"

"In a few days it'll be too late. I need you now." There was some static over the line, a buzzing, then it went dead. They had been disconnected.

Ted hung up. When he looked up, Laura was gone.

He found her sitting in the passenger seat of the BMW, her face unreadable. "What's the matter?" he asked, sliding behind the wheel. "Why did you run off like that?"

"Don't you know?"

"I have a pretty good idea, but I'd like to hear it from you."

She closed her eyes, waiting for the thumping of her heart to stop before speaking. "It's not going to work with us, is it, Ted? I mean, we have no future together."

Ted turned around in his seat so he could face her. "I wouldn't exactly say that."

"No?" Her tone was sarcastic. "What *would* you say? Exactly?"

This was the moment he had dreaded, the moment he had refused to think about, hoping it would come far enough into his relationship with Laura not to make any difference. But he had been kidding himself. Laura was not the kind of woman to take half measures now or two months from now. That much he knew.

"You heard what I told Lloyd. I'm not going."

"But you want to go. Badly." She gave him a sad smile. "Admit it, Ted. There is only one thing that will make you truly happy. And that's to do what you've been doing for the last sixteen years. I would have to be blind not to see that."

"I won't deny that I love my work. But I love you, too. More than I've ever loved anyone in my life."

The words, spoken with such sincerity, brought tears to her eyes. But she fought them. She wouldn't cry, dammit. She would not hold him that way. "And I love you. That's why I won't ask you to choose between your career and me. If I did and you chose me, I would always wonder if you did it out of decency. I could never live with that uncertainty, Ted, wondering if you would have been happier the other way around."

He took her chin between his fingers and raised it gently. "There are compromises we could make, you know. One of my best friends in London is a perfect example that a couple doesn't have to live under the same roof three hundred and sixty-five days a year to be happy."

"What about the other couples? Those who don't make it? Are they in the minority or the majority?"

"It's all what you make of it, darling. Some can do it, others can't."

"I won't take the chance that we might fall into the latter group."

He smiled. "I thought you liked taking chances."

She shook her head. "Not with this." An ambulance sped by, sirens wailing. Her gaze followed the blinking red lights until they disappeared. "I would go crazy knowing you were facing danger every minute of the day."

Slowly, he pulled his hand away. "What are you saying?"

"I'm saying that what we had was wonderful—for the time it lasted. I want you to go to Belfast, Ted. I want you to go where you belong."

"I belong with you."

"Not tonight. Not after I saw the look on your face as you talked to Lloyd. Not after I heard the excitement in your voice, sensed the adrenaline pumping through your veins."

He wanted to deny it. He wanted to tell her he loved her too much to give her up, that he was ready to settle down. But under her level gaze, the words remained unspoken. She was right. The call to Lloyd had brought a rush of excitement but also a deep regret that for the first time in sixteen years, he wouldn't be part of the action, that his camera wouldn't be the one to record the images, that he wouldn't be there to make a difference. He felt pulled from both sides, like a contestant in a tug-of-war.

"I won't leave you now," he said stubbornly. "I'll wait and see what happens with the *Sentinel,* then—"

She gave another firm shake of her head. "No. You heard Lloyd. This can't wait. As for the *Sentinel,* your staying won't change its destiny." After a while, she added, "I know a charter pilot in Dallas. I could give him a call when we get home and see if he's in. I'm sure he'll be able to take you wherever you want to go."

It was pointless to argue with her now. He would go to Belfast and call her from there. Maybe, after she'd had time to think, to realize that a part-time relationship was better than no relationship at all, she would change her mind.

He inserted the key into the ignition, put the car in gear, and headed back to Lost Creek.

After trying three different numbers, Laura was finally able to locate Dale Anderson at Dallas/Fort Worth Airport. The pilot had just returned from Orlando, Florida, but as she had predicted, he was willing to fly anywhere.

"You give me a few hours to catch up on my sleep," he told her. "And I'll be ready to take off at eleven o'clock tomorrow morning."

Their lovemaking was different that night. It had an edge to it, a desperation that not even their shattering climax could erase. Later, as Ted held her, Laura could already feel the distance build between them, slowly, irrevocably.

At six A.M., pretending to be asleep so she wouldn't have to face tearful good-byes, she listened to Ted as he got out of bed and went back into his room to pack.

By six-thirty on Tuesday morning, thirteen hours after Barbara had stormed out of the house, Malcolm was frantic.

Thinking she had gone to her mother's house as she often did when she was distraught, he had flown to Houston on Jerry Orbach's Lear, which was available to him day or night. But the house had been dark and silent when he had arrived, and the driveway empty. He had rung the bell for al-

most ten minutes, hoping Barbara was inside, sulk-
ing. Convinced she wasn't, he had come back home
and stayed up as he kept calling Deirdre's house.

Now, as he paced his bedroom, glaring at the
phone and willing it to ring, he felt the panic
mount. Where was she? The polls would open in
less than an hour. The media would be there in
force, expecting to see Barbara at his side. What
the hell was he supposed to tell them?

He hadn't dared to call any of her friends for
fear they would start a rumor that she was missing.
He could do nothing. Except wait.

Laura was awakened by the patter of rain against
the window. With a half smile, she reached over
the other side of the bed, her hand ready to stroke
the strong, hard back. But all she found was a cold,
empty space and with it the painful realization that
Ted was gone.

With a strangled sob, she clutched his pillow
against her chest and buried her face in it. Why did
she have to be so damned noble? Why couldn't she
have asked him to choose, as so many other women
would have done? He would have chosen her. And
she would have made him happy. She would have
made him forget about places like Bosnia, and Ireland and Ruanda. They were other things in life
worth photographing. Some of them were right
here in Texas.

But at the same time, she kept remembering Mildred's words: *"He's got the wanderlust, you know.
He can never stay in any one place for very long."*

He wouldn't have been happy in Burnet. She had done the right thing.

Her movements slow and stiff, she got up and went through her morning rituals in an automated fashion. Somehow, she managed to get showered and dressed. She even managed to get herself to the *Sentinel.* On her desk, a daily calendar was already displaying today's date, Tuesday, November 8, a bleak reminder that in a few hours the fate of the newspaper would be decided.

Trying not to think about Ted, she sat down in front of her computer and went to work.

She was about to take a coffee break when she saw it.

It was a small column on page three of the Friday, May 23, 1993 edition.

"More than two hundred guests attended a fundraising dinner for Mayor Malcolm Kandall last night. The $500 plate event, hosted by Political Action Committee Chairman Jerry Orbach, was held at the Four Seasons Hotel and raised more than a hundred thousand dollars for Mayor Kandall who is seeking a second term."

Below the short paragraph was a snapshot showing a grinning Malcolm standing next to Jerry Orbach. Just behind them, and slightly out of focus, was a man who bore a striking resemblance to Enzio Scarpati.

Laura fell back against her chair. There it was. The connection she had been searching for all these weeks. How could she have overlooked Jerry Orbach? Five years ago, the auto dealer had been implicated in a drug deal with Hidalgo County's corrupt sheriff, Paul Montenegro. Although Orbach was later released for insufficient evidence, many believed he was guilty.

Orbach was the connection, she thought, as she reread the article, not Malcolm Kandall. But how? How could Jerry be in a position to help Enzio Scarpati with his drug operation when he was still being watched by the FBI?

Unless Enzio Scarpati was at that fund-raiser for only one purpose—to meet Malcolm Kandall. Now *that* made more sense.

She glanced at the photograph again, focusing her attention on the man she believed to be Scarpati. He had the same thick black hair, the same olive complexion, the same wart on the side of his nose. A few days ago, she might have had doubts; but after meeting him in the hospital last week, she was certain it was him.

"Good news?"

At the sound of Mildred's voice, Laura looked up. "I found it, Mildred."

Mildred quickly closed the door. "You found something on Malcolm Kandall?"

"See for yourself." She pulled back so Mildred could look at the screen. "Enzio Scarpati was lying after all," she continued as Mildred read. "And now I can prove it." She was already dialing Quentin's number. When he came on the line, she told him what she had discovered.

"I'll call my private investigator in New York right away," he said, sounding more excited than he had in days. "It shouldn't be too difficult to trace Scarpati's whereabouts the night of May 23, 1993."

No sooner had Laura hung up than the phone rang. Realizing it was her private line, and half hoping it was Ted, Laura answered it immediately. "Laura Spencer."

The voice at the other end was slurred and Laura couldn't make out what the woman was saying.

"I can't understand you. Who is this?"

"Barbara . . ." A sob caught in her throat. "Barbara Kandall."

"Barbara." Laura gripped the phone with both hands. "What's wrong? Why are you crying?"

"Need to talk to you." Laura heard the tinkling of ice cubes. Barbara was drinking—heavily, judging from the way she talked.

"I'm listening, Barbara."

"I know . . ." There was a short pause. "I know who killed J.B."

3 2

Her heart began to beat wildly. "Who is it?"

"Not on the phone. Need to . . . to explain. In person."

"All right." Afraid Barbara would hang up on her, Laura didn't argue. "Tell me where you are."

"Houston. My mother's house." Barbara started to cry. "Such a mess," she said between sobs. "Such an ugly mess."

"Barbara, listen to me. Don't drink anymore. It's only going to make things worse. I'll help you. That's why you called me, isn't it? So I could help?"

"Yes."

"All right. Give me your mother's address."

"You have to come alone. No police. No one."

"I promise." Then, in a gentler voice. "The address, Barbara?"

"It's 101 Inwood. Across from the River Oaks Country Club."

Cradling the phone in her left shoulder, Laura wrote down the information. "I've got it."

"When . . . will you be here?"

"I don't know. I'm going to try to catch the first

commuter flight available. If I can't, I'll have to drive down. But I'll be there. One way or another."

It had taken Ted a little under three hours to make the drive from Austin to Dallas/Fort Worth Airport. Once there, he had tried to call Sandra at home but there had been no answer. He would call her later, from the plane.

Now, as he waited for the faulty landing gear on Dale Anderson's plane to be repaired, Ted paced the small lounge, unable to sit down and map out his strategy as he usually did before an important assignment.

He kept thinking about Laura, about the way she had looked when he had left her this morning, soft and vulnerable. When he had kissed her warm cheek, he had been tempted to say the hell with Belfast and get back in bed with her.

Now that the time to leave was nearing, he was beginning to have serious doubts about his decision. He was no longer sure that flying from one corner of the globe to another with a camera around his neck was what he wanted. Oh, sure, photography was his passion. But when he compared it to what he had with Laura, it just didn't measure up.

As a slender woman with long, red hair walked into the lounge, his heart lurched. "Laura!"

It wasn't until the woman turned a questioning glance in his direction that he realized she was a stranger.

He stood there for a full minute, feeling miserable. Then, as an overhead speaker announced the next flight, he picked up a phone and dialed the *Sentinel* where he knew Laura would be hard at work.

"Laura's not here," Mildred told him when he was put through. "She went to Houston."

"Houston? What in the world is she doing there?"

"Barbara Kandall called her. She said she knows who killed J.B."

"What?"

"That was my reaction, too, at first." Mildred's tone was upbeat, and reassuring. "But I was right there when Laura took the call, Ted. It wasn't a trick this time. It was really Barbara on the phone."

"Did Laura notify the police?"

"Oh no. Barbara explicitly said no police. She wanted to talk to Barbara alone."

What had she gotten herself into this time? Ted wondered as a cold knot settled in his stomach. How did he know she was not walking into another trap? One set by Malcolm?

He was tempted to call Amos, then thought better of it. If Barbara was on the level, the arrival of a police officer could ruin everything. And Laura would never forgive him.

He glanced at the clock on the wall. "When did she leave, Mildred?"

"About an hour ago. She missed the last morning flight and didn't want to wait for the next one, so she drove down."

Ted did some fast thinking. Houston was a three-and-a-half-hour drive from Austin. If he and Dale left within the next hour, they would reach Houston at approximately the same time as Laura. "Is my aunt at the Fentons' estate?" he asked.

"Yes."

Still holding the receiver, he disconnected the call and dialed the hangar. "Dale," he said when the pilot came on the line. "There's been a change of plans. We're going to Houston."

"Why won't you do it?" Sandra cried in exasperation as her father stared stubbornly out the Firebird window. "What would it cost you to just tell Ted you're sorry? *He* did it. Or tried to anyway."

"Unlike Ted I have nothing to be sorry about," Charles snapped. "He's the one who accused me of being a murderer if you recall."

"I *don't* recall. I was six years old."

"Then you'll have to take my word for it."

"But that was years ago, Daddy. And he's apologized time and time again since then. Why can't you forgive him?"

"There are some things a father can't easily forget. Or forgive."

"A less rigid father would have."

"That's enough, Sandra. I agreed to let you drive me to the polls, not to railroad me into a discussion about your brother."

She hated to upset him, but dammit, she wasn't going to let Ted go back to England without making one last attempt to patch things up between the two men she loved most in the world.

"Why do you resent him so much? Is it because he hurt you? Or because he had the courage to break away from the mold—something *you* were never able to do."

She threw him a quick glance, hoping she had cracked a piece of the armor he wore so well, but his expression remained just as neutral as before.

"Carrying on the Kandall tradition was *my* choice, Sandra. It was a contribution to our family history I was proud to make. Ted, on the other hand, was never interested in traditions."

"So what? Look what he's accomplished." She pulled into the parking lot of the Omega Elementary School where a few voters were beginning to trickle in. When her remark was met with another stony silence, she turned to face him. "I don't get you, Daddy. You talk as if Ted were some kind of monster, a man with no heart, no love for his family. But he's nothing like that. He is caring, warm, funny, and generous. And he loves his family."

"I told you I didn't want to talk about him." Charles's eyes flashed wtih anger, and Sandra pulled back as if he had slapped her. "Ted has been out of my life for a long time, and that's how I want it to stay."

Anger rose to her throat, choking her. "That's a horrible thing to say after all he's done to protect you. Why, if it weren't for him, you'd be in jail right now ..."

She stopped, breathless and horrified that she had allowed herself to go this far, to almost blurt it all out.

Charles pinned her with an eaglelike stare. "What did you say?"

She turned to pick up her purse from the back seat. "Nothing. Let's go in before it starts pouring."

In spite of his diminished strength, his hand closed over her wrist like a vise. "We're not going anywhere until you tell me what you meant by that remark. What did he tell you? What lies did he put in your head now?"

"Oh, Daddy." She shook her head. "You don't know him at all, do you?"

"Tell me what he said, dammit!"

For a moment, she was torn between the fear of hurting him and the need to have everything out in the open, to prove to him how much Ted cared. It was the look in his eyes, hard and unforgiving, that made the decision for her.

"He knows about Mom," she said in a whisper. "We both know."

He let go of her wrist. "What the devil are you talking about?"

She glanced toward the parking lot. More people were arriving now, their heads bent against the forceful wind. In the distance, rain clouds had gathered, turning the skies a stormy shade of gray. After a moment, she turned around in her seat and met her father's gaze. "We know you killed her."

She wasn't sure what she saw first, shock or horror. The two emotions, too strong for him to hold back, kept flashing through his eyes as he stared at her in total disbelief. "My God." The two words floated past dry, white lips.

"Ted found Mom's necklace in the attic a couple of weeks ago. It was hidden inside your old golf bag."

He opened his mouth as if to speak, but no sound came out.

"Ted was shattered," Sandra continued. "I've never seen him looking so torn and defeated. But he still found the strength to comfort me, to hold me. And when I begged him not to say anything, to keep what we knew a secret, he agreed. It wasn't an easy decision for him, Daddy. You know how he felt about Mom. But he agreed anyway. He did it for you, to spare you more pain. He did it because he loves you . . ."

Her sentence hung in the air as Charles fell back against his seat. She saw him close his eyes, heard his shallow breath. "Daddy?" She shook him.

He gave her hand a gentle pat. "I'm all right."

"You scared me."

"Don't be scared. I'm a tough old nut. It's going to take a lot more than an argument with my daughter to kill me."

"Don't talk like that."

His breathing had improved, but he was still pale. "I want to hear the rest of your story, Sandra. What was Ted doing in the attic?"

She told him everything, how she had gone to London, talked Ted into coming back, and how she had come up with the idea of an exhibition to cover Ted's real reason for being in Austin.

He didn't interrupt her. Sitting up straight now, he stared at the steady rain as it pounded across the parking lot.

It wasn't until she started telling him about the arguments she had heard night after night that he turned to look at her. "You heard all that?"

She nodded. "Every word. Including when Mom told you there was another man in her life and that she was leaving you."

He closed his eyes. "Dear God."

"I wanted to come to you the following morning, but I was too scared."

"So you went to your brother instead."

"No. I didn't say anything to him until the other day when I was trying to convince him to give you another chance. When he heard about that mystery lover, he went to the attic, hoping to find out his identity. He thought maybe *he* was the killer. Instead he found the necklace in your golf bag."

"And so he assumed *I* had put it there."

She looked up, startled by his choice of words. "Well ... Yes. I mean, you did. Didn't you?"

He shook his head, slowly, repeatedly, while his eyes stayed riveted to hers. "No, Sandra. I didn't. I'm as astounded to find out where it's been all these years as you are." His voice was husky, almost gruff. "And I didn't kill your mother."

Sandra fell back against her seat. "But the chain ... the arguments, the things you said ..."

"I won't deny I was angry. And yes, if I had known right there and then who the man was, I might very well have killed him. But not your mother." His blue eyes filled with tears. "I could never hurt her. I loved her too much. As painful as it was for me to see her go, I would have done that rather than harm one hair on her head."

"Then how did Mom's chain end up in your golf bag?"

"I don't know, Sandra." He shook his head. "I just don't know."

"We'll have to tell Ted—"

"No." The tone of his voice left no room for discussion. "Since he was so quick to believe I had murdered his mother, let him continue to think that."

"But that's cruel—"

"You heard me, Sandra." Then, opening the door, he stepped out of the Firebird, snapped his umbrella open, and headed toward the school building.

The Pine Brook firehouse, where voters in Malcolm's district voted, was packed when he arrived on that chilly, rainy Tuesday morning.

As Malcolm had expected, the media was there, waiting for him to step out of his chauffeur-driven car. Ever the consumate actor, he waved and smiled at the cameras, revealing none of the turmoil that was taking place inside.

"Are you confident the elections will go as you hope, Mr. Kandall?"

"Absolutely. The people of Texas have shown they're ready for a change. They want a governor who will take charge, who will restore the luster to our great state." He cast a satisfied glance at the people around him. "The turnout here this morning confirms that."

"Isn't Mrs. Kandall with you?"

"She's nursing a bad cold," he improvised. "And didn't want to pass it on to anyone. She'll be in as soon as the early-morning rush is over."

He fended off another question by raising his hand. "My campaigning is over, ladies and gentlemen. I would like to thank all of you for the support and loyalty you've shown during the past eighteen months. Win or lose, I'll try to never disappoint you. Now if you don't mind, I'd like to go and cast my vote."

Half an hour later, he was back home. "Any calls?" he asked Dolores.

The housekeeper shook her head. "No, sir. Nothing."

He waited until noon, then decided he couldn't wait any longer. He had to start making calls before Barbara's absence became too conspicuous. But first he would make one more attempt to call his mother-in-law's house in Houston.

Malcolm's shoulders sagged with relief when Barbara answered the phone. "Barbara! Thank god I found you. I've been worried sick—"

"Go 'way, Malcolm."

He could tell by the sound of her voice that she had been drinking. "Barbara, I'm coming down. We have to talk."

"Too late for that." He heard her sniffle. "Will only talk to Laura."

He felt as if someone had shot ice through his veins. "No! Not Laura." He ran shaking fingers through his hair. "You didn't call her, did you, Barbara? You didn't say anything to her. Answer me, dammit." Hearing no response, he tapped impatiently on the plungers. "Barbara? Hello? Hello?"

He let the phone drop back in the cradle. She had hung up.

That dumb bitch. She had done it. She had called the fucking press. By six o'clock tonight, the story would be in all the newscasts.

Forcing himself to stay in control, he took a long, head-clearing breath. He had to stop her from talking to Laura. Without wasting another second, he called the private airfield where Jerry kept his plane. "We're going back to Houston," he instructed the pilot. "As soon as you can make it."

He was almost out the door when he remembered the gun.

Retracing his steps to the study, he walked over to his desk and unlocked the drawer where he kept his Beretta. He had bought it two years ago after the house next door was robbed. He had wanted Barbara to take instructions with him, but she had categorically refused. Years ago in college, her best friend had been shot at point-blank range by a jealous lover, right in front of Barbara. She had been terrified of guns ever since. The mere sight of one made her break into a cold sweat. If she put up a fuss, all he had to do was wave it at her and she would do exactly as he said.

After checking to make sure it was properly loaded, he snapped the clip back in place and slid it into his breast pocket. He didn't expect to have to use it, but it never hurt to be prepared.

3 3

By the time Laura reached the western outskirts of Houston, the light rain that had fallen during most of her trip had turned into a nasty downpour that made the roads slick and reduced visibility to near zero.

Deirdre Fenton lived on a three-acre estate, west of downtown, in the prestigious section known as River Oaks. Brilliantly lit, the house was a stunning study of early English Tudor and stood like a gigantic sentry at the end of the long, graveled driveway.

Feeling a little apprehensive, although she wasn't sure why, Laura drove through the iron gates, which had been left open, and stopped in front of the ornately carved front door.

Flipping the hood of her London Fog over her head, she ran the short distance to the door. She couldn't hear any sound coming from behind the solid brick structure, yet someone had to be expecting her, otherwise why would the gates be open and all the lights on?

She pressed the bell, praying someone in the house had realized Barbara's condition, and had

had the good sense to take the liquor away from her.

When there was no answer, she rang again. When that, too, remained unanswered, she knocked loudly, calling Barbara's name and identifying herself. After a few more seconds, she gripped the knob and turned it, surprised to find the door unlocked.

"Barbara?" She pushed the door wide open. "Is anybody home?"

She was greeted by an eerie silence.

She hesitated, but for only a moment. She hadn't come all this distance for nothing. If Barbara was here, she had to find her. If not, she would wait until she returned.

Closing the door behind her, Laura walked across the elegant, two-story foyer and into a luxurious living room. At any other time she would have loved to linger, to admire the rich old wood, the imported damask, and the antique carpets. But there was no time for such frivolity now. She had to look for Barbara.

She found her in the kitchen, sound asleep in a window seat, her head cradled against a mound of blue-and-white-checkered pillows. Clasped against her chest was an empty glass. On the floor, laying on its side, was an empty bottle of vodka.

The stench of stale liquor was overpowering, but Laura ignored it. She removed her raincoat, laid it over the back of a chair, and hurried toward the sleeping woman. "Barbara?" She shook her several times, calling her name, trying to elicit some sort of response from her. It was useless. Barbara remained totally unresponsive.

Taking the glass from the sleeping woman's hand, Laura took it to the sink along with the empty bottle. She had no choice but to wait for Barbara to wake up. Then, hopefully, with a cup of strong coffee and some food in her stomach, she would be coherent enough to finish the conversation she had started earlier. And since there seemed to be no servants in the house and no Mrs. Fenton, Laura thought as she glanced around the immaculate kitchen, she would have to handle the task herself.

Walking around the butcher block island, she started opening cupboards. When she spotted a can of Maxwell House coffee, she went to work.

It wasn't until Ted saw a sign for Rice University that he realized he was heading in the wrong direction.

Cursing under his breath, he peered through the window of the Audi he had rented at Houston Intercontinental Airport. Although it was only four o'clock in the afternoon, the skies were almost black from the storm and the roads sleek and dangerous. He had expected to arrive here much earlier, but there had been interminable delays in landing because of the continuous lightning.

Spotting an intersection, he made a U-turn, not bothering to check if the maneuver was legal or not.

As he drove north on Greenbriar, he hit the redial button on the car phone. He had been trying to call Laura from the plane every ten minutes, but either she had been out of range or the storm had interfered with the signals. As the operator's voice came on the line again, he pressed the disconnect button and dialed Deirdre's house. As before, there was no answer.

"What the hell is going on there?"

At last, he saw the sign for the Kirby Drive turn-off. If the traffic didn't get any worse, he should be at the Fentons in about twenty minutes.

As the tantalizing aroma of French roast coffee wafted through the Fentons' kitchen, Barbara began to stir. Relieved, Laura filled a mug, set it on a tray next to another mug filled with thick mushroom soup, and carried everything to the kitchen table. "Hello, Barbara." Laura sat on the edge of the window seat. "How do you feel?"

After a few attempts to open her eyes, Barbara finally succeeded. They were bloodshot and unfocused. "Who . . ."

"I'm Laura Spencer. You sent for me, remember?"

Barbara mumbled something unintelligible and slowly sat up, groaning. "My head."

"Here." Laura handed her two Excedrins she had found in an upstairs bathroom, and a glass of water.

"What's that?"

"Aspirin. Go ahead. Take them. You'll feel better."

Like an obedient child, Barbara did as she was told.

"Good girl." Laura handed her the coffee. "Now this. It's hot, so take small sips." She helped her until Barbara had drunk half and could manage the rest without scalding herself.

"Now the soup," Laura said, watching some of the color return to Barbara's cheeks. "It'll be easier if you sip it, but I can get you a spoon if you prefer."

Barbara shook her head. "This is fine."

Something deep in Laura's heart tugged as she watched the woman drink her soup. With her hair disheveled, her expensive linen dress all wrinkled, and her eyes downcast, she looked like a sad, disoriented child.

It took another few minutes before she was sober enough to answer a few questions. Trying to sound as unthreatening as possible, Laura said gently, "Are you here alone, Barbara?"

She nodded. "Mother is in California for a couple of weeks and the servants have the week off."

"We can talk freely then, without fear of being interrupted." When Barbara didn't answer, Laura probed gently. "Do you remember calling me at the *Sentinel*? Asking me to come here?"

"Yes."

"You said you knew who killed J.B."

This time Barbara closed her eyes. But even then the pain was visible, and heartbreaking. Whatever she had been keeping to herself had become an unbearable burden. "Let me help you, Barbara."

"You came alone?"

Laura nodded. "Yes. It's just you and me."

It seemed to take Barbara forever to make up

her mind. She kept staring out the window with
that same forlorn expression. When she finally
turned her attention back to Laura, her voice was
steady. "Malcolm," she said. "It was Malcolm who
killed J.B."

Stunned, Laura could only stare at her.

"I found a shirt with blood on it," Barbara went
on. "The same shirt he had worn the day of the
Jaycees dinner—the day J.B. was killed. When I
questioned him about the stain, he told me he had
cut himself that morning."

"You didn't believe him?"

"No." She turned back toward the window. "I
followed him upstairs. He was in our bedroom, with
one of his suits rolled up in his arms. It was the
suit he had worn that night . . ." A tear rolled down
her cheek. She made no attempt to wipe it off.
"The sleeve was bloody, too."

Suddenly Laura remembered the black Corvette
parked in the driveway of the Kandalls' home the
day she had gone to see Barbara. And she remembered Shirley's description of the car she had
passed on the way to Lost Creek.

*"It made a lot of noise when it went by. Like one
of those fancy race cars."*

Corvettes were noisy. That's what Laura had
been trying to remember the day of the preliminary
hearing. "Did he admit to killing J.B.?"

"Not at first." Barbara's voice was flat as if she
was reciting something she didn't fully understand.
"After a while, he knew there was no point in lying
anymore." Her fingers went to touch her cheek.
"He hit me. He's never done that before."

"Why did he do it?" Laura asked in a whisper. "Why did he kill J.B.?"

"On the day of the MediaTech conference, J.B. took me home."

"I know. You were sick."

"I wasn't sick." She took another sip of her soup. "I was drunk. I have a drinking problem, you see. A serious one."

"I didn't know."

"Few people do. Between Malcolm, my mother, and the woman my husband hired to look after me, they manage to keep me in line. Occasionally, however, I slip."

"And that's what J.B. had on Malcolm?" Laura asked, astounded that something so insignificant could lead to murder. "Your drinking problem?"

"No. It's what I told J.B. when he took me home that caused Malcolm to ..." She leaned her head back. "It's all my fault. If I had kept quiet, if I hadn't started to drink that day, none of this would have happened. J.B. would still be alive."

"Shhh." Laura took the mug from her and set it on the table. "Don't blame yourself."

"Talking to J.B. was always so easy. He had a strong shoulder, and a sympathetic ear."

"What did you tell him that was so damaging?"

"Secrets. Secrets I had kept hidden inside me for the past sixteen years, secrets I could no longer cope with. When Malcolm found out, he was furious. We had a terrible fight." She buried her head in her hands and sobbed helplessly.

If time hadn't been so critical, Laura would have gladly listened to the rest of her story, for it was obvious this woman needed help. But it was equally important to get Barbara back to Burnet where she could make an official statement. No doubt Malcolm had already disposed of the incriminating shirt and suit jacket, but if both the housekeeper *and* Barbara had seen the stained shirt, it might be enough for Amos to make an arrest.

Laura rose to her feet, aware they had been sitting here, talking, for almost half an hour. "Why don't you tell me the rest in the car, Barbara? Right now we have to get to the airport."

"Why? Where are we going?"

"Back to Burnet to talk to Sheriff Wilson. We'll take the first flight available. You're up to doing that, aren't you?"

Barbara tested her legs and stood slowly. "I think so."

"Come on then. Let's go."

"Over my dead body," a threatening voice said behind her.

As Barbara cried out in alarm, Laura spun around.

Malcolm Kandall stood in the doorway, a gun pointed at her.

3 4

If the situation hadn't been so serious, Laura would have laughed.

With rain dripping from his face, his hair all matted down, and his eyes wild with panic, Malcolm Kandall looked more like an escapee from the insane asylum than the handsome, sophisticated politician who had charmed millions of Texans.

"You couldn't leave it alone, could you?" he said between clenched teeth. "You had to keep meddling. You had to keep pushing."

Laura tried to affect a calm she was far from feeling. "I was trying to save my mother from a prison sentence."

"Well, you're not going to save anybody now. Not even yourself."

"Malcolm, please," Barbara whimpered. "Put that gun away. You know how I hate them."

"She's right," Laura interjected. "You've got enough problems right now without adding to them by—"

"Shut up." He circled around the two women. His face was white and he was visibly shaken, but his hand was steady, his gaze unfaltering. He waved the gun in Barbara's direction. "Move away from her."

Barbara, a terrified look in her eyes, flattened herself against the wall. "What?"

"Are you deaf? I said move away from Laura."

From the corner of her eye, Laura saw Barbara retreat further against the wall.

"And you." He jerked the gun back in Laura's direction. "Step back."

Laura knew she was in no position to argue. She did as she was told.

With his left hand, Malcolm yanked at the blue silk cord tied around the swag curtain and held it out to Barbara. "Tie her hands behind her back."

Barbara, her eyes still on the gun, shook her head. "No."

Malcolm quickly assessed the situation. Yelling and waving the gun at her wasn't helping him. He had to switch tactics. "Barbara, listen to me—"

"Put the gun away."

"I can't. But I'll lower it." He brought his arm down to his side. "Is that better?"

Barbara nodded but didn't take her eyes off the gun. "I don't want anyone hurt."

"You should have thought of that before you called her down here. Before you spilled your guts to her."

"What are you going to do to her?"

"You know the answer to that. We have to get rid of her. If we don't she'll send both of us to prison for a very long time."

"Don't listen to him, Barbara. You won't go to prison. You didn't do anything wrong."

"I don't want anyone else hurt," Barbara said obstinately.

"It's either her or us. She'll destroy you as well. And you know why, don't you?"

As tears ran down her cheeks, Barbara remained silent.

"Do it," he ordered, shaking the cord at her. "Tie her up." He raised the gun again. "Or I'll start shooting. Right here."

Shocked, Laura watched as Barbara, apparently terrified he would do just that, took a hesitant step forward, toward Malcolm.

Laura knew she had to think of something. Quickly. Taking advantage of Malcolm's momentary distraction, she snatched the percolator from the counter and hurled it at Malcolm's face.

With a scream, he stumbled back and went crashing into the hutch.

Laura didn't waste a moment. "Come on," she said, grabbing Barbara's hand and pulling her along. "My car's outside." As they ran past Malcolm, Laura plucked her purse and coat from the kitchen table. "Quick."

Barbara stumbled twice on the way to the door, but Laura managed to hold her up. Outside the downpour had turned into a light but steady drizzle.

"Get in," Laura said as she held the Mustang's passenger door open.

Barbara hesitated and glanced toward the house. "Malcolm. Shouldn't we check . . ."

"The coffee was cold. He'll be fine. You can call an ambulance from the car if you want. *After* we call the police. Come on, get in." With a sigh of impatience at the woman's indecision, she shoved her in and ran to the driver's side.

As she pumped the gas pedal, her eyes kept darting toward the front door. "Come on," she urged as the engine refused to catch. "Start."

She kept pumping. Once. Twice. Three times. Nothing happened. "Don't do this to me, dammit! Not now."

As the engine finally caught, the driver's door was yanked open. Malcolm stood glaring at her, a bloody gash running from his forehead to his eyebrow.

"You bitch. Get out of the car."

Laura cried out in pain as he grabbed hold of her left arm and dragged her out. A searing heat spread across her upper chest, reminding her she wasn't as well recovered as she had thought. "You bastard," she yelled. "You won't get away with this. Too many people know where I am—"

Malcolm's vicious slap caught her unprepared. Her head whipped to the side and back. Enraged by the pain and the humiliation, she threw herself at him, fingers clawing, nails raking his face, feet kicking. But she was no match for him. And she was hurting too badly to practice any of the self-defense moves she had been taught.

Grabbing her right arm, Malcolm twisted it and spun her around, pinning her back to his chest. "How would you like to have your head blown off right this minute?'' he asked as the cold barrel of the gun pressed against her temple.

She prepared to let herself go limp, hoping he'd believe she had fainted, when a screech of tires and a blast of horns filled the courtyard, startling them both.

3 5

Scarcely able to believe the scene caught in his headlights, Ted tore out of the car. "Malcolm!"

"Ted, watch out!" Laura cried. "He's got a gun. And he killed J.B."

The shock brought him to a stop, but only temporarily. His eyes locked on his uncle, he moved steadily forward. "Let her go."

"Stay where you are," Malcolm ordered. "You take one more step and I swear, I'll blow her away."

Ted had no choice but to stop. He had been in too many similar situations not to take guns, and the people who held them, seriously. "Take it easy." He wished he'd had the foresight to bring a weapon. Since he hadn't, he would have to rely on what he had—his head and his body.

A whimper made him glance off to the side. Standing beside the Mustang, Barbara was crying softly, her fists clenched and held against her mouth.

"Why don't you let Laura go, Uncle Malcolm?" he said, his tone even and unthreatening. "Then we'll talk. Just you and me."

"Shut up. And keep your hands where I can see them."

Ted spread his arms wide. "Don't be a fool, Uncle Malcolm. Whatever mess you got yourself into isn't worth killing for. If anything, it'll make things worse."

"Don't give me any of your two-bit logic, boy. And don't try to play hero with me. If you do, you'll be a dead one."

Barbara had stopped crying. "Listen to him, Ted." Her hands were now crossed over her chest and although she still looked terrified, she seemed to have come out of her trance. "He has nothing to lose. He's already killed two people."

"Two?" Ted's head snapped back toward Malcolm. He looked like a trapped animal. His eyes were wild, darting to a black car parked on the other side of the Mustang. But the hand that held the gun to Laura's head was steady as a rock. "Who did he kill besides J.B.?"

"Don't say another word, Barbara!" Malcolm warned.

"Or what?" Her voice was loud and clear now and growing stronger. "What will you do? Kill me, too? Kill all three of us?"

"Shut up!"

"Can't you see it's over? That short of a blood-bath, you'll never get away?"

"Who did he kill, Barbara?"

As if all strength had suddenly drained from her, she leaned against the Mustang. "Your mother."

The words penetrated Ted's mind but refused to register. "What did you say?"

"It was an accident. They were having an affair. Elizabeth was going to leave Charles for Malcolm. But that's not what Malcolm wanted. He wanted her, yes, but he also wanted his career, his wealthy wife, his brilliant future."

A blind, killing rage came over Ted. "You bastard," he hissed under his breath. "You dirty, double-crossing bastard."

Shoulders low, he sprang. Then, in a move he hadn't tried since his high school football days, he caught Malcolm in a blindside tackle that would have made his coach proud.

There was a grunt, then a solid thump as Malcolm pitched forward and hit the fender of the Mustang. The gun went flying out of Malcolm's hand.

"Call 911," Ted shouted as Barbara screamed. As she dove into the Mustang, Ted grabbed hold of Malcolm's jacket, spun him around, and smashed his fist into the man's face.

Malcolm went down without a whimper.

From behind him, Ted heard a groan. Laura was on the ground, trying to pull herself up.

In two leaps, he was at her side, hugging her to him. "Thank God you're all right." It wasn't until he saw the blood seeping through her blouse that he realized she was hurt. "Jesus, you're bleeding!"

"It's nothing. The wound reopened, that's all." Tears streamed down her face as she watched him pull a handkerchief from his back pocket and slide it underneath her blouse. "What are you doing here?" she asked in a voice that trembled with emotion. "You should be somewhere above the Atlantic by now."

"I changed my plans."

"Why?"

Gently, he pressed the handkerchief to the wound. "Because I love you. And because I don't want to be separated from you. Not even for one minute."

"But Belfast ... Your job ..."

As she held the temporary bandage in place, he helped her up to her feet. "Not nearly as important as you. I always knew that. I just wasn't ready to admit it."

"And you are now?"

"Yes. I wouldn't have come back if I weren't."

"Oh, Ted." Before she could say another word, the wail of a siren pierced through the air. Moments later, headlights flooded the courtyard and a half-dozen squad cars surrounded them.

"And ... we're finished."

The emergency room doctor at Houston Memorial Hospital, a young intern who looked more like a high school student than a surgeon, sewed up the last stitch on Laura's chest and gave her a quick, teasing smile. "That should hold up. Provided you don't suddenly decide to test it by joining a commando team or something."

"Now why would you say something like that, Dr. Ryan?"

"Oh." He secured a thick square of gauze over the wound with surgical tape. "One hears things."

"Well, rest assured. My crime-chasing days are

over. At least for a while." As he held her arm,
she slid cautiously from the table where she had
been lying for the last forty-five minutes. "Now if
you don't mind, I'd like to go home."

"Take these with you." He took a small bottle
from a glassed-in medicine cabinet and handed it
to her. "If the pain gets too severe once the local
anesthetic wears off, take one pill every four
hours."

"Thank you, Doctor."

She found Ted in the waiting room. His face was
pale, his jaw clenched. He hadn't heard her approach and gave a start when she laid a hand on
his shoulder.

"Laura." He stood up and enveloped her in his
arms, holding her as if she were a life raft. "Are
you all right? They wouldn't let me come in with
you."

"I'm fine." There were so many things she
wanted to say to him, but the words eluded her.
So she returned the embrace and remained silent.

"You were right about Malcolm all along," he
said, releasing her at last. "And about Barbara."

She looked into his eyes and saw all those emotions reflected in them—sadness, disappointment,
anger. "We don't have to talk about that now if
you don't want to."

"I want to." They both sat down. "I had to go
and give a statement and while I was at the police
station, Barbara asked to talk to me. I knew you'd
be in with Dr. Ryan for a while, so I went to see
her."

"How is she?"

"Better than I expected. She's much stronger than people think. Malcolm was the one who was stifling her." He waited for a nurse wheeling a cart to walk by before speaking again. "She told me everything that happened that day in Aspen. She had been looking for Malcolm. When she finally found him, he was on the balcony of Charles's library—with my mother."

"Then what Barbara said earlier is true? Malcolm and your mother were having an affair?"

Ted nodded. "The two of them were arguing. According to Barbara, my mother was in a terrible state. She was threatening to tell Charles everything. When she tried to leave, Malcolm wouldn't let her go. They struggled. In the next moment, my mother was toppling over the balcony. Malcolm tried to stop the fall, but it happened so fast, all he could get hold of was her necklace."

"How horrible."

"When Malcolm realized Barbara had seen the whole thing, he fell apart. He begged for her forgiveness, swearing he had never truly loved Elizabeth, that she was the one who had come on to him."

"Why didn't she call the police?"

"She wanted to. Malcolm told her he would rather die than be in prison. He was like a small, lost child, sobbing in her arms and telling her he loved her. Her tender heart couldn't take it. She loved him too much. So she agreed not to say anything. She helped him pull himself together and they returned to the party."

"You said Malcolm got hold of your mother's necklace. What happened to it?"

"When Barbara realized Malcolm was incapable of thinking clearly, she took it from him and dropped it in the first golf bag she saw, unaware it belonged to my father. She had meant to retrieve it later, but when she tried to do that, she couldn't recognize which bag it was. Eventually, the guests were allowed to go home and those who had come to golf took their clubs with them. Barbara had no choice but wait for one of the guests to return the chain. When no one did, she assumed it had been lost somehow."

"I don't understand. The necklace was in your father's golf bag all along and he didn't know it?"

He told her about his foray into his father's attic two weeks ago, and his reaction after finding the chain.

"Oh, Ted."

"Barbara started drinking shortly after that. At first, it helped her forget the part she had played in my mother's death. But after a while, the problem became so serious, she couldn't stop."

"She never considered going to a rehabilitation clinic?"

"Many times. J.B. knew about her drinking and had encouraged her to have it treated. So did her mother, and Joan Alden, Barbara's best friend. But Malcolm wouldn't allow it. He was terrified that if the news of her alcoholism leaked out, his career would be over."

"That sentence J.B. told Lenox the afternoon of the MediaTech luncheon, '*Things have finally come full circle,'* puzzled me for so long," Laura murmured. "I couldn't imagine what he was talking about, but I do now. He must have realized that Malcolm was responsible for your mother's death. I always had the feeling that like you, J.B. never believed Elizabeth had committed suicide."

"I'm glad that much was settled. Maybe now she'll be able to rest in peace."

Laura took his hand and held it against her cheek. "Has Malcolm confessed?"

"Not yet. He's not saying a word until he speaks to his attorney." Ted gave a short, mirthless laugh. "You want to know the ironic part to all this? According to the latest election recap, Malcolm is leading by more than seven hundred thousand votes. They expect him to win by a landslide. Even if the story were to break now and no one else voted for him, he would still win the election."

"Knowing how badly he wanted to be governor, having to give it up will hurt him more than a thirty-year prison sentence."

He threw her a quick glance. "Is that what you think he'll get?"

"With one charge of murder in the first degree and one for involuntary manslaughter, yes, that sounds about right."

"What about Barbara?"

"She could be charged with conspiracy, or at the very least of being an accessory after the fact. But since I suspect she'll be testifying against her husband, even though she can't be forced to, they'll probably make a deal with her." Then, as she saw a uniformed policeman walk through the double doors, she sprang up. "Amos! Has anyone thought of notifying him?"

"I made sure the arresting officer at the station did. Amos and two deputies are flying down on a police helicopter."

"What about my mother?"

Ted smiled. "She should be released within the next hour or so. I called Lenox and told him to go pick her up and bring her back to Lost Creek. I hope that's all right. I didn't think she should be alone."

Laura's eyes filled with tears. "I couldn't have done better myself. Thank you, Ted."

He stood up. "I told the police I'd bring you over so you could give a formal statement. What do you say we get that out of the way and go home? Dale's plane is waiting for us at the airport."

Home. No word had ever sounded more wonderful. Or more right. Smiling up at him, she wrapped an arm around his waist. "Let's do that."

Sitting in a cell no bigger than his closet at home, Malcolm glared as his attorney, a well-dressed man with heavy jowls and long, white sideburns, walked in.

"About time you got here," Malcolm mumbled as the guard locked them in.

"Couldn't help the delay. Air traffic over Houston was a nightmare."

Yeah. Tell me about it. If it hadn't been for that, I would have arrived here long before Laura, and I wouldn't be sitting here.

"So." Pulling up a chair so it wouldn't touch the dingy wall, Sam Garret sat down. "Want to tell me what this mess is all about?"

There wasn't much point in lying to him. Not with Barbara singing like a bloody canary and two witnesses as credible as Ted and Laura.

He told Sam everything, from the beginning of his affair with his sister-in-law, which he would regret until the day he died, to the moment the Houston police had arrived at the Fentons' estate.

"Christ." Sam ran a hand through his hair.

"Don't give me that shocked look," Malcolm snapped. "Just get me the hell out of here."

Sam gave a slow, sad shake of his head. "I'm an attorney, Malcolm. Not a miracle worker. I can almost guarantee you'll be held without bail."

Malcolm started to pace the cell. Maybe Enzio could do something. He had connections. He could arrange for bail. He might even be able to help him get out of the country.

He stopped in front of Sam's chair. "I want to make a call."

"To whom?"

"Never mind that. Arrange it."

Five minutes later, Malcolm was dialing Enzio's number from a pay phone outside his cell.

He never got any further than some snotty nose asshole who had apparently replaced Tony Cordero.

"Mr. Scarpati is in conference," the man said in a heavy Brooklyn accent. "What did you say the name was again?"

Malcolm's jaw clenched. "Kandall. Malcolm Kandall. Enzio and I—"

"Just a moment."

When the man returned, all politeness was gone from his voice. "Mr. Scarpati's never heard of you. Check the phone book. You probably have the wrong guy."

"I don't have the wrong guy—"

To his amazement, the man hung up. Malcolm stood looking at the receiver for a few seconds before he finally hung up. Conference, hell. Enzio was right there, in his office. He was sure of it. And the only reason he didn't want to talk to him was because he no longer had any use for Malcolm Kandall. That's how Enzio was.

That son of a bitch. After all the risks he had taken for him, the bastard was discarding him like yesterday's garbage.

For a moment, the thought of exposing Enzio for the crook he was was so overwhelming that he almost asked the guard to get the D.A. What he wouldn't give to see that grease ball in handcuffs. But that wasn't possible. Without witnesses, it would be his word against Enzio's. And once the mobster found out Malcolm had blown the whistle on him, Malcolm's life wouldn't be worth a plugged nickel. Even behind bars.

Behind bars. As Malcolm was returned to his cell, all hope of beating this rap left him. Sitting down, he put his head between his hands.

For the first time in his life, he felt totally helpless.

3 6

By the time Ted and Laura arrived in Austin two hours later, the airport was mobbed. The media, along with hundreds of onlookers, pushed and shoved to get a better look at the two people a television anchor had dubbed "Texas's mighty duo."

Exhausted but clearheaded, Laura held Ted's hand as she faced the glare of cameras.

"You might as well talk to them and get it over with," he suggested, his arm firmly anchored around her waist. "We won't get any peace until you do."

In a voice that grew stronger with each sentence, she told reporters what they already knew, that Malcolm Kandall had confessed to J.B.'s murder and that he was being brought back to Burnet County where he would be formally charged.

A reporter in a back row raised his hand. "Did you know he had killed your stepfather when you went down to Houston, Miss Spencer?"

"No."

"What about those earlier reports of a possible Mafia connection between Malcolm Kandall and Enzio Scarpati. Are they true?"

"I'm afraid I'm not at liberty to discuss that."

Another reporter directed the next question at Ted. "Mr. Kandall, did your uncle confess to killing your mother?"

"Yes. But since that incident falls under a different jurisdiction, we've been asked not to comment on it either." He smiled. "I'm sorry. You'll have to ask us something we can talk about."

"Miss Spencer, how do you feel knowing that the man who tried to destroy you and your newspaper also killed your stepfather?"

"Angry. And sad. No position in the world, no matter how powerful, is worth killing for. Malcolm Kandall understands that now. I wished he had understood it a little earlier. If he had, J.B. would still be alive."

A television anchor Laura knew, held a mike to her. "I understand that a special late-afternoon edition of the *Sentinel* with an exclusive account of the events went on the stands a little over an hour ago. Have you had any feedback on that yet, Miss Spencer? And on the status of the *Sentinel*?"

Laura smiled. She and Milton Shank had been in constant communication for the last two hours, she dictating her story to him over the phone and he calling back with the latest local developments. "The response has been phenomenal," she said with a touch of pride in her voice. "Not only have we had to go back to press twice, but I just learned that advertisers are calling by the dozens."

As a photographer focused his camera on her, she smiled broadly. "I'm pleased to report that the

Sentinel is alive and well. And will be for a very long time."

In the limousine that was taking them back to Lost Creek, Laura snuggled into Ted's arms. "You were very good with the press this time. Very diplomatic." She looked up, a small smile on her lips. "And no punches. Is this the new Ted Kandall? Or just another side of the very complex man I know and love?"

"Let's just say it's an improved version of the old model." Looking down at her, he added, "You didn't do too badly yourself. J.B. would have been proud."

Her eyes clouded. "Now that I know why he died, I feel as though I could have prevented it."

"Nonsense."

"It's true. If I hadn't been so damned preoccupied with the fate of the paper, J.B. would have come to me with what he had found out. We would have talked it over the way we did with almost everything. Together we would have decided what to do about Malcolm. He chose to handle the situation alone because he didn't want to add to my problems."

"Don't do this to yourself, darling."

They were interrupted by yet another election recap.

"In a bizarre twist of events," the radio announcer said. "Malcolm Kandall, who, earlier tonight, was charged with J.B. Lawson's murder, has won the gubernatorial elections by a landslide. In a written statement received by this station a few minutes ago, Mr. Kandall conceded the governorship and congratulated Governor Thorne on a job well done. No other comments were made."

Ted turned the radio off. "Well, I'm glad *that* chapter is closed. Somehow I'll sleep better tonight knowing Malcolm Kandall will not be our next governor."

Although it was nearly midnight when Ted and Laura arrived at Lost Creek, every light in the house shone brightly. As the limousine pulled up into the courtyard, the front door flew open and Shirley came running out, arms outstretched. "Oh, my baby."

Laughing and crying, she hugged Laura to her chest. "Are you all right, baby? Lenox said your wound had reopened." She pulled back, a worried expression on her face. "Oh, God, I didn't hurt you, did I?"

Laura laughed. "I'm fine. Stop treating me as if I were made of glass." She held her mother at arm's length. "Look at you." She grinned as she took in the white studded jeans, the matching jacket, and the fringed white boots. "Where did you get the clothes?"

Arms extended, Shirley made a graceful pirouette. "You like? They're new. I figured after what I had been through, I deserved some new threads. So Lenox took me shopping."

Astounded, Laura glanced at Lenox, who was standing just behind Shirley. "You took my mother shopping?"

He held back a smile. "I did, although I must

admit it isn't something I would want to do on a regular basis."

"Oh, don't listen to him." Her past resentments obviously forgotten, Shirley gave the stoic butler a pat on the back. "He enjoyed himself. I could tell. And he doesn't have bad taste either. For a Brit, that is."

He bowed slightly. "Thank you, ma'am." Turning to Ted and Laura, he added, "I took the liberty of preparing a light supper, Miss Laura. Shall I bring it in here?"

"That would be fine, Lenox."

"Why don't I give you a hand with that, old man?" Ted said, wrapping an arm around Lenox's shoulders. "That way, Laura and her mother can have some private time together."

"You don't have to do that," Laura protested.

Ted waved the remark away and walked out of the room.

Shirley took Laura by the hand and led her toward the sofa. "That was very thoughtful of him to do that." She gave her an amused, sidelong glance. "Amos told me Ted wasn't going back to England. Is that true? Should I not be reading anything into that either?"

Laura smiled. "Well ... Maybe you can read a *little* into it."

Shirley squeezed her hand. "Good. Because I'm beginning to like this young man a lot."

Laura pretended to be mildly alarmed. "I'm not sure if that's good or bad." Then, noticing Shirley's thoughtful expression, she asked, "Something on your mind, Mom?"

"Actually there is." Shirley glanced at her fingernails, which were freshly manicured and painted a vampish shade of red. "I don't know how to tell you this."

Laura's smile faded. "Tell me what?"

"A friend of mine, a man I knew in Germany called me this evening. He heard the news of my release on TV and contacted me through the Burnet sheriff's department. He lives in L.A. now. He owns a nightclub there." She looked up. "He wants to give me a job, Laura. And a long-term contract."

"In Los Angeles?"

Shirley nodded.

"What about your plans to buy the Golden Parrot?"

Shirley shrugged. "I don't think it would have worked. Like you said, it would have been a lot of work and responsibility."

She's doing it again, Laura thought, remembering a similar conversation she and her mother had had sixteen years ago. And with the same insouciance she had shown then. It didn't matter to her that they hadn't had a chance to celebrate her release from jail yet, or the saving of the *Sentinel,* or Ted's decision to stay in Texas. A new adventure beckoned and she was off.

Cut it out, Laura. You're not a teenager anymore. You're all grown up now. As for Shirley, she'll always be Shirley. You know that.

"You're not upset with me, are you, baby?"

Laura gazed into the misty brown eyes and shook her head. "No. Of course not. I'm glad for you, Mom. I'm sure you'll be a hit in L.A." She forced a smile. "When is all this supposed to happen anyway?"

"I start this Friday."

"Oh."

"You *are* upset." Before Laura could deny it, Shirley's face took on one of those tragic looks of hers. This one reminded Laura of Lana Turner in *Madame X.* "Oh, Laura, I'm nothing but a series of disappointments to you, aren't I?"

"No, you're not."

"I've always been a terrible mother."

"Stop it."

"It's true. I never did any of the things other mothers did for their daughters—like teaching you how to sew, going to PTA meetings, baking for your Girl Scout troop, singing you lullabies."

Laura smiled. "You sang me lullabies."

Shirley raised an eyebrow. "I did?"

"Sure." Standing up, Laura assumed a dramatic pose, with one hand on her breast and the other extended toward some imaginary lover. Then, in a remarkably good imitation of her mother, she sang, "Good Morning Heartache."

As Shirley broke into peals of laughter, the two women fell into each other's arms and hugged again. "Oh, baby," Shirley murmured. "You are so good for me. How am I going to manage without you?"

She would manage, Laura thought as a tear ran down her cheek. She always did.

3 7

Ted was about to go up and join Laura, who had already gone to bed when the doorbell rang. He saw Lenox walk across the foyer to answer it. A few moments later, he was back.

"There is someone here to see you, sir."

A bewildered expression on his face, Ted rose slowly from his chair as his father came into the room. "Dad." He was so shocked that he couldn't think of anything else to say.

"I know it's late but Sheriff Wilson called me just a little while ago, so I took a chance . . ."

His voice had lost its sarcastic edge and his eyes, the same eyes that had stared at him with such disdain weeks ago, were now watching him with mild apprehension. "Oh."

Say something intelligent for crying out loud, Ted thought. Something with more than one syllable in it. Swallowing, he pointed at a chair. "Please sit down. Would you like something to drink? Coffee? A soda?"

Charles, looking emaciated in a cardigan that was too big for him, shook his head. "Nothing for me, thanks." He sat on the sofa and rested his cane against the armrest. "I would have waited until morning, but your sister said something about you having to leave for Belfast."

"That trip has been canceled." He paused. "I'm staying in Texas. Permanently."

Although Ted saw a look of surprise in Charles's eyes, he couldn't tell whether the news pleased him or not.

"She also told me about your visit to the attic the other day."

Ted felt a quick burst of anger. "She shouldn't have done that."

"Don't be upset with her. It was my fault. I made her mad and it all came out before she realized what she was doing. She's a lot like you in that respect, you know. She talks before she thinks."

A faint smile tugged at Ted's lips. "And you were always a harsh judge of human weaknesses."

"True." He paused. "About your mother's necklace—"

"I'll go get it." Moments later, Ted was back and handed Charles the chain. At the look of anguish on his father's face as his fingers moved over the broken clasp, Ted's throat tightened.

"It was Malcolm all along," Charles murmured. "My own brother."

"I know. I'm sorry I jumped to the wrong conclusions, Dad."

"What else could you do? The evidence was damning. Even Sandra believed it."

"She wouldn't have if I hadn't been so adamant that you were the murderer."

"Yet you agreed not to turn me in."

"It wasn't an easy decision. There were a lot of feelings bottled up inside me. But in the end I couldn't do it."

"And you were willing to go back to England without me knowing what you had done for me. Why? Were you afraid I wouldn't be grateful?"

He still didn't get it, Ted thought with a pinch of regret. He was trying, but he still didn't get it. "Gratitude was never what I was after." When Charles didn't reply, he asked, "What about you, Dad? What are *you* after? What do you want?"

For a moment, Charles seemed lost in the contemplation of a Jack Bryant sculpture on the coffee table. "It's too late for me to have any kind of expectation."

"That's not true. You didn't come here tonight because it was too late for us. You came because you know there is hope."

"So much has happened . . ."

"It can all be reversed, forgotten."

"Just like that?"

Ted leaned back in his chair and crossed his legs. "What? Too impulsive for you?"

An expression Ted hadn't seen in many years flitted across the tired old blue eyes. "Something like that."

"Well then, why don't we take it one day at a time? Just to see how it goes."

Charles was thoughtful for a while. "That would be fine."

Ted knew that was the most he would get out of him at this point. For Charles, that was a lot. And for the time being, it was enough. "I'm going to do a picture book," he said casually. "I'm going to call it *The Many Faces of Texas*. Would you like to help me with my research?"

"Me?"

"Sure. Who in this state knows and loves Texas more than you do? Who can talk about it with more passion? Or with more pride?"

Charles's expression was one of mild surprise. "What would I have to do?"

Ted shrugged. "Tell me places I should photograph and why, talk about some of the changes that have taken place throughout the state in the last fifty years, that sort of things."

Charles nodded slowly. "Sure. I can do that."

"Good. I'll call you."

As Charles picked up his cane and rose, Ted did the same. Silently, they walked out together. When they reached the old Bentley Charles drove so rarely these days, he paused. "Thanks, son," he said, his voice thick with emotion. "You've made this visit a lot easier than I thought it would be."

Son. How long had it been since Ted had heard that word? "You're welcome."

Then, an incredible thing happened. Charles opened his arms.

Ted felt his eyes fill with tears. Pushing them back, he let himself be enfolded in the unfamiliar embrace. Emotions rushed to the surface, almost choking him. One by one, the feelings he had kept buried deep inside him all these years vanished. He closed his arms around his father's frail body.

"Welcome home, son," Charles murmured.

"It's good to be here, Dad."

*　　*　　*

"You were restless last night." Ted said.

Ted and Laura stood on the porch, watching the sun rise over the hills. He was behind her, his arms wrapped around her waist. The morning sun felt warm on his skin, but the real warmth came from deep within. It came from holding her, from the knowledge that he loved her and that she loved him.

Laura sighed. "I kept thinking about my mother."

"Are you still upset that she's leaving?"

"No." She leaned her head back against his chest. "I'm just worried that she's being exploited by that so-called old friend of hers, that the only reason he's hiring her is because of all the publicity she's been getting. With her there, his club will be packed with the curious for weeks, maybe months."

"Is that so bad? Knowing how Shirley loves the attention?"

"No. But what happens afterward? When she's no longer news?"

Ted tightened his hold on her. "I don't know, darling. But I do know that if you tried to stop her, she wouldn't listen. She might even resent you for it."

"I know, which is why I don't intend to say anything." She chuckled. "Funny though, isn't it? How things never really change? Even though you think they have."

"What do you mean?"

"I was so sure my mother had turned a new leaf, that she was finally ready to settle down, to be a family. But she's still the same old Shirley—carefree, delightful, exuberant. And fickle."

"You do know she loves you very much, don't you?"

"But she loves the limelight more. And now that I finally understand that, I can accept it. With no bitterness."

Ted kissed the top of her head. "What about you? Sherlock? Got any plans for the future? Some well-deserved rest perhaps? That trip to Hawaii you say you always wanted to take?"

She laughed. "I'm afraid I haven't had much time to think about travel in the last few days."

"Well, would you like to think about it now?"

"Mmm." She turned her head sideways. "Would you be joining me?"

He nuzzled her ear. "Don't grooms usually accompany their brides on a honeymoon?"

She turned around, eyes wide, lips parted. "Did you say honeymoon? As in ... *marriage*?"

"What's the matter? The word scares you?"

"No. I thought ... I thought it scared *you*. I thought you were dead set against marriage."

Amusement danced in his eyes. "I was at one time. But I changed my mind. Women aren't the only ones with that prerogative, you know. Guys can do it, too."

"But ..." She took a slow, careful breath. "Are you sure you gave this enough consideration? Maybe you just feel sorry for me because my mother is leaving. Or maybe you feel it's the right thing to do now that you've decided to stay. If that's the—"

"God Almighty, woman! Do you always talk so much when a man proposes to you?"

She swallowed. "No. Only when the man is the right one."

"Is that a yes?"

"Only if you're sure ..."

"I'm sure." He rested his forehead against hers. "I've never been so sure of anything in my whole life. And no, I didn't make that decision because I feel sorry for you. Or because it's the right thing to do. I want to marry you because I adore you. Because I can't live without you. Because I want to go to sleep every night with you in my arms and I want to wake up the same way. Feel free to stop me when you've heard enough."

"Oh, Ted." Half laughing and half crying, she threw her arms around his neck. "I love you."

"You still haven't given me an answer."

"Yes, I'll marry you. Yes! yes! yes!"

She would have squeezed in another yes, but he wouldn't let her. Pulling her to him, he crushed her mouth with his.